MIXED COMPANY

MIXED COMPANY
IRWIN SHAW

NEW ENGLISH LIBRARY/TIMES MIRROR

To
GUS LOBRANO
and
WILLIAM MAXWELL

First published in Great Britain by
Jonathan Cape Ltd.
© by Irwin Shaw

First NEL Paperback Edition
November 1977

NEL Books are published by
New English Library from Barnard's Inn,
Holborn, London EC1N 2JR.

Made and printed in Great Britain by
Hunt Barnard Printing Ltd.,
Aylesbury, Bucks.

45003344 9

CONTENTS

The Girls in Their Summer Dresses

Fifth Avenue was shining in the sun when they left the Brevoört and started walking toward Washington Square. The sun was warm, even though it was November, and everything looked like Sunday morning – the buses, and the well-dressed people walking slowly in couples and the quiet buildings with the windows closed.

Michael held Frances's arm tightly as they walked downtown in the sunlight. They walked lightly, almost smiling, because they had slept late and had a good breakfast and it was Sunday. Michael unbuttoned his coat and let it flap around him in the mild wind. They walked, without saying anything, among the young and pleasant-looking people who somehow seem to make up most of the population of that section of New York City.

'Look out,' Frances said, as they crossed Eighth Street. 'You'll break your neck.'

Michael laughed and Frances laughed with him.

'She's not so pretty, anyway,' Frances said. 'Anyway, not pretty enough to take a chance breaking your neck looking at her.'

Michael laughed again. He laughed louder this time, but not as solidly. 'She wasn't a bad-looking girl. She had a nice complexion. Country-girl complexion. How did you know I was looking at her?'

Frances cocked her head to one side and smiled at her husband under the tip-tilted brim of her hat. 'Mike, darling . . . ' she said.

Michael laughed, just a little laugh this time. 'O.K.,' he said. 'The evidence is in. Excuse me. It was the complexion. It's not the sort of complexion you see much in New York. Excuse me.'

Frances patted his arm lightly and pulled him along a little faster toward Washington Square.

'This is a nice morning,' she said. 'This is a wonderful morning. When I have breakfast with you it makes me feel good all day.'

'Tonic,' Michael said. 'Morning pick-up. Rolls and coffee with Mike and you're on the alkali side, guaranteed.'

'That's the story. Also, I slept all night, wound around you like a rope.'

'Saturday night,' he said. 'I permit such liberties only when the week's work is done.'

'You're getting fat,' she said.

'Isn't it the truth? The lean man from Ohio.'

'I love it,' she said, 'an extra five pounds of husband.'

'I love it, too,' Michael said gravely.

'I have an idea,' Frances said.

'My wife has an idea. That pretty girl.'

'Let's not see anybody all day,' Frances said. 'Let's just hang around with each other. You and me. We're always up to our neck in people, drinking their Scotch, or drinking our Scotch, we only see each other in bed . . . '

'The Great Meeting Place,' Michael said. 'Stay in bed long enough and everybody you ever knew will show up there.'

'Wise guy,' Frances said. 'I'm talking serious.'

'O.K., I'm listening serious.'

'I want to go out with my husband all day long. I want him to talk only to me and listen only to me.'

'What's to stop us?' Michael asked. 'What party intends to prevent me from seeing my wife alone on Sunday? What party?'

'The Stevensons. They want us to drop by around one o'clock and they'll drive us into the country.'

'The lousy Stevensons,' Mike said. 'Transparent. They can whistle. They can go driving in the country by themselves. My wife and I have to stay in New York and bore each other *tête-à-tête*.'

'Is it a date?'

'It's a date.'

Frances leaned over and kissed him on the tip of the ear.

'Darling,' Michael said. 'This is Fifth Avenue.'

'Let me arrange a programme,' Frances said. 'A planned Sunday in New York for a young couple with money to throw away.'

'Go easy.'

'First let's go see a football game. A professional football

8

game,' Frances said, because she knew Michael loved to watch them. 'The Giants are playing. And it'll be nice to be outside all day today and get hungry and later we'll go down to Cavanagh's and get a steak as big as a blacksmith's apron, with a bottle of wine, and after that, there's a new French picture at the Filmarte that everybody says . . . Say, are you listening to me?'

'Sure,' he said. He took his eyes off the hatless girl with the dark hair, cut dancer-style, like a helmet, who was walking past him with the self-conscious strength and grace dancers have. She was walking without a coat and she looked very solid and strong and her belly was flat, like a boy's, under her skirt, and her hips swung boldly because she was a dancer and also because she knew Michael was looking at her. She smiled a little to herself as she went past and Michael noticed all these things before he looked back at his wife. 'Sure,' he said, 'we're going to watch the Giants and we're going to eat steak and we're going to see a French picture. How do you like that?'

'That's it,' Frances said flatly. 'That's the programme for the day. Or maybe you'd just rather walk up and down Fifth Avenue.'

'No,' Michael said carefully. 'Not at all.'

'You always look at other women,' Frances said. 'At every damn woman in the City of New York.'

'Oh, come now,' Michael said, pretending to joke. 'Only pretty ones. And, after all, how many pretty women *are* there in New York? Seventeen?'

'More. At least you seem to think so. Wherever you go.'

'Not the truth. Occasionally, maybe. I look at a woman as she passes. In the street. I admit, perhaps in the street I look at a woman once in a while . . . '

'Everywhere,' Frances said. 'Every damned place we go. Restaurants, subways, theatres, lectures, concerts,'

'Now, darling,' Michael said, 'I look at everything. God gave me eyes and I look at women and men and subway excavations and moving pictures and the little flowers of the field. I casually inspect the universe.'

'You ought to see the look in your eye,' Frances said, 'as you casually inspect the universe on Fifth Avenue.'

'I'm a happily married man.' Michael pressed her elbow tenderly, knowing what he was doing. 'Example for the whole twentieth century, Mr and Mrs Mike Loomis.'

'You mean it?'

9

'Frances, baby . . .'

'Are you *really* happily married?'

'Sure,' Michael said, feeling the whole Sunday morning sinking like lead inside him. 'Now what the hell is the sense in talking like that?'

'I would like to know.' Frances walked faster now, looking straight ahead, her face showing nothing, which was the way she always managed it when she was arguing or feeling bad.

'I'm wonderfully happily married,' Michael said patiently. 'I am the envy of all men between the ages of fifteen and sixty in the State of New York.'

'Stop kidding,' Frances said.

'I have a fine home,' Michael said. 'I got nice books and a phonograph and nice friends. I live in a town I like the way I like and I do the work I like and I live with the woman I like. Whenever something good happens, don't I run to you? When something bad happens, don't I cry on your shoulder?'

'Yes,' Frances said. 'You look at every woman that passes.'

'That's an exaggeration.'

'Every woman.' Frances took her hand off Michael's arm. 'If she's not pretty you turn away fairly quickly. If she's halfway pretty you watch her for about seven steps . . .'

'My lord, Frances!'

'If she's pretty you practically break your neck . . .'

'Hey, let's have a drink,' Michael said, stopping.

'We just had breakfast.'

'Now listen, darling,' Mike said, choosing his words with care, 'it's a nice day and we both feel good and there's no reason why we have to break it up. Let's have a nice Sunday.'

'I could have a fine Sunday if you didn't look as though you were dying to run after every skirt on Fifth Avenue.'

'Let's have a drink,' Michael said.

'I don't want a drink.'

'What do you want, a fight?'

'No,' Frances said so unhappily that Michael felt terribly sorry for her. 'I don't want a fight. I don't know why I started this. All right, let's drop it. Let's have a good time.'

They joined hands consciously and walked without talking among the baby carriages and the old Italian men in their Sunday clothes and the young women with Scotties in Washington Square Park.

'I hope it's a good game today,' Frances said after a while, her tone a good imitation of the tone she had used at breakfast and at the beginning of their walk. 'I like professional football games. They hit each other as though they're made out of concrete. When they tackle each other,' she said, trying to make Michael laugh, 'they make divots. It's very exciting.'

'I want to tell you something,' Michael said very seriously. 'I have not touched another woman. Not once. In all the five years.'

'All right,' Frances said.

'You believe that, don't you?'

'All right.'

They walked between the crowded benches, under the scrubby city park trees.

'I try not to notice it,' Frances said, as though she were talking to herself. 'I try to make believe it doesn't mean anything. Some men're like that, I tell myself, they have to see what they're missing.'

'Some women're like that, too,' Michael said. 'In my time I've seen a couple of ladies.'

'I haven't even looked at another man,' Frances said, walking straight ahead, 'since the second time I went out with you.'

'There's no law,' Michael said.

'I feel rotten inside, in my stomach, when we pass a woman and you look at her and I see that look in your eye and that's the way you looked at me the first time, in Alice Maxwell's house. Standing there in the living-room, next to the radio, with a green hat on and all those people.'

'I remember the hat,' Michael said.

'The same look,' Frances said. 'And it makes me feel bad. It makes me feel terrible.'

'Sssh, please, darling, ssh . . .'

'I think I would like a drink now,' Frances said.

They walked over to a bar on Eighth Street, not saying anything, Michael automatically helping her over kerbstones, and guiding her past automobiles. He walked, buttoning his coat, looking thoughtfully at his neatly shined heavy brown shoes as they made the steps toward the bar. They sat near a window in the bar and the sun streamed in, and there was a small cheerful fire in the fireplace. A little Japanese waiter came over and put down some pretzels and smiled happily at them.

'What do you order after breakfast?' Michael asked.

'Brandy, I suppose,' Frances said.

'Courvoisier,' Michael told the waiter. 'Two Courvoisier.'

The waiter came with the glasses and they sat drinking the brandy, in the sunlight. Michael finished half his and drank a little water.

'I look at women,' he said. 'Correct. I don't say it's wrong or right. I look at them. If I pass them on the street and I don't look at them, I'm fooling you, I'm fooling myself.'

'You look at them as though you want them,' Frances said, playing with her brandy glass. 'Every one of them.'

'In a way,' Michael said, speaking softly and not to his wife, 'in a way that's true. I don't do anything about it, but it's true.'

'I know it. That's why I feel bad.'

'Another brandy,' Michael called. 'Waiter, two more brandies.'

'Why do you hurt me?' Frances asked. 'What're you doing?'

Michael sighed and closed his eyes and rubbed them gently with his fingertips. 'I love the way women look. One of the things I like best about New York is the battalions of women. When I first came to New York from Ohio that was the first thing I noticed, the million wonderful women, all over the city. I walked around with my heart in my throat.'

'A kid,' Frances said. 'That's a kid's feeling.'

'Guess again,' Michael said. 'Guess again. I'm older now. I'm a man getting near middle age, putting on a little fat and I still love to walk along Fifth Avenue at three o'clock on the east side of the street between Fiftieth and Fifty-seventh Streets; they're all out then, making believe they're shopping, in their furs and their crazy hats, everything all concentrated from all over the world into eight blocks, the best furs, the best clothes, the handsomest women, out to spend money and feeling good about it, looking coldly at you, making believe they're not looking at you as you go past.'

The Japanese waiter put the two drinks down, smiling with great happiness.

'Everything is all right?' he asked.

'Everything is wonderful,' Michael said.

'If it's just a couple of fur coats,' Frances said, 'and forty-five-dollar hats . . .'

'It's not the fur coats. Or the hats. That's just the scenery for that particular kind of woman. Understand,' he said, 'you don't have to listen to this.'

'I want to listen.'

'I like the girls in the offices. Neat, with their eyeglasses, smart, chipper, knowing what everything is about, taking care of themselves all the time.' He kept his eye on the people going slowly past outside the window. 'I like the girls on Forty-fourth Street at lunchtime, the actresses, all dressed up on nothing a week, talking to the good-looking boys, wearing themselves out being young and vivacious outside Sardi's, waiting for producers to look-at them. I like the salesgirls in Macy's, paying attention to you first because you're a man, leaving lady customers waiting, flirting with you over socks and books and phonograh needles. I got all this stuff accumulated in me because I've been thinking about it for ten years and now you've asked for it and here it is.'

'Go ahead,' Frances said.

'When I think of New York City, I think of all the girls, the Jewish girls, the Italian girls, the Irish, Polack, Chinese, German, Negro, Spanish, Russian girls, all on parade in the City. I don't know whether it's something special with me or whether every man in the city walks around with the same feeling inside him, but I feel as though I'm at a picnic in this city. I like to sit near the women in the theatres, the famous beauties who've taken six hours to get ready and look it. And the younger girls at the football games, with the red cheeks, and when the warm weather comes, the girls in their summer dresses . . . ' He finished his drink. 'That's the story. You asked for it, remember. I can't help but look at them. I can't help but want them.'

'You want them,' Frances repeated without expression. 'You said that.'

'Right,' Michael said, being cruel now and not caring, because she had made him expose himself. 'You brought this subject up for discussion; we will discuss it fully.'

Frances finished her drink and swallowed two or three times extra. 'You say you love me?'

'I love you, but I also want them. O.K.'

'I'm pretty, too,' Frances said. 'As pretty as any of them.'

'You're beautiful,' Michael said, meaning it.

'I'm good for you,' Frances said, pleading. 'I've made a good wife, a good housekeeper, a good friend. I'd do any damn thing for you.'

'I know,' Michael said. He put his hand out and grasped hers.

'You'd like to be free to . . . ' Frances said.

'Sssh.'

13

'Tell the truth.' She took her hand away from under his.

Michael flicked the edge of his glass with his finger. 'O.K.,' he said gently. 'Sometimes I feel I would like to be free.'

'Well,' Frances said defiantly, drumming on the table, 'anytime you say . . .'

'Don't be foolish.' Michael swung his chair around to her side of the table and patted her thigh.

She began to cry, silently, into her handkerchief, bent over just enough so that nobody else in the bar would notice. 'Some day,' she said, crying, 'you're going to make a move . . .'

Michael didn't say anything. He sat watching the bartender slowly peel a lemon.

'Aren't you?' Frances asked harshly. 'Come on, tell me. Talk. Aren't you?'

'Maybe,' Michael said. He moved his chair back again. 'How the hell do I know?'

'You know,' Frances persisted. 'Don't you know?'

'Yes,' Michael said after a while, 'I know.'

Frances stopped crying then. Two or three snuffles into the handkerchief and she put it away and her face didn't tell anything to anybody. 'At least do me one favour,' she said.

'Sure.'

'Stop talking about how pretty this woman is, or that one. Nice eyes, nice breasts, a pretty figure, good voice,' she mimicked his voice. 'Keep it to yourself. I'm not interested.'

'Excuse me.' Michael waved to the waiter. 'I'll keep it to myself.'

Frances flicked the corner of her eyes. 'Another brandy,' she told the waiter.

'Two,' Michael said.

'Yes, ma'am. Yes, sir,' said the waiter, backing away.

Frances regarded him coolly across the table. 'Do you want me to call the Stevensons?' she asked. 'It'll be nice in the country.'

'Sure,' Michael said. 'Call them up.'

She got up from the table and walked across the room towards the telephone. Michael watched her walk, thinking what a pretty girl, what nice legs.

The Eighty-Yard Run

The pass was high and wide and he jumped for it, feeling it slap flatly against his hands, as he shook his hips to throw off the half-back who was diving at him. The centre floated by, his hands desperately brushing Darling's knee as Darling picked his feet up high and delicately ran over a blocker and an opposing linesman in a jumble on the ground near the scrimmage line. He had ten yards in the clear and picked up speed, breathing easily, feeling his thigh pads rising and falling against his legs, listening to the sound of cleats behind him, pulling away from them, watching the other backs heading him off toward the sideline, the whole picture, the men closing in on him, the blockers fighting for position, the ground he had to cross, all suddenly clear in his head, for the first time in his life not a meaningless confusion of men, sounds, speed. He smiled a little to himself as he ran, holding the ball lightly in front of him with his two hands, his knees pumping high, his hips twisting in the almost girlish run of a back in a broken field. The first half-back came at him and he fed him his leg, then swung at the last moment, took the shock of the man's shoulder without breaking stride, ran right through him, his cleats biting securely into the turf. There was only the safety man now, coming warily at him, his arms crooked, hands spread. Darling tucked the ball in, spurted at him, driving hard, hurling himself along, his legs pounding, knees high, all two hundred pounds bunched into controlled attack. He was sure he was going to get past the safety man. Without thought, his arms and legs working beautifully together, he headed right for the safety man, stiff-armed him, feeling blood spurt instantaneously from the man's nose on to his hand, seeing his face go awry, head turned, mouth pulled to one side. He pivoted away, keeping the arm locked, dropping the safety man as he ran easily toward the goal line, with the drumming of cleats diminishing behind him.

How long ago? It was autumn then, and the ground was getting hard because the nights were cold and leaves from the maples around the stadium blew across the practice fields in gusts of wind, and the girls were beginning to put polo coats over their sweaters when they came to watch practice in the afternoons . . . Fifteen years. Darling walked slowly over the same ground in the spring twilight, in his neat shoes, a man of thirty-five dressed in a double-breasted suit, ten pounds heavier in the fifteen years, but not fat, with the years between 1925 and 1940 showing in his face.

The coach was smiling quietly to himself and the assistant coaches were looking at each other with pleasure the way they always did when one of the second-stringers suddenly did something fine, bringing credit to them, making their $2,000 a year a tiny bit more secure.

Darling trotted back, smiling, breathing deeply but easily, feeling wonderful, not tired, though this was the tail end of practice and he'd run eighty yards. The sweat poured off his face and soaked his jersey and he liked the feeling, the warm moistness lubricating his skin like oil. Off in a corner of the field some players were punting and the smack of leather against the ball came pleasantly through the afternoon air. The freshmen were running signals on the next field and the quarter back's sharp voice, the pound of the eleven pairs of cleats, the 'Dig now *dig*!' of the coaches, the laughter of the players all somehow made him feel happy as he trotted back to midfield, listening to the applause and shouts of the students along the sidelines, knowing that after that run the coach would have to start him Saturday against Illinois.

Fifteen years, Darling thought, remembering the shower after the workout, the hot water steaming off his skin and the deep soapsuds and all the young voices singing with the water streaming down and towels going and managers running in and out and the sharp sweet smell of oil of wintergreen and everybody clapping him on the back as he dressed and Packard, the captain, who took being captain very seriously, coming over to him and shaking his hand and saying, 'Darling, you're going to go places in the next two years.'

The assistant manager fussed over him, wiping a cut on his leg with alcohol and iodine, the little sting making him realise suddenly how fresh and whole and solid his body felt. The manager slapped a piece of adhesive tape over the cut, and Darling noticed the sharp clean white of the tape against the ruddiness of the skin, fresh from the shower.

He dressed slowly, the softness of his shirt and the soft warmth of his wool socks and his flannel trousers a reward against his skin after the harsh pressure of the shoulder harness and thigh and hip pads. He drank three glasses of cold water, the liquid reaching down coldly inside of him, soothing the harsh, dry places in his throat and belly left by the sweat and running and shouting of practice.

Fifteen years.

The sun had gone down and the sky was green behind the stadium and he laughed quietly to himself as he looked at the stadium, rearing above the trees, and knew that on Saturday when the 70,000 voices roared as the team came running out on to the field part of that enormous salute would be for him. He walked slowly, listening to the gravel crunch satisfactorily under his shoes in the still twilight. feeling his clothes swing lightly against his skin, breathing the thin evening air, feeling the wind move softly in his damp hair, wonderfully cool behind his ears and at the nape of his neck.

Louise was waiting for him at the road, in her car. The top was down and he noticed all over again, as he always did when he saw her, how pretty she was, the rough blonde hair and the large, inquiring eyes and the bright mouth, smiling now.

She threw the door open. 'Were you good today?' she asked.

'Pretty good,' he said. He climbed in, sank luxuriously into the soft leather, stretched his legs far out. He smiled, thinking of the eighty yards. 'Pretty damn good.'

She looked at him seriously for a moment, then scrambled around, like a little girl, kneeling on the seat next to him, grabbed him, her hands along his ears, and kissed him as he sprawled, head back, on the seat cushion. She let go of him, but kept her head close to his, over his. Darling reached up slowly and rubbed the back of his hand against her cheek, lit softly by a street lamp a hundred feet away. They looked at each other, smiling.

Louise drove down to the lake and they sat there silently, watching the moon rise behind the hills on the other side. Finally, he reached over, pulled her gently to him, kissed her. Her lips grew soft, her body sank into his, tears formed slowly in her eyes. He knew, for the first time, that he could do whatever he wanted with her.

'Tonight,' I'll call for you at seven-thirty. Can you get out?'

17

She looked at him. She was smiling, but the tears were still full in her eyes. 'All right,' she said. 'I'll get out. How about you? Won't the coach raise hell?'

Darling grinned. 'I got the coach in the palm of my hand,' he said. 'Can you wait till seven-thirty?'

She grinned back at him. 'No,' she said.

They kissed and she started the car and they went back to town for dinner. He sang on the way home.

Christian Darling, thirty-five years old, sat on the frail spring grass, greener now than it ever would be again on the practice field, looked thoughtfully up at the stadium, a deserted ruin in the twilight. He had started on the first team that Saturday and every Saturday after that for the next two years, but it had never been as satisfactory as it should have been. He never had broken away, the longest run he'd ever made was thirty-five yards, and that in a game that was already won, and then that kid had come up from the third team, Diedrich, a blank-faced German kid from Wisconsin, who ran like a bull, ripping lines to pieces Saturday after Saturday, ploughing through never getting hurt, never changing his expression, scoring more points, gaining more ground than all the rest of the team put together, making everybody's All-American carrying the ball three times out of four, keeping everybody else out of the headlines. Darling was a good blocker and he spent his Saturday afternoons working on the big Swedes and Polacks who played tackle and end for Michigan, Illinois, Purdue, hurling into huge pile-ups, bobbing his head wildly to elude the great raw hands swinging like meat-cleavers at him as he went charging in to open up holes for Diederich coming through like a locomotive behind him. Still, it wasn't so bad. Everybody liked him and he did his job and he was pointed out on the campus and the boys always felt important when they introduced their girls to him at their proms, and Louise loved him and watched him faithfully in the games, even in the mud, when your own mother wouldn't know you, and drove him around in her car keeping the top down because she was proud of him and wanted to show everybody that she was Christian Darling's girl. She bought him crazy presents because her father was rich, watches, pipes, humidors, an icebox for beer for his room, curtains, wallets, a fifty-dollar dictionary.

'You'll spend every cent your old man owns,' Darling protested once when she showed up at his rooms with seven

18

different packages in her arms and tossed them on to the couch.

'Kiss me,' Louise said, 'and shut up.'

'Do you want to break your poor old man?'

'I don't mind. I want to buy you presents.'

'Why?'

'It makes me feel good. Kiss me. I don't know why. Did you know that you're an important figure?'

'Yes,' Darling said gravely.

'When I was waiting for you at the library yesterday two girls saw you coming and one of them said to the other, "That's Christian Darling. He's an important figure".'

'You're a liar.'

'I'm in love with an important figure.'

'Still, why the hell did you have to give me a forty-pound dictionary?'

'I wanted to make sure,' Louise said, 'that you had a token of my esteem. I want to smother you in tokens of my esteem.'

Fifteen years ago.

They'd married when they got out of college. There'd been other women for him, but all casual and secret, more for curiosity's sake, and vanity, women who'd thrown themselves at him and flattered him, a pretty mother at a summer camp for boys, an old girl from his home town who'd suddenly blossomed into a coquette, a friend of Louise's who had dogged him grimly for six months and had taken advantage of the two weeks that Louise went home when her mother died. Perhaps Louise had known, but she'd kept quiet, loving him completely, filling his rooms with presents, religiously watching him battling with the big Swedes and Polacks on the line of scrimmage on Saturday afternoons, making plans for marrying him and living with him in New York and going with him there to the nightclubs, the theatres, the good restaurants, being proud of him in advance, tall, white-teethed, smiling, large, yet moving lightly, with an athlete's grace, dressed in evening clothes, approvingly eyed by magnificently dressed and famous women in theatre lobbies, with Louise adoringly at his side.

Her father, who manufactured inks, set up a New York office for Darling to manage and presented him with three hundred accounts, and they lived on Beekman Place with a view of the river with fifteen thousand dollars a year between them, because everybody was buying everything in those days,

19

including ink. They saw all the shows and went to all the speakeasies and spent their fifteen thousand dollars a year and in the afternoons Louise went to the art galleries and the matinées of the more serious plays that Darling didn't like to sit through and Darling slept with a girl who danced in the chorus of *Rosalie* and with the wife of a man who owned three copper mines. Darling played squash three times a week and remained as solid as a stone barn and Louise never took her eyes off him when they were in the same room together, watching him with a secret, miser's smile, with a trick of coming over to him in the middle of a crowded room and saying gravely, in a low voice, 'You're the handsomest man I've ever seen in my whole life. Want a drink?'

Nineteen twenty-nine came to Darling and to his wife and father-in-law, the maker of inks, just as it came to everyone else. The father-in-law waited until 1933 and then blew his brains out, and when Darling went to Chicago to see what the books of the firm looked like he found out all that was left were debts and three or four gallons of unbought ink.

'Please, Christian,' Louise said, sitting in their neat Beekman Place apartment, with a view of the river and prints of paintings by Dufy and Braque and Picasso on the wall, 'please, why do you want to start drinking at two o'clock in the afternoon?'

I have nothing else to do,' Darling said, putting down his glass, emptied of its fourth drink. 'Please pass the whisky.'

Louise filled his glass. 'Come take a walk with me,' she said. 'We'll walk along the river.'

'I don't want to walk along the river,' Darling said, squinting intensely at the prints of paintings by Dufy, Braque and Picasso.

'We'll walk along Fifth Avenue.'

'I don't want to walk along Fifth Avenue.'

'Maybe,' Louise said gently, 'you'd like to come with me to some art galleries. There's an exhibition by a man named Klee...'

'I don't want to go to any art galleries. I want to sit here and drink Scotch whisky,' Darling said. 'Who the hell hung those goddam pictures up on the wall?'

'I did,' Louise said.

'I hate them.'

'I'll take them down,' Louise said.

'Leave them there. It gives me something to do in the afternoon. I can hate them,' Darling took a long swallow. 'Is that the way people paint these days?'

'Yes, Christian. Please don't drink any more.'

'Do you like painting like that?'

'Yes, dear.'

'Really?'

'Really.'

Darling looked carefully at the prints once more. 'Little Louise Tucker. The middle-western beauty. I like pictures with horses in them. Why should you like pictures like that?'

'I just happen to have gone to a lot of galleries in the last few years . . . '

'Is that what you do in the afternoon?'

'That's what I do in the afternoon,' Louise said.

'I drink in the afternoon.'

Louise kissed him lightly on the top of his head as he sat there squinting at the pictures on the wall, the glass of whisky held firmly in his hand. She put on her coat and went out without saying another word. When she came back in the early evening, she had a job on a woman's fashion magazine.

They moved downtown and Louise went out to work every morning and Darling sat home and drank and Louise paid the bills as they came up. She made believe she was going to quit work as soon as Darling found a job, even though she was taking over more responsibility day by day at the magazine, interviewing authors, picking painters for the illustrations and covers, getting actresses to pose for pictures, going out for drinks with the right people, making a thousand new friends whom she loyally introduced to Darling.

'I don't like your hat,' Darling said, once when she came in in the evening and kissed him, her breath rich with Martinis.

'What's the matter with my hat, Baby?' she asked, running her fingers through his hair. 'Everybody says it's very smart.'

'It's too damned smart,' he said. 'It's not for you. It's for a rich, sophisticated woman of thirty-five with admirers.'

Louise laughed. 'I'm practising to be a rich, sophisticated woman of thirty-five with admirers,' she said. He stared soberly at her. 'Now, don't look so grim, Baby. It's still the same simple little wife under the hat.' She took the hat off, threw it into a corner, sat on his lap. 'See? Homebody Number One.'

'Your breath could run a train,' Darling said, not wanting to be mean, but talking out of boredom, and sudden shock at seeing his wife curiously a stranger in a new hat, with a new expression in her eyes under the little brim, secret, confident, knowing.

Louise tucked her head under his chin so he couldn't smell her breath. 'I had to take an author out for cocktails,' she said. 'He's a boy from the Ozark Mountains and he drinks like a fish. He's a Communist.'

'What the hell is a Communist from the Ozarks doing writing for a woman's fashion magazine?'

Louise chuckled. 'The magazine business is getting all mixed up these days. The publishers want to have a foot in every camp. And, anyway, you can't find an author under seventy these days who isn't a Communist.'

'I don't think I like you to associate with all those people, Louise,' Darling said. 'Drinking with them.'

'He's a very nice, gentle boy,' Louise said. 'He reads Ernest Dowson.'

'Who's Ernest Dowson?'

Louise patted his arm, stood up, fixed her hair. 'He's an English poet.'

Darling felt that somehow he had disappointed her. 'Am I supposed to know who Ernest Dowson is?'

'No, dear, I'd better go in and take a bath.'

After she had gone, Darling went over to the corner where the hat was lying and picked it up. It was nothing, a scrap of straw, a red flower, a veil, meaningless on his big hand, but on his wife's head a signal of something . . . big city, smart and knowing women drinking and dining with men other than their husbands, conversation about things a normal man wouldn't know much about, Frenchmen who painted as though they used their elbows instead of brushes, composers who wrote whole symphonies without a single melody in them, writers who knew all about politics and women who knew all about writers, the movement of the proletariat, Marx, somehow mixed up with five-dollar dinners and the best-looking women in America and fairies who made them laugh and half-sentences immediately understood and secretly hilarious and wives who called their husbands 'Baby'. He put the hat down, a scrap of straw and a red flower, and a little veil. He drank some whisky straight and went into the bathroom, where his wife was lying deep in her bath, singing to herself and smiling from time to time like a little girl, paddling the water gently with her hands, sending up a slightly spicy fragrance from the bath salts she used.

He stood over her, looking down at her. She smiled up at him, her eyes half closed, her body pink and shimmering in the warm, scented water. All over again, with all the old suddenness, he was hit deep inside him with the knowledge of how beautiful she was, how much he needed her.

'I came in here,' he said, 'to tell you I wish you wouldn't call me "Baby".'

She looked up at him from the bath, her eyes quickly full of sorrow, half-understanding what he meant. He knelt and put his arms around her, his sleeves plunged heedlessly in the water, his shirt and jacket soaking wet as he clutched her wordlessly, holding her crazily tight, crushing her breath from her, kissing her desperately, searchingly, regretfully.

He got jobs after that, selling real estate and automobiles, but somehow, although he had a desk with his name on a wooden wedge on it, and he went to the office religiously at nine each morning, he never managed to sell anything and he never made any money.

Louise was made assistant editor, and the house was always full of strange men and women who talked fast and got angry on abstract subjects like mural painting, novelists, labour unions. Negro short-story writers drank Louise's liquor, and a lot of Jews, and big solemn men with scarred faces and knotted hands who talked slowly but clearly about picket lines and battles with guns and lead pipes at mine shaft-heads and in front of factory gates. And Louise moved among them all, confidently, knowing what they were talking about, with opinions that they listened to and argued about just as though she were a man. She knew everybody, condescended to no one, devoured books that Darling had never heard of, walked along the streets of the city, excited, at home, soaking in all the million tides of New York without fear, with constant wonder.

Her friends liked Darling and sometimes he found a man who wanted to get off in the corner and talk about the new boy who played full-back for Princeton, and the decline of the double wing-back, or even the state of the stock market, but for the most part he sat on the edge of things, solid and quiet in the high storm of words. 'The dialectics of the situation . . . The theatre has been given over to expert jugglers . . . Picasso? What man has a right to paint old bones and collect ten thousand dollars for them? . . . I stand firmly behind Trotsky . . .

Poe was the last American critic. When he died they put lilies on the grave of American criticism. I don't say this because they panned my last book, but . . . '

Once in a while he caught Louise looking soberly and consideringly at him through the cigarette smoke and the noise and he avoided her eyes and found an excuse to get up and go into the kitchen for more ice or to open another bottle.

'Come on,' Cathal Flaherty was saying, standing at the door with a girl, 'you've got to come down and see this. It's down on Fourteenth Street, in the old Civic Repertory, and you can only see it on Sunday nights and I guarantee you'll come out of the theatre singing.' Flaherty was a big young Irishman with a broken nose who was the lawyer for a longshoreman's union, and he had been hanging around the house for six months on and off, roaring and shutting everybody else up when he got in an argument. 'It's a new play, *Waiting for Lefty*; it's about taxi-drivers.'

'Odets,' the girl with Flaherty said. 'It's by a guy named Odets.'

'I never heard of him,' Darling said.

'He's a new one,' the girl said.

'It's like watching a bombardment,' Flaherty said. 'I saw it last Sunday night. You've got to see it.'

'Come on, Baby,' Louise said to Darling, excitement in her eyes already. 'We've been sitting in the Sunday *Times* all day; this'll be a great change.'

'I see enough taxi-drivers every day,' Darling said, not because he meant that, but because he didn't like to be around Flaherty, who said things that made Louise laugh a lot and whose judgement she accepted on almost every subject. 'Let's go to the movies.'

'You've never seen anything like this before,' Flaherty said. 'He wrote this play with a baseball bat.'

'Come on,' Louise coaxed. 'I bet it's wonderful.'

'He has long hair,' the girl with Flaherty said. 'Odets. I met him at a party. He's an actor. He didn't say a goddam thing all night.'

'I don't feel like going down to Fourteenth Street,' Darling said, wishing Flaherty and his girl would get out. 'It's gloomy.'

'Oh, hell!' Louise said loudly. She looked coolly at Darling, as though she'd just been introduced to him and was making up her mind about him, and not very favourably. He saw her looking at him, knowing there was something new and danger-

24

ous in her face and he wanted to say something, but Flaherty was there and his damned girl, and anyway, he didn't know what to say.

'I'm going,' Louise said, getting her coat. 'I don't think Fourteenth Street is gloomy.'

'I'm telling you,' Flaherty was saying, helping her on with her coat, 'it's the Battle of Gettysburg, in Brooklynese.'

'Nobody could get a word out of him,' Flaherty's girl was saying as they went through the door. 'He just sat there all night.'

The door closed. Louise hadn't said good night to him. Darling walked across the room four times, then sprawled out on the sofa, on top of the Sunday *Times*. He lay there for five minutes looking at the ceiling, thinking of Flaherty walking down the street talking in that booming voice, between the girls holding their arms.

Louise had looked wonderful. She'd washed her hair in the afternoon and it had been very soft and light and clung close to her head as she stood there angrily putting her coat on. Louise was getting prettier every year, partly because she knew by now how pretty she was, and made the most of it.

'Nuts,' Darling said, standing up. 'Oh, nuts.'

He put on his coat and went down to the nearest bar and had five drinks off by himself in a corner before his money ran out.

The years since then had been foggy and downhill. Louise had been nice to him, and in a way, loving and kind, and they'd fought only once, when he said he was going to vote for Landon. ('Oh, Christ,' she said, 'doesn't *anything* happen inside your head? Don't you read the papers? The penniless Republican!') She'd been sorry later and apologised for hurting him, but apologised as she might to a child. He'd tried hard, had gone grimly to the art galleries, the concert-halls, the bookshops, trying to gain on the trail of his wife, but it was no use. He was bored, and none of what he saw or heard or dutifully read made much sense to him, and finally he gave it up. He had thought, many nights as he ate dinner alone, knowing that Louise would come home late and drop silently into bed without explanation, of getting a divorce, but he knew the loneliness, the hopelessness, of not seeing her again would be too much to take. So he was good, completely devoted, ready at all times to go any place with her, do anything she wanted. He even got a small job, in a broker's office and paid his own way, bought his own liquor.

Then he'd been offered the job of going from college to college as a tailor's representative. 'We want a man,' Mr Rosenberg had said, 'who as soon as you look at him, you say, "There's a university man".' Rosenberg had looked approvingly at Darling's broad shoulders and well-kept waist, at his carefully brushed hair and his honest, wrinkle-less face. 'Frankly, Mr Darling, I am willing to make you a proposition. I have inquired about you, you are favourably known on your old campus. I understand you were in the backfield with Alfred Diederich.'

Darling nodded. 'Whatever happened to him?'

'He is walking around in a cast for seven years now. An iron brace. He played professional football and they broke his neck for him.'

Darling smiled. That, at least, had turned out well.

'Our suits are an easy product to sell, Mr Darling,' Rosenberg said. 'We have a handsome, custom-made garment. What has Brooks Brothers got that we haven't got? A name. No more.'

'I can make fifty, sixty dollars a week,' Darling said to Louise that night. 'And expenses. I can save some money and then come back to New York and really get started here.'

'Yes, Baby,' Louise said.

'As it is,' Darling said carefully, 'I can make it back here once a month, and holidays and the summer. We can see each other often.'

'Yes, Baby.' He looked at her face, lovelier now at thirty-five than it had ever been before, but fogged over now as it had been for five years with a kind of patient, kindly, remote boredom.

'What do you say,' he asked. 'Should I take it?' Deep within him he hoped fiercely, longingly, for her to say, 'No, Baby, you stay right here,' but she said, as he knew she'd say, 'I think you'd better take it.'

He nodded. He had to get up and stand with his back to her, looking out the window, because there were things plain on his face that she had never seen in the fifteen years she'd known him. 'Fifty dollars is a lot of money,' he said. 'I never thought I'd ever see fifty dollars again.' He laughed, Louise laughed, too.

Christian Darling sat on the frail green grass of the practice field. The shadow of the stadium had reached out and covered him. In the distance the lights of the university shone a little mistily in the light haze of evening. Fifteen years. Flaherty even now was calling for his wife, buying her a drink, filling whatever bar they were in with that voice of his and that easy laugh. Darling half-closed his eyes, almost saw the boy fifteen years ago reach for the pass, slip the half-back, go skittering lightly down the field, his knees high and fast and graceful, smiling to himself because he knew he was going to get past the safety man. That was the high point, Darling thought, fifteen years ago, on an autumn afternoon, twenty years old and far from death, with the air coming easily into his lungs, and a deep feeling inside him that he could do anything, knock over anybody, outrun whatever had to be outrun. And the shower after and the three glasses of water and the cool night air on his damp head and Louise sitting hatless in the open car with a smile and the first kiss she ever really meant. The high point, an eighty-yard run in the practice, and a girl's kiss and everything after that a decline. Darling laughed. He had practised the wrong thing, perhaps. He hadn't practised for 1929 and New York City and a girl who would turn into a woman. Somewhere, he thought, there must have been a point where she moved up to me, was even with me for a moment, when I could have held her hand, if I'd known, held tight, gone with her. Well, he'd never known. Here he was on a playing field that was fifteen years away and his wife was in another city having dinner with another and better man, speaking with him a different, new language, a language nobody had ever taught him.

Darling stood up, smiled a little, because if he didn't smile he knew the tears would come. He looked around him. This was the spot. O'Connor's pass had come sliding out just to here . . . the high point. Darling put up his hands, felt all over again the flat slap of the ball. He shook his hips to throw off the half-back, cut back inside the centre, picked his knees high as he ran gracefully over two men jumbled on the ground at the line of scrimmage, ran easily, gaining speed, for ten yards, holding the ball lightly in his two hands, swung away from the half-back diving at him, ran, swinging his hips in the almost girlish manner of a back in a broken field, tore into the safety man, his shoes drumming heavily on the turf, stiff-armed, elbow locked, pivoted, raced lightly and exultantly for the goal line.

It was only after he had sped over the goal line and slowed to a trot that he saw the boy and girl sitting together on the turf, looking at him wonderingly.

He stopped short, dropping his arms. 'I . . . ' he said, gasping a little, though his condition was fine and the run hadn't winded him. 'I – once I played here.'

The boy and the girl said nothing. Darling laughed embarrassedly, looking hard at them sitting there, close to each other, shrugged, turned and went toward his hotel, the sweat breaking out on his face and running down into his collar.

Act of Faith

'Present it in a pitiful light,' Olson was saying, as they picked their way through the mud toward the orderly room tent. 'Three combat-scarred veterans, who fought their way from Omaha Beach to – what was the name of the town we fought our way to?'

'Konigstein,' Seeger said.

'Konigstein.' Olson lifted his right foot heavily out of a puddle and stared admiringly at the three pounds of mud clinging to his overshoe. 'The backbone of the Army. The non-commissioned officer. We deserve better of our country. Mention our decorations in passing.'

'What decorations should I mention?' Seeger asked. 'The marksman's medal?'

'Never quite made it,' Olson said. 'I had a cross-eyed scorer at the butts. Mention the Bronze Star, the Silver Star, the Croix de Guerre, with palms, the unit citation, the Congressional Medal of Honour.'

'I'll mention them all,' Seeger grinned. 'You don't think the C.O.'ll notice that we haven't won most of them, do you?'

'Gad, sir,' Olson said with dignity, 'do you think that one Southern military gentleman will dare doubt the word of another Southern military gentleman in the hour of victory?'

'I come from Ohio,' Seeger said.

'Welch comes from Kansas,' Olson said, coolly staring down a second lieutenant who was passing. The lieutenant made a nervous little jerk with his hand as though he expected a salute, then kept it rigid, as a slight superior smile of scorn twisted at the corner of Olson's mouth. The lieutenant dropped his eyes and splashed on through the mud. 'You've heard of Kansas,' Olson said. 'Magnolia-scented Kansas.'

'Of course,' said Seeger. 'I'm no fool.'

'Do your duty by your men, Sergeant.' Olson stopped to wipe the rain off his face and lectured him. 'Highest ranking noncom present took the initiative and saved his comrades, at great personal risk, above and beyond the call of you-know-what, in the best traditions of the American Army.'

'I will throw myself in the breach,' Seeger said.

'Welch and I can't ask more,' said Olson, approvingly.

They walked heavily through the mud on the streets between the rows of tents. The camp stretched drearily over the Rheims plain, with the rain beating on the sagging tents. The division had been there over three weeks by now, waiting to be shipped home, and all the meagre diversions of the neighbourhood had been sampled and exhausted, and there was an air of watchful suspicion and impatience with the military life hanging over the camp now, and there was even reputed to be a staff sergeant in C Company who was laying odds they would not get back to America before July Fourth.

'I'm redeployable,' Olsen sang. 'It's so enjoyable . . . ' It was a jingle he had composed to no recognisable melody in the early days after the victory in Europe, when he had added up his points and found they only came to 63. 'Tokyo, wait for me . . . '

They were going to be discharged as soon as they got back to the States, but Olson persisted in singing the song, occasionally adding a mournful stanza about dengue fever and brown girls with venereal disease. He was a short, round boy who had been flunked out of air cadets' school and transferred to the infantry, but whose spirits had not been damaged in the process. He had a high, childish voice and a pretty baby face. He was very good-natured, and had a girl waiting for him at the University of California, where he intended to finish his course at Government expense when he got out of the Army, and he was just the type who is killed off early and predictably and sadly in motion pictures about the war, but he had gone through four campaigns and six major battles without a scratch.

Seeger was a large, lanky boy, with a big nose, who had been wounded at Saint Lô, but had come back to his outfit in the Siegfried Line, quite unchanged. He was cheerful and dependable, and he knew his business and he had broken in five or six second lieutenants who had been killed or wounded and the C.O. had tried to get him commissioned in the field, but the war had ended while the paperwork was being fumbled over at headquarters.

They reached the door of the orderly tent and stopped. 'Be brave, Sergeant,' Olson said. 'Welch and I are depending on you.'

'O.K.,' Seeger said, and went in.

The tent had the dank, Army-canvas smell that had been so much a part of Seeger's life in the past three years. The company clerk was reading a July, 1945, issue of the *Buffalo Courier-Express,* which had just reached him, and Captain Taney, the company C.O., was seated at a sawbuck table he used as a desk, writing a letter to his wife, his lips pursed with effort. He was a small, fussy man, with sandy hair that was falling out. While the fighting had been going on, he had been lean and tense and his small voice had been cold and full of authority. But now he had relaxed, and a little pot belly was creeping up under his belt and he kept the top button of his trousers open when he could do it without too public loss of dignity. During the war Seeger had thought of him as a natural soldier, tireless, fanatic about detail, aggressive, severely anxious to kill Germans. But in the past few months Seeger had seen him relapsing gradually and pleasantly into a small-town wholesale hardware merchant, which he had been before the war, sedentary and a little shy, and, as he had once told Seeger, worried, here in the black champagne fields of France, about his daughter, who had just turned twelve and had a tendency to go after the boys and had been caught by her mother kissing a fifteen-year-old neighbour in the hammock after school.

'Hello, Seeger,' he said, returning the salute in a mild, off-hand gesture. 'What's on your mind?'

'Am I disturbing you, sir?'

'Oh, no. Just writing a letter to my wife. You married, Seeger?' He peered at the tall boy standing before him.

'No, sir.'

'It's very difficult,' Taney sighed, pushing dissatisfiedly at the letter before him. 'My wife complains I don't tell her I love her often enough. Been married fifteen years. You'd think she'd know by now.' He smiled at Seeger. 'I thought you were going to Paris,' he said. 'I signed the passes yesterday.'

'That's what I came to see you about, sir.'

'I suppose something's wrong with the passes.' Taney spoke resignedly, like a man who has never quite got the hang of Army regulations and has had requisitions, furloughs, requests for court-martial returned for correction in a baffling flood.

'No, sir,' Seeger said. 'The passes're fine. They start to-

31

morrow. Well, it's just . . . ' He looked around at the company clerk, who was on the sports page.

'This confidential?' Taney asked.

'If you don't mind, sir.'

'Johnny,' Taney said to the clerk, 'go stand in the rain some place.'

'Yes, sir,' the clerk said, and slowly got up and walked out.

Taney looked shrewdly at Seeger, spoke in a secret whisper. 'You pick up anything?' he asked.

Seeger grinned. 'No, sir, haven't had my hands on a girl since Strasbourg.'

'Ah, that's good.' Taney leaned back, relieved, happy he didn't have to cope with the disapproval of the Medical Corps.

'It's – well,' said Seeger, embarrassed, 'it's hard to say – but it's money.'

Taney shook his head sadly. 'I know.'

'We haven't been paid for three months, sir, and . . . '

'Damn it!' Taney stood up and shouted furiously. 'I would like to take every bloody chair-warming old lady in the Finance Department and wring their necks.'

The clerk stuck his head into the tent. 'Anything wrong? You call for me, sir?'

'No,' Taney shouted. 'Get out of here.'

The clerk ducked out.

Taney sat down again. 'I suppose,' he said, in a more normal voice, 'they have their problems. Outfits being broken up, being moved all over the place. But it is rugged.'

'It wouldn't be so bad,' Seeger said. 'But we're going to Paris tomorrow. Olsen, Welch and myself. And you need money in Paris.'

'Don't I know it.' Taney wagged his head. 'Do you know what I paid for a bottle of champagne on the Place Pigalle in September . . . ?' He paused significantly. 'I won't tell you. You won't have any respect for me for the rest of your life.'

Seeger laughed. 'Hanging,' he said, 'is too good for the guy who thought up the rate of exchange.'

'I don't care if I never see another franc as long as I live.' Taney waved his letter in the air, although it had been dry for a long time.

There was silence in the tent and Seeger swallowed a little embarrassedly, watching the C.O. wave the flimsy sheet of paper in regular sweeping movements. 'Sir,' he said, 'the truth is, I've come to borrow some money for Welch, Olson and myself.

32

We'll pay it back out of the first pay we get, and that can't be too long from now. If you don't want to give it to us, just tell me and I'll understand and get the hell out of here. We don't like to ask, but you might just as well be dead as be in Paris broke.'

Taney stopped waving his letter and put it down thoughtfully. He peered at it, wrinkling his brow, looking like an aged book-keeper in the single gloomy light that hung in the middle of the tent.

'Just say the word, Captain,' Seeger said, 'and I'll blow . . . '

'Stay where you are son,' said Taney. He dug in his shirt pocket and took out a worn, sweat-stained wallet. He looked at it for a moment. 'Alligator,' he said, with automatic, absent pride. 'My wife sent it to me when we were in England. Pounds don't fit in it. However . . . ' He opened it and took out all the contents. There was a small pile of francs on the table in front of him. He counted them. 'Four hundred francs,' he said. 'Eight bucks.'

'Excuse me,' Seeger said humbly. 'I shouldn't have asked.'

'Delighted,' Taney said vigorously. 'Absolutely delighted.' He started dividing the francs into two piles. 'Truth is, Seeger, most of my money goes home in allotments. And the truth is, I lost eleven hundred francs in a poker game three nights ago, and I ought to be ashamed of myself. Here . . . ' he shoved one pile toward Seeger. 'Two hundred francs.'

Seeger looked down at the frayed, meretricious paper, which always seemed to him like stage money, anyway. 'No, sir,' he said, 'I can't take it.'

'Take it,' Taney said. 'That's a direct order.'

Seeger slowly picked up the money, not looking at Taney. 'Some time, sir,' he said, 'after we get out, you have to come over to my house and you and my father and my brother and I'll go on a real drunk.'

'I regard that,' Taney said, gravely, 'as a solemn commitment.'

They smiled at each other and Seeger started out.

'Have a drink for me,' said Taney, 'at the Café de la Paix. A small drink.' He was sitting down to write his wife he loved her when Seeger went out of the tent.

Olson fell into step with Seeger and they walked silently through the mud between the tents.

'Well, *mon vieux?*' Olson said finally.

'Two hundred francs,' said Seeger.

Olson groaned. 'Two hundred francs! We won't be able to pinch a whore's behind on the Boulevard des Capucines for two hundred francs. That miserable, penny-loving Yankee!'

'He only had four hundred,' Seeger said.

'I revise my opinion,' said Olson.

They walked disconsolately and heavily back toward their tent.

Olson spoke only once before they got there. 'These raincoats,' he said, patting his. 'Most ingenious invention of the war. Highest saturation point of any modern fabric. Collect more water per square inch, and hold it, than any material known to man. All hail the quartermaster!'

Welch was waiting at the entrance of their tent. He was standing there peering excitedly and short-sightedly out at the rain through his glasses, looking angry and tough, like a big-city hack driver, individual and incorruptible even in the ten-million coloured uniform. Every time Seeger came upon Welch unexpectedly, he couldn't help smiling at the belligerent stance, the harsh stare through the steel-rimmed G.I. glasses, which had nothing at all to do with the way Welch really was. 'It's a family inheritance,' Welch had once explained. 'My whole family stands as though we were getting ready to rap a drunk with a beer glass. Even my old lady.' Welch had six brothers, all devout, according to Welch, and Seeger from time to time idly pictured them standing in a row, on Sunday mornings in church, seemingly on the verge of general violence, amid the hushed Latin and Sabbath millinery.

'How much?' Welch asked loudly.

'Don't make us laugh,' Olson said, pushing past him into the tent.

'What do you think I could get from the French for my combat jacket?' Seeger said. He went into the tent and lay down on his cot.

Welch followed them and stood between the two of them, a superior smile on his face. 'Boys,' he said, 'on a man's errand.'

'I can just see us now,' Olson murmured, lying on his cot with his hands clasped behind his head, 'painting Montmarte red. Please bring on the naked dancing girls. Four bucks worth.'

'I am not worried,' Welch announced.

'Get out of here.' Olson turned over on his stomach.

'I know where we can put our hands on sixty-five bucks.'

34

Welch looked triumphantly first at Olson, then at Seeger.

Olson turned over slowly and sat up. 'I'll kill you,' he said, 'if you're kidding.'

'While you guys are wasting your time,' Welch said, 'fooling around with the infantry, I used my head. I went into Reems and used my head.'

'Rance,' Olson said automatically. He had had two years of French in college and he felt, now that the war was over, that he had to introduce his friends to some of his culture.

'I got to talking to a captain in the Air Force,' Welch said eagerly. 'A little fat old paddle-footed captain that never got higher off the ground than the second floor of Com Z headquarters, and he told me that what he would admire to do more than anything else is take home a nice shiny German Luger pistol with him to show to the boys back in Pacific Grove, California.'

Silence fell on the tent and Welch and Olson looked tentatively at Seeger.'

'Sixty-five bucks for a Luger, these days,' Olson said, 'is a very good figure.'

'They've been sellin' for as low as thirty-five,' said Welch hesitantly. 'I'll bet,' he said to Seeger, 'you could sell yours now and buy another one back when you get some dough and make a clear twenty-five on the deal.'

Seeger didn't say anything. He had killed the owner of the Luger, an enormous S.S. major, in Coblenz, behind some paper bales in a warehouse, and the major had fired at Seeger three times with it, once knicking his helmet, before Seeger hit him in the face at twenty feet. Seeger had kept the Luger, a long, heavy, well-balanced gun, very carefully since then, lugging it with him, hiding it at the bottom of his bedroll, oiling it three times a week, avoiding all opportunities of selling it, although he had been offered as much as a hundred dollars for it and several times eighty and ninety, while the war was still on, before German weapons became a glut on the market.

'Well,' said Welch, 'there's no hurry. I told the captain I'd see him tonight around eight o'clock in front of the Lion D'Or Hotel. You got five hours to make up your mind. Plenty of time.'

'Me,' said Olson, after a pause. 'I won't say anything.'

Seeger looked reflectively at his feet and the other two men avoided looking at him. Welch dug in his pocket. 'I forgot,' he said. 'I picked up a letter for you.' He handed it to Seeger.

'Thanks,' Seeger said. He opened it absently, thinking about the Luger.

'Me,' said Olson, 'I won't say a bloody word. I'm just going to lie here and think about that nice fat Air Force captain.'

Seeger grinned a little at him and went to the tent opening to read the letter in the light. The letter was from his father, and even from one glance at the handwriting, scrawly and hurried and spotted, so different from his father's usual steady, handsome, professional script, he knew something was wrong.

'Dear Norman,' it read, 'some time in the future you must forgive me for writing this letter. But I have been holding this in so long, and there is no one here I can talk to, and because of your brother's condition I must pretend to be cheerful and optimistic all the time at home, both with him and your mother, who has never been the same since Leonard was killed. You're the oldest now, and although I know we've never talked very seriously about anything before you have been through a great deal by now, and I imagine you must have matured considerably, and you've seen so many different places and people . . . Norman, I need help. While the war was on and you were fighting, I kept this to myself. It wouldn't have been fair to burden you with this. But now the war is over, and I no longer feel I can stand up under this alone. And you will have to face it some time when you get home, if you haven't faced it already, and perhaps we can help each other by facing it together . . . '

'I'm redeployable,' Olson was singing softly, on his cot. 'It's so enjoyable. In the Pelilu mud. With the tropical crud . . . ' He fell silent after his burst of song.

Seeger blinked his eyes, at the entrance of the tent, in the wan rainy light, and went on reading his father's letter, on the stiff white stationery with the University letterhead in polite engraving at the top of each page.

'I've been feeling this coming on for a long time,' the letter continued, 'but it wasn't until Sunday morning that something happened to make me feel it in its full force. I don't know how much you've guessed about the reason for Jacob's discharge from the Army. It's true he was pretty badly wounded in the leg at Metz, but I've asked around, and I know that men with worse wounds were returned to duty after hospitalisation. Jacob got a medical discharge, but I don't think it was for the shrapnel wound in his thigh. He is suffering now from what I suppose you call combat fatigue, and he is subject to fits of depression and hallucinations. Your mother and I thought that as time went by and the war and the Army receded, he would grow better. Instead, he is growing worse. Last Sunday morning when I came down into the living-room from upstairs he was crouched in his old uniform, next to the window, peering out . . .'

'What the hell,' Olson was saying, 'if we don't get the sixty-five bucks we can always go the Louvre. I understand the Mona Lisa is back.'

'I asked Jacob what he was doing,' the letter went on. 'He didn't turn round. 'I'm observing,' he said. 'V-1's and V-2's. Buzz-bombs and rockets. They're coming in by the hundreds.' I tried to reason with him and he told me to crouch and save myself from flying glass. To humour him I got down on the floor beside him and tried to tell him the war was over, that we were in Ohio, 4,000 miles away from the nearest spot where bombs had fallen, that America had never been touched. He wouldn't listen. "These're the new rocket bombs," he said, "for the Jews".'

'Did you ever hear of the Pantheon?' Olson asked loudly.

'No,' said Welch.

'It's free.'

'I'll go,' said Welch.

Seeger shook his head a little and blinked his eyes before he went back to the letter.

'After that,' his father went on, 'Jacob seemed to forget about the bombs from time to time, but he kept saying that the mobs were coming up the street armed with bazookas and Browning automatic rifles. He mumbled incoherently a good deal of the time and kept walking back and forth saying, "What's the situation? Do you know what the situation is?" And he told me he wasn't worried about himself, he was a soldier and he expected to be killed, but he was worried about Mother and myself and Leonard and you. He seemed to forget that Leonard was dead. I tried to calm him and get him back to bed before your mother came down, but he refused and wanted to set out immediately to rejoin his division. It was all terribly disjointed and at one time he took the ribbon he got for winning the Bronze Star and threw it in the fireplace, then he got down on his hands and knees and picked it out of the ashes and made me pin it on him again, and he kept repeating, "This is when they are coming for the Jews".'

'The next war I'm in, said Olson, 'they don't get me under the rank of colonel.'

37

It had stopped raining by now and Seeger folded the unfinished letter and went outside. He walked slowly down to the end of the company street, and facing out across the empty, soaked French fields, scarred and neglected by various armies, he stopped and opened the letter again.

'I don't know what Jacob went through in the Army,' his father wrote, 'that has done this to him. He never talks to me about the war and he refuses to go to a psychoanalyst, and from time to time he is his own bouncing, cheerful self, playing in tennis tournaments and going around with a large group of girls. But he has devoured all the concentration camp reports, and I have found him weeping when the newspapers reported that a hundred Jews were killed in Tripoli some time ago. 'The terrible thing is, Norman, that I find myself coming to believe that it is not neurotic for a Jew to behave like this today. Perhaps Jacob is the normal one, and I, going about my business, teaching economics in a quiet classroom, pretending to understand that the world is comprehensible and orderly, am really the mad one. I ask you once more to forgive me for writing you a letter like this, so different from any letter or conversation I've ever had with you. But it is crowding me, too. I do not see rockets and bombs, but I see other things.

'Wherever you go these days – restaurants, hotels, clubs, trains – you seem to hear talk about the Jews, mean, hateful, murderous talk. Whatever page you turn to in the newspapers you seem to find an article about Jews being killed somewhere on the face of the globe. And there are large, influential newspapers and well-known columnists who each day are growing more and more outspoken and more popular. The day that Roosevelt died I heard a drunken man yelling outside a bar, "Finally, they got the Jew out of the White House". And some of the people who heard him merely laughed and nobody stopped him. And on V.E. Day, in celebration, hoodlums in Los Angeles savagely beat a Jewish writer. It's difficult to know what to do, whom to fight, where to look for allies.

'Three months ago, for example, I stopped my Thursday night poker game, after playing with the same men for over ten years. John Reilly happened to say that the Jews were getting rich out of this war, and when I demanded an apology he refused, and when I looked around at the faces of the men who had been my friends for so long, I could see they were not with me. And when I left the house no one said good-night to me. I know the poison was spreading from Germany before the war

38

and during it, but I had not realised it had come so close.

'And in my economics class, I find myself idiotically hedging in my lectures. I discover that I am loath to praise any liberal writer or any liberal act and find myself somehow annoyed and frightened to see an article of criticism of existing abuses signed by a Jewish name. And I hate to see Jewish names on important committees, and hate to read of Jews fighting for the poor, the oppressed, the cheated and hungry. Somehow, even in a country where my family has lived a hundred years, the enemy has won this subtle victory over me – he has made me disfranchise myself from honest causes by calling them foreign, Communist, using Jewish names connected with them as ammunition against them.

'And, most hateful of all, I find myself looking for Jewish names in the casualty lists and secretly being glad when I discover them there, to prove that there at least, among the dead and wounded, we belong. Three times, thanks to you and your brothers, I have found our name there, and, may God forgive me, at the expense of your blood and your brother's life, through my tears, I have felt that same twitch of satisfaction . . .

'When I read the newspapers and see another story that Jews are still being killed in Poland, or Jews are requesting that they be given back their homes in France, or that they be allowed to enter some country where they will not be murdered, I am annoyed with them, I feel they are boring the rest of the world with their problems, they are making demands upon the rest of the world by being killed, they are disturbing everyone by being hungry and asking for the return of their property. If we could all fall through the crust of the earth and vanish in one hour, with our heroes and poets and prophets and martyrs, we would be doing the memory of the Jewish race a service . . .

'This is how I feel today, son. I need some help. You've been to the war, you've fought and killed men, you've seen the people of other countries. Maybe you understand things that I don't understand. Maybe you see some hope somewhere. Help me. Your loving father.'

Seeger folded the letter slowly, not seeing what he was doing because the tears were burning in his eyes. He walked slowly and aimlessly across the dead autumn grass of the empty field, away from the camp.

He tried to wipe away his tears, because with his eyes full

and dark, he kept seeing his father and brother crouched in the old-fashioned living-room in Ohio and hearing his brother, dressed in the old, discarded uniform, saying, 'These're the new rocket bombs. For the Jews.'

He sighed, looking out over the bleak, wasted land. Now, he thought, now I have to think about it. He felt a slight, unreasonable twinge of anger at his father for presenting him with the necessity of thinking about it. The Army was good about serious problems. While you were fighting, you were too busy and frightened and weary to think about anything, and at other times you were relaxing, putting your brain on a shelf, postponing everything to that impossible time of clarity and beauty after the war. Well, now, here was the impossible, clear, beautiful time, and here was his father, demanding that he think. There are all sorts of Jews, he thought, there are the sort whose every waking moment is ridden by the knowledge of Jewishness, who see signs against the Jew in every smile on a stretcher, every whisper, who see pogroms in every newspaper article, threats in every change of the weather, scorn in every hand-shake, death behind each closed door. He had not been like that. He was young, he was big and healthy and easy going and people of all kinds had seemed to like him all his life, in the Army and out. In America, especially, what was going on in Europe had seemed remote, unreal, unrelated to him. The chanting, bearded old men burning in the Nazi furnaces, and the dark-eyed women screaming prayers in Polish and Russian and German as they were pushed naked into the gas chambers had seemed as shadowy and almost as unrelated to him as he trotted out on to the Stadium field for a football game, as they must have been to the men named O'Dwyer and Wickersham and Poole who played in the line beside him.

They had seemed more related in Europe. Again and again in the towns that had been taken back from the Germans, gaunt grey-faced men had stopped him humbly, looking searchingly at him, and had asked, peering at his long, lined, grimy face, under the anonymous helmet, 'Are you a Jew?' Sometimes they asked it in English, sometimes French, or Yiddish. He didn't know French or Yiddish, but he learned to recognise the phrase. He had never understood exactly why they had asked the question, since they never demanded anything from him, rarely even could speak to him, until, one day in Strasbourg, a little bent old man and a small, shapeless woman had stopped him, and asked, in English, if he was Jewish.

'Yes,' he said, smiling at them.

The two old people had smiled widely, like children. 'Look,' the old man had said to his wife. 'A young American soldier. A Jew. And so large and strong.' He had touched Seeger's arm reverently with the tips of his fingers, then had touched the Garand he was carrying. 'And such a beautiful rifle . . . '

And there, for a moment, although he was not particularly sensitive, Seeger got an inkling of why he had been stopped and questioned by so many before. Here, to these bent, exhausted old people, ravaged of their families, familiar with flight and death for so many years, was a symbol of continuing life. A large young man in the uniform of the liberator, blood, as they thought, of their blood, but not in hiding, not quivering in fear and helplessness, but striding secure and victorious down the street, armed and capable of inflicting terrible destruction on his enemies.

Seeger had kissed the old lady on the cheek and she had wept and the old man had scolded her for it, while shaking Seeger's hand fervently and thankfully before saying good-bye.

And, thinking back on it, it was silly to pretend that, even before his father's letter, he had been like any other American soldier going through the war. When he had stood over the huge dead S.S. major with the face blown in by his bullets in the warehouse in Coblenz, and taken the pistol from the dead hand, he had tasted a strange little extra flavour of triumph. How many Jews, he'd thought, had this man killed; how fitting it is that I've killed him. Neither Olson nor Welch, who were like his brothers, would have felt that in picking up the Luger, its barrel still hot from the last shots its owner had fired before dying. And he had resolved that he was going to make sure to take this gun back with him to America, and plug it and keep it on his desk at home, as a kind of vague, half-understood sign to himself that justice had once been done and he had been its instrument.

Maybe, he thought, maybe I'd better take it back with me, but not as a memento. Not plugged, but loaded. America by now was a strange country for him. He had been away a long time and he wasn't sure what was waiting for him when he got home. If the mobs were coming down the street towards his house, he was not going to die singing and praying.

41

When he was taking basic training he'd heard a scrawny, clerklike-looking soldier from Boston talking at the other end of the PX bar, over the watered beer. 'The boys at the office,' the scratchy voice was saying, 'gave me a party before I left. And they told me one thing. "Charlie," they said, "hold on to your bayonet. We're going to be able to use it when you get back. On the Yids".'

He hadn't said anything then, because he'd felt it was neither possible nor desirable to fight against every random overheard voice raised against the Jews from one end of the world to another. But again and again, at odd moments, lying on a barracks cot, or stretched out trying to sleep on the floor of a ruined French farmhouse, he had heard that voice, harsh, satisfied, heavy with hate and ignorance, saying above the beery grumble of apprentice soldiers at the bar, 'Hold on to your bayonet . . . '

And the other stories – Jews collected stories of hatred and injustice and inklings of doom like a special, lunatic kind of miser. The story of the naval officer, commander of a small vessel off the Aleutians, who, in the officers' wardroom, had complained that he hated the Jews because it was the Jews who had demanded that the Germans be beaten first and the forces in the Pacific had been starved in consequence. And when one of his junior officers, who had just come aboard, had objected and told the commander that he was a Jew, the commander had risen from the table and said, 'Mister, the Constitution of the United States says I have to serve in the same Navy with Jews, but it doesn't say I have to eat at the same table with them.' In the fogs and the cold, swelling Arctic seas off the Aleutians, in a small boat, subject to sudden, mortal attack at any moment . . .

And the two young combat engineers in an attached company on D-Day, when they were lying off the coast right before climbing down into the landing barges. 'There's France,' one of them had said.

'What's it like?' the second one had asked, peering out across the miles of water toward the smoking coast.

'Like every place else,' the first one had answered. 'The Jews've made all the dough during the war.'

'Shut up!' Seeger had said, helplessly thinking of the dead, destroyed, wandering, starving Jews of France. The engineers had shut up, and they'd climbed down together into the heaving boat, and gone into the beach together.

And the million other stories. Jews, even the most normal and best adjusted of them, became living treasuries of them, scraps of malice and bloodthirstiness, clever and confusing and cunningly twisted so that every act by every Jew became suspect and blameworthy and hateful. Seeger had heard the stories, and had made an almost conscious effort to forget them. Now, holding his father's letter in his hand, he remembered them all.

He stared unseeingly out in front of him. Maybe, he thought, maybe it would've been better to have been killed in the war, like Leonard. Simpler. Leonard would never have to face a crowd coming for his mother and father. Leonard would not have to listen and collect these hideous, fascinating little stories that made of every Jew a stranger in any town, on any field, on the face of the earth. He had come so close to being killed so many times, it would have been so easy, so neat and final.

Seeger shook his head. It was ridiculous to feel like that, and he was ashamed of himself for the weak moment. At the age of twenty-one, death was not an answer.

'Seeger!' It was Olson's voice. He and Welch had sloshed silently up behind Seeger, standing in the open field. 'Seeger, *mon vieux,* what're you doing – grazing?'

Seeger turned slowly to them. 'I wanted to read my letter,' he said.

Olson looked closely at him. They had been together so long, through so many things, that flickers and hints of expression on each other's faces were recognised and acted upon. 'Anything wrong?' Olson asked.

'No,' said Seeger. 'Nothing much.'

'Norman,' Welch said, his voice young and solemn. 'Norman, we've been talking. Olson and me. We decided – you're pretty attached to that Luger, and maybe – if you – well . . . '

'What he's trying to say,' said Olson, 'is we withdraw the request. If you want to sell it, O.K. If you don't, don't do it for our sake. Honest.'

Seeger looked at them, standing there, disreputable and tough and familiar. 'I haven't made up my mind yet,' he said.

'Anything you decide,' Welch said oratorically, 'is perfectly all right with us. Perfectly.'

They walked aimlessly and silently across the field, away from camp. As they walked, their shoes making a wet, sliding sound in the damp, dead grass, Seeger thought of the time Olson had covered him in the little town outside Cherbourg, when Seeger had been caught going down the side of a street by four Germans with a machine gun on the second story of a house on the corner and Olson had had to stand out in the middle of the street with no cover at all for more than a minute, firing continuously, so that Seeger could get away alive. And he thought of the time outside Saint Lô when he had been wounded and had lain in a minefield for three hours and Welch and Captain Taney had come looking for him in the darkness and had found him and picked him up and run for it, all of them expecting to get blown up any second.

And he thought of all the drinks they'd had together and the long marches and the cold winter together, and all the girls they'd gone out with together, and he thought of his father and brother crouching behind the window in Ohio waiting for the rockets and the crowds armed with Browning automatic rifles.

'Say,' He stopped and stood facing them. 'Say, what do you guys think of the Jews?'

Welch and Olson looked at each other, and Olson glanced down at the letter in Seeger's hand.

'Jews?' Olson said finally. 'What're they? Welch, you ever hear of the Jews?'

Welch looked thoughtfully at the grey sky. 'No,' he said. 'But remember, I'm an uneducated fellow.'

'Sorry, Bud,' Olson said, turning to Seeger. 'We can't help you. Ask us another question. Maybe we'll do better.'

Seeger peered at the faces of his friends. He would have to rely upon them, later on, out of uniform, on their native streets, more than he had ever relied on them on the bullet-swept street and in the dark minefield in France. Welch and Olson stared back at him, troubled, their faces candid and tough and dependable.

'What time,' Seeger asked, 'did you tell that captain you'd meet him?'

'Eight o'clock,' Welch said. 'But we don't have to go. If you have any feeling about that gun . . . '

'We'll meet him,' Seeger said. 'We can use that sixty-five bucks.'

'Listen,' Olson said, 'I know how much you like that gun and I'll feel like a heel if you sell it.'

'Forget it,' Seeger said, starting to walk again. 'What could I use it for in America?'

'Flacker: All right now, Kid, now you'd better talk,' Andrew dictated. 'Business: Sound of the door closing, the slow turning of the key in the lock. Buddy: You're never going to get me to talk, Flacker. Business: Sound of a slap. Flacker: Maybe that'll make you think different, Kid. Where is Jerry Carmichael? Buddy: (Laughing) Wouldn't you like to know, Flacker? Flacker: Yeah. (Slowly, with great threat in his voice) And I'm going to find out. One way or another. See? Business: Siren fades in, louder, fades out. Announcer: Will Buddy talk? Will Flacker force him to disclose the whereabouts of the rescued son of the railroad king? Will Dusty Blades reach him in time? Tune in Monday at the same time, etcetera, etcetera . . . '

Andrew dropped on to the couch and put his feet up. He stretched and sighed as he watched Lenore finish scratching his dictation down in the shorthand notebook. 'Thirty bucks,' he said. 'There's another thirty bucks. Is it the right length?'

'Uhuh,' Lenore said. 'Eleven and a half pages. This is a very good one, Andy.'

'Yeah,' Andrew said, closing his eyes. 'Put it next to Moby Dick on your library shelf.'

'It's very exciting,' Lenore said, standing up. 'I don't know what they're complaining about.'

'You're a lovely girl.' Andrew put his hands over his eyes and rubbed around and around. 'I have wooden hinges on my eyelids. Do you sleep at night?'

'Don't do that to your eyes.' Lenore started to put on her coat. 'You only aggravate them.'

'You're right.' Andrew dug his fists into his eyes and rotated them slowly. 'You don't know how right you are.'

'Tomorrow. At ten o'clock?' Lenore asked.

'At ten o'clock. Dig me out of the arms of sleep. We shall leave Dusty Blades to his fate for this week and go on with the further adventures of Ronnie Cook and His Friends, forty dollars a script. I always enjoy writing Ronnie Cook much better than Dusty Blades. See what ten dollars does to a man.' He opened his eyes and watched Lenore putting her hat on in front of the mirror. When he squinted, she was not so plain-looking. He felt very sorry for Lenore, plain as sand, with her flat-coloured face and her hair pulled down like rope, and never a man to her name. She was putting on a red hat with a kind of ladder arrangement going up one side. It looked very funny and sad on her. Andrew realised that it was a new hat. 'That's a mighty fine hat,' he said.

'I thought a long time before I bought this hat,' Lenore said, flushing because he'd noticed it.

'Har-*riet!*' The governess next door screamed in the alley to the next-door neighbour's little girl. 'Harriet, get away from there this minute!'

Andrew turned over on his stomach on the couch and put a pillow over his head. 'Have you got any ideas for Ronnie Cook and His Friends for tomorrow?' he asked Lenore.

'No. Have you?'

'No.' He pulled the pillow tight around his head.

'You'll get them by tomorrow,' Lenore said. 'You always do.'

'Yeah,' said Andrew.

'You need a vacation,' Lenore said.

'Get out of here.'

'Good-bye,' Lenore started out. 'Get a good night's sleep.'

'Anything you say.'

Andrew watched her with one eye as she went off the porch on which he worked and through the living-room and dining-room, towards the stairs. She had nice legs. You were always surprised when a girl with a face like that had nice legs. But she had hair on her legs. She was not a lucky girl. 'Oh, no,' Andrew said as the door closed behind her, 'you are not a lucky girl.'

He closed his eyes and tried to sleep. The sun came in through the open windows and the curtains blew softly over his head and the sun was warm and comforting on his closed eyes. Across the street, on the public athletic field, four boys were shagging flies. There would be the neat pleasant crack of the bat and a long time later the smack of the ball in the fielder's glove. The tall trees outside, as old as Brooklyn, rustled a little from time to time as little spurts of wind swept across the baseball field.

'Har-*riet*!' The governess called. 'Stop that or I will make you stand by yourself in the corner all afternoon! Harriet! I demand you to stop it!' The governess was French. She had the only unpleasant French accent Andrew had ever heard.

The little girl started to cry. 'Mamma! Mamma! Mamma, she's going to hit me!' The little girl hated the governess and the governess hated the little girl, and they continually reported each other to the little girl's mother. 'Mamma!'

'You are a little liar,' the governess screamed. 'You will grow up, and you will be a liar all your life. There will be no hope for you.'

'Mamma!' wailed the little girl.

They went inside the house and it was quiet again.

'Charlie,' one of the boys on the baseball field yelled, 'hit it to me, Charlie!'

The telephone rang, four times, and then Andrew heard his mother talking into it. She came on to the porch.

'It's a man from the bank,' she said. 'He wants to talk to you.'

'You should've told him I wasn't home,' Andrew said.

'But you are home,' his mother said. 'How was I to know that . . . '

'You're right.' Andrew swung his legs over and sat up. 'You're perfectly right.'

He went into the dining-room, to the telephone, and talked to the man at the bank.

'You're a hundred and eleven dollars overdrawn,' said the man at the bank.

Andrew squinted at his mother, sitting across the room, on a straight chair, with her arms folded in her lap, her head turned just a little, so as not to miss anything.

'I thought I had about four hundred dollars in the bank,' Andrew said into the phone.

'You are a hundred and eleven dollars overdrawn,' said the man at the bank.

Andrew sighed. 'I'll check it.' He put the phone down.

'What's the matter?' his mother asked.

'I'm a hundred and eleven dollars overdrawn,' he said.

'That's shameful,' his mother said. 'You ought to be more methodical.'

'Yes.' Andrew started back to the porch.

'You're awfully careless.' His mother followed him. 'You really ought to keep track of your money.'

'Yes.' Andrew sat down on the couch.

'Give me a kiss,' his mother said.

'Why?'

'No particular reason.' She laughed.

'O.K.' He kissed her and she held him for a moment. He dropped down on the couch. She ran her finger under his eye.

'You've got rings under your eyes,' she said.

'That's right.'

She kissed him again and went to the rear of the house. He closed his eyes. From the rear of the house came the sound of the vacuum-cleaner. Andrew felt his muscles getting stiff in protest against the vacuum-cleaner. He got up and went to her bedroom, where she was running the machine back and forth under the bed. She was down on one knee and was bent over, looking under the bed.

'Hey!' Andrew yelled. 'Hey, Mom!'

She turned off the machine and looked up at him. 'What's the matter?'

'I'm trying to sleep,' he said.

'Well, why don't you sleep?'

'The vacuum-cleaner. It's shaking the house.'

His mother stood up, her face setting into stern lines. 'I've got to clean the house, don't I?'

'Why do you have to clean the house while I'm trying to sleep?'

His mother bent down again. 'I can't use it while you're working. I can't use it while you're reading. I can't use it until ten o'clock in the morning because you're sleeping.' She started the machine. 'When am I supposed to clean the house?' she called over the noise of the cleaner. 'Why don't you sleep at night like everybody else?' And she put her head down low and vigorously ran the machine back and forth.

Andrew watched her for a moment. No arguments came to him. The sound of the cleaner so close to him made his nerves jump. He went out of the room, closing the door behind him.

The telephone was ringing and he picked it up and said, 'Hello.'

'Ahndrew?' his agent's voice asked. His agent was from Brooklyn, too, but he had a very broad A, with which he impressed actors and sponsors.

'Yes, this is Ahndrew.' Andrew always made this straight-faced joke with his agent, but the agent never seemed to catch on. 'You didn't have to call. The Dusty Blades scripts are all through. You'll get them tomorrow.'

'I called about something else, Ahndrew,' his agent said, his voice very smooth and influential on the phone. 'The complaints're piling up on the Blades scripts. They're as slow as gum. Nothing ever happens. Ahndrew, you're not writing for the *Atlantic Monthly*.'

'I know I'm not writing for the *Atlantic Monthly*.'

'I think you've rather run out of material,' his agent said lightly, soothingly. 'I think perhaps you ought to take a little vacation from the Blades scripts.'

'Go to hell, Herman,' Andrew said, knowing that Herman had found somebody to do the scripts more cheaply for him.

'That's hardly the way to talk, Ahndrew,' Herman said, his voice still smooth, but hurt. 'After all, I have to stand in the studio and listen to the complaints.'

'Sad, Herman,' Andrew said. 'That's a sad picture,' and hung up.

He rubbed the back of his neck reflectively, feeling again the little lump behind his ear.

He went into his own room and sat at his desk looking blankly at the notes for his play that lay, neatly piled, growing older, on one side. He took out his cheque-book and his last month's vouchers and arranged them in front of him.

'One hundred and eleven dollars,' he murmured, as he checked back and added and subtracted, his eyes smarting from the strain, his hands shaking a little because the vacuum-cleaner was still going in his mother's room. Out on the athletic field more boys had arrived and formed an infield and were throwing the ball around the bases and yelling at each other.

Dr Chalmers, seventy-five dollars. That was for his mother and her stomach.

Eighty dollars rent. The roof over his head equalled two Ronnie Cook's and His Friends. Five thousand words for rent.

Buddy was in the hands of Flacker. Flacker could torture him for six pages. Then you could have Dusty Blades speeding to the rescue with Sam, by boat, and the boat could spring a leak because the driver was in Flacker's pay, and there could be a fight for the next six pages. The driver could have a gun. You could use it, but it wouldn't be liked, because you'd done at least four like it already.

Furniture, and a hundred and thirty-seven dollars. His

mother had always wanted a good dining-room table. She didn't have a maid, she said, so he ought to get her a dining-room table. How many words for a dining-room table?

'Come on, Baby, make it two,' the second baseman out on the field was yelling. 'Double 'em up!'

Andrew felt like picking up his old glove and going out there and joining them. When he was still in college he used to go out on a Saturday at ten o'clock in the moring and shag flies and jump around the infield and run and run all day, playing in pick-up games until it got too dark to see. He was always tired now and even when he played tennis he didn't move his feet right, because he was tired, and hit flat-footed and wild.

Spain, one hundred dollars. Oh, Lord.

A hundred and fifty to his father, to meet his father's pay-roll. His father had nine people on his pay-roll, making little tin gadgets that his father tried to sell to the dime stores, and at the end of every month Andrew had to meet the pay-roll. His father always gravely made out a note to him.

Flacker is about to kill Buddy out of anger and desperation. In bursts Dusty, alone. Sam is hurt. On the way to the hospital. Buddy is spirited away a moment before Dusty arrives. Flacker, very smooth and oily. Confrontation. 'Where is Buddy, Flacker?' 'You mean the little lad?' 'I mean the little lad, Flacker!'

Fifty dollars to Dorothy's piano teacher. His sister. Another plain girl. She might as well learn how to play the piano. Then one day they'd come to him and say, 'Dorothy is ready for her debut. All we're asking you to do is rent Town Hall for a Wednesday evening. Just advance the money.' She'd never get married. She was too smart for the men who would want her and too plain for the men she'd want herself. She bought her dresses in Saks. He would have to support, for life, a sister who would only buy her dresses in Saks and pay her piano teacher fifty dollars a month every month. She was only twenty-four, she would have a normal life expectancy of at least forty years, twelve times forty, plus dresses at Saks and Town Hall from time to time . . .

His father's teeth – ninety dollars. The money it cost to keep a man going in his losing fight against age.

The automobile. Nine hundred dollars. A nine-hundred-dollar cheque looked very austere impressive, like a penal institution. He was going to go off in the automobile, find a place in the mountains, write a play. Only he could never get

50

himself far enough ahead on Dusty Blades and Ronnie Cook and His friends. Twenty thousand words a week, each week, recurring like Sunday on the calendar. How many words was *Hamlet*? Thirty, thirty-five thousand?

Twenty-three dollars to Best's. That was Martha's sweater for her birthday. 'Either you say yes or no,' Martha said Saturday night. 'I want to get married and I've waited long enough.' If you married you paid rent in two places, light, gas, telephone twice, and you bought stockings, dresses, toothpaste, medical attention, for your wife.

Flacker plays with something in his pocket. Dusty's hand shoots out, grabs his wrist, pulls his hand out. Buddy's little pen-knife, which Dusty had given him for a birthday present, is in Flacker's hand. 'Flacker, tell me where Buddy Jones is, or I'll kill you with my bare hands.' A gong rings. Flacker has stepped on an alarm. Doors open and the room fills with his henchmen.

Twenty dollars to Macy's for books. Parrington, *Main Currents in American Thought*. How does Dusty Blades fit into the *Main Current of American Thought*?

Ten dollars to Dr Farber. 'I don't sleep at night. Can you help me?'

'Do you drink coffee?'

'I drink one cup of coffee in the morning. That's all.'

Pills, to be taken before retiring. Ten dollars. We ransom our lives from doctors' hands.

If you marry, you take an apartment downtown because it's silly to live in Brooklyn this way; and you buy furniture, four rooms full of furniture, beds, chairs, dish-rags, relatives. Martha's family was poor and getting no younger and finally there would be three families, with rent and clothes and doctors and funerals.

Andrew got up and opened the closet door. In it, stacked in files, were the scripts he had written in the last four years. They stretched from one end of a wide closet across to another, bridge from one wall to another of a million words. Four years' work.

Next script. The henchmen close in on Dusty. He hears the sounds of Buddy screaming in the next room . . .

How many years more?

The vacuum-cleaner roared.

Martha was Jewish. That meant you'd have to lie your way into some hotels, if you went at all, and you never could

51

escape from one particular meanness of the world around you; and when the bad time came there you'd be, adrift on that dangerous sea.

He sat down at his desk. One hundred dollars again to Spain. Barcelona had fallen and the long dusty lines were beating their way to the French border with the planes over them, and out of a sense of guilt at not being on a dusty road, yourself, bloody-footed and in fear of death, you gave a hundred dollars, feeling at the same time that it was too much and nothing you ever gave could be enough. Three-and-a-third The Adventures of Dusty Blades to the dead and dying of Spain.

The world loads you day by day with new burdens that increase on your shoulders. Lift a pound and you find you're carrying a ton. 'Marry me,' she says, 'marry me.' Then what does Dusty do? What the hell can he do that he hasn't done before? For five afternoons a week now, for a year, Dusty has been in Flacker's hands, or the hands of somebody else who is Flacker but has another name, and each time he has escaped. How now?

The vacuum roared in the hallway outside his room.

'Mom!' he yelled. 'Please turn that thing off!'

'What did you say?' his mother called.

'Nothing.'

He added up the bank balances. His figures showed that he was four hundred and twelve dollars overdrawn instead of one hundred and eleven dollars, as the bank said. He didn't feel like adding the figures over. He put the vouchers and the bank's sheet into an envelope for his income-tax returns.

'Hit it out, Charlie!' a boy called on the field. 'Make it a fast one!'

Andrew felt like going out and playing with them. He changed his clothes and put on a pair of old spikes that were lying in the back of the closet. His old pants were tight on him. Fat. If he ever let go, if anything happened and he couldn't exercise, he'd blow up like a house, if he got sick and had to lie in bed and convalesce . . . Maybe Dusty has a knife in a holster up his sleeve . . . How plant that? The rent, the food, the piano teacher, the people at Saks who sold his sister dresses, the nimble girls who painted the tin gadgets in his father's shop, the teeth in his father's mouth, the doctors, the doctors, all living on the words that would have to come out of his head. See here, Flacker, I know what you're up to. Business: Sound of a shot. A groan. Hurry, before the train gets to the crossing! Look! He's gaining on us! Hurry! will he make it? Will Dusty Blades head off the desperate gang of counterfeiters and murderers in the race for the yacht? Will I be able to keep it up? The years, the years ahead . . . You grow fat and the lines become permanent under your eyes and you drink too much and you pay more to the doctors because death is nearer and there is no stop, no vacation from life, in no year can you say, 'I want to sit this one out; kindly excuse me'.

His mother opened the door. 'Martha's on the phone.'

Andrew clattered out in his spiked shoes, holding the old, torn fielder's glove. He closed the door to the dining-room to show his mother this was going to be a private conversation.

'Hello,' he said. 'Yes.' He listened gravely. 'No,' he said. 'I guess not. Good-bye. Good luck, Martha.'

He stood looking at the phone. His mother came in and he raised his head and started down the steps.

'Andrew,' she said, 'I want to ask you something.'

'What?'

'Could you spare fifty dollars, Andrew?'

'Oh, God!'

'It's important. You know I wouldn't ask you if it wasn't important. It's for Dorothy.'

'What does she need it for?'

'She's going to a party, a very important party, a lot of very big people're going to be there and she's sure they'll ask her to play . . . '

'Do the invitations cost fifty dollars apiece?' Andrew kicked the top step and a little piece of dried mud fell off the spiked shoes.

'No, Andrew.' His mother was talking in her asking-for-money voice. 'It's for a dress. She can't go without a new dress, she says. There's a man there she's after.'

'She won't get him, dress or no dress,' Andrew said. 'Your daughter's a very plain girl.'

'I know,' his mother's hand waved a little, helpless and sad. 'But it's better if she at least does the best she can. I feel so sorry for her, Andrew . . . '

'Everybody comes to me!' Andrew yelled, his voice suddenly high. 'Nobody leaves me alone! Not for a minute!'

He was crying now and he turned to hide it from his mother. She looked at him, surprised, shaking her head. She put her arms around him. 'Just do what you want to, Andrew, that's all. Don't do anything you don't want to do.'

'Yeah,' Andrew said. 'Yeah. I'm sorry. I'll give you the money. I'm sorry I yelled at you.'

'Don't give it to me if you don't want to, Andrew.' His mother was saying this honestly, believing it.'

He laughed a little. 'I want to, Mom. I want to.'

He patted her shoulder and went down towards the baseball field, leaving her standing there puzzled at the top of the steps.

The sun and the breeze felt good on the baseball field, and he forgot for an hour, but he moved slowly. His arms hurt at the shoulder when he threw, and the boy playing second base called him Mister, which he wouldn't have done even last year, when Andrew was twenty-four.

Strawberry Ice Cream Soda

Eddie Barnes looked at the huge Adirondack hills, browning in the strong summer afternoon sun. He listened to his brother Lawrence practice finger-exercises on the piano outside the house, onetwothreefour*five*, onetwothreefour*five*, and longed for New York. He lay on his stomach in the long grass of the front lawn and delicately peeled his sunburnt nose. Morosely he regarded a grasshopper, stupid with sun, wavering on a bleached blade of grass in front of his nose. Without interest he put out his hand and captured it.

'Give honey,' he said, listlessly. 'Give honey or I'll kill yuh . . .'

But the grasshopper crouched unmoving, unresponsive, oblivious to Life or Death.

Disgusted, Eddie tossed the grasshopper away. It flew uncertainly, wheeled, darted back to its blade of grass, alighted and hung there dreamily, shaking a little in the breeze in front of Eddie's nose. Eddie turned over on his back and looked at the high blue sky.

The country! Why anybody ever went to the country . . . What things must be doing in New York now, what rash, beautiful deeds on the steaming, rich streets, what expeditions, what joy, what daring sweaty adventure among the trucks, the trolley cars, the baby carriages! What cries, hoarse and humorous, what light laughter outside the red-painted shop where lemon ice was sold at three cents the double scoop, true nourishment for a man at fifteen.

Eddie looked around him, at the silent, eternal, granite-streaked hills. Trees and birds, that's all. He sighed, torn with thoughts of distant pleasure, stood up, went over to the window behind which Lawrence seriously hammered at the piano, onetwothreefour*five*.

'Lawrrrence,' Eddie called, the rrr's rolling with horrible gentility in his nose, 'Lawrrrence, you stink.'

Lawrence didn't even look up. His thirteen-year-old fingers, still pudgy and babyish went onetwothreefour*five*, with unswerving precision. He was talented and he was dedicated to his talent and some day they would wheel a huge piano out on to the stage of Carnegie Hall and he would come out and bow politely to the thunder of applause and sit down, flipping his coat-tails back, and play, and men and women would laugh and cry and remember their first loves as they listened to him. So now his fingers went up and down, up and down, taking strength against the great day.

Eddie looked through the window a moment more, watching his brother, sighed and walked around to the side of the house, where a crow was sleepily eating the radish seeds that Eddie had planted three days ago in a fit of boredom. Eddie threw a stone at the crow and the crow silently flew up to the branch of an oak and waited for Eddie to go away. Eddie threw another stone at the crow. The crow moved to another branch. Eddie wound up and threw a curve, but the crow disdained it. Eddie picked his foot up the way he'd seen Carl Hubbell do and sizzled one across not more than three feet from the crow. Without nervousness the crow walked six inches up the branch. In the style now of Dizzy Dean, with terrifying speed, Eddie delivered his fast one. It was wild and the crow didn't even cock his head. You had to expect to be a little wild with such speed. Eddie found a good round stone and rubbed it professionally on his back pocket. He looked over his shoulder to hold the runner close to the bag, watched for the signal. Eddie Hubbell Dean Mungo Feller Ferrell Warnecke Gomez Barnes picked up his foot and let go his high hard one. The crow slowly got off his branch and regretfully sailed away.

Eddie went over, kicked away the loose dirt, and looked at his radish seeds. Nothing was happening to them. They just lay there, baked and inactive, just as he had placed them. No green, no roots, no radishes, no anything. He was sorry he'd ever gone in for farming. The package of seeds had cost him a dime, and the only thing that happened to them was that they were eaten by crows. And now he could use that dime. Tonight he had a date.

'I got a date,' he said aloud, savouring the words. He went to the shade of the grape arbour to think about it. He sat down on the bench under the cool flat leaves, and thought about it. He'd never had a date before in his life. He had

56

thirty-five cents. Thirty-five cents ought to be enough for any girl, but if he hadn't bought the radish seeds, he'd have had forty-five cents, really prepared for any eventuality. 'Damn crow,' he said, thinking of the evil black head feeding on his dime.

Many times he'd wondered how you managed to get a date. Now he knew. It happened all of a sudden. You went up to a girl where she was lying on the raft in a lake and you looked at her, chubby in a blue bathing suit, and she looked seriously at you out of serious blue eyes where you stood dripping with lake water, with no hair on your chest, and suddenly you said, 'I don't s'pose yuh're not doing anything t'morra night, are yuh?' You didn't know quite what you meant, but she did, and she said, 'Why, no, Eddie. Say about eight o'clock?' And you nodded and dived back into the lake and there you were.

Still, those radish seeds, that crow-food, that extra dime . . .

Lawrence came out, flexing his fingers, very neat in clean khaki shorts and a white blouse. He sat down next to Eddie in the grape arbour.

'I would like a strawberry ice cream soda,' he said.

'Got any money?' Eddie asked, hopefully.

Lawrence shook his head.

'No strawberry ice cream soda,' Eddie said.

Lawrence nodded seriously. 'You got any money?' he asked.

'Some,' Eddie said carefully. He pulled down a grape leaf and cracked it between his hands, held up the two parts and looked at them critically.

Lawrence didn't say anything, but Eddie sensed a feeling developing in the grape arbour, like a growth. 'I gotta save my money,' Eddie said harshly. 'I got a date, I got thirty-five cents. How do I know she won't want a banana-split tonight?'

Lawrence nodded again, indicating that he understood, but sorrow washed up in his face like a high tide.

They sat in silence, uncomfortably, listening to the rustle of the grape leaves.

'All the time I was practising,' Lawrence said, finally, 'I kept thinking, "I would like a strawberry ice cream soda, I would like a strawberry ice cream soda . . . " '

Eddie stood up abruptly. 'Aaah, let's get outa here. Let's go down to the lake. Maybe something's doing down the lake.'

They walked together through the fields to the lake, not saying anything, Lawrence flexing his fingers mechanically.

'Why don't yuh stop that fer once?' Eddie asked, with distaste. 'Just fer once?'

'This is good for my fingers. It keeps them loose.'

'Yuh give me a pain.'

'All right,' Lawrence said. 'I won't do it now.'

They walked on again, Lawrence barely up to Eddie's chin, frailer, cleaner, his hair mahogany dark and smooth on his high pink, baby brow. Lawrence whistled. Eddie listened with disguised respect.

'That's not so bad,' Eddie said. 'You don't whistle half-bad.'

'That's from the Brahms second piano concerto,' Lawrence stopped whistling for a moment. 'It's easy to whistle.'

'Yuh give me a pain,' Eddie said, mechanically, 'a real pain.'

When they got to the lake, there was nobody there. Flat and unruffled it stretched across, like a filled blue cup, to the woods on the other side.

'Nobody here,' Eddie said, staring at the raft, unmoving and dry in the still water. 'That's good. Too many people here all the time.' His eyes roamed the lake, to the farthest corner, to the deepest cove.

'How would yuh like to go rowing in a boat out in that old lake?' Eddie asked.

'We haven't got a boat,' Lawrence answered reasonably.

'I didn't ask yuh that. I asked, "How'd yuh like to go rowing?"'

'I'd like to go rowing if we had a . . .'

'Shut up!' Eddie took Lawrence's arm, led him through tall grass to the waer's edge, where a flat-bottomed old boat was drawn up, the water just lapping at the stern, high, an old red colour, faded by sun and storm. A pair of heavy oars lay along the bottom of the boat.

'Jump in,' Eddie said, 'when I tell yuh to.'

'But it doesn't belong to us.'

'Yuh want to go rowing, don't yuh?'

'Yes, but . . .'

'Then jump in when I give yuh the word.'

Lawrence neatly took off his shoes and socks while Eddie hauled the boat into the water.

'Jump in!' Eddie called.

Lawrence jumped. The boat glided out across the still lake. Eddie rowed industriously once they got out of the marsh grass.

'This isn't half bad, is it?' He leaned back on his oars for a moment.

'It's nice,' Lawrence said. 'It's very peaceful.'

'Aaah,' said Eddie, 'yuh even talk like a pianist.' And he rowed. After a while he got tired and let the boat go with the wind. He lay back and thought of the night to come, dabbling his fingers in the water, happy. 'They oughta see me now, back on a Hunnerd and Seventy-third Street,' he said. 'They oughta see me handle this old boat.'

'Everything would be perfect,' Lawrence agreed, picking his feet up out of the puddle that was collecting on the bottom of the boat, 'if we only knew that when we got out of this boat, we were going to get a strawberry ice cream soda.'

'Why don't yuh think of somethin' else? Always thinkin' of one thing! Don't yuh get tired?'

'No,' Lawrence said, after thinking it over.

'Here!' Eddie pushed the oars towards his brother. 'Row! That'll give yuh somethin' else t' think about.'

Lawrence took the oars gingerly. 'This is bad for my hands,' he explained as he pulled dutifully on the oars. 'It stiffens the fingers.'

'Look where yuh're goin'!' Eddie cried impatiently. 'In circles. What the hell's the sense of goin' in circles?'

'That's the way the boat goes,' Lawrence said, pulling hard. 'I can't help it if that's the way the boat goes.'

'A pianist. A regular pianist. That's all yuh are. Gimme those oars.'

Gratefully Lawrence yielded the oars up.

'It's not my fault if the boat goes in circles. That's the way it's made,' he persisted quietly.

'Aaah, shut up!' Eddie pulled savagely on the oars. The boat surged forward, foam at the prow.

'Hey, out there in the boat! Hey!' A man's voice called over the water.

'Eddie,' Lawrence said, 'there's a man yelling at us.'

'Come on in here, before I beat your pants off!' the man called. 'Get out of my boat!'

'He wants us to get out of his boat,' Lawrence interpreted. 'This must be his boat.'

'You don't mean it,' Eddie snorted with deep sarcasm. He turned around to shout at the man on the shore, who was waving his arms now. 'All right,' Eddie called. 'All right. We'll give yuh yer old boat. Keep your shirt on.'

The man jumped up and down. 'I'll beat yer heads off,' he shouted.

Lawrence wiped his nose nervously. 'Eddie,' he said, 'why don't we row over to the other side and walk home from there?'

Eddie looked at his brother contemptuously. 'What're yuh – afraid?'

'No,' Lawrence said, after a pause. 'But why should we get into an argument?'

For answer Eddie pulled all the harder on the oars. The boat flew through the water. Lawrence squinted to look at the rapidly nearing figure of the man on the bank.

'He's a great big man, Eddie,' Lawrence reported. 'You never saw such a big man. And he looks awfully sore. Maybe we shouldn't've gone out in this boat. Maybe he doesn't like people to go out in his boat, Eddie, are you listening to me?'

With a final heroic pull, Eddie drove the boat into the shore. It grated with a horrible noise on the pebbles of the lake bottom.

'Oh, my God,' the man said, 'that's the end of that boat.'

'That doesn't really hurt it, mister,' Lawrence said. 'It makes a lot of noise, but it doesn't do any damage.'

The man reached over and grabbed Lawrence by the back of his neck with one hand and placed him on solid ground. He was a very big man, with tough bristles that grew all over his double chin and farmer's muscles in his arms that were quivering with passion now under a mat of hair. There was a boy of about thirteen with him, obviously, from his look, his son, and the son was angry, too.

'Hit 'im, Pop,' the son kept calling. 'Wallop 'im!'

The man shook Lawrence again and again. He was almost too overcome with anger to speak. 'No damage, eh? Only noise, eh?' he shouted into Lawrence's paling face. 'I'll show you damage. I'll show you noise.'

Eddie spoke up. Eddie was out of the boat now, an oar gripped in his hand, ready for the worst. 'That's not fair,' he said. 'Look how much bigger yuh are than him. Why'n't yuh pick on somebody yuh size?'

The farmer's boy jumped up and down in passion, exactly as his father had done. 'I'll fight him, Pop. I'll fight 'im! I'm his size! Come on, kid, put yer hands up!'

The farmer looked at his son, looked at Lawrence. Slowly he released Lawrence. 'O.K.,' he said. 'Show him, Nathan.'

Nathan pushed Lawrence. 'Come into the woods, kid,' he said belligerently. 'We can settle it there.'

'One in the eye,' Eddie whispered out of the corner of his mouth. 'Give 'im one in the eye, Larry!'

But Lawrence stood with eyes lowered, regarding his hands.

'Well?' the farmer asked.

Lawrence still looked at his hands, opening and closing them slowly.

'He don't wanna fight,' Nathan taunted Eddie. 'He just wants t' row in our boat, he don't wanna fight.'

'He wants to fight, all right,' Eddie said staunchly, and under his breath. 'Come on, Larry, in the kisser, a fast one in the puss . . . '

But Larry stood still, calmly, seeming to be thinking of Brahms and Beethoven, of distant concert halls.

'He's yella, that's what's the matter with him!' Nathan roared. 'He's a coward; all city kids're cowards!'

'He's no coward,' Eddie insisted, knowing in his deepest heart that his brother was a coward. With his knees he nudged Lawrence. 'Bring up yuh left! Please, Larry, bring up yuh left! '

Deaf to all pleas, Lawrence kept his hands at his sides.

'Yella! Yella! Yella!' Nathan screamed loudly.

'Well,' the farmer wanted to know, 'is he goin' to fight or not?'

'Larry!' Fifteen years of desperation was in Eddie's voice, but it made no mark on Lawrence. Eddie turned slowly towards home. 'He's not goin' to fight,' he said flatly. And then, as one throws a bone to a neighbour's noisy dog, 'Come on, you . . . '

Slowly Lawrence bent over, picked up his shoes and socks, took a step after his brother.

'Wait a minute, you!' the farmer called. He went after Eddie, turned him around. 'I want to talk to ye.'

'Yeah?' Eddie said sadly, with little defiance. 'What do yuh wanna say?'

'See that house over there?' the farmer asked, pointing.

'Yeah,' Eddie said. 'What about it?'

'That's my house,' the farmer said. 'You stay away from it. See?'

'O.K. O.K.,' Eddie said wearily, all pride gone.

'See that boat there?' the farmer asked, pointing at the source of all the trouble.

'I see it,' Eddie said.

'That's my boat. Stay away from it or I'll beat hell outa ye. See?'

'Yeah, yeah. I see,' Eddie said. 'I won't touch yer lousy boat.' And once more, to Lawrence, 'Come on, *you* . . .'

'Yella! Yella! Yella!' Nathan kept roaring, jumping up and down, until they passed out of earshot, across the pleasant fields, ripe with the soft sweet smell of clover in the late summer afternoon. Eddie walked before Lawrence, his face grimly contracted, his mouth curled in shame and bitterness. He stepped on the clover blossoms fiercely, as though he hated them, wanted to destroy them, the roots under them, the very ground they grew in.

Holding his shoes in his hands, his head bent on his chest, his hair still mahogany smooth and mahogany dark, Lawrence followed ten feet back in the footsteps, plainly marked in the clover, of his brother.

'Yella,' Eddie was muttering, loud enough for the villain behind him to hear clearly, 'Yella! Yella as a flower. My own brother,' he marvelled. 'If it was me I'd'a been glad to get killed before I let anybody call me that. I would let 'em cut my heart out first. My own brother. Yella as a flower. Just one in the eye! Just *one*! Just to show 'im . . . But he stands there, takin' guff from a kid with holes in his pants. A pianist. Lawrrrence! They knew what they were doin' when they called yuh Lawrrrence! Don't talk to me! I don't want yuh ever to talk to me again as long as yuh live! Lawrrrrence!'

In sorrow too deep for tears, the two brothers reached home, ten feet, ten million miles apart.

Without looking around, Eddie went to the grape arbour, stretched out on the bench. Lawrence looked after him, his face pale and still, then went into the house.

Face downward on the bench, close to the rich black earth of the arbour, Eddie bit his fingers to keep the tears back. But he could not bite hard enough, and the tears came, a bitter tide, running down his face, dropping on the black soft earth in which the grapes were rooted.

'Eddie!'

Eddie scrambled around, pushing the tears away with iron hands. Lawrence was standing there, carefully pulling on doeskin gloves over his small hands. 'Eddie,' Lawrence was saying, stonily disregarding the tears. 'I want you to come with me.'

Silently, but with singing in his heart so deep it called new tears to his wet eyes, Eddie got up, blew his nose, and followed after his brother, caught up with him, walked side by side with him across the field of clover, so lightly that the red and purple blossoms barely bent in their path.

Eddie knocked sternly at the door of the farmhouse, three knocks, solid, vigorous, the song of trumpets caught in them.

Nathan opened the door. 'What do ye want?' he asked suspiciously.

'A little while ago,' Eddie said formally, 'yuh offered to fight my brother. He's ready now.'

Nathan looked at Lawrence, standing there, straight, his head up, his baby lips compressed into a thin tight line, his gloved hands creased in solid fists. He started to close the door. 'He had his chance,' Nathan said.

Eddie kept the door open firmly. 'Yuh offered; remember that,' he reminded Nathan politely.

'He shoulda fought then,' Nathan said stubbornly. 'He had his chance.'

'Come on,' Eddie almost begged. 'Yuh wanted to fight before.'

'That was before. Lemme close the door.'

'Yuh can't do this!' Eddie was shouting desperately. 'Yuh offered!'

Nathan's father, the farmer, appeared in the doorway. He looked bleakly out. 'What's goin' on here?' he asked

'A little while ago,' Eddie spoke very fast, 'this man here offered to fight this man here.' His eloquent hand indicated first Nathan, then Lawrence. 'Now we've come to take the offer.'

The farmer looked at his son. 'Well?'

'He had his chance,' Nathan grumbled sullenly.

'Nathan don't want t' fight,' the farmer said to Eddie. 'Get outa here.'

Lawrence stepped up, over to Nathan. He looked Nathan squarely in the eye. 'Yella,' he said to Nathan.

The farmer pushed his son outside the door. 'Go fight him,' he ordered.

'We can settle it in the woods,' Lawrence said.

'Wipe him up, Larry!' Eddie called as Lawrence and Nathan set out for the woods, abreast, but a polite five yards apart. Eddie watched them disappear behind trees, in silence.

The farmer sat down heavily on the porch, took out a pack-

63

age of cigarettes, offered them to Eddie. 'Want one?'

Eddie looked at the cigarettes, suddenly took one. 'Thanks,' he said.

The farmer struck a match for the cigarettes, leaned back against a pillar, stretched comfortably, in silence. Eddie licked the tobacco of his first cigarette nervously off his lips.

'Sit down,' the farmer said; 'ye cin never tell how long kids'll fight.

'Thanks,' Eddie said, sitting, pulling daringly at the cigarette, exhaling slowly, with natural talent.

In silence they both looked across the field to the woods that shielded the battlefield. The tops of the trees waved a little in the wind and the afternoon was collecting in deep blue shadows among the thick brown tree-trunks where they gripped the ground. A chicken hawk floated lazily over the field, banking and slipping with the wind. The farmer regarded the chicken hawk without malice.

'Some day,' the farmer said, 'I'm going to get that son of a gun.'

'What is it?' Eddie asked, carefully holding the cigarette out so he could talk.

'Chicken hawk. You're from the city, ain't ye?'

'Yeah.'

'Like it in the city?'

'Nothing like it.'

The farmer puffed reflectively. 'Some day I'm goin' to live in the city. No sense in livin' in the country these days.'

'Oh, I don't know,' Eddie said. 'The country's very nice. There's a lot to be said for the country.'

The farmer nodded, weighing the matter in his own mind. He put out his cigarette. 'Another cigarette?' he asked Eddie.

'No, thanks,' Eddie said. 'I'm still working on this.'

'Say,' said the farmer, 'do you think your brother'll damage my kid?'

'It's possible,' Eddie said. 'He's very tough, my brother. He has dozens a' fights, every month. Every kid back home's scared stiff a' him. Why.' said Eddie, sailing full into fancy, 'I remember one day, Larry fought three kids all in a row. In a half a hour. He busted all their noses. In a half-hour! He's got a terrific left jab – one, two, bang! like this – and it gets 'em in the nose.'

'Well, he can't do Nathan's nose any harm.' The farmer

laughed. 'No matter what you did to a nose like that it'd be a improvement.'

'He's got a lot of talent, my brother,' Eddie said, proud of the warrior in the woods. 'He plays the piano. He's a very good piano-player. You ought to hear him.'

'A little kid like that,' the farmer marvelled. 'Nathan can't do nothing.'

Off in the distance, in the gloom under the trees, two figures appeared, close together, walked slowly out into the sunlight of the field. Eddie and the farmer stood up. Wearily the two fighters approached, together, their arms dangling at their sides.

Eddie looked first at Nathan. Nathan's mouth had been bleeding and there was a lump on his forehead and his ear was red. Eddie smiled with satisfaction. Nathan had been in a fight. Eddie walked slowly towards Lawrence. Lawrence approached with head high. But it was a sadly battered head. The hair was tangled, an eye was closed, the nose was bruised and still bled. Lawrence sucked in the blood from his nose from time to time with his tongue. His collar was torn, his pants covered with forest loam, with his bare knees skinned and raw. But in the one eye that still could be seen shone a clear light, honourable, indomitable.

'Ready to go home now, Eddie?' Lawrence asked.

'Sure,' Eddie started to pat Lawrence on the back, pulled his hand back. He turned and waved at the farmer. 'So long.'

'So long,' the farmer called. 'Any time you want to use the boat, just step into it.'

'Thanks.' Eddie waited while Lawrence shook hands gravely with Nathan.

'Good night,' Lawrence said. 'It was a good fight.'

'Yeah,' Nathan said.

The two brothers walked away, close together, across the field of clover, fragrant in the long shadows. Half the way they walked in silence, the silence of equals, strong men communicating in a language more eloquent than words, the only sound the thin jingle of the thirty-five cents in Eddie's pocket.

Suddenly Eddie stopped Lawrence. 'Let's go this way,' he said, pointing off to the right.

'But home's this way, Eddie.'

'I know. Let's go into town. Let's get ice cream sodas,' Eddie said; 'let's get strawberry ice cream sodas.'

5

Material Witness

Lester Barnum walked down the steps, across the street and around the corner without looking back. He was a small worn-out, neat, married-looking man, walking slowly, as though he never got enough sleep, his head lowered politely and humbly into his grey overcoat, his grey face pursed vaguely and undramatically over some inner problem.

A year in jail, he thought. He shook his head and turned to look at the huge grey prison that had held him, but he had gone around the corner without realising it, and the jail and the year were behind him and out of sight. He walked aimlessly on, looking without real interest at the free men about him.

He hadn't liked the men he'd met in prison. In the movies, cell blocks were invariably inhabited by warm, great-hearted, harmless persons, but in the year he had spent behind bars no convicts of that particular type had turned up. There had only been rough, large, desperate men who had put pepper in his coffee, nails in his bed, and occasionally, in moments of extreme emotion, had hit him with mop-handles and slop buckets. And there was always a small, pasty-faced man turning up every month or so, whispering gratingly into his ear in the exercise yard, 'Talk an' the next stop is Woodlawn. Fer yer own good . . .'

Everybody took it for granted that he owned some secret, deadly information – the police, the district attorney, the convicts. Barnum sighed as he walked listlessly along the bustling, free steets. He stopped irresolutely at a corner. No direction was more inviting than any other direction, no street offered any final destination. There was no home for him to go to. For the first time in his forty-three years there was no definite, appointed place where his clothes were hanging, his bed ready to be slept in. His wife had gone to St Louis with an automobile mechanic and had taken his two daughters with her 'I might as well tell you,' she'd said flatly in the visiting-room at the jail after he'd been there three months. 'This has been going on a long time, but now he's going to St Louis and I guess it's about time you found out.' And she'd pulled at one of the curly little hats she was always wearing and adjusted her corset a little angrily as though Barnum had insulted her and she'd started west. And he'd found out that the printing shop he'd worked in for seventeen years had been unionised and his job had been taken over, at a much higher salary, by a Rumanian with a beard.

Barnum whistled bleakly through his teeth, thinking vaguely of the years behind him when he had led an ordinary, simple existence, bringing home the comic papers to his children every evening, dozing after dinner while his wife complained of one thing after another, a plain, unnoticed, uncomplicated life, in which he never talked to such important, improbable persons as district attorneys and Irish detectives, never had pepper put in his coffee by exasperated swindlers and dope-peddlers.

It had all started because he'd turned down Columbus Avenue, instead of Broadway. A year ago he'd been walking slowly and quietly home from work, worrying over the fact that the Boss had marched back and forth behind him in the shop all afternoon, muttering, 'I can't stand it! There are limits! I can't stand it!' Barnum hadn't known what it was that the Boss couldn't stand, but, vaguely, it had worried him, as there was always the possibility that the thing that the Boss couldn't stand might be Barnum. But he had been walking wearily home, knowing there would be haddock for dinner and that he would have to mind the children that evening because his wife was going to some woman's club where, she said, instruction was to be had in knitting.

Dimly Barnum had felt the evening was not going to be pleasant – dull, aimless, like thousands of other evenings in his life.

Then it had happened. A tall, very dark man had walked swiftly past Barnum, holding his hands in his pockets. Suddenly another man, in a grey hat and topcoat, had leaped out of a doorway and tapped the tall dark man on the shoulder. 'Here you are, you son of a bitch,' the man in the grey hat had said loudly and the dark man had started to run and the man in the grey hat had pulled a gun from under his armpit and yelled, 'Not this time, Spanish!' and shot the dark man four times. The dark man slid quietly to the pavement and the man in the grey coat said, 'How do you like that?' and looked once, coldly, at Barnum, who was standing there, with his mouth open. 'Aah!' the man in the grey coat said loudly, pulling up one corner of his mouth in a snarl – and then he'd disappeared.

Barnum just stood there looking at the tall dark man who was lying quietly on the sidewalk, looking not so tall now, with the blood coming from him. After a while Barnum closed his mouth. He moved dreamily over to the man lying on the sidewalk. The man's eyes looked up at Barnum, calmly dead.

'Say – say, mister! What happened?' a man in a butcher's apron was standing next to Barnum, looking down excitedly.

'I saw it,' Barnum said slowly. 'This fellow walked past me and a man in a grey hat jumped out of a doorway and he said, 'Here you are, you son of a bitch!' and then he said, 'Not this time, Spanish,' and he went bang! bang! bang! bang! and he said, 'How do you like that?' and he looked at me and he went "Aaah!" and he disappeared and this gentleman was dead.'

'What happened?' A fat lady ran across the street from a millinery shop, shouting as she ran.

'A man's been shot,' the butcher said. 'He saw it.' He pointed at Barnum.

How did it happen?' the milliner asked, respectfully. Three more men had run up by this time, and four small boys, all looking at the corpse.

'Well,' Barnum said, feeling important as the babel of talk died down as he began to speak, 'I was walking along and this fellow walked past me and a man in a grey hat jumped out of a doorway and he said, "Here you are, you son of a bitch!" and this fellow started to run and the man in the grey hat pulled out a gun and he said, "Not this time, Spanish," and he went bang! bang! bang! bang!' Barnum shouted the bangs and pointed his finger violently at the corpse on the sidewalk. 'And he said, "How do you like that?" and he looked at me and he went "Aaah!" Barnum curled his lip into an imitation of the murderer's snarl. 'And he disappeared and this gentleman was dead.'

By now there were fifty people gathered around Barnum and the corpse. 'What happened?' the latest arrival asked.

'I was walking along,' Barnum said in a loud voice, conscious of every eye upon him, 'and this fellow walked past me . . .'

'Lissen, Buddy.' A small, rough-looking man nudged his elbow, 'Why don't you go home? You didn't see nuthin'.'

'I saw,' Barnum said excitedly. 'I saw with my own eyes. A man in a grey hat jumped out of a doorway . . . ' Barnum leaped to demonstrate, the crowd respectfully falling back to give him room, as Barnum landed catlike, his knees bent but tense. 'And he said, 'Here you are, you son of a bitch!'' And this fellow' – with a wave for the corpse – 'started to run . . . ' Barnum took two quick little steps to show how the dead man had started to run ' . . . and the man in the grey hat pulled out a gun and said . . . '

'Why don't you go home?' the rough little man said pleadingly. 'It's nothin' to me, but you're only complicating yerself. Why don't you go home?'

Barnum looked at him coldly for a moment.

'Then what happened?' a voice demanded from the crowd.

' "Not this time, Spanish!" ' Barnum cried. 'And he went bang! bang! bang! bang!' Barnum moved his hand as though he was firing a heavy gun and fighting the recoil. 'And he said, 'How do you like that?' and he looked at me and he went "Aaah!" ' Barnum snarled it out, with every eye upon him. 'And he disappeared, and this gentleman was dead.'

'As a good friend of yours,' the small rough man said, earnestly, 'I advise you to go home. You didn't see nuthin' . . . '

'What happened?' A voice shouted across the bobbing heads. By now it seemed to Barnum nearly a thousand people must be congregated around him, all with their eyes fixed eagerly on him, who never, even in his own home, could get three people at one time, even his wife and two children, to listen to him for as long as a minute without interruption.

'I was walking along,' Barnum said in a loud, ringing voice, 'and this fellow . . . '

'Mistuh!' The small man shook his head despairingly. 'Why're you doing this? What's it goin' to get you? Trouble!'

'This fellow,' Barnum went on, disregarding the small, rough man, 'walked past me and a man in a grey hat jumped out of a doorway . . . ' Once more Barnum demonstrated. ' "There you are, you son of a bitch!" he hollered and this fellow started to run and the man in the grey hat pulled out a gun . . . ' Barnum snatched an imaginary pistol from under his armpit, pointed it at the corpse. 'And he yelled, "Not this time, Spanish!" and he went bang! bang! bang! bang! and he said, 'How do you like that?' and he looked at me and went "Aaah!" and he disappeared and this gentleman was dead.' Barnum was sweating heavily now from his leaps and snarls and the unaccustomed strain of talking so that a thousand people could hear every word, and his eyes were rolling with excitement. 'And it was all over,' Barnum said dramatically, 'and this gentleman was lying there looking up at me before you could blink your eyes.'

'Jesus Christ!' one of the four little boys in the inner circle said in deep admiration.

'Whoever you are,' the small man said to Barnum, 'you're a dope. Remember I told you. Goodbye.' And he pushed his way out of the crowd.

A big man with a red face tapped Barnum's arm. He smiled engagingly at Barnum. 'Did you really see it?' he asked.

'Did I see it!' Barnum waved his hand. 'The bullets went past my head.'

'What happened?' the red-faced man asked.

'I was walking along,' Barnum began while the red-faced man listened with deep interest. 'And this fellow was walking in front of me . . . '

'Louder!' a voice cried deep in the crowd.

'I WAS WALKING ALONG,' Barnum shouted, 'AND THIS FELLOW WAS WALKING IN FRONT OF ME AND A MAN IN A GREY HAT . . . ' And Barnum went through the story, with gestures, while the red-faced man listened with respect.

'You saw the murderer close up?' the red-faced man inquired.

'Like you.' Barnum stuck his face right next to the other man's.

'You'd know his face again if you saw it?'

'Like my wife's . . . '

'Good,' said the red-faced man, taking Barnum by the elbow and starting out through the crowd, as the sirens of radio cars howled to a halt at the corner. 'You'll come with me to the police station and when we catch the murderer you'll identify him. You're a material witness. I'm glad I found you.'

Barnum, a year later, sighed in retrospect. For a whole year the murderer was not caught, and he sat in jail and lost his wife and children and a bearded Rumanian took his job and highwaymen and forgers beat him with mop handles and slop buckets. Every three days he would be taken down to look at some new collection of thugs. Each time he would have to shake his head because the man in the grey hat was not among them and then the young district attorney would say, sneeringly, 'You're one hell of a fine material witness, Barnum. Get him the hell out of here!' and the detectives would wearily drag him back to his cell. 'We're pertectin' yuh,' the detectives would say when Barnum would ask to be freed. 'Yuh wanna go out and have 'em blow yer brains out? That was Sammy Spanish that was killed. He's an important figure. You know too much. Take it easy; yuh're getting yer three squares a day, ain't yuh?'

'I don't know anything,' Barnum would say wearily, in a low voice, as they locked him into his cell, but they never paid any attention. Luckily, the district attorney got a good job with an insurance company and gave up looking for the murderer of Sammy Spanish, otherwise Barnum was sure he'd have been kept until either he or the district attorney died.

Walking aimlessly down the street, with the year behind him, homeless, wifeless, childless, jobless, Barnum sighed. He stood on a corner, rubbing his chin sadly, trying to decide which way to turn. A car swung around the corner past him, too close to a car parked just below the corner. There was the sound of the grating of fenders and then the forlorn wail of brakes and the crumpling of metal. A man jumped out of the parked car waving his hands.

'Where the hell do you think you're going?' he cried to the driver of the other car, looking wildly at his mashed fender. 'Lemme see your licence! Somebody's got to pay for that fender and it ain't going to be me, brother!' While the reckless driver was getting out of his car the owner of the damaged car turned sadly to Barnum.

'Did you see that?' he asked.

Barnum looked hurriedly at him, at the fender, at the street around him. 'Oh, no,' he said. 'I didn't see anything.'

And he turned and walked swiftly back in the direction from which he had come.

Sailor off the Bremen

They sat in the small white kitchen, Ernest and Charley and Preminger and Dr Stryker, all bunched around the porcelain-topped table, so that the kitchen seemed to be overflowing with men. Sally stood at the stove turning griddle-cakes over thoughtfully, listening intently to what Preminger was saying.

'So,' Preminger said, carefully working his knife and fork, 'everything was excellent. The comrades arrived, dressed like ladies and gentlemen at the opera, in evening gowns and what do you call them?'

'Tuxedos,' Charley said. 'Black ties.'

'Tuxedos,' Preminger nodded, speaking with his precise educated German accent. 'Very handsome people, mixing with all the other handsome people who came to say goodbye to their friends on the boat; everybody very gay, everybody with a little whisky on the breath; nobody would suspect they were Party members, they were so clean and upper class.' He laughed lightly at his own joke. He looked like a young boy from a nice Middle Western college, with crew-cut hair and a straight nose and blue eyes and an easy laugh. His laugh was a little high and short, and he talked fast, as though he wanted to get a great many words out to beat a certain deadline, but otherwise, being a Communist in Germany and a deck officer on the *Bremen* hadn't made any obvious changes in him. 'It is a wonderful thing,' he said, 'how many pretty girls there are in the Party in the United States. Wonderful!'

They all laughed, even Ernest, who put his hand up to cover the empty spaces in the front row of his teeth every time he smiled. His hand covered his mouth and the fingers cupped around the neat black patch over his eye, and he smiled secretly and swiftly behind that concealment, getting his merriment over with swiftly, so he could take his hand down and compose his face into its usual unmoved, distant expression, cultivated from the time he got out of the hospital. Sally watched him from the stove, knowing each step: the grudging smile, the hand, the consciousness and memory of deformity, the wrench to composure, the lie of peace when he took his hand down.

She shook her head, dumped three brown cakes on to a plate.

'Here,' she said, putting them before Preminger. 'Better than Childs Restaurant.'

'Wonderful,' Preminger said, dousing them with syrup. 'Each time I come to America I feast on these. There is nothing like it in the whole continent of Europe.'

'All right,' Charley said, leaning across the kitchen table, practically covering it, because he was so big, 'finish the story.'

'So I gave the signal,' Preminger said, waving his fork. 'When everything was nice and ready, everybody having a good time, stewards running this way, that way, with champagne, a nice little signal and we had a very nice little demonstration. Nice signs, good loud yelling, the Nazi flag cut down, one, two, three, from the pole. The girls standing together singing like angels, everybody running there from all parts of the ship, everybody getting the idea very, very clear – a very nice little demonstration.' He smeared butter methodically on the top cake. 'So then, the rough business. Expected. Naturally. After all, we all know it is no cocktail party for Lady Astor.' He pursed his lips and squinted at his plate, looking like a small boy making believe he's the head of a family. 'A little pushing, expected, maybe a little crack over the head here and there, expected. Justice comes with a headache these days, we all know that. But my people, the Germans. You must always expect the worst from them. They organise like lightning. Method. How to treat a riot on a ship. Every steward, every oiler, every sailor, was there in a minute and a half. Two men would hold a comrade, the other would beat him. Nothing left to accident.'

'The hell with it,' Ernest said. 'What's the sense in going through the whole thing again? It's all over.'

'Shut up,' Charley said.

'Two stewards got hold of Ernest,' Preminger said softly. 'And another one did the beating. Stewards are worse than sailors. All day long they take orders, they hate the world. Ernest was unlucky. All the others did their jobs, but they were human beings. The steward is a member of the Nazi Party. He is an Austrian; he is not a normal man.'

'Sally,' Ernest said, 'give Mr Preminger some more milk.'

'He kept hitting Ernest,' Preminger tapped absently on the porcelain top with his fork, 'and he kept laughing and laughing.'

'You know who he is?' Charley asked. 'You're sure you know who he is?'

'I know who he is. He is twenty-five years old, very dark and good-looking, and he sleeps with at least two ladies a voyage.' Preminger slopped his milk around in the bottom of his glass. 'His name is Lueger. He spies on the crew for the Nazis. He had sent two men already to concentration camps. He is a very serious character. He knew what he was doing.' Preminger said clearly, 'when he kept hitting Ernest in the eye. I tried to get to him, but I was in the middle of a thousand people, screaming and running. If something happens to that Lueger that will be a very good thing.'

'Have a cigar,' Ernest said, pulling two out of his pocket.

'Something will happen to him,' Charley said, taking a deep breath, and leaning back from the table. 'Something will damn sure happen to him.'

'You're a dumb kid,' Ernest said, in the weary tone he used now in all serious discussions. 'What do you prove if you beat up one stupid sailor?'

'I don't prove anything,' Charley said. 'I don't prove a goddamn thing. I am going to have a good time with the boy that knocked my brother's eye out. That's all.'

'It's not a personal thing,' Ernest said, in a tired voice. 'It is the movement of Fascism. You don't stop Fascism with a personal crusade against one German. If I thought it would do some good, I'd say, sure, go ahead . . . '

'My brother, the Communist,' Charley said bitterly. 'He goes out and he gets ruined and still he talks dialectics. The Red Saint with the long view. The long view gives me a pain in the ass. I am taking a very short view of Mr Lueger. I am going to kick the living guts out of his belly. Preminger, what do you say?'

'Speaking as a Party member,' Preminger said, 'I approve of your brother's attitude, Charley.'

'Nuts,' Charley said.

'Speaking as a man, Charley,' Preminger went on, 'please put Lueger on his back for at least six months. Where is that cigar, Ernest?'

Dr Stryker spoke up in his dry, polite, dentist's voice. 'As you know,' he said, 'I am not the type for violence.' Dr Stryker weighed a hundred and thirty-three pounds and it was almost possible to see through his wrists, he was so frail. 'But as Ernest's friends, I think there would be a definite satisfaction for all of us, including Ernest, if this Lueger was taken care of. You may count on me for anything within my powers.' He was very scared, Dr Stryker, and his voice was even drier than usual, but he spoke up after reasoning the whole thing out slowly and carefully, disregarding the fear, the worry, the possible great damage. 'That is my opinion,' he said.

'Sally,' Ernest said, 'talk to these damn fools.'

'I think,' Sally said slowly, looking steadily at her husband's face, always stiffly composed now, like a corpse's face. 'I think they know what they're talking about.'

Ernest shrugged. 'Emotionalism. A large useless gesture. You're all tainted by Charley's philosophy. He's a football player. He has a football player's philosophy. Somebody knocks you down, you knock him down, everything is fine.'

'I want a glass of milk, too,' Charley said. 'Please, Sally.'

'Whom're you playing this week?' Ernest said.

'Georgetown.'

'Won't that be enough violence for one week?' Ernest asked.

'Nope,' Charley said. 'I'll take care of Georgetown first, then Lueger.'

'Anything I can do,' Dr Stryker said. 'Remember, anything I can do. I am at your service.'

'The coach'll be sore,' Ernest said, 'if you get banged up, Charley.'

'The hell with the coach. Please shut up, Ernest. I have got my stomach full of Communist tactics. No more. Get this in your head, Ernest.' Charley stood up and banged the table. 'I am disregarding the class struggle, I am disregarding the education of the proletariat, I am disregarding the fact that you are a good Communist. I am acting strictly in the capacity of your brother. If you'd had any brains you would have stayed away from that lousy boat. You're a painter, an artist, you make water-colours, what the hell is it your business if lunatics're running Germany? But all right. You've got no brains. You go and get your eye beat out. O.K. Now I step in. Purely personal. None of your business. Shut your trap. I will fix everything to my own satisfaction. Please go and lie down in the bedroom. We have arrangements to make here.'

Ernest stood up, hiding his mouth, which was twitching, and

walked into the bedroom and closed the door and lay down on the bed, in the dark, with his eye open.

The next day, an hour before sailing time, Charley and Dr Stryker and Sally went down to the *Bremen*, and boarded the ship on different gangplanks. They stood separately on the A Deck, up forward, waiting for Preminger. Preminger came, very boyish and crisp in his blue uniform, looked coldly past them, touched a steward on the arm, a dark, good-looking young steward, said something to him, and went aft. Charley and Dr Stryker examined the steward closely, so that two weeks later, on a dark street, there would be no mistake, and left, leaving Sally there, smiling at Lueger.

'Yes,' Sally said two weeks later, 'it is very clear. I'll have dinner with him, and I'll go to a movie with him, and I'll get him to take at least two drinks, and I'll tell him I live on West Twelfth Street, near West Street. There is a whole block of apartment houses there, and I'll get him down to West Twelfth Street between a quarter to one and one in the morning, and you'll be waiting there, you and Stryker, under the Ninth Avenue L, and you'll say, 'Pardon me, can you direct me to Sheridan Square?' and I'll start running.'

'That's right,' Charley said; 'that's fine.' He blew reflectively on his huge hands, knotted and cleat-marked from last Saturday's game. 'That is the whole story for Mr Lueger. You'll go through with it now?' he asked. 'You're sure you can manage it?'

'I'll go through with it,' Sally said. 'I had a long talk with him today when the boat came in. He is very . . . anxious. He likes small girls like me, he says, with black hair. I told him I lived alone, downtown. He looked at me very significantly. I know why he manages to sleep with two ladies a voyage, like Preminger says. I'll manage it.'

'What is Ernest going to do tonight?' Dr Stryker asked. In the two weeks of waiting his voice had become so dry he had to swallow desperately every five words. 'Somebody ought to take care of Ernest tonight.'

'He's going to Carnegie Hall tonight,' Sally said. 'They're playing Brahms and Debussy.'

'That's a good way to spend an evening,' Charley said. He opened his collar absently, and pulled down his tie. 'The only place I can go with Ernest these days is the movies. It's dark, so I don't have to look at him.'

'He'll pull through,' Dr Stryker said professionally. 'I'm making him new teeth; he won't be so self-conscious, he'll adjust himself.'

He hardly paints any more,' Sally said. 'He just sits around the house and looks at his old pictures.'

'Mr Lueger,' Charley said. 'Our pal Mr Lueger.'

'He carries a picture of Hitler,' Sally said. 'In his watch. He showed me. He says he's lonely.'

'How big is he?' Stryker asked nervously.

'He's a large, strong man,' Sally said.

'I think you ought to have an instrument of some kind, Charley,' Stryker said dryly. 'Really, I do.'

Charley laughed. He extended his two hands, palms up, the broken fingers curled a little, broad and muscular. 'I want to do this with my own hands,' he said. 'I want to take care of Mr Lueger with my bare fists. I want it to be a very personal affair.'

'There is no telling what . . . ' Stryker said.

'Don't worry, Stryker,' Charley said. 'Don't worry one bit.'

At twelve that night Sally and Lueger walked down Eighth Avenue from the Fourteenth Street subway station. Lueger held Sally's arm as they walked, his fingers moving gently up and down, occasionally grasping tightly the loose cloth of her coat and the firm flesh of her arm just above the elbow.

'Oh,' Sally said. 'Don't. That hurts.'

Lueger laughed. 'It does not hurt much,' he said. He pinched her playfully. 'You don't mind if it hurt, nevertheless,' he said. His English was very complicated, with a thick accent.

'I mind,' Sally said. 'Honest, I mind.'

'I like you,' he said, walking very close to her. 'You are a good girl. You are made excellent. I am happy to accompany you home. You are sure you live alone?'

'I'm sure,' Sally said. 'Don't worry. I would like a drink.'

'Aaah,' Lueger said. 'Waste time.'

'I'll pay for it,' Sally said. She had learned a lot about him in one evening. 'My own money. Drinks for you and me.'

'If you say so,' Lueger said, steering her into a bar. 'One drink, because we have something to do tonight.' He pinched her hard and laughed, looking obliquely into her eyes with a kind of technical suggestiveness he used on the two ladies during a voyage on the *Bremen*.

Under the Ninth Avenue L on Twelfth Street, Charley and Dr Stryker leaned against an elevated post, in deep shadow.

'I . . . I . . . ' Stryker said. Then he had to swallow to wet his throat so that the words would come out. 'I wonder if they're coming,' he said finally in a flat, high whisper.

'They'll come,' Charley said, keeping his eyes on the little triangular park up Twelfth Street where it joins Eighth Avenue. 'That Sally has guts. That Sally loves my dumb brother like he was the President of the United States. As if he was a combination of Lenin and Michelangelo. And he had to go and get his eye batted out.'

'He's a very fine man,' Stryker said. 'Your brother Ernest. A man with true ideals. I am very sorry to see what has happened to his character since . . . Is that them?'

'No,' Charley said. 'It's two girls from the Y.W.C.A. on the corner.'

'He used to be a very merry man,' Stryker said, swallowing rapidly. 'Always laughing. Always sure of what he was saying. Before he was married we used to go out together all the time and all the time the girls, my girl and his, no matter who they were, would give all their attention to him. All the time, I didn't mind. I love your brother Ernest as if he were my young brother. I could cry when I see him sitting now, covering his eye and his teeth, not saying anything, just listening to what other people have to say.'

'Yeah,' Charley said. 'Yeah. Why don't you keep quiet, Stryker?'

'Excuse me,' Stryker said, talking fast and dry. 'I don't like to bother you. But I must talk. Otherwise, if I just stand here keeping still, I will suddenly start running and I'll run right up to Forty-second Street. I can't keep quiet at the moment, excuse me.'

'Go ahead and talk, Stryker,' Charley said gently, patting him on the shoulder. 'Shoot your mouth right off, all you want.'

'I am only doing this because I think it will help Ernest,' Stryker said, leaning hard against the post, in the shadow, to keep his knees straight. 'I have a theory. My theory is that when Ernest finds out what happens to this Lueger, he will pick up. It will be a kind of springboard to him. It is my private notion of the psychology of the situation. We should have brought an instrument with us, though. A club, a knife, brass knuckles.' Stryker put his hands in his pockets, holding them tight against the cloth to keep them from trembling: 'It will be very bad if we mess this up. Won't it be very bad, Charley? Say, Charley . . . '

'Sssh,' said Charley.

Stryker looked up the street. 'That's them. That's Sally, that's her coat. That's the bastard. The lousy German bastard.'

'Sssh, Stryker. Sssh.'

'I feel very cold, Charley. Do you feel cold? It's a warm night, but I . . . '

'For Christ's sake, shut up!'

'We'll fix him,' Stryker whispered. 'Yes, Charley, I'll shut up, sure, I'll shut up, depend on me, Charley . . . '

Sally and Lueger walked slowly down Twelfth Street. Lueger had his arm around Sally's waist and their hips rubbed as they walked.

'That was a very fine film tonight,' Lueger was saying. 'I enjoy Deanna Durbin. Very young, fresh, sweet. Like you.' He grinned at Sally in the dark and held tighter to her waist. 'A small young maid. You are just the kind I like.' He tried to kiss her. Sally turned her head away.

'Listen, Mr Lueger,' she said, not because she liked him, but because he was a human being and thoughtless and unsuspecting and because her heart was softer than she had thought. 'Listen, I think you'd better leave me here.'

'I do not understand English,' Lueger said, enjoying this last coyness.

'Thank you very much for a pleasant evening,' Sally said desperately, stopping in her tracks. 'Thank you for taking me home. You can't come up. I was lying to you. I don't live alone . . . '

Lueger laughed. 'Little frightened girl. That's nice. I love you for it.'

'My brother,' Sally said. 'I swear to God I live with my brother.'

Lueger grabbed her and kissed her, hard, bruising her lips against his teeth, his hands pressing harshly into the flesh of her back. She sobbed into his mouth with the pain, helpless. He released her. He was laughing.

'Come,' he said, holding her close. 'I am anxious to meet your brother. Little liar.'

'All right,' she said, watching Charley and Stryker move out from the L shadow. 'All right. Let's not wait. Let's walk fast. Very fast. Let's not waste time.'

79

Lueger laughed happily. 'That's it. That's the way a girl should talk.'

They walked swiftly toward the elevated ramp, Lueger laughing, his hand on her hip in certainty and possession.

'Pardon me,' Stryker said. 'Could you direct me to Sheridan Square?'

'Well,' said Sally, stopping, 'it's . . .'

Charley swung and Sally started running as soon as she heard the wooden little noise a fist makes on a man's face. Charley held Lueger up with one hand and chopped the lolling head with the other. He carried Lueger back into the shadows against a high iron railing. He hung Lueger by his overcoat against one of the iron points, so he could use both hands on him. Stryker watched for a moment, then turned and looked toward Eighth Avenue.

Charley worked very methodically, getting his two hundred pounds behind short, accurate, smashing blows that made Lueger's head jump and loll and roll against the iron spikes. Charley hit him in the nose three times, squarely, using his fist the way a carpenter uses a hammer. Each time Charley heard the sound of bone breaking, cartilage tearing. When he got through with the nose, Charley went after the mouth, hooking along the side of the jaws with both hands, until teeth fell out and the jaw hung open, smashed, loose, with the queer looseness of flesh that is no longer moored to solid bone. Charley started crying, the tears running down into his mouth, the sobs shaking him as he swung his fists. Even then Stryker didn't turn around. He just put his hands to his ears and looked steadfastly at Eighth Avenue.

When he started on Lueger's eye, Charley talked. 'You bastard. Oh, you lousy goddamn bastard,' came out with the sobs and the tears as he hit at the eye with his right hand, cutting it, smashing it, tearing it again and again, his hand coming away splattered with blood each time. 'Oh, you dumb, mean, skirt-chasing sonofabitch, bastard.' And he kept hitting with fury and deliberation at the shattered eye . . .

A car came up Twelfth Street from the waterfront and slowed down at the corner. Stryker jumped on the running board. 'Keep moving,' he said, very tough, 'if you know what's good for you.'

He jumped off the running board and watched the car speed away.

Charley, still sobbing, pounded Lueger in the chest and belly.

With each blow Lueger slammed against the iron fence with a noise like a carpet being beaten, until his coat ripped off the spike and he slid to the sidewalk.

Charley stood back, his fists swaying, the tears still coming, the sweat running down his face inside his collar, his clothes stained with blood.

'O.K.,' he said. 'O.K., you bastard.'

He walked swiftly up under the L in the shadows, and Stryker hurried after him.

Much later, in the hospital, Preminger stood over the bed in which Lueger lay, unconscious, in splints and bandages.

'Yes,' he said to the detective and the doctor. 'That's our man. Lueger. A steward. The papers on him are correct.'

'Who do you think done it?' the detective asked in a routine voice. 'Did he have any enemies?'

'Not that I know of,' Preminger said. 'He was a very popular boy. Especially with the ladies.'

The detective started out of the ward. 'Well,' he said, 'he won't be a very popular boy when he gets out of here.'

Preminger shook his head. 'You must be very careful in a strange city,' he said to the interne, and went back to the ship.

The Climate of Insomnia

Cahill let himself into the silent house, softly closing the door behind him. He hung up his hat and coat, noticing the pleasant, frail smell of damp and night that came up from the cloth. Then he saw the note on the telephone table. It was scrawled in the maid's grave, childish handwriting, which always amused him a little when he saw it. 'Mr Reeves called,' the message read. 'He must talk to you. Very important, he says.'

Cahill started to take up the phone under the mirror. Then he glanced at his watch. It was past one. Too late, he decided; it will have to wait till morning. He looked at himself in the dim glass, noting with satisfaction that his face was still thin and rather young-looking and that his eyes, despite the three drinks after the meeting that night, were not bloodshot. With dissatisfaction, he noted also that the grey was gaining over the black at his temples and that the lines under his eyes were now permanent. He sighed with agreeable melancholy, thinking gently: 'Older, older . . .

He put out the light and started upstairs. He was a large, bulky man, but he moved gracefully up the carpeted steps of his home. He touched the smooth wood of the banister, smelling the mixed but orderly aromas of living that the house breathed into the still darkness – the lemony fragrance of furniture polish, the autumnal dust of chrysanthemums from the living-room, the hint of his wife's perfume, lingering here after the day's comings and goings.

He walked past the adjoining doors behind which slept his son and his daughter. He thought of the dark-haired, seventeen-year-old girl lying neatly in the quilted bed, the almost womanly mouth relaxed into childishness by sleep. He brushed the door with his fingertips sentimentally. As he passed his son's door, he could hear a low, dreamy mumble, then, more clearly, Charlie's voice calling, 'Intercept! Intercept!' Then the voice stopped. Cahill grinned, reflecting on what vigorous, simple dreams of green fields and sunny afternoons visited the sleep of his fifteen-year-old son. Cahill, the miser, he thought, quietly going past the closed doors, counting his treasures at midnight.

He went into the bathroom and undressed there, so as not to wake his wife. After he had put on his pyjamas and slippers, he stood for a moment in front of the medicine chest, debating whether or not to take the sedative for his stomach that Dr Manners had prescribed for him on Tuesday. He patted his stomach thoughtfully. It bulged a little, as it had been doing for seven or eight years now, but it felt relaxed and healthy. The hell with it, he thought. I am going to break the tyranny of the Pill.

Unmedicined, he put out the bathroom light and padded into the bedroom. He sat carefully on the edge of his bed and silently took off his slippers, moving with domestic caution, watching his wife, in the next bed. She did not stir. A little moonlight filtered in through the curtained windows and softly outlined the head against the pillows. She slept steadily, not moving even when Cahill inadvertently knocked against the base of the lamp on the bed table, making a resonant metallic noise. She looked young, pretty, defenceless in the obscure light, although Cahill noticed with a grimace, that she had her hair up in curlers, leaving only a small bang loose in front as a sop to marital attractions. A woman must be awfully certain of her husband, he thought, to appear in bed night after night in those grim ringlets. He grinned to himself as he got under the covers, amused at his strong feelings on the subject.

As the warmth of the blankets slowly filled in around him, he stretched, enjoying the softness of the bed, his muscles luxuriously delivering him over to the long weariness of the day. The curtains, folded in moonlight, rustled gently at the windows. A fragile tenuous sense of peace settled drowsily upon him. His son and his daughter slept youthfully and securely beyond the bedroom wall. His first class the next morning was not until ten o'clock. His wife confidently clamped her hair in ludicrous curls, knowing nothing could disturb her marriage. At the meeting, he had spoken quite well, and Professor Edwards, who was the head of the department, had come over afterward and approved of it. In the next morning's second class, Philosophy 12, there were three of the brightest young people in the college – two boys and a girl, and the girl was rather pretty, too – and they had all made it plain that they admired him enormously, and were constantly quoting him in the classes of other instructors. Cahill moved softly under the covers as the pleasant, half-formed images of contentment drifted across his brain. Tomorrow, he thought, will be clear and warmer – that's what the paper says. I'll wear my new brown tweed suit.

Just before he dozed off, he thought of the message from Joe Reeves. Important, he thought a little irritably, important – now, what could that be? He twitched a little, uneasily, nearly coming back to wakefulness. Then, with the steady breathing of his wife sounding from the next bed, he dropped off to sleep.

The siren must have been wailing for some time before Cahill woke, because it entered harshly into his dream, and somehow he was back in London, in the cold billet, and the planes were overhead and the guns were going off, and he had the old feeling that neighbours were dying by chance in burning buildings on the street outside his window. He could feel himself moaning softly and shivering under the blankets and hoping he would be alive in the morning, and then he awoke.

He gazed blindly at the dark ceiling, feeling the cold, unreasonable sweat come out on his body. What is it? he thought. What is it? Then he realised that he was at home, in his own bed, and that the war was over. The noise of the siren howled down the quiet street outside – a police car going to investigate a burglary or pick up a drunk – echoing among the untouched homes, behind their undamaged lawns. He shook his head, irritated with himself for his nervousness. He looked across at his wife. She slept, unperturbed, her breath coming evenly, her arms primly down at her sides, her captured hair untossed on the pillows, happily beyond the reach of sirens and the memory of sirens.

He felt tremblingly awake. Every sound now reached him clearly and with individual significance: the wind troubling the curtains in a starched rhythm; the insubstantial creak of the stairs reacting to the obscure strain that years put upon old houses; the distant crashing of a truck's gears past a far-away street corner, attacking all insomniacs within a radius of a mile; the even intake and exhalation of his wife's breath, too mild to be called a snore but now as annoying as a suddenly loud clock, holding the hours of the night too strictly to account, reminding the would-be-sleeper that every moment of wakefulness now would be answered by weariness tomorrow.

Cahill looked at the low radium gleam of the clock on the bed table. Four-thirty. He fell back on his pillow heavily. Too late to take a sleeping pill. If he took a pill now, he'd be doped all day; he wouldn't have time to sleep it off. The ubiquitous problem of modern civilisation, he thought: Is it too late for a pill? Too early? Which way will it be worse tomorrow? All over the country, sleepy, nervous hands reaching out for the clock, troubled heads calculating. It will wear off in six hours, but I have to get up in four. Sleep, he thought, the first great natural resource to be exhausted by modern man. The erosion of the nerves, not to be halted by any reclamation project, private or public.

He lay rigid in his bed, conscious now of various dull, unpleasant sensations in his body. His eyelids felt harsh and granular and seemed to scrape his eyeballs when he blinked. He was too warm, but a damp breeze from the window felt cold and uncomfortable on his forehead. The muscles of his right leg felt cramped, and he had a curious sensation that the tendon running up from his ankle had grown too short during the night. His stomach, just under the diaphragm, was moving in little spasms. He put his hand on the spot and felt the sick, erratic fluttering. He could taste the whisky he had drunk, high and sour in his throat. That damned siren, he thought. I was feeling so well . . .

Then Cahill remembered the message. It must be something really pressing, he thought, for Joe Reeves to call like that. Cahill couldn't recall another occasion, in all the time he'd known Joe, when Joe had left that sort of a message for him. Early in his college career, Joe had decided to be urbane, debonair, off-hand, and his manner of treating all matters light-heartedly and without urgency had become, if anything, more pronounced with the years. And there was nothing off-handed about leaving a disturbing note like that waiting for a man to pick up at one o'clock in the morning. After all, he saw Joe almost every day, at lunch. You'd think a man could wait until noon the next day. Unless it was a matter of the most drastic importance . . .

Cahill twisted restlessly in his bed, trying to keep his eyes closed, sullenly inviting sleep. I will think about this tomorrow, he thought. I will think about this tomorrow. But the restful emptiness of mind he sought evaded him. Unpleasantly, he remembered that Joe had good reason to call him. Subconsciously, he realised he had been waiting for just such a message, and dreading it. For the twentieth time, he wondered if Joe had heard what he, Cahill, had said about him at the Faculty Club two weeks before. He had felt guilty about it ever since, and ashamed of himself. Even giving himself the excuse that he had drunk a little too much had not helped. In a discussion about teaching techniques, the subject of Joe's popularity with his classes had come up, and Cahill had said cruelly, 'Joe Reeves charms his classes into believing they're learning a great deal about economics when what they're really learning is how charming Joe Reeves can be.' It was a stupid thing to say, even though it was partly true, and Lloyd and Evarts, who had been listening to him, had chuckled maliciously. Reeves had seemed rather cool for the last two weeks, and Cahill was almost certain that the remark had got back to him, as was almost inevitable in the narrow companionship of a college town. It was too bad. He and Joe Reeves had been close friends for over twenty years, and even though the relationship by now had more the form than the substance of the earlier friendship (how really remain friendly with any man after you are married?), it was silly to risk it for a light and mischievous judgement over a glass of whisky. And it didn't even represent what Cahill really felt about Reeves. True, there was a superficiality about Reeves, especially in recent years, that came with his easy success with everyone – university presidents, faculty wives, students – but buried beneath that were the shrewdness, the good sense, the honourable instincts that had attracted Cahill to him in the first place. Jealousy, Cahill thought, ashamed of himself. How can a grown man give himself to it so easily? Probably, Cahill thought, Reeves had heard about the remark the very next morning and had mulled it over for the last two weeks, growing angrier and angrier, until this evening, when he had decided to have a showdown with Cahill about it. And Cahill couldn't deny having said it, or disguise in any way the envy and criticism that had called it forth, and that would be the end of the friendship. Joe, for all his easy assurance, was terribly touchy, vain, unforgiving. Cahill pondered on what it would be like not to be friendly with Joe. They had gone through college together, travelled through Europe together, lent each other money, books, opinions, neckties, celebrated together, mourned, exulted together. Even now, they and their wives had dinner together once or twice a week and made free of each other's homes in a carefully preserved informality that was pleasant, if not quite honest, and that kept alive for them a kind of gentle memory of their exciting younger days. And now, for a phrase, for a drop of wanton acid, to lose it all.

Cahill stared bitterly at the ceiling. The tongue, he thought, grows looser and more destructive with the years. Give a talkative man enough listeners and he will bring down stone with his indiscretions.

The curtains scraped in their humble starch at the windows, rasping across his consciousness. Of course, Cahill thought, it is possible that Joe did not hear what I said about him. The message could be about a dozen other things. What things? Joe was so intimately connected with his life, with the people and events of his past, with the problems and promises of the present, that the message might be concerned with his wife, his children, his job, his health, his finances, anything.

Edith moved a little in the next bed, sighing – a forlorn, sleep-bound, homeless, unremembered intake of breath – then settled back into that steady almost snore. Cahill looked over at her shadowed face. She slept, resting, secure, masked, giving no information, volunteering no help. Suddenly, he disliked and mistrusted her. Just to be so calmly and happily unconscious at a moment like this, when her husband lay awake, remorseful and torn by doubt, was a kind of wilful absence, a tacit infidelity, a form of uncaring callousness.

Cahill considered his wife coldly. Her face looked surprisingly young. Twenty-eight, you might say – thirty. Frivolity, he thought has preserved her youth. Age needed some assistance from thought and feeling to carve lines into a face, and in Edith's case age had had to work unaided. Still, she looked pretty attractive, despite the net and curlers. Why was she so finickingly careful about the way she looked? Not for his sake, that was sure. Another man? How could anyone ever possibly know? Lectures in other towns took him away from home quite often. And then there were the whole long days that were hers to spend unquestioned. Maybe Joe had something to say on this subject – something that couldn't wait.

Unwillingly, Cahill remembered the evening, the week before, at the Crowells', when he'd gone out on to the darkened porch and come upon Joe and Edith sitting close to each other, both of them speaking in low, urgent whispers. They'd seemed embarrassed when they saw Cahill, and Edith had looked startled. And Joe's rather heavy standard joke about

87

being caught in the act had not served to clear the air. Cahill had been troubled for a moment; then he had dismissed it from his mind. There could be a hundred reasons, all innocent, for Joe and Edith to be talking secretly together. They'd always been friendly, right from the beginning. They kissed each time they met, Cahill suddenly recalled. Why was that? He, Cahill, never kissed Joe's wife, except ceremonially, on New Year's Eve and birthdays. The whole modern world, Cahill thought with distaste, kisses too damned much. Sly, without innocence, full of subtle invitation and hidden implication, these public embraces of the married. And, considered coldly, Joe was ripe for experiment. He and his wife didn't get along at all well. She bored Joe; that was plain enough. He was impatient with her in discussions, and she often gave the impression that she had been crying before guests arrived. And she was one of those women who are always going off on long visits to their families, in the Midwest. No woman who had a happy married life remained that attached to her mother and father. And in those bachelor-like periods God knew what Joe did with himself Also, Cahill remembered, Joe had not been spectacularly celibate in his youth, and in his speech, at least, gave no indication that he had reformed. Another thing: Edith, Cahill remembered, always laughed at Joe's jokes. Damaging, Cahill thought, very damaging. She laughed markedly seldom at his. Well, the truth was he wasn't terribly witty, and a woman might be expected to catch on in eighteen years of marriage. He mourned briefly over the fact that he was not witty, and mourned even more bitterly because now, at the age of forty, he realised it. When he was younger, he had had a higher opinion of himself. Edith had laughed at his jokes then, and so had other people, but now he knew that it was not wit so much as the good humour and vitality of youth that had created an air of cheerfulness about him. That was gone, there was no doubt about that, and it would be unseemly and embarrassing to pretend it wasn't. I must turn, as gracefully as possible, he thought, into a grave old man. Let people like Joe Reeves, who had the talent, say the bright things. He thought of Reeves, with his arched, actor's eyebrows and his dry, knowing delivery, at the centre of things at parties, surrounded by eagerly listening, easily laughing people. Of course, Cahill thought bleakly, that's bound to be attractive to women. Also, Reeves wasn't fat. He had never exercised in all his life, but he was still as thin and straight and young-looking as ever.

God has a vicious habit, Cahill thought, of putting all the gifts in one basket. Weighing the matter objectively, a woman would have to be crazy to prefer Cahill to Joe Reeves. Cahill thought of all the stories he'd heard, through the years, of good friends who had switched wives. And of the man he had met during the war who had arrived back from Europe to find his brother and his wife waiting for him on the dock with the brave, honourable, up-to-date news that they were in love with each other and wanted to marry, but not without his permission. What permission would he be able to give Joe Reeves and his sleeping wife, and what permission had they already given themselves?

Hating Edith, Cahill twitched under the rumpled covers and groaned softly. I should have taken the pill when I woke up, regardless of the time, he thought.

It might not be Edith, Cahill thought, violently keeping his eyes shut; it might be about the Mitchell girl. There was no doubt about it, he'd been a fool about that, and trouble waited there inevitably. Dora Mitchell had been in one of his classes the year before and had decided that she was in love with him. She was nineteen years old, with a dark, unstable look to her and a kind of solemn, uncertain beauty that Cahill thought most attractive. They had met several times out of class, by accident. (At least, Cahill had thought it was by accident until Dora had told him that she waited for him outside his classroom and on the steps of the library building.) And then, more times than he wished to remember, Cahill had met her in quiet bars and had taken her on drives to the country and to a small inn for tea, fifteen miles out of town. He had been flattered by her devotion, and some obscure, middle-aged hunger in him had fed on her youth and her ingenuous high estimate of him. He had known enough, of course, never to touch her. In fact, he had never even kissed her. But who, seeing them together in a clandestine corner of the Red Wheel Inn – the animated, unaccustomedly high-spirited man and the tall, adoring girl – would ever believe that? And he know they'd been observed several times. And, besides that, Dora had once or twice wept and rather hysterically declared she could not go on this way and had even suggested, with the melodrama born of a hundred movies full of Other Women, that she have a heart-to-heart talk with Edith.

Cahill shuddered in his bed. It was all too possible that Dora had gone to Reeves, whom she knew, and unburdened herself to him, sobbing and overflowing with grandiose, youthful passion. Perhaps she had been to see Reeves that very night, and that's why Reeves had been so anxious to have Cahill call him. Tenderness, Cahill thought, the blind, many-edged weapon for the cutting down of fools. Bitterly, he made himself imagine what it would be like the day his own daughter, Elizabeth, herself only two years younger than Dora, found out (from a malicious sorority sister, a newspaper report, from a process server for divorce proceedings, from Dora herself over ice-cream sodas after a basketball game). Grotesque, he thought, for a few hours of gentle conversation, for an illusory, ephemeral buttressing of the vanity, for the titillating suggestion of sin without the sin itself, to risk so much! Maybe, he thought despairingly, I should go to a psychoanalyst; the urge for self-destruction has overcome me.

That, of course, was out of the question. He couldn't afford it. He could be as mad as Peter the Great, or as any lunatic screaming in a padded cell, and he couldn't pay the first bill of the rawest young practitioner, just past his initial reading of Freud and Jung. Absolutely sane or raving like an ape in a tree, he would still have to conduct classes in Philosophy 22, Philosophy 12, Philosophy 53A, for Students in Pre-Educational courses. Money. He thought about money and groaned again. Still three payments on the car. Elizabeth's tuition, due in two weeks. Butter, how many cents a pound? Roast beef once a week, eighty cents a pound, and Charles, his son, and Margaret, the maid, between them devoured four whole ribs each time. Insurance, he calculated in the darkness, in a well-remembered, dreadful night-time litany, taxes, clothes, dentist, doctor, gifts to his wife's large family, amusement. Perhaps, he thought, Reeves had called him to tell him about promotion. God knew he was up for it, and Old Man Edwards was almost due to retire, and that would leave some room near the top. Reeves was very friendly with the president. Dinner there once a month. First names and private confidences. Reeves had been in to see the president that afternoon. Cahill knew because Lloyd, in his own department, who had all the gossip of the university at his fingertips, had told him so. Perhaps Reeves had been given the good word and wanted to pass it on. Cahill played luxuriously with the idea of promotion. Twelve, fifteen hundred more a year. No more Philosophy 53A, the dullest course in the curriculum. No eight-o'clock classes. Then the glow passed. Probably, he thought, it's the other way around. The president had never been any more than polite to him, and it was to be remembered that he had been passed over twice on the promotion lists, for Kennedy and O'Rourke, younger men than he. It wouldn't be too surprising, all things considered, if they had decided to get rid of him. He was far from being the most popular instructor on the campus. To be absolutely honest, he wouldn't blame them for firing him. Ever since he'd come back from the war, the job had bored him. Not that there was anything else that he particularly wanted to do. Just sit, perhaps, and stare into an open fire. Drink more whisky than was good for him. Not pretend to anyone that he knew anything much, or not pretend he thought it was valuable that anyone learn anything much. Dangerous doctrine for professors, assistant professors, instructors, tutors. Probably others had caught on. Come to think of it, the last time he had seen the president at a faculty meeting, the president had been . . . frosty. That was the word – frosty. Purge by frost. Execution, university style. The polite death among the library shelves. He could almost hear Joe Reeves's troubled voice on the phone, warning him, trying to break it to him gently, trying to cheer him up with lies about other jobs, in other colleges.

Cahill lay in bed thinking about what it would be like not to have a job. Rent, taxes, roast beef, tuition, clothes. The advantage of marrying a rich wife. Nothing, finally, was crucial. There was always the net of fat relatives to fall back on, like a high-wire artist who slipped in the circus. Edith's father had worked for the Pennsylvania Railroad and had retired on a pension of a hundred and thirty-five dollars a month. Not much of a net there. Cahill thought of the rich wives he might have married. Rowena . . . Rowena what? Twenty years ago, in Chicago. Shipping. Father in Lake steamers. How could a man be expected to marry a girl named Rowena? Also, she had weighed a hundred and seventy pounds. No exaggeration. Maybe a hundred and eighty. Amorous as the gilded fly, too. Who wanted a wife like that, Lake steamers or no Lake steamers, especially at that weight? Anyway, that had been his one chance of marrying into wealth. Some people were lucky, of course. They met pretty girls, very nice, whose fathers controlled the Chase National Bank or owned mining empires in Central America. Still, if he had married Rowena – Rowena Grumman, that was it; good God, what a name – he wouldn't be trembling like this tonight. Seven hundred dollars in the bank, debts three fifty-five, and that was that. One month and then relief. For this relief, very little thanks. He supposed that nine-tenths of the people in the country walked, as he did, on this thin edge of disaster all their lives, smiling, dissembling, not sleeping some nights, hoping their nerve would hold out as they saw the edge crumbling, crumbling. And then the people in China, scouring sidewalks for lost grains of rice, running before the armies with two pans and a blanket on their backs, dying politely, with Oriental good manners, of starvation. Maybe Reeves ought to call them up, too. Perhaps he had an important message for the Chinese as well. Still, all the philosophical identification in the world would not help if the frost set in. Somehow, he thought regretfully, I should have arranged things better. Somewhere, I missed a chance, was too lazy, too stupid, too complacent.

Of course, Reeves might be calling him about something entirely different. Maybe Elizabeth. Reeves had a nephew, name of Richard, and he and Elizabeth had been seeing a good deal of each other recently. Fact was, last Saturday night Cahill had surprised them kissing at the door. Quite a shock. Item: What do you do when you see your seventeen-year-old daughter kissing the nephew of your best friend? Bringing up a daughter was a little like sitting over one of those dud bombs that had been dropped into cellars during the war. A year might go by, two years. Nothing might happen. Or, the world was full of women who had gone bad, and at one time they had all been seventeen and some father's dewy darling. Ministers' daughters, admirals' daughters, daughters of the leaders of society. How could any father know what obscure, shameful invitations of the flesh his daughter was accepting and succumbing to among the college pennants and dimity and framed photographs in the next room? And Elizabeth was no help. She had always been a secretive, self-willed child, going her own way, disdainful of help or advice, not lying, exactly but never telling any more of the truth than she was forced to. He tried to think of her as someone else's daughter, in order to get an objective impression of her. Handsomely developed, prematurely womanly, he would have to say, with a promising, challenging look in her eye, a hidden, guarded sensuality, very much like her mother's. Oh, God, he thought torturedly, I hope the message isn't about her!

Or Reeves might want to talk to him about Charlie. Cahill considered the question of Charlie. In addition to eating an enormous amount of expensive roast beef when he got the chance, Charlie did very badly in his studies (was it possible that he was fundamentally stupid?) and got into trouble regularly with all authorities. A smooth-tongued truant, a brawler in schoolyards, a mischievous vandal in locker rooms, Charlie had been the occasion, again and again, for long visits of apology on the part of Cahill to parents of broken-nosed children, angry and insulted teachers even, once, to the police station, when Charlie had broken into the country-club tennis shop and stolen a dozen cans of balls and two lengths of chrome twist. At what moment did the high-spirited school-boy turn into the juvenile delinquent? Cahill thought of Charlie's sly, blond, unruly face. Consider your son objectively. What did you see? The insolence of the radio-and-comic-book age. The violence and irresponsibility of the double- and triple-featured generation of movie gangsters and movie sensualists. The restless superficiality of the book-haters, who slid into whisky, divorce courts, bankruptcy, worse, as the years wore on. Cahill had a vision of himself at the age of seventy, supporting his son, paying various blonde women alimony for him, bailing him out of magistrates' courts, and trying to hush up charges of drunken driving and cop-fighting. Tomorrow, he thought gloomily, I am going to have a serious talk with that young man. Though who knew what good it might do? John Dillinger's father probably had several talks with his son on the farm back in Indiana, and old Mr Capone no doubt had the parish priest in to talk sternly to his dark-eyed boy in the crowded home in Brooklyn.

Cahill hoped that Reeves was not going to talk to him about Charlie when they finally met the next day.

The bed now seemed intolerably warm, and Cahill could feel the sweat collecting in the crease of his chest. He threw back the covers. They made a loud, electric crackle and static electricity from the friction jumped in strange blue flashes around him. Edith stirred a little at the noise but did not wake. Cahill glared gloomily at her, listening to her breathe. If she had been home, as she had said she was going to be, that evening, it would have been she who had talked to Reeves. He'd have given her some inkling of what it was he wanted to talk to Cahill about and he'd have been spared this agonising night of conjecture. Tomorrow, Cahill thought, I'm going to damn well ask her a question or two, too. No, he thought, I'll be sly. If I seem to be quizzing her, she'll get suspicious or angry and sulk for days, and there'll be hell to pay around the house, and I'll have to give in to her on everything from now to Easter Sunday. I'll be nonchalant, elaborately offhand – pretend to be reading the paper, mix it up with questions about the kids, surprise her into revelations, if there are any. Then he was ashamed of himself for plotting this way against his wife, sleeping so trustfully and innocently in the next bed. He had an impulse to go over to her and hold her in his arms. He even sat up, tentatively. Then he thought better of it. Edith was terribly grouchy when he woke her in the middle of the night, and could be depended on to make him suffer for it the next day. He stared at her, resenting her. The business of the two beds, now. Until the war, they'd slept in one big old bed, as married people should. You felt really married, two people defending themselves as a unit against the world, if each night you retired into the warm fortress of the marital bed. Two beds brought with them the inevitable warning of division, oneness, loneliness, rejection. And when he'd come back from the war, Edith had said she couldn't sleep that way any more; she'd got too used to sleeping alone. And, like a fool, he'd consented. The two beds, with the extra mattresses and blankets, had cost nearly three hundred dollars, too. All his terminal-leave pay. Your bonus for fighting the war was that your wife made you sleep alone. Beds fit for heroes to sleep in – singularly.

It was silly to worry about that any more. It was a battle he'd lost, definitely, a long time ago. Each night to its own insomnia. Tonight, he thought – by now a little light-headed and oratorical, even in his thoughts – we take up the problem of the message of Joseph Reeves.

The thing was to systematise it, attack the problem scientifically. Like *Time* magazine: Business, Politics, National Affairs, Science, Religion, Sex. Everything in its neat, crisp department. Two minutes with each one and you're ready with enough facts and opinions to carry you until the next publication date.

National Affairs. In the twentieth century, Reeves had said at lunch three days before, National Affairs had become a euphemism for butchery. Butchery accomplished, butchery in progress, butchery contemplated. Slaughter in three tenses, with a corresponding rise in the budget. In the last few months,

Reeves had become more and more obsessed with the idea of war. At the same lunch, they'd had a gloomy conversation about the possibility that it would break out soon. Reeves, so optimistic about other things, sombrely dug around in newspapers and magazines to find new and disturbing items about the imminence of conflict and the dreadful new tools that might be employed. Cahill had even tried to avoid Reeves recently, because it was a subject he preferred not to reflect on. And his friend's dark flood of statistics about the range of atomic missiles and the mortal potential of biologic agents was not calculated to improve the delicate lunchtime appetite. Also, Reeves had made an unpleasant survey of the various and all too frequent occasions in history on which whole nations and, in fact, whole civilisations had committed suicide, deducing from that that it was entirely possible, and, indeed, probable, that in the next few years just such a widespread immolation would take place. To preserve his sanity, Cahill thought, resentfully trying to crowd Reeves's apocalyptic arguments out of his mind, a man must keep himself from speculating on these matters. Impotent and haunted, frozen in the slow, massive tide of events beyond his control, the night waker could only hope to ignore the question, or at least think about it in daylight, when the nerves were steadier. War, he thought angrily and helplessly, war. He remembered the cemeteries of Normandy and the sound shells made going over his head. At this moment, in a dozen places on the crust of the earth, machine guns were flicking and men were joyfully and devotedly putting other men to death and inviting the Americans, the Russians, the Berbers, the Malayans, the Yugoslavs, the Finns, and the Bulgars to join them.

Read a newspaper, listen to a news broadcast, wake for a quarter-hour in your own bed some time before dawn, and death came familiarly to hand. When he'd come home in 1945, he'd thought all that was behind him. My limit, he always said – not seriously, but meaning it, too – is one war. But other people, of more influence, seemed to have other limits. It was one thing, at the age of thirty-three, bravely to don the uniform and sail off to a relatively old-fashioned war, in which comprehensible weapons like machine-guns and bombs were being used. It was quite another, seven years later, a sedentary forty, to contemplate exposing yourself to the atom and the microbe, feeling, too, all the while, that your well-run home, enclosing your wife and children, might at any moment dissolve in radioactive dust or become the harbour for the germs of plague. He looked over at his wife, comfortably at rest. How, he wondered, does anyone sleep this year?

The dim light of dawn was washing through the curtains now. God, Cahill thought, his hot eyes resentfully taking it in. I am going to be a wreck today. Masochistically, he continued with his list. Politics. There we have a subject, he reflected, to keep a man's eyes open a night or two. According to Lloyd again, after Reeves had visited the president's office that afternoon, he had been called into a secret session of the committee of state senators who were down from the capital investigating Communist influence on the campus. Lloyd, who had been active in several questionable organisations for years, and who didn't trust Reeves, had been none too happy about that. 'A company man,' Lloyd had said resentfully, in Cahill's presence. 'He'd sell his best friend for a smile from the stockholders.' Lloyd had peered meaningfully at Cahill when he said it, too, and Cahill was sure that the phrase 'his best friend' had not been a random choice of words. Cahill thought of various things that Reeves might have told the committee and twitched uneasily. Back in the years before the war, when Communism was an almost respectable doctrine, Cahill had been on various committees with people he was sure belonged to the Party and had let his name be used again and again on a flood of well-meaning petitions and statements that, if not promulgated by the Communists, certainly had their endorsement. Once, he and Reeves had even gone to a kind of polite, open Party meeting, at which several people he knew had made amorphous speeches about Communism's being twentieth-century Americanism, and stuff like that. He had been invited to join, he remembered, although he couldn't remember who had actually come up to him and spoken the fateful words. He hadn't joined, and he'd never gone to another meeting, but what if the committee, armed with informers' information, demanded of him whether he had ever attended a meeting and if he had ever been asked to join. What would he do? Perjure himself, and say he had never gone, or tell the truth, and leave himself open to the next question. Was Professor Kane there? Did Mr Ryan, instructor in chemistry, make a speech about the working of the Communist Party? Will you kindly look over this list of names and check off the ones you can swear were present? What do you do in a situation like that? Professor Kane had been there and had made a speech, but Cahill knew that he had quietly resigned from the Party at the time of the Pact and had had no more to do with it. Still, who knew what Kane had told the committee? Kane was a friend of his, and needed the job. And if Cahill told the truth, Kane would be out of his job, disgraced, in a month. And poor Ryan. He'd been suspended on suspicion already, and his wife was sick, and he'd had to pay a lawyer to defend him. And, Communist or no, he'd always seemed to Cahill to be a very decent, shy, undangerous man. Cahill had given Ryan fifty dollars towards his defence, secretly, in cash. It was hard to understand just why. He was opposed to Ryan's politics, but he liked Ryan and felt sorry for him, and fifty dollars was not much, one way or another. Cahill had told Reeves about the fifty dollars and had even asked Reeves to help, too. Reeves, coldly, saying Ryan had it coming to him, had refused. What if Reeves had been trapped into saying something about the fifty dollars to the committee? What could Cahill tell them when he was questioned? How would he act? Would he be brave, considered, honourable? Just what was honourable in a situation like this? Was there honour in perjury? Or did honour lie in destroying your friends? Or destroying yourself? Did he actually believe that Ryan, for example, was an innocent, idealistic fellow, or did he believe that Ryan, the soft-voiced, scholarly, shyly smiling family man Ryan, was a potential traitor, a patient murderer, a dangerous conspirator against all the values that he, Cahill, held dear? I am too weary, Cahill thought pettishly, to decide this this morning. What if they asked about the meeting? What day was it? What year? Who invited you? The mists of memory shifted thickly around the fact. Whatever you answered was bound to be wrong. And if you said honestly, 'I don't remember,' how would that look on the record and in the newspapers? Like evasion, guilt, worthy only of disbelief and disdain.

So much for the crisp, neat two minutes of Politics. It was simpler in a magazine, where another issue was coming out in seven days, with another capsule of highly polished, anonymous, streamlined facts. A new man, Cahill thought, should be published every week, under a different title, anonymously. Each issue built around a different fact. The honourable man. The perjured man. The sensual man. The devout man. The economic man. Fifty-two times a year, something new and interesting in each copy. No irreconcilable facts to be found in any single volume. For Christmas, we plan to give you the friendly man, to be followed shortly by the betraying man, all in fine, unlimited editions. And, as a dividend to our subscribers, bound in blood, stitched with nerve ends, and illustrated by the leading artists of the age, with copious notes, the doubtful man, on which our editors have been working continuously for three hundred years at great personal expense.

There was a soft, sighing sound at the window, and Cahill saw that the wind had grown stronger and that it had begun to snow. A thin shower of snow sifted in through the open window, making a pale pattern on the floor. Fair and warmer, Cahill thought angrily, that's what the forecasters said. The liars of science, portentously inaccurate instruments, confidently deluding you with false visions of the future. Like Dr Manners, armed with stethoscope and X-ray, patting him heartily on the back last Tuesday, telling him of course he occasionally must expect to feel a twinge here, a pain there; he was not as young as he used to be. How many men died on Sunday who had been told during the week by their doctors that they were not as young as they used to be? The breezy assumption on the part of the medical profession that agony was the ordinary condition of life. Manners, he thought resentfully, would be considerably less breezy, with himself if it were his chest that trembled to the tone of pain, secret and until now distant, but there, warning, definite. Experimentally, Cahill lifted his left arm and stretched it. Again, as always in the last few months, there was the small answering pressure, dull, lurking, across his chest, across his heart. 'A slight irregularity,' Manners had said. 'Just nerves. Nothing to worry about.' Nothing for Manners to worry about, perhaps. And the constriction across the stomach; that, too, according to Manners, was nerves. Nerves, the modern equivalent for Fate, the substitute for the medieval Devil, which attacked mankind in the form of obscure, and often mortal, ills. Nerves, the perfect formula for the lazy diagnostician. Or – and Cahill could feel his breath catching in his throat at the thought – perhaps Manners, out of kindness, was hiding the true information from him. A hearty clap on the back, an innocuous prescription for sugar water and belladonna, and, after the door had closed, a thoughtful, sorrowful shrug, and the fateful entry in the case history of Philip Cahill 'Prognosis negative'.

Cahill put the palm of his hand under his pyjama jacket, on the warm skin of his abdomen, as though by the touch of flesh on flesh he might discover the dreadful secret that lay there. Within him under his hand, he could feel a faint, erratic quivering. Not good, he thought, not good at all. His mind touched regretfully on the edge of the word he was afraid to say. The papers were so damned full of it, the posters on the buses, even the radio. And if it occurred in the stomach, it was fatal at least eighty per cent of the time, and you almost never found out about it before it was too late. Maybe that was what Reeves had called about. Maybe Manners had gone to see Reeves and explained to him and asked what Reeves thought should be done. The services that friends had to do for each other. You start out as gay children, playing tennis with each other, racing each other across the lakes of summer, roaring jubilantly together on your first drunks, and twenty years later, all that far in the past, you have to go in and announce to your friend that his death is at hand.

Ridiculous, Cahill thought. I'm not going to lie here any longer. He got out of bed and stood up. His legs felt weary and uncertain, and there was the tense, stretched sensation in his stomach as he put on his robe and slippers. He looked over at Edith. She still slept, the rhythm of her breathing unchanged. Walking slowly, his slippers shuffling across the rug, he went silently out of the bedroom. He descended the stairs, holding the banister, shivering a little in the night-frozen house. In the hall below, he went over to the telephone, on the table under the mirror. He hesitated, staring at the phone. The clock in the living-room said ten minutes to seven. He picked up the phone and dialled Joe Reeves's number. While he listened to the long succession of buzzes in the receiver, he stared at himself in the mirror. His face was haggard, his eyes thick and glazed and encircled completely by muddy blue shadows. His rumpled hair looked slack and lustreless, his face exhausted and – hunted. He looked for a moment, then turned his back on the mirror.

Finally, there was the sound of someone picking up the receiver at the other end. Whoever it was fumbled a long time with the instrument, and Cahill said impatiently, 'Hello! Hello!' Then he heard a sleepy, dark voice mumbling irritatedly, 'Mr Reeves's residence. Who that calling?'

'Hello,' Cahill said eagerly. 'Violet?'

'Yes. This Violet. Who calling?'

'Violet,' Cahill said, making his voice even and clear, because he remembered with what suspicion Violet regarded the telephone, 'this is Mr Cahill.'

'Who?'

'Cahill. Mr Cahill. '

'It's an awful early hour of the mawnin', Mr Cahill,' Violet said aggrievedly.

'I know,' Cahill said, 'but Mr Reeves has a message for me. He especially asked me to call him as soon as I could. Is he up yet?'

'I dunno, Mr Cahill,' said Violet. He could hear her yawn enormously at the other end of the wire. 'He's not here.'

'What's that?'

'He's gone. Went last night. He and Mis' Reeves. They gone for the week-end. I'm the only livin' soul in the house. And' – her voice took on a tone of impatient complaint – 'I'm freezin' here in my night-shirt in this drafty old hall.'

Cahill could sense that Violet was on the verge of hurling the receiver down on the hook – an amusing trick of hers, with which she concluded telephone conversations in mid-message. It was not amusing now. 'Violet,' he said urgently, 'don't hang up. Where did they go?'

'Don't ask me,' Violet said. 'They didn't tell me. You know Mr Reeves. He was sittin' around the house last night, real restless, like he is, and all of a sudden he jumped up and said to Mis' Reeves, "Let's get into the car and get away from here for a couple of days." They just packed one little bag. Mis' Reeves was wearing slacks and she didn't even bother to change 'em. They just gone for a ride, I guess. They'll be back by Monday, never you worry.'

Slowily, Cahill put the receiver down. He looked up and saw that Elizabeth was standing at the foot of the stairs, in an almost transparent nightgown, her bathrobe carelessly open and hanging loose from her shoulders. Her dark hair was down, flowing thickly around her throat. Her face was creamy with sleep and her eyes were half closed in an amused, almost condescending smile. 'Daddy,' she said, 'who on earth are you calling at this fantastic hour? One of your other girls?'

Cahill stared dully at her. Though the frail rayon of her night-dress, he could see, very plainly, the swell of her breasts, rising generously from the exposed, rich skin of her bare bosom. 'None of your business,' he said harshly. 'Now go upstairs. And when you come down again, make sure you're

100

decently covered! This is your home. It is not a burlesque house! is that clear?'

He could see the incredulous, hurt grimace gripping her features, and then the blush, rising from her bosom, flaming on her cheeks. 'Yes,' she said faintly. 'Yes, Daddy,' She turned, hugging the robe around her ashamedly. Cahill watched her walk slowly and painfully up the stairs. He wanted to say something, call her back, but by now he knew there was nothing to say and that the child would not come back.

He went into the living-room and sank into a chair, feeling cold. Wildly, he contemplated the thought of living until Monday.

God on Friday Night

Sol let himself quietly into the house and walked softly down the long hall towards the kitchen, the only sound the fashionable creaking of his pale tan shoes. He saw his mother bending over the stove, red-faced, peering into the roaster, basting a chicken.

'Ma,' he said softly.

Ma grunted, busily pushing the potatoes.

'It's me, Ma. It's Sol.'

Ma closed the oven and stood up wearily, her hands pushing helpfully at the hip.

'Kiss Mama,' she said.

Sol kissed her and she sat down and looked at him. 'You don't look so good, Sol. You don't look the way you looked when you were a young boy.'

Every time she saw him she told him the same thing.

'What do you want, Ma?' Sol sighed, voicing the hopeless argument. 'I'm not a young boy any more. I'm a man thirty-three years old.'

'Even so.' Ma wiped her forehead and looked anxiously at him. 'The life you lead.'

'A man who makes his living entertaining in night clubs can't live like a prize horse,' Sol said. He sat down across the table and stretched his hand out tenderly to cover hers. 'How're yuh, Ma?'

Ma sighed. 'What do you expect? My kidneys. Always my kidneys. A woman with a family gets old like an express train.' She looked closely at her son. 'Sol, darling,' she said, 'you wear the worst clothes I've ever seen on a man's back. You belong on a merry-go-round.'

'In my profession,' Sol said with sober pride, 'this is the way they dress.'

'They should not be allowed out in the daytime.' She shook her head. 'That tie. That material would be good to line closets with.'

'Violet picked out this tie.'

'How is Violet? Why can't she come visit her mother-in-law once in a while? Is the Bronx another world?'

'Violet's all right,' Sol said flatly, looking at the glitter on his shoe tips. 'Only . . . '

Ma sighed, her large, fashionably supported bosom heaving under the black net. 'O.K, Baby, tell Mama.'

Sol leaned over anxiously. 'I must talk to you, private.'

Ma looked around the kitchen. 'Are we in Grand Central Station?'

'Real private, Ma. I don't want *nobody* to hear this. *Nobody.* Not even Pop.'

'What've you done, Sol? There was a note of stern alarm in Ma's voice, and she grabbed Sol's arm tightly. 'Tell Mama the truth.'

'I ain't done nothing. Honest. At least nothing bad. Don't worry, Ma.'

'Nobody's sick?'

'Nobody's sick.'

'All right.' Ma sat back in her chair, holding her feet off the floor to take the weight off them. 'Do you want to stay for dinner? You can always cut an extra portion out of a chicken.'

'Lissen, Ma,' Sol said intensely, 'you got to lissen to me and you got to promise you won't tell nobody.'

'I promise. All right, I promise. Will you stay to dinner?'

'Yeah,' Sol said. 'Well . . . ' He hesitated. 'This is complicated.'

Lawrence came into the kitchen, throwing his books on the floor. 'Hiya, Sol, Hello, Mom. Am I hungry, oh, Momma, am I hungry . . . Mom, whatta ye got to eat? Oh, am I hungry!'

'I'm talkin' to Ma, private,' Sol said.

'I'm hungry,' Lawrence said, looking in the icebox. 'Go ahead and talk. I'll forget it, anyway.'

'I want to talk to Ma private,' Sol said in measured tones.

'What the hell's so private?' Lawrence asked, gesturing with a bottle of milk. 'What're you, a German spy? Boy, am I hungry!'

'Don't say "hell", Larry,' Ma said. 'And get out of here.'

'I'm taking the bottle with me,' Lawrence announced, marching towards the door. He patted his mother on the head. 'Mata Hari.' He went out.

'A brilliant boy,' Ma said. 'He leads his class.'

Sol cleared his throat.

'Yes, Sol,' Ma said. 'I'm listening.'

'I been thinking, Ma,' he began in a low thoughtful voice, twisting his heavy gold ring slowly around on his finger. 'I ain't a good boy.'

'That's not such private news.' Ma laughed at the expression on Sol's face. She pinched his arm. 'You got a good heart, Sol,' she said. 'My baby Sol, with a heart like a house.'

'I have done things, Ma,' Sol said slowly, choosing his words with great care, 'that were not so good.'

'If we were all angels, we wouldn't need aeroplanes,' Ma said with finality. 'Let me look at the chicken.'

She went over and looked at the chicken. 'That butcher!' she said. 'He is selling me eagles.' She closed the oven door and sat down again.

'I have done things,' Sol said quietly, 'that God wouldn't like.'

'I think God has other things on His mind, these days, Sol.'

'Ma,' Sol said, not looking at his mother, 'Ma, would you light candles on Friday night and make the prayer?'

There was silence in the kitchen, broken only by the small crackle from the oven, where the chicken was browning.

'I haven't lighted candles for a long time, Sol.' Ma said gently. 'Ever since the day I married your father. He was a Socialist, your father.'

'Would yuh light 'em now, Ma?' Sol pleaded. 'Every Friday night?'

'What is it, Sol? Why should I light candles?'

Sol took a deep breath and stood up and walked back and forth in the kitchen. 'Violet,' he said, 'Violet's goin' to have a baby.'

'Oh!' Ma gasped, fanning herself. 'Oh! Well! That blonde girl! Oh! A grandchild! Oh, Sol, Baby!' She grabbed Sol and kissed him. 'My Sol!'

'Don't cry, Ma. Ma, please . . . ' Sol patted her solid wide back. 'It's all right.'

'It's about time, Sol. I thought you'd never . . . ' She kissed him on the forehead and smiled widely. 'I thought Violet was beginning to look very good in the breasts. Congratulations from the bottom of my heart. We'll name him after my father.'

'Yeah,' Sol said. 'Thanks. How about the candles now, Ma?'

'What do you need candles for? I had five children without burning a single candle.'

'Violet's different,' Sol said uneasily. 'She's not like you.'

'She is just built for children,' Ma declared. 'She is built like a horse. When I had you I weighed ninety-five pounds. Including you. She doesn't need candles.'

'You don't know, Ma,' Sol looked intently into his mother's eyes. 'Today Violet slipped in the bathtub.'

'Well?'

'She coulda killed herself. As it is, she fainted.'

'So you want me to pray because your wife doesn't know how to take a bath. Sol?' Ma waved him away. 'Every day millions of people fall down in bathtubs.'

'Lissen, Ma,' Sol said, holding both her hands. 'Nuthin' can happen to Violet. And nuthin' can happen to the kid. See Ma? We been tryin' to have a kid for years now and . . .' He stopped.

Ma shook her head in wonderment. 'That big blonde horse.'

'We want that kid, Ma. We gotta have that kid. Everybody should have a kid. What've I got if I haven't got a son?'

'Sssh, Baby,' Ma said. 'Sure, you're right. Only don't yell. You're too nervous to yell.'

'All right. I won't yell.' Sol wiped the sweat off his forehead with a blue silk handkerchief with a green monogram. 'All right. What I want to say is, Violet's dumpin' herself in the bathtub was a omen.'

'A what?'

'A omen. It's a . . .'

'I know.'

'It shows us we can't take any chances, Ma.'

'Loose in the head, my baby Sol,' Ma said. 'Too much night life.'

'We got to pray to God, Ma,' Sol said, 'that nuthin' happens to that baby.'

'If you want to pray to God, go ahead and pray. Did *I* make the baby?' Ma asked. 'Let Violet pray.'

Sol swallowed. 'Violet's not fit to pray,' he said gently. 'She's a first-class girl and I would lay down on railroad tracks for her, but she ain't fit to pray to God.'

'That's no way to talk about your own wife, Solly,' Ma said. 'Shame on you.'

'I love her like she was my right arm,' Sol said. 'But she's not a very good woman, Ma. What's the sense in kiddin' ourselves? Violet has a weak character, Ma, and she has done two or three or five things . . . Give Violet four drinks, Ma, and

105

she says "Yes" to the man from Macy's. She's young, she'll outgrow it an' settle down, but right now . . . ' Sol nervously lit a cigarette. 'Right now, Ma, Violet's prayers'd carry top weight in the field.'

'Sol, Sol,' Ma said gravely, 'why can't *you* pray?'

Sol sat quietly, observing his cigarette. The blush came up over his purple collar, like dye soaking in cloth. 'I am not one hundred per cent perfect in any respect, myself,' he said. 'First of all, Ma, in my business if yuh don't tell the customers dirty jokes, yuh might just as well apply to the W.P.A.'

'You should've been a doctor, like I said.'

'I know, Ma,' Sol said patiently. 'But I'm not. I'm a man who has to play in cheap night clubs in Philadelphia and Lowell, Massachusetts, and Boston, weeks at a time. Yuh don't know how lonely it can get at night in Lowell, Massachusetts.'

'A lot, Sol?'

'A lot, Ma, a lot,' Sol cast his eyes up at the kitchen ceiling.

'A boy with a face like yours,' Ma shrugged. 'Girls're funny.'

'If I prayed, Ma, the words'd stick in my throat.'

'So you want me. I don't even believe in God, Baby.'

'That's all right, Ma,' Sol said. 'You're a good woman. Yuh never hurt anybody in all yer life.'

Ma sighed hugely. 'I'll have to go down to Mrs Aaronson and get her to teach me the prayer. Sol, darling, you're a nuisance.'

Sol kissed her, his eyes shining.

'I got to see what's happening to that bird,' Ma said, bending over the chicken. 'I'll pray that it's a boy,' she said, 'while I'm at it.'

Every Friday night the candles were lighted and Ma steadfastly said the old words: '*Burach ee, burach shmoi, Burach ee, burach shmoi. Burach ee, burach shmoi. Burach ata adanoi eluchainu melach huoilom. Chaleck necht shil shabos.*' And then she prayed for a boy.

It was on a Friday night that Sol and Violet brought the baby over to Ma's for the first time.

Sol held the smiling and pink and robust boy in his arms as if he were wood.

'See, Ma?' he said, holding the baby out.

Ma put her hands out slowly, and gently rubbed the little soft head. 'Hair,' she said. 'He's got hair.' She chuckled and

106

took the baby's hand out and kissed it. 'Take him into the bedroom, Violet,' she said. 'I'm busy here for a minute.'

She turned and lighted the seven candles in the window, one by one.

'The last stronghold of religion,' Lawrence said. 'All of a sudden. This house.'

'Shut up,' Ma said. 'City College philosopher.'

And she said, *'Burach ee, burach shmoi. Burach ee . . .'* as the candles burned.

Mike Pilato purposefully threw open the door of Victor's shack. Above him the sign that said, 'Lunch, Truckmen Welcome', shook a little, and the pale shadows its red bulbs threw in the twilight waved over the State Road.

'Victor,' Mike said, in Italian.

Victor was leaning on the counter, reading Walter Winchell in a spread-out newspaper. He smiled amiably. 'Mike,' he said, 'I am so glad to see you.'

Mike slammed the door. 'Three hundred dollars, Victor,' he said, standing five feet tall, round and solid as a pumpkin against the door. 'You owe me three hundred dollars, Victor, and I am here tonight to collect.'

Victor shrugged slightly and closed the paper on Walter Winchell.

'As I've been telling you for the past six months,' he said, 'business is bad. Business is terrible. I work and I work and at the end . . . ' He shrugged again. 'Barely enough to feed myself.'

Mike's cheeks, farmer-brown, and wrinkled deeply by wind and sun, grew dark with blood. 'Victor, you are lying in my face,' he said slowly, his voice desperately even. 'For six months, each time it comes time to collect the rent you tell me, "Business is bad". What do I say? I say, "All right, Victor, don't worry, I know how it is".'

'Frankly, Mike,' Victor said sadly, 'there has been no improvement this month.

Mike's face grew darker than ever. He pulled harshly at the ends of his iron-grey moustache, his great hands tense and swollen with anger, repressed but terrible. 'For six months Victor,' Mike said, 'I believed you. Now I no longer believe you.'

'Mike,' Victor said reproachfully.

'My friends, my relatives,' Mike said, 'they prove it to me.

108

Your business is wonderful, ten cars an hour stop at your door; you sell cigarettes to every farmer between here and Chicago; on your slot machine alone . . . ' Mike waved a short thick arm at the machine standing invitingly against a wall, its wheels stopped at two cherries and a lemon. Mike swallowed hard, stood breathing heavily, his deep chest rising and falling sharply against his sheepskin coat. 'Three hundred dollars!' he shouted. 'Six months at fifty dollars! I built this shack with my own hands for you, Victor. I didn't know what kind of a man you were. You were an Italian, I trusted you! Three hundred dollars or get out tomorrow! Finish! That's my last word.'

Victor smoothed his newspaper down delicately on the counter, his hands making a dry brushing sound in the empty lunchroom. 'You misunderstand,' he said gently.

'I misunderstand nothing!' Mike yelled. 'You are on my land in my shack and you owe me three hundred dollars . . . '

'I don't owe you anything,' Victor said, looking coldly at Mike. 'That is what you misunderstand. I have paid you every month, the first day of the month, fifty dollars.'

'Victor!' Mike whispered, his hands dropping to his sides. 'Victor, what are you saying . . . ?'

'I have paid the rent. Please do not bother me any more.' Calmly Victor turned his back on Mike and turned two handles on the coffee urn. Steam, in a thin little plume, hissed up for a moment.

Mike looked at Victor's narrow back, with the shoulder blades jutting far out, making limp wings in the white shirt. There was finality in Victor's pose, boredom, easy certainty. Mike shook his head slowly, pulling hard at his moustache. 'My wife,' Mike said, to the disdainful back, 'she told me not to trust you. My wife knew what she was talking about, Victor.' Then, with a last flare of hope, 'Victor, do you really mean it when you said you paid me?'

Victor didn't turn around. He flipped another knob on the coffee urn. 'I mean it.'

Mike lifted his arm, as though to say something, pronounce warning. Then he let it drop and walked out of the shack, leaving the door open. Victor came out from behind the counter, looked at Mike moving off with his little rolling limp down the road and across the cornfield. Victor smiled and closed the door and went back and opened the paper to Walter Winchell.

Mike walked slowly among the cornstalks, his feet crunching unevenly in the October earth. Absently he pulled at his moustache. Dolores, his wife, would have a thing or two to say. 'No,' she had warned him, 'do not build a shack for him. Do not permit him on to your land. He travels with bad men; it will turn out badly. I warn you!' Mike was sure she would not forget this conversation and would repeat it to him word for word when he got home. He limped along unhappily. Farming was better than being a landlord. You put seed into the earth and you knew what was coming out. Corn grew from corn, and the duplicity of Nature was expected and natural. Also no documents were signed in the compact with Nature, no leases and agreements necessary, a man was not at a disadvantage if he couldn't read or write. Mike opened the door to his house and sat down heavily in the parlour, without taking his hat off. Rosa came and jumped on his lap, yelling, 'Poppa, Poppa, tonight I want to go to the movies, Poppa, take me to the movies!'

Mike pushed her off. 'No movies,' he said harshly. Rosa stood in a corner and watched him reproachfully.

The door from the kitchen opened, and Mike sighed as he saw his wife coming in, wiping her hands on her apron. She stood in front of Mike, round, short, solid as a plough horse, canny, difficult to deceive.

'Why're you sitting in the parlour?' she asked.

'I feel like sitting in the parlour,' Mike said.

'Every night you sit in the kitchen,' Dolores said. 'Suddenly you change.'

'I've decided,' Mike said loudly, 'that it's about time I made some use of this furniture. After all, I paid for it, I might as well sit in it before I die.'

'I know why you're sitting in the parlour,' Dolores said.

'Good! You know!'

'You didn't get the money from Victor.' Dolores wiped the last bit of batter from her hands. 'It's as plain as the shoes on your feet.'

'I smell something burning,' Mike said.

'Nothing is burning. Am I right or wrong?' Dolores sat in the upright chair opposite Mike. She sat straight, her hands neatly in her lap, her head forward and cocked a little to one side, her eyes staring directly and accusingly into his. 'Yes or no?'

'Please attend to your own department,' Mike said miserably. 'I do the farming and attend to the business details.'

'Huh!' Dolores said disdainfully.

'Are you starving?' Mike shouted. 'Answer me, are you starving?'

Rosa started to cry because her father was shouting.

'Please, for the love of Jesus,' Mike screamed at her, 'don't cry!'

Dolores enfolded Rosa in her arms . . . 'Baby, baby,' she crooned, 'I will not let him harm you.'

'Who offered to harm her?' Mike screamed, banging on a table with his fist like a mallet. 'Don't lie to her!'

Dolores kissed the top of Rosa's head soothingly. 'There, there,' she crooned. 'There.' She looked coldly at Mike. 'Well. So he didn't pay.'

'He . . . ' Mike started loudly. Then he stopped, spoke in a low, reasonable voice. 'So. To be frank with you, he didn't pay. That's the truth.'

'What did I tell you?' Dolores said as Mike winced. 'I repeat the words. "Do not permit him on to your land. He travels with bad men; it will turn out badly, I warn you!" Did I tell you?'

'You told me,' Mike said wearily.

'We will never see that money again,' Dolores said, smoothing Rosa's hair. 'I have kissed it good-bye.'

'Please,' said Mike. 'Return to the kitchen. I am hungry for dinner. I have made plans already to recover the money.'

Dolores eyed him suspiciously. 'Be careful, Mike,' she said. 'His friends are gangsters and he plays poker every Saturday night with men who carry guns in their pockets.'

'I am going to the law,' Mike said. 'I'm going to sue Victor for three hundred dollars.'

Dolores stared to laugh. She pushed Rosa away and stood up and laughed.

'What's so funny?' Mike asked angrily. 'I tell you I'm going to sue a man for money he owes me, you find it funny! Tell me the joke.'

Dolores stopped laughing. 'Have you got any papers? No! You trust him, he trusts you, no papers. Without papers you're lost in a court. You'll make a fool of yourself. They'll charge you for the lawyers. Please, Mike, go back to your farming.'

Mike's face set sternly, his wrinkles harsh in his face with the grey stubble he never managed completely to shave. 'I want my dinner, Dolores,' he said coldly, and Dolores discreetly moved into the kitchen, saying, 'It is not my business, my love; truly, I merely offer advice.'

Mike walked back and forth in the parlour, limping, rolling a little from side to side, his eyes on the floor, his hands plunged into the pockets of his denims like holstered weapons, his mouth pursed with thought and determination. After a while he stopped and looked at Rosa, who prepared to weep once more.

'Rosa, baby,' he said sitting down and taking her gently on his lap. 'Forgive me.'

Rosa snuggled to him. They sat that way in the dimly lit parlour.

'Poppa,' Rosa said finally.

'Yes,' Mike said.

'Will you take me to the movies tonight, Poppa?'

'All right,' Mike said. 'I'll take you to the movies.'

The next day Mike went into town, dressed in his neat black broadcloth suit and his black soft hat and his high brown shoes. He came back to the farm like a business-man in the movies, busily, preoccupied, sober, but satisfied.

'Well?' Dolores asked him, in the kitchen.

He kissed her briskly, kissed Rosa, sat down, took his shoes off, rubbed his feet luxuriously, said paternally to his son, who was reading *Esquire* near the window, 'That's right, Anthony, study.'

'Well?' asked Dolores.

'I saw Dominic in town,' Mike said, watching his toes wiggling. 'They're having another baby.'

'Well,' asked Dolores. 'The case? The action?'

'All right,' Mike said. 'What is there for dinner?'

'Veal,' Dolores said. 'What do you mean "all right"?'

'I've spoken to Judge Collins. He is filling out the necessary papers for me and he will write me a letter when I am to appear in court. Rosa, have you been a good girl?'

Dolores threw up her hands. 'Lawyers. We'll throw away a fortune on lawyers. Good money after bad. We could put in an electric pump with the money.'

'Lawyers will cost us nothing.' Mike stuffed his pipe elaborately. 'I have different plans. Myself. I will take care of the case myself.' He lit up, puffed deliberately.

Dolores sat down across the table from him, spoke slowly, carefully. 'Remember, Mike,' she said. 'This is in English. They conduct the court in English.'

'I know,' said Mike. 'I am right. Justice is on my side. Why should I pay a lawyer fifty, seventy-five dollars to collect my own money? There is one time you need lawyers – when you are wrong. I am not wrong. I will be my own lawyer.'

'What do you know about the law?' Dolores challenged him.

'I know Victor owes me three hundred dollars.' Mike puffed three times, quickly, on his pipe. 'That's all I need to know.'

'You can hardly speak English, you can't even read or write, nobody will be able to understand you. They'll all laugh at you, Mike.'

'Nobody will laugh at me. I can speak English fine.'

'When did you learn?' Dolores asked. 'Today?'

'Dolores!' Mike shouted. 'I tell you my English is all right.'

'Say Thursday,' Dolores said.

'I don't want to say it,' Mike said, banging the table. 'I have no interest in saying it.'

'Aha,' Dolores crowed. 'See? He wants to be a lawyer in an American court, he can't even say Thursday.'

'I can,' Mike said. 'Keep quiet, Dolores.'

'Say Thursday.' Dolores put her head to one side, spoke coquettishly, slyly, like a girl asking her lover to say he loved her.

'Stirday,' Mike said, as he always said. 'There!'

Dolores laughed, waving her hand. 'And he wants to conduct a law case! Holy Mother! They will laugh at you!'

'Let them laugh!' Mike shouted. 'I will conduct the case! Now I want to eat dinner! Anthony!' he yelled. 'Throw away that trash and come to the table.'

On the day of the trial, Mike shaved closely, dressed carefully in his black suit, put his black hat squarely on his head, and with Dolores seated grimly beside him drove early into town in the 1933 family Dodge.

Dolores said nothing all the way into town. Only after the car was parked and they were entering the courthouse, Mike's shoes clattering bravely on the legal marble, did Dolores speak. 'Behave yourself,' she said. Then she pinched his arm. Mike smiled at her, braced his yoke-like shoulders, took off his hat. His rough grey hair sprang up like steel wool when his hat was off, and Mike ran his hand through it as he opened the door to the court-room. There was a proud, important smile on his face as he sat down next to his wife in the first row and patiently waited for his case to be called.

When Victor came, Mike glared at him, but Victor, after a quick look, riveted his attention on the American flag behind the Judge's head.

'See,' Mike whispered to Dolores. 'I have him frightened. He doesn't dare look at me. Here he will have to tell the truth.'

'Sssh!' hissed Dolores. 'This is a court of law.'

'Michael Pilato,' the clerk called, '*versus* Victor Fraschi.'

'Me!' Mike said loudly, standing up.

'Sssh,' said Dolores.

Mike put his hat in Dolores's lap, moved lightly to the little gate that separated the spectators from the principals in the proceedings. Politely, with a deep ironic smile, he held the gate open for Victor and his lawyer. Victor passed through without looking up.

'Who's representing you, Mr Pilato?' the Judge asked when they were all seated. 'Where's your lawyer?'

Mike stood up and spoke in a clear voice. 'I represent myself. I am my lawyer.'

'You ought to have a lawyer,' the Judge said.

'I do not need a lawyer,' Mike said loudly. 'I am not trying to cheat anybody.' There were about forty people in the courtroom and they all laughed. Mike turned and looked at them, puzzled. 'What did I say?'

The Judge rapped with his gavel and the case was opened. Victor took the stand, while Mike stared, coldly accusing, at him. Victor's lawyer, a young man in a blue pin-stripe suit and a starched tan shirt, questioned him. Yes, Victor said, he had paid each month. No, there were no receipts, Mr Pilato could neither read nor write and they had dispensed with all formalities of that kind. No, he did not understand on what Mr Pilato based his claim. Mike looked incredulously at Victor, lying under solemn oath, risking Hell for three hundred dollars.

Victor's lawyer stepped down and waved to Mike gracefully. 'Your witness.'

Mike walked dazedly past the lawyer and up to the witness stand, round, neat, his bull neck, deep red-brown and wrinkled, over his pure white collar, his large scrubbed hands politely but awkwardly held at his sides. He stood in front of Victor, leaning over a little toward him, his face close to Victor's.

'Victor,' he said, his voice ringing through the courtroom, 'tell the truth, did you pay me the money?'

'Yes,' said Victor.

Mike leaned closer to him. 'Look in my eye, Victor,' Mike said, his voice clear and patient, 'and answer me. Did you pay me the money?'

Victor lifted his head and looked unflinchingly into Mike's eyes. 'I paid you the money.'

Mike leaned even closer. His forehead almost touched Victor's now. 'Look me *straight* in the eye, Victor.'

Victor looked bravely into Mike's eyes, less than a foot away now.

'Now, Victor,' Mike said, his eyes narrowed, cold, the light in them small and flashing and grey, 'DID YOU PAY ME THE MONEY?'

Victor breathed deeply. 'Yes,' he said.

Mike took half a step back, almost staggering, as though he had been hit. He stared incredulously into the perjurer's eyes, as a man might stare at a son who had just admitted he has killed his mother, beyond pity, beyond understanding, outside all the known usage of human life. Mike's face worked harshly as the tides of anger and despair and vengeance rolled up in him.

'You're a goddamn liar, Victor!' Mike shouted terribly. He leapt down from the witness platform, seized a heavy oak armchair, raised it murderously above Victor's head.

'Mike, oh Mike!' Dolores's wail floated above the noise of the courtroom.

'Tell the truth, Victor!' Mike shouted, his face brick red, his teeth white behind his curled lips, almost senseless with rage, for the first time in his life threatening a fellow-creature with violence. 'Tell it fast!'

He stood, the figure of Justice, armed with the chair, the veins pulsing in his huge wrists, the chair quivering high above Victor's head in his huge gnarled hands, his tremendous arms tight and bulging in their broadcloth sleeves. 'Immediately, Victor!'

'Pilato!' shouted the Judge. 'Put that chair down!'

Victor sat stonily, his eyes lifted in dumb horror to the chair above his head.

'Pilato,' the Judge shouted, 'you can be sent to jail for this!' He banged sternly but helplessly on his desk. 'Remember, this is a court of law!'

'Victor?' Mike asked, unmoved, unmoving. 'Victor? Immediately, please.'

'No,' Victor screamed, cringing in his seat, his hands now

115

held in feeble defence before his eyes. 'I didn't pay! I didn't!'

'Pilato,' screamed the Judge, 'this is not evidence!'

'You were lying?' Mike said inexorably, the chair still held, axe-like, above him.

'Mike, oh Mike,' wailed Dolores.

'It was not my idea,' Victor babbled. 'As God is my judge, I didn't think it up. Alfred Lotti, he suggested it, and Johnny Nolan. I am under the influence of corrupt men. Mike, for the love of God, please don't kill me, Mike, it would never have occurred to me myself, forgive me, forgive me . . . '

'Guiness!' the Judge called to the court policeman. 'Are you going to stand there and let this go on? Why don't you do something?'

'I can shoot him,' Guiness said. 'Do you want me to shoot the plaintiff?'

'Shut up,' the Judge said.

Guiness shrugged and turned his head toward the witness stand, smiling a little.

'You were lying?' Mike asked, his voice low, patient.

'I was lying,' Victor cried.

Slowly, with magnificent calm, Mike put the chair down neatly in its place. With a wide smile he turned to the Judge. 'There,' he said.

'Do you know any good reason,' the Judge shouted, 'why I shouldn't have you locked up?'

Victor was crying with relief on the witness stand, wiping the tears away with his sleeve.

'There is no possible excuse,' the Judge said, 'for me to admit this confession as evidence. We are a court of law in the State of Illinois, in the United States. We are not conducting the Spanish Inquisition, Mr Pilato.'

'Huh?' Mike asked, cocking his head.

'There are certain rules,' the Judge went on, quickly, his voice high, 'which it is customary to observe. It is not the usual thing, Mr Pilato,' he said harshly, 'to arrive at evidence by bodily threatening to brain witnesses with a chair.'

'He wouldn't tell the truth,' Mike said simply.

'At the very least, Mr Pilato,' the Judge said, 'you should get thirty days.'

'Oh, Mike,' wept Dolores.

'Mr Fraschi,' the Judge said, 'I promise you that you will be protected. That nobody will harm you.'

'I did it,' sobbed Victor, his hands shaking uncontrollably

in a mixture of fear, repentance, religion, joy at delivery from death. 'I did it. I will not tell a lie. I'm a weak man and influenced by loafers. I owe him three hundred dollars. Forgive me, Mike, forgive me . . . '

'He will not harm you,' the Judge said patiently. 'I guarantee it. You can tell the truth without any danger. Do you owe Mr Pilato three hundred dollars?'

'I owe Mr Pilato three hundred dollars,' Victor said, swallowing four times in a row.

The young lawyer put three sheets of paper into his brief-case and snapped the lock.

The Judge sighed and wiped his brow with a handkerchief as he looked at Mike. 'I don't approve of the way you conducted this trial, Mr Pilato,' he said. 'It is only because you're a working man who has many duties to attend to on his land that I don't take you and put you away for a month to teach you more respect for the processes of law.'

'Yes, sir,' Mike said faintly.

'Hereafter,' the Judge said, 'kindly engage an attorney when you appear before me in this court.'

'Yes, sir,' Mike said.

'Mr Pilato,' the Judge said, 'it is up to you to decide when and how he is to pay you.'

Mike turned and walked back to Victor. Victor shrank into his chair. 'Tomorrow morning, Victor,' Mike said, waving his finger under Victor's nose, 'at eight-thirty o'clock, I am coming into your store. The money will be there.'

'Yes,' said Victor.

'Is that all right?' Mike asked the Judge.

'Yes,' said the Judge.

Mike strode over to the young lawyer. 'And you,' he said, standing with his hands on his hips in front of the young man with the pin-stripe suit. 'Mr Lawyer. You knew he didn't pay me.' A boy with an education. You should be ashamed of yourself.' He turned to the Judge, smiled broadly, bowed. 'Thank you,' he said. 'Good morning.' Then, triumphantly, smiling broadly, rolling like a sea captain as he walked, he went through the little gate. Dolores was waiting with his hat. He took the hat, put Dolores's arm through his, marched down the aisle, nodding, beaming to the spectators. Someone applauded and by the time he and Dolores got to the door all the spectators were applauding.

He waited until he got outside, in the bright morning sunshine down the steps of the courthouse, before he said anything to Dolores. He put his hat on carefully, turning to her, grinning. 'Well,' he said, 'did you observe what I did?'

'Yes,' she said. 'I was never so ashamed in my whole life!'

'Dolores!' Mike was shocked. 'I got the money, I won the case.'

'Acting like that in a court of law!' Dolores started bitterly toward the car. 'What are you, a Red Indian?'

Dolores got into the car and slammed the door and Mike limped slowly around and got into the other side. He started the car without a word and, shaking his head from time to time, drove slowly toward home.

The City Was in Total Darkness

Dutcher stood at the bar, feeling clean after his shower and still thirsty, looking at the girls, glad that he was alone, listening with one ear to the conversation around him. 'The British and French,' a man in a hound's-tooth check jacket was saying, 'will shuttle back and forth over Germany from Paris to Warsaw. And besides, he has no oil. Everybody knows Hitler has no oil.'

' "Darling," she says to me,' a large blonde woman said loudly to another large blonde woman, ' "darling, I haven't seen you in forever. Where've you been – in the summer theatre?" She knows goddamn well I just finished two pictures for Fox!'

'It's a bluff,' the man in the hound's-tooth check said. 'He's going to back down, Russia or no Russia. He has no oil. Where are you today without oil?'

'Mr Dutcher,' The barman brought over the phone and plugged it in. 'For you.'

It was Machamer on the phone. 'What're you doing tonight, Ralph?' Machamer asked, his voice, as always, grating and noisy.

'I'm drinking tonight,' Dutcher said. 'I'm drinking and waiting for something good to happen to me.'

'We're going to Mexico,' Machamer said. 'Want to come along?'

'Who's we?'

'Dolly and me. Want to come along?'

'What part of Mexico?' Dutcher asked. 'What distant part of that verdant land? Vera Cruz, Mexico City . . . ?'

Machamer laughed. 'Tia Juana. I got to be back on Tuesday to look for a job. Just overnight. For the races. Want to go?'

'Without oil,' the man in the check was saying, 'a war is absolutely impractical.' Dutcher looked gravely at him, considering whether or not he wanted to go to Mexico. He had avoided people after playing tennis in the afternoon, because he'd wanted to be alone, by himself, with the decks clear for something special and significant to happen to him on this special and significant week-end.

'Have they got bullfights in Tia Juana?' he asked Machamer.

'Maybe,' Machamer said. 'They have them sometimes. Come on, this is Labour Day, there's nobody in Hollywood.'

'I'm tired,' Dutcher said. 'I've been listening to the radio for seven nights and I played tennis and I'm thirsty.'

'You can lie down in the back of the car, with a bottle,' Machamer said. Machamer was a young writer and very impressed with Dutcher's two novels and constantly was after him. 'I'll drive.'

'I never saw a bullfight,' Dutcher said. 'Did you ever see one there?'

'Oh, nuts!' Machamer said. 'Dolly and I'll be over in fifteen minutes to pick you up.'

'Tonight,' Dutcher said, 'I would like to have a startling adventure.'

'Oh, nuts,' Machamer said. 'Fifteen minutes.'

Dutcher gravely put the phone back on its pedestal. 'I've got to find another bar,' he said to the barman. 'Whenever people want to find me they call me here. It's bad for the reputation. In two years nobody'll give me a job.' The barman grinned. 'Another Rum Collins,' Dutcher said, looking steadfastly at a slender girl down the bar who had long thick black hair and tremendous full breasts that jutted out like pennants in front of her. The barman looked too. 'Doesn't it break your heart?' the barman said.

'California,' Dutcher said. 'Specialty of the country.'

'That cameraman,' one of the blonde ladies was saying, 'he made me look like William S. Hart's mother. I told him, too, but *loud*!'

In Poland, now, the tanks were roaring over the dusty plains, German boys were climbing into bombers now, Dutcher thought, fiddling with the controls, peering at the instruments, thinking in this one minute when they were waiting and there was nothing to do, 'Is this the last time?' and then getting the signal and sweeping off the field toward Warsaw. Cavalry, Dutcher remembered, the Poles had wonderful cavalry. He could just see a wonderful Polish cavalryman sitting on his plodding mount, retreating, sleepless, from the border, sinking from the horse, listening to the bombers overhead, thinking of

120

sleep and home and the English Air Force, kicking his horse wearily, saying, 'Son of a bitch'. And the rich and their women, like the rich and their women everywhere, leaving quietly out the back way, while the dawn broke and the light came up and the boy in the bomber could get a good clear view of the cavalryman on the long, open road below.

Dutcher looked at the girl with breasts like pennants. He sat at the bar, making believe he was staring blankly ahead, making believe nothing was happening inside him, feeling lust rise within him as definitely as water rising in a filling glass. General, non-particular lust, he thought, looking at the girl, pretty, with her black hair and long throat and bright print dress and that amazing bosom. I ought to be ashamed, Dutcher thought. The reader of Spinoza, the admirer of John Milton, the advocate of moral and economic reforms, a sufferer from general and indiscriminate lust ten times daily at the sight of a face, a ruffle, at the sound of a woman's laugh.

'We live on two planes,' Dutcher said to the bartender. The bartender smiled weakly.

Hollywood, Dutcher thought, Hollywood had a great deal to do with it. It was the product of the neighbourhood, and everywhere you went it was pushed in your face like cheese in Wisconsin, and you tried to keep yourself from thinking about *Murder at Midnight* and sex rushed in to fill the vacuum. *Murder at Midnight* was the picture he was writing. It had a long, complicated story about a night-club singer who got drunks to spend money on her, but who was genuine, all the way through, as everyone always said in the conferences. She had a small son from whom she bravely tried to conceal the tawdriness of her profession, and she got mixed up in a murder and she fled town in the rain with her son and the cops picked up an innocent man . . . Dutcher shook his head. He never could get the story straight. Anyway, this was the week-end. And he'd be through in two weeks and have enough money for eight months in New York. Why'm I kidding myself? he thought. I look at them in New York, too.

Hollywood, you could always blame everything on Hollywood. That was the nicest thing about Hollywood.

'Sacred and profane,' he told the bartender. 'That's the whole explanation.'

Machamer came in with Dolly. 'On to Mexico,' Machamer said.

'Sit down,' Dutcher said, 'and give me some good arguments.

121

Dolly, you look beautiful.' Dolly looked as thin and as plain and nervous as ever, and Dutcher was always very careful, in this city of magnificent women, to be gallant and flattering to her. 'Give me Dolly,' he said to Machamer, 'and I'll go to Mexico.'

Dolly laughed. Her laugh was high and very nervous and always made Dutcher a little uncomfortable.

'Poor Dutcher,' Dolly said. 'Poor lonesome Dutcher.

'Get me a girl,' Dutcher said, suddenly, not thinking about it or why he was saying it, 'and I'll go with you.'

'Now, Dutcher,' Machamer protested. 'Eight o'clock Saturday night, Labour Day week-end.'

'On a high moral plane,' Dutcher said. 'I just want to have somebody to talk to.'

'You have plenty of girls,' Machamer said.

'I'm tired of them,' Dutcher said. 'Tonight I'm tired of them. War, *Murder at Midnight*, the fickleness of the male character, I'm tired of them. Tonight I'm in the mood for a new face.' Dutcher waved his hands elaborately, embroidering on the theme, although already half-sorry that he'd said anything about a girl 'A face moody, passionate, with the eyes cynical and despairing, the mouth lost and contemptuous and stormy, the hair tossed and black . . . '

'He wants a character out of Thomas Wolfe,' Machamer said.

'A face for the week-end,' Dutcher said, his tongue sliding joyfully in his mouth after the Rum Collins, 'a face tragic and tortured by the guilt of a slaughtering and slaughtered world . . . '

Dolly jumped off her stool. 'I'm going to call Maxine,' she said.

'Who's Maxine?' Dutcher asked, warily.

'She's very pretty,' Dolly said. 'She's an actress at Republic.'

'Oh, God,' Dutcher said.

'Don't be such a snob,' said Dolly. 'Give me a nickel.'

'What do you expect at eight o'clock Saturday night?' Machamer gave her a nickel. 'Heddy LaMarr?'

'She's very pretty,' Dolly repeated. 'She just got in from New York and she may not be busy . . . ' She started toward the phone.

'On a high moral plane!' Dutcher shouted after her. 'Remember!'

Dolly strode out of sight toward the telephone booth.

Dutcher watched her and then turned to Machamer. 'When you read the papers,' he said, 'and you read about aeroplanes bombing people and then being shot down, do you ever think about what it's like up there, with the bullets coming at you and the plane bucking and all of a sudden just air below . . . ?'

'All the time,' Machamer said soberly.

'During the Spanish War I used to dream about being machine-gunned by aeroplanes. I'd run and run along alleyways between garages and the planes would always come back and get me from an open side. 'Dutcher finished his drink. 'I wonder what garages had to do with it. The trouble with the human race is it's too brave. You can get people to do anything – fly around and get shot at twenty thousand feet up, walk into hand-grenades, fight naval battles. If the human race wasn't so damn courageous, this would be a much better world to live in. That's the sum total of my thinking in two months in Hollywood.'

'Einstein is resting easy,' Machamer said. 'He's still got a good lead.'

'I know,' said Dutcher. 'But he doesn't have to think in this climate.'

Dolly slipped in between them. 'It's all settled,' she said. 'Maxine is dying to go. She's heard about you.'

'Good or bad?' Dutcher asked.

'She's just heard about you. She says you mustn't get fresh.'

Dutcher wrinkled his nose. 'Did she say "fresh"?'

'Yes,' Dolly said.

'I don't like Maxine.'

'Nuts,' Machamer said, and pulled him away from the bar and out to his car.

The big car sped toward Mexico, Dutcher sprawled luxuriously on the back seat with his head in Maxine's lap. Occasionally he moved his head lazily because Maxine was wearing a suit trimmed all the way down the front with red fox and the fur got into his nose and tickled him.

'He was an Italian,' Maxine was saying. 'He had large estates in Italy and he had a good job in New York, fifteen thousand a year, but he didn't like Mussolini.'

'A character,' Dutcher said softly. 'A beautiful character.'

'We were engaged to be married,' Maxine said, speaking loudly, talking to Dolly, 'but two weeks later he gave up his job. He relaxed; my little Wop relaxed.' She laughed a little

123

sadly, stroked Dutcher's head absently. 'As soon as I meet a man he relaxes.'

Machamer turned on the radio, and a man in London said that Hitler had not as yet answered Chamberlain's ultimatum and an orchestra played 'I May Be Wrong, But I think You're Wonderful.'

Dutcher looked thoughtfully up at Maxine's face. It was a round, full face, with a little full mouth that looked as though it had been created in God's mind with a careful brilliant smear of lipstick already on it. 'You're very pretty,' he said seriously.

Maxine smiled. 'I'm not so bad.' She patted him in appreciation. 'I'm a little fat at the moment. I drank too much wine in New York. Dolly, I heard that Gladys is marrying Eddie Lane. Is that true?'

'In October,' Dolly said.

Maxine sighed. 'That Gladys. Eddie Lane's ole man is good for five hundred thousand a year. She was in my class at high school. Oil. Old man Lane is up to his navel in oil. Eddie Lane chased me for two years like a kid after a fire truck. What a goddamn fool I was to go to New York.'

Dutcher laughed, looking up at her. 'You have a nice, refreshing outlook on finance.'

Maxine laughed with him. 'Money is money,' she said. 'I'll get a little fatter and even Republic won't have me, and then where'll I be?'

'I'll write a play,' Machamer said, at the wheel, 'and you can act in it in New York. They like them fat in New York.'

'I tried that, too,' Maxine said grimly. 'I thought of another way out. I had my stepfather insured...'

'Holy God!' Dutcher said. 'For how much?'

'Fifty thousand.'

'We're in the dough,' Dutcher said. 'Stop and buy me a Lincoln.'

'Hah,' said Maxine. 'I paid his insurance three years, then he went and got married on me. A little Irish biddy he saw waiting on table in San Luis Obispo.'

They all laughed. 'You're wonderful,' Dutcher said. He pulled her down and kissed her. She kissed politely, with reserve, carefully, yet with a hint of vulgar accomplishment.

Unsatisfactory, Dutcher thought, letting his head fall back, yet ... Reader of Spinoza, admirer of John Milton...

'This is Berlin,' a voice said on the radio. 'The city is in total darkness. The Fuehrer has not replied as yet to the English ultimatum. There is constant troop movement at the Berlin railroad stations and trains are pouring toward the Polish frontier.'

A band played 'Begin the Beguine', and Maxine talked to Dolly about another friend of theirs who had married a seventy-year-old man with fourteen blocks of real estate in downtown Cleveland.

'The city is in total darkness,' Dutcher murmured. He lay back comfortably. This wasn't so bad, racing through the night to a new country, with a new girl, even though it was only Tia Juana and only an ordinarily pretty girl, getting a little fat, and a little hard and not exactly the girl you'd pick to take with you on a visit to your old Professsor of Ethics at Amherst. Still it was better than sitting at a bar all alone, thinking, 'I'll wait another ten minutes and then go out and buy another paper, see what *they* have to say.'

He turned and buried his face in the red fox. There was a heavy smell of perfume, which was pleasant over the old smell of leather and gasoline in the back of the car. 'Prince Matchabelli,' Dutcher said. 'This fox fell into a well of Prince Matchabelli and drowned. A beautiful death. Machamer, did I ever tell you about Cynthia Messmore, who was a classmate of mine at P.S. 99 and Miss Finch's? She married old Shamus Goonan, from the eleventh assembly district . . .'

'No!' Machamer said in tones of wonder.

'A brilliant match,' Dutcher said. 'He was on the W.P.A. three days a week and he was good for seven hundred and sixty dollars a year, as long as he stayed sober. Sewer construction, he was a sewer construction magnate, he was up to his navel in . . .'

'Are you making fun of me?' Maxine's voice was hard, and Dutcher knew he ought to stop, but he couldn't. He sat up.

'I never should've left P.S. 99,' he said sadly. 'Sex is the opium of the people. Turn on the radio, Machamer.'

Dolly was shaking her head at him, but Dutcher made believe he was looking out the window. Mean, he thought, I've been mean. And I liked it. Tonight I want to be everything . . . mean, angry, noble, gracious, lordly, docile, everything. I want my emotions to be engaged. I can't love her, I can't make her love me, but I can make her angry at me and then win her over, then . . .

'This is Paris,' a voice said. 'All the lights are out. The Cabi-

125

net has been in conference since seven o'clock this evening.'

Machamer turned the radio off.

Dutcher felt Maxine eyeing him. He turned and looked pleasantly at her. After all, he thought, regarding her, she *is* a pretty girl, with a fine figure and we *are* going to be together until tomorrow night . . .

'Is that how you're going to the races tomorrow?' Maxine asked. 'Without a tie?'

Dutcher felt at his collar. He was wearing a polo shirt, open at the throat. 'I guess so,' he said. 'It's awfully hot.'

'I won't go with you,' Maxine said, 'unless you wear a tie.'

'I haven't got a tie.'

'I won't go with you,' Maxine said firmly.

'We live in a tropical climate,' Dutcher said. 'We mustn't ever forget that. I'm a Northern man. I sweat like . . . '

'I have an extra tie,' Machamer said. 'You can wear that.'

Dutcher nodded. 'If it'll make Maxine happy . . . ' He smiled at her.

'I wouldn't be seen in front of all those people with a man who wasn't wearing a tie.'

'You're right,' Dutcher said, smiling pleasantly at her. 'Now that I think of it, you're absolutely right.'

Maxine smiled back at him. At least, he thought, I haven't thought of Murder at Midnight since the trip began. At least, she's done that.

They stopped in San Diego and drank at a bar among a lot of sailors from the naval base. Dolly took some of the pills she was always taking and for a moment gripped Machamer's arm and leaned over and kissed his neck. It was nearly two o'clock and the bar was closing and the sailors were drunk.

'The United States will not get into any war,' a big blond farm boy jutting out of his flimsy blue uniform announced. 'I have the guarantee of my Congressman.'

'Where you from?' Dutcher asked.

'Arkansas.'

Dutcher nodded as though this convinced him. The sailor gulped down what was left of his beer.

'Let the Japs come over,' he called. 'We'll sweep 'em from the seas. I'd like to see the Japs just try and come over. I'd just like to see . . . '

Maxine was smiling at the sailor.

'I'm hungry,' Dutcher said herding Maxine and Dolly toward the door. 'I hate discussions of relative naval strength.

'That was heartening,' Machamer said, as they walked toward the bright lights of a waffle shop down the street. 'An official representative of the United States armed forces says we won't get into a war.'

'He was a nice-looking boy,' Maxine said as they entered the waffle shop. 'If you took him out of that sailor suit.'

The waffle shop was crowded, and they sat at a table that had not been cleared. Maxine and Dolly went to the ladies' room and Machamer and Dutcher were left at the table, looking at each other in the garish waffle-room light, across the dirty dishes and spilled coffee on the table.

'She's all right,' Machamer said loudly, grinning at Dutcher. 'Dolly did all right for you, didn't she? She's got a wonderful figure.'

'Machamer,' Dutcher said, 'if I had a cement-mixer and I wanted somebody to make a speech while it was going, I would pick you.'

Machamer looked around him apologetically. 'Isn't it funny, how loud I talk?'

'Everybody in the Square Deal Waffle Shop now knows you think Maxine has a wonderful figure.'

The waitress, very pale and harried-looking at two in the morning, rattled the dishes between them as she cleared the table.

'You're having a good time, aren't you?' Machamer asked. 'She makes you laugh, doesn't she?'

'She makes me laugh,' Dutcher said.

Dolly and Maxine came back. Dutcher watched Maxine walk down the aisle between the tables, her red fox shaking down the front of her suit and all the men in the place watching her. That suit, Dutcher thought, is one-half inch too tight, in all directions. Everything she wears, always, I bet, is one-half inch too tight. Even her nightgowns.

'You know what I'm thinking of?' Dutcher said to Maxine as she sat down.

'What?' Maxine asked, all newly powdered and rouged.

'Your nightgowns.'

Maxine frowned. 'That's not a nice thing to say.'

'Dutcher's a very vulgar man,' Machamer said. 'You ought to read his books.'

'The English,' Maxine said, 'just declared war on the Germans. The woman in the ladies' room told us.'

That's how I found out, Dutcher thought. In the ladies'

room in a waffle shop in San Diego, a woman told an actress from Republic, who drank too much wine in New York, that the English declared war on Germany, and that's how I found out.

'This fork is dirty,' Maxine said loudly to the waitress, who was putting their waffles down on the table. 'You have some nerve giving us dirty forks.'

The waitress sighed and put down a clean fork.

'They'll get away with murder,' Maxine said, 'if you let them.'

All through the room, people knifed slabs of butter and poured syrup and ate waffles, Dutcher noted, as he started on his. There was no change, just the usual restaurant noise of voices and plates.

'This waffle stinks,' Maxine said. 'That's my honest opinion. And they make a specialty of them! San Diego!'

Dutcher put his hand gently on hers to calm her.

'You got the hand of a day-labourer,' Maxine said. 'What do you do, hammer in nails with them at the studio?'

'It's the disgraceful heritage of my wasted youth,' Dutcher said.

Maxine turned his hand over and carefully examined the palm. 'You got a heart line that's branched many times,' she said.

'Tell me more,' said Dutcher.

'You're fickle, jealous, selfish.' Maxine leaned over his hand very seriously. 'And in the long run you're not going to be very successful.'

'What a catch!' Dolly said.

'Tell me more,' said Dutcher.

'You're moody,' Maxine ran her finger lightly over his palm. 'You're a very moody man.'

'They don't come any moodier,' said Dutcher.

'Your life line is short.'

Dutcher took his hand back gravely. 'Thank you very much,' he said, his hands still aware of the soft, promising feel of Maxine's fingers. 'Now I'm all cleared up about myself. I certainly am glad I brought you down to San Diego.'

'It's all there in the palm,' Maxine said defensively. 'I didn't put it there.' She drew her collar around her. 'Let's get out of this joint.' She walked toward the door, with all the men in the room watching her.

'You're not her type,' Dolly whispered to Dutcher. 'She told me in the ladies' room. She likes you, but you're not her type.'

Dutcher shrugged. 'Palmists don't like me. It's something I've always noticed.'

He caught up with Maxine and held her elbow as they walked toward the car. 'Now,' he said, 'we come to a most delicate point. 'We – uh . . . We have to go to a hotel – and – I . . .'

'I want my own room,' Maxine said firmly.

'I just thought I'd ask,' Dutcher shrugged.

'A gentleman doesn't ask,' Maxine said.

'What does a gentleman do for girls?' Dutcher asked.

'He doesn't talk about it! It just happens.'

'It never occurred to me before,' Dutcher said as they got into the car. 'But you're absolutely right.'

'They could only get a two-room suite at the hotel, because it was all filled up, and there were some other people from Hollywood in the lobby and Dutcher tried to appear as though he were in no way connected with Maxine. If only she didn't have that red fox, he thought. And all day tomorrow, at the races, there would be people he knew, and he'd have to try to be eight paces in front of her or at the betting windows or at the bar . . .

Upstairs, Maxine primly put her bag down next to Dolly's in one of the two rooms. Machamer looked at Dutcher.

'We have the west wing,' Dutcher said, and walked into the next room.

'Look.' Machamer followed him. 'This was supposed to be a holiday for Dolly and me. She lives at home and her mother prays to God every night to save her sinful daughter's soul.' Dolly came in and looked at them. Then she giggled.

'Go in and talk to Maxine,' Machamer shouted to Dutcher.

Dutcher shrugged. 'I see my duty,' he said.

He went into the next room. Maxine was sitting neatly on the bed, her hands folded, her eyes reflectively on the ceiling. 'Maxine, old girl,' Dutcher said.

'Don't make fun of me.'

'I'm tired,' Dutcher said wearily. 'There's a war on. I give up. There're two beds inside. I promise not to touch you. For Machamer and Dolly . . .'

'Let Machamer be a gentleman!' Maxine said loudly. 'For one night.'

Dutcher went back into the other room. She says let Mach-

9   129

amer be a gentleman for one night,' he said. He took off one shoe. 'I'm going to sleep.'

Dolly kissed Machamer. She hung on, her arms wound around his neck and Dutcher made a big business of carefully arranging his shoes neatly in line under a chair. Dolly came over and kissed Dutcher lightly. 'You sure make a big hit with the girls,' she said, and went in.

Machamer and Dutcher put on their pyjamas and turned off the light and Machamer got into bed. Dutcher went to the door of the girls' room. 'Latest bulletin,' he announced 'Machamer has promised not to lay a hand on me. Good-night.'

The girls laughed and Machamer roared and Dutcher joined them, the two rooms resounding wildly with laughter, as Dutcher climbed into his bed.

Outside, the newsboys, far off along the dark streets of San Diego, cried that England had declared war.

Dutcher lay in his bed and listened to the newboys' cries, swelling and wailing in the streets, and looked up at the dark ceiling; and the hour and the war, which had been kept off all night by drink and speed and laughter and lust, like lions warded off by a trainer's chair, now closed in on him. The cavalryman in Poland now lay across the dusty Polish road, his mouth open in surprise and death and his dead horse beside him and the boy in the German bomber flew back from Warsaw, saying to himself, 'One more time. I came back one more time.'

'It's for Dolly's sake,' Machamer's voice came across the small dark abyss between the beds, grating, but young and sorrowful. 'It's nothing to me, but she's crazy to grab every hour. Do you want to go to sleep, Ralph?'

'No.'

'She wants to grab everything. Everything. She hates to go to sleep. She always has her hands on me. She's going to die.' Dutcher heard Machamer sigh and the bedsprings click gently and the newsboys coming near. 'She's sick; the doctors can't cure her; she has Bright's disease. She gets numb, she feels as though an eye is falling out, an ear . . . That's why she takes those pills. She doesn't tell anybody except me. Her family doesn't know, and her boss . . . '

Dutcher lay rigid in his bed, looking up at the ceiling.

'I don't love her,' Machamer's voice was harsh but small.

130

'I tell her I do, but . . . I like other girls . . . I tell her I do. She doesn't want to lose an hour.'

'Sssh,' Dutcher said gently. 'Don't talk so loud.'

'Even now,' Machamer marvelled. 'Even now my voice would break down a wall. Are you sad, Dutcher?'

'Yes,' said Dutcher.

'It came funny, didn't it?' Machamer asked.

'You hardly felt it.' Dutcher talked with his eyes closed, his head straight back on the pillow. 'You were waiting for it six years and expecting it, and each time a shot was fired you'd say "Here it is", but it wasn't, and you read the papers every day, and by the time it came you didn't feel it at all. We'll feel it later, we'll feel it later . . .'

'What're you going to do now?'

Dutcher laughed. 'Go to sleep.'

'Good night,' Machamer said.

'Good night.'

The bomber was coming down to a landing and the boy banked and looked down to see that the landing gear was out and he, Dutcher, was on his way with a fat citizen in a red fox-trimmed suit to a rat-eaten Mexican race-track, where the youngest horse running was at least nine years old, where the Hollywood people in their scarves and dark glasses and buckskin shoes, with their agents and beauty-contest winners for the week-end gambled their crazy, easy money in the dusty Mexican heat, talking of sex and dollars, saying over and over, 'Colossal, terrific, he's hot this year, it lost Metro a million'. The war was on, and it was on here, too, among these idle, unbombed, frivolous people. I'd stay here, in Hollywood, Dutcher thought, if I could bear *Murder at Midnight* and all the Murders at Midnight to come. I don't want to write any more books. An honest book is a criticism. Why should I torture myself into criticising this poor, corrupt, frantic, tortured, agony-stricken world? Later, later, let the criticism come later . . .'

The newsboys wailed in the streets below.

Here I am, Dutcher thought, in a hotel room far from home, with a dying and unloved girl, cheated of an hour, and a movie writer who wanders like a refugee from studio to studio, week in week out, beggary plain on his face, looking for a job, and a palm-reader who could have been bought for the night with three compliments and ten minutes of polite charade. Fickle, jealous, selfish, moody, not successful, short of life.

131

'England, England . . . ' The boys' voices, wavering in the night wind, came faintly through the window, I'm ashamed of myself, Dutcher thought. I meet the tragic hour in a mournful and ludicrous costume.

Now is the time, Dutcher thought, for some noble and formidable act. Who will supply me with a noble and formidable act?'

'I would like to speak to the continent of Europe,' Dutcher said aloud.

'Huh?' Machamer murmured.

'Nothing.' Dutcher pulled the covers up to his chin. 'You know what I'm going to do?'

'Huh?'

'I'm going to get married. I'm going to have a wife and live on a farm and grow corn and wheat and grapes and watch the snow fall and slaughter pigs and become involved with the seasons. For a little while I want to become involved in an eternal motion.'

'Sure,' said Machamer. 'I just dreamed Mervyn LeRoy was offering me a job. Isn't it too bad, isn't it too bad . . . ' His voice trailed off.

'Involved with the seasons,' Dutcher said, rolling it on his tongue. 'Involved with the seasons.' He closed his eyes.

Now the bomber stopped and the boy jumped out, feeling the ground solid under his feet and cold in the early morning. The boy grinned and the sweat of relief ran down under his arms and he said, 'I made it, I made it again,' as he went off across the field to report to his commanding officer.

The Monument

'I do not want any of his private stock,' McMahon said firmly. He blew on a glass and wiped it carefully. 'I have my own opinion of his private stock.'

Mr Grimmet looked sad, sitting across the bar on his high stool, and Thesing shrugged like a salesman, not giving up the fight, but moving to a new position to continue the attack. McMahon picked up another glass in his clean, soft bartender's hands. He wiped it, his face serious and determined and flushed right up to the bald spot that his plastered-down hair couldn't cover. There was nobody else in the bar at the front part of the restaurant.

It was three o'clock in the afternoon. In the rear three waiters stood arguing. Every day at three o'clock the three waiters gathered in the back and argued.

'Fascism,' one waiter said, 'is a rehearsal for the cemetery.'

'You read that some place,' another waiter said.

'All right,' said the first waiter. 'I read it some place.'

'An Italian,' the third waiter said to the first waiter. 'You are one lousy Italian.'

Mr Grimmet turned around and called to the waiters 'Please reserve discussions of that character for when you go home. This is a restaurant, not Madison Square Garden.'

He turned back to watching McMahon wiping the glasses. The three waiters looked at him with equal hate.

'Many of the best bars in the city,' Thesing said in his musical salesman's voice, 'use our private stock.'

'Many of the best bars in the city,' McMahon said, using the towel very hard, 'ought to be turned into riding academies.'

'That's funny,' Thesing said, laughing almost naturally. 'He's very funny, isn't he, Mr Grimmet?'

'Listen, Billy,' Mr Grimmet said, leaning forward, disregarding Thesing, 'listen to reason. In a mixed drink nobody can tell how much you paid for the rye that goes into it. That is the supreme beauty of cocktails.'

McMahon didn't say anything. The red got a little deeper on his cheeks and on his bald spot and he put the clean glasses down with a sharp tinkle and the tinkle went through the shining lines of the other glasses on the shelves and sounded thinly through the empty restaurant. He was a little fat man, very compact. He moved with great precision and style behind a bar and you could tell by watching him whether he was merry or sad or perturbed, just from the way he mixed a drink or put down a glass. Just now he was angry and Mr Grimmet knew it. Mr Grimmet didn't want a fight, but there was money to be saved. He put out his hand appealingly to Thesing.

'Tell me the truth, Thesing,' he said. 'Is your private stock bad?'

'Well,' Thesing said slowly, 'a lot of people like it. It is very superior for a blended product.'

'Blended varnish,' McMahon said, facing the shelves. 'Carefully matched developing fluid.'

Thesing laughed, the laugh he used from nine to six. 'Witty,' he said, 'the sparkling bartender.' McMahon wheeled and looked at him, head down a little on his chest. 'I meant it,' Thesing protested. 'I sincerely meant it.'

'I want to tell you,' Mr Grimmet said to McMahon, fixing him with his eye, 'that we can save seven dollars a case on the private stock.'

McMahon started whistling the tenor aria from *Pagliacci*. He looked up at the ceiling and wiped a glass and whistled. Mr Grimmet felt like firing him and remembered that at least twice a month he felt like firing McMahon.

'Please stop whistling,' he said politely. 'We have a matter to discuss.'

McMahon stopped whistling and Mr Grimmet still felt like firing him.

'Times're not so good,' Mr Grimmet said in a cajoling tone of voice, hating himself for descending to such tactics before an employee of his. 'Remember, McMahon, Coolidge is no longer in the White House. I am the last one in the world to compromise with quality, but we must remember, we are in business and it is 1938.'

'Thesing's private stock,' McMahon said, 'would destroy the stomach of the healthy horse.'

'Mussolini!' the first waiter's voice came out from the back of the restaurant. 'Every day on Broadway I pass forty-five actors who could do his act better.'

'I am going to tell you one thing,' Mr Grimmet said with obvious calmness to McMahon. 'I am the owner of this restaurant.'

McMahon whistled some more from *Pagliacci*. Thesing moved wisely down the bar a bit.

'I am interested in making money,' Mr Grimmet said. 'What would you say, Mr McMahon, if I ordered you to use the private stock?'

'I would say, "I'm through, Mr Grimmet". Once and for all.'

Mr Gimmet rubbed his face unhappily and stared coldly at the waiters in the back of the restaurant. The waiters remained silent and stared coldly back at him. 'What's it to you?' Mr Grimmet asked McMahon angrily. 'What do you care if we use another whisky. Do you have to drink it?'

'In my bar, Mr Grimmet,' McMahon said, putting down his towel and the glasses and facing his employer squarely, 'in my bar, good drinks are served.'

'Nobody will know the difference!' Mr Grimmet got off his stool and jumped up and down gently. 'What do Americans know about liquor? Nothing! Read any book on the subject!'

'True,' Thesing said judiciously. 'The general consensus of opinion is that Americans do not know the difference between red wine and a chocolate malted milk.'

'In my bar,' McMahon repeated, his face very red, his wide hands spread on the bar, 'I serve the best drinks I know how to serve.'

'Stubborn!' Mr Grimmet yelled. 'You are a stubborn Irishman! You do this out of malice! You are anxious to see me lose seven dollars on every case of liquor because you dislike me. Let us get down to the bedrock of truth!'

'Keep your voice down,' McMahon said, speaking with great control. 'I want to remind you of one or two things. I have worked for you since Repeal, Mr Grimmet. In that time, how many times did we have to enlarge the bar?'

'I am not in the mood for history, McMahon!' Mr Grimmet shouted. 'What good is a bar as long as the *Normandie* if it is not run on a businesslike basis?'

'Answer my question,' McMahon said. 'How many times?'

'Three,' Mr Grimmet said; 'all right, three.'

'We are three times as big now as we were six years ago,' McMahon said in a professor's tone, explaining proposition one, going on to proposition two. 'Why do you think that is?'

'Accident!' Mr Grimmet looked ironically up to the ceiling. 'Fate! Roosevelt! The hand of God! How do I know?'

'I will tell you,' McMahon said, continuing in the professorial vein. 'People who come into this bar get the best Manhattans, the best Martinis, the best Daiquiris that are made on the face of the earth. They are made out of the finest ingredients, with great care, Mr Grimmet.'

'One cocktail tastes like another,' Mr Gimmet said. 'People make a big fuss and they don't know anything!'

'Mr Gimmet,' McMahon said with open contempt, 'it is easy to see that you are not a drinking man.'

Mr Grimmet's face reflected his desperate search for a new line of defence. His eyebrows went up with pleasure as he found it. He sat down and spoke softly across the bar to McMahon. 'Did it ever occur to you,' he asked, 'that people come into this place because of the food that is served here?'

'I will give you my final opinion of Greta Garbo,' the first waiter's voice sounded out defiantly. 'There is nobody like her.'

For a moment McMahon looked straight into Mr Grimmet's eyes. A slight, bitter smile played at one corner of his mouth. He breathed deeply, like a man who has just decided to bet on a horse that has not won in fourteen races. 'Shall I tell you what I think of the food that is served in your restaurant, Mr Grimmet?' McMahon asked flatly.

'The best chefs,' Mr Grimmet said quickly, 'the best chefs in the City of New York.'

McMahon nodded slowly. 'The best chefs,' he said, 'and the worst food.'

'Consider,' Mr Grimmet called. 'Consider what you're saying.'

'Anything a cook can disguise,' McMahon said, talking now to Thesing, disregarding Mr Grimmet, 'is wonderful here. Anything with a sauce. Once I ate a sirloin steak in this restaurant . . . '

'Careful, McMahon,' Mr Grimmet jumped off his stool and ran around to face McMahon.

'What can be done to disguise a sirloin steak?' McMahon asked reasonably. 'Nothing. You broil it. Simply that. If it was good when it was cut off the steer, it's good on your plate. If it was bad . . . '

'I pay good prices!' Mr Grimmet yelled. 'I'll have no allusions . . . '

'I would not bring a dog into this restaurant to eat sirloin steak,' McMahon said. 'Not a young dog with the teeth of a lion.'

'You're fired!' Mr Grimmet pounded on the bar. 'This restaurant will now do without your services.'

McMahon bowed. 'That is satisfactory to me,' he said. 'Perfectly satisfactory.'

'Well, now, everybody. Boys!' Thesing said pacifically. 'Over a little thing like private stock rye . . . '

McMahon began taking off his apron. 'This bar has a reputation. It is my reputation. I am proud of it. I am not interested in remaining at a place in which my reputation will be damaged.'

McMahon threw his apron, neatly folded, over a towel rack and picked up the little wooden wedge on which was printed, in gold letters. 'William McMahon, *In Charge*'. Mr Grimmet watched him with trouble in his eyes as McMahon lifted the hinged piece of the bar that permitted the bartenders to get out into the restaurant proper.

'What is the sense,' Mr Grimmet asked as the hinges creaked, 'of taking a rash step, Billy?' Once more Mr Grimmet hated himself for his dulcet tone of voice, but William McMahon was one of the five finest bartenders in the City of New York.

McMahon stood there, pushing the hinged piece of the bar a little back and forth. 'Once and for all,' he said. He let the hinged piece fall behind him.

'I'll tell you what I'll do, Billy,' Mr Grimmet went on swiftly, hating himself more and more. 'I'll make a compromise. I will give you five dollars more per week.' He sighed to himself and then looked brightly at McMahon.

McMahon knocked his shingle thoughtfully against the bar.

'I will try to make you understand something, Mr Grimmet,' he said, gently. 'I am not as fundamentally interested in money as I am fundamentally interested in other things.'

'You are not so different from the rest of the world,' Mr Grimmet said with dignity.

'I have been working for twenty-five years,' McMahon said, knocking the shingle that said 'William McMahon, *In Charge*'. 'and I have constantly been able to make a living. I do not work only to make a living. I am more interested in making something else. For the last six years I have worked here night

137

and day. A lot of nice people come in here and drink like ladies and gentlemen. They all like this place. They all like me.'

'Nobody is saying anything about anybody not liking you,' Mr Grimmet said impatiently. 'I am discussing a matter of business principle.'

'I like this place,' McMahon looked down at the shingle in his hand. 'I think this is a very nice bar. I planned it. Right?' He looked up at Mr Grimmet.

'You planned it. I will sign an affidavit to the effect that you planned it,' Mr Grimmet said ironically. 'What has that got to do with Thesing's private stock?'

'If something is right here,' McMahon went on, without raising his voice, 'people can say it's William McMahon's doing. If something is wrong here they can say it's William McMahon's fault. I like that, Mr Grimmet. When I die people can say, "William McMahon left a monument, the bar at Grimmet's Restaurant. He never served a bad drink in his whole life".' McMahon took his coat out of the closet next to the bar and put it on. 'A monument. I will not have a monument made out of Thesing's private stock. Mr Grimmet, I think you are a dumb bastard.'

McMahon bowed a little to the two men and started out. Mr Grimmet gulped, then called, his words hard and dry in the empty restaurant. 'McMahon!' The bartender turned around. 'All right,' Mr Grimmet said. 'Come back.'

McMahon gestured toward Thesing.

'Any liquor you say,' Mr Grimmet said in a choked voice. 'Any goddamn whisky you want!'

McMahon smiled and went back to the closet and took his coat off and took the shingle out of his pocket. He went back of the bar and slipped on his apron, as Thesing and Grimmet watched.

'One thing,' Mr Grimmet said, his eyes twitching from the strain, 'one thing I want you to know.'

'Yes, sir,' said McMahon.

'I don't want you to talk to me,' Mr Grimmet said, 'and I don't want to talk to you. Ever.'

Thesing quietly picked up his hat and stole out of the door.

'Yes, sir,' said McMahon.

Mr Grimmet walked swiftly into the kitchen.

'I will tell you something about debutantes,' the first waiter was saying in the rear of the restaurant, 'they are overrated.'

McMahon tied the bow in his apron strings and, neatly, in the centre of the whisky shelves above the bar, placed the shingle, 'William McMahon, *In Charge*'.

Return to Kansas City

Arline opened the bedroom door and softly went over between the twin beds, the silk of her dress making a slight rustle in the quiet room. The dark shades were down and the late afternoon sun came in only in one or two places along the sides of the window frames, in sharp, thin rays.

Arline looked down at her husband, sleeping under the blankets. His fighter's face with the mashed nose was very peaceful on the pillow and his hair was curled like a baby's and he snored gently because he breathed through his mouth. A light sweat stood out on his face. Eddie always sweated, any season, any place. But now, when she saw Eddie begin to sweat, it made Arline a little angry.

She stood there, watching the serene, glove-marked face. She sat down on the other bed, still watching her husband. She took a lace-bordered handkerchief out of a pocket and dabbed at her eyes. They were dry. She sniffed a little and the tears started. For a moment she cried silently, then she sobbed aloud. In a minute the tears and the sobs were regular, loud in the still room.

Eddie stirred in his bed. He closed his mouth, turned over on his side.

'Oh, my,' Arline sobbed, 'oh, my God.'

She saw, despite the fact that Eddie's back was toward her, that he had awakened.

'Oh,' Arline wept, 'sweet Mother of God.'

She knew that Eddie was wide awake listening to her and he knew that she knew it, but he hopefully pretended he hadn't been roused. He even snored experimentally once or twice. Arline's sobs shook her and the mascara ran down her cheeks in straight black lines.

Eddie sighed and turned around and sat up, rubbing his hair with his hands.

'What's the matter?' he asked. 'What's bothering you, Arline?'

'Nothing,' Arline sobbed.

'If nothing's the matter,' Eddie said mildly, 'what're you crying for?'

Arline didn't say anything. She stopped sobbing aloud and turned the grief inward upon herself and wept all the more bitterly, in silence. Eddie wiped his eye with the heel of his hand, looked wearily at the dark shades that shut out the slanting rays of the sun.

'There are six more rooms in this house, Arline darling,' he said. 'If you have to cry why is it necessary to pick the exact room where I am sleeping?'

Arline's head sank low on her breast, her beautiful beauty-shop straw-coloured hair falling tragically over her face. 'You don't care,' she murmured, 'you don't care one dime's worth if I break my heart.'

She squeezed the handkerchief and the tears ran down her wrist.

'I care,' Eddie said, throwing back the covers neatly and putting his stockinged feet on to the floor. He had been sleeping in his pants and shirt, which were very wrinkled now. He shook his head two or three times as he sat on the edge of the bed and hit himself smartly on the cheek with the back of his hand to awaken himself. He looked unhappily across at his wife, sitting on the other bed, her hands wrung in her lap, her face covered by her careless hair, sorrow and despair in every line of her. 'Honest, Arline, I care.' He went over and sat next to her on the bed and put his arm around her. 'Baby,' he said. 'Now, baby.'

She just sat there crying silently, her round, soft shoulders shaking now and then under his arm. Eddie began to feel more and more uncomfortable. He squeezed her shoulders two or three times, exhausting his methods of consolation. 'Well,' he said finally, 'I think maybe I'll put the kid in the carriage and take him for a walk. A little air. Maybe when I come back you'll feel better.'

'I won't feel better,' Arline promised him, without moving. 'I won't feel one ounce better.'

'Arline,' Eddie said.

'The kid.' She sat up erect now and looked at him. 'If you paid as much attention to me as to the kid.'

'I pay equal attention. My wife and my kid.' Eddie stood up and padded around the room uneasily in his socks.

Arline watched him intently, the creased flannel trousers

141

and the wrinkled shirt not concealing the bulky muscles.

'The male sleeping beauty,' she said. 'The long-distance sleeping champion. My husband.'

'I don't sleep so awful much,' Eddie protested.

'Fifteen hours a day,' Arline said. 'Is it natural?'

'I had a hard workout this morning,' Eddie said, standing at the window. 'I went six fast rounds. I got to get rest. I got to store up my energy. I am not so young as some people any more. I got to take care of myself. Don't I have to store up energy?'

'Store up your energy!' Arline said loudly. 'All day long you store up energy. What is your wife supposed to do when you are storing up energy?'

Eddie let the window shade fly up. The light shot into the room, making it harder for Arline to cry.

'You ought to have friends,' Eddie suggested without hope.

'I have friends.'

'Why don't you go out with them?'

'They're in Kansas City,' Arline said.

There was silence in the room. Eddie sat down and began putting on his shoes.

'My mother's in Kansas City,' Arline said. 'My two sisters are in Kansas City. My two brothers. I went to high school in Kansas City. Here I am, in Brooklyn, New York.'

'You were in Kansas City two and a half months ago,' Eddie said, buttoning his collar and knotting his tie. 'A mere two and a half months ago.'

'Two and a half months are a long time,' Arline said, clearing away the mascara lines from her cheeks, but still weeping 'A person can die in two and a half months.'

'What person?' Eddie asked.

Arline ignored him. 'Mama writes she wants to see the baby again, After all, that is not unnatural, a grandmother wants to see her grandchild. Tell me, is it unnatural?'

'No,' said Eddie, 'it is not unnatural.' He combed his hair swiftly. 'If Mama wants to see the baby,' he said, 'explain to me why she can't come here. Kindly explain to me.'

'My husband is of the opinion that they are handing out gold pieces with movie tickets in Kansas City,' Arline said with cold sarcasm.

'Huh?' Eddie asked, honestly puzzled. 'What did you say?'

'How can Mama afford to come here?' Arline asked. 'After all, you know, there are no great prizefighters in *our* family.

I had to *marry* to bring one into the family. Oh, my God!' Once more she wept.

'Lissen, Arline.' Eddie ran over to her and spoke pleadingly, his tough, battered face very gentle and sad. 'I can't afford to have you go to Kansas City every time I take a nap in the afternoon. We have been married a year and a half and you have gone to Kansas City five times. I feel like I am fighting for the New York Central Railroad, Arline!'

Arline shook her head obstinately. 'There is nothing to do in New York,' she said.

'There is nothing to do in New York!' Eddie's mouth opened in surprise. 'My God! There's something to do in Kansas City?' he cried. 'What the hell is there to do in Kansas City? Remember, I have been in that town myself. I married you in that town.'

'I didn't know how it was going to be,' Arline said flatly. 'It was nice in Kansas City. I was an innocent young girl.'

'Please,' said Eddie. 'Let us not rake up the past.'

'I was surrounded by my family,' Arline went on shakily. 'I went to high school there.'

She bent over and grief took possession once more. Eddie licked his lips uncomfortably. They were dry from the morning's workout and the lower lip was split a little and smarted when he ran his tongue over it. He searched his brain for a helpful phrase.

'The kid,' he ventured timidly, 'why don't you play more with the kid?'

'The kid!' Arline cried defiantly. 'I take very good care of the kid. I have to stay in every night minding the kid while you are busy storing up your energy.' The phrase enraged her and she stood up, waving her arms. 'What a business! You fight thirty minutes a month, you got to sleep three hundred and fifty hours. Why, it's laughable. It is very laughable! You are some fighter!' She shook her fist at him in derision. 'With all the energy you store up you ought to be able to beat the German Army!'

'That is the business I am in,' Eddie tried to explain gently. 'That is the nature of my profession.'

'Don't tell me that!' Arline said. 'I have gone out with other fighters. They don't sleep all the time.'

'I am not interested,' Eddie said. 'I do not want to hear anything about your life before our marriage.'

'They go to night clubs,' Arline went on irresistibly, 'and

143

they dance and they take a drink once in a while and they take a girl to see a musical show!'

Eddie nodded. 'They are after something,' he said. 'That is the whole story.'

'I wish to God you were after something!'

'I meet the type of fighter you mention, too,' Eddie said. 'The night-club boys. They knock my head off for three rounds and then they start breathing through the mouth. By the time they reach the eighth round they wish they never saw a naked lady on a dance floor. And by the time I get through with them they are storing up energy, flat on their backs, With five thousand people watching them. You want me to be that kind of a fighter?'

'You're wonderful,' Arline said, wrinkling her nose, sneering. 'My Joe Louis. Big-Purse Eddie Megaffin. I don't notice you bringing back the million-dollar gate.'

'I am progressing slowly,' Eddie said, looking at the picture of Mary and Jesus over his bed. 'I am planning for the future.'

'I am linked for life to a goddamn health-enthusiast,' Arline said despairingly.

'Why do you talk like that, Arline?'

'Because I want to be in Kansas City,' she wailed.

'Explain to me,' Eddie said, 'why in the name of God you are so crazy for Kansas City?'

'I'm lonesome,' Arline wept with true bitterness. 'I'm awful lonesome. I'm only twenty-one years old, Eddie.'

Eddie patted her gently on the shoulder. 'Look, Arline.' He tried to make his voice very warm and at the same time logical. 'If you would only go easy. If you would go by coach and not buy presents for everybody, maybe I can borrow a coupla bucks and swing it.'

'I would rather die,' Arline said. 'I would rather never see Kansas City again for the rest of my life than let them know my husband has to watch pennies like a streetcar conductor. A man with his name in the papers every week. It would be shameful!'

'But, Arline, darling' – Eddie's face was tortured – 'you go four times a year, you spread presents like the W.P.A. and you always buy new clothes . . . '

'I can't appear in Kansas City in rags!' Arline pulled at a stocking, righting it on her well-curved leg. 'I would rather . . . '

'Some day, darling,' Eddie interrupted. 'We're working up. Right now I can't.'

'You can!' Arline said. 'You're lying to me, Eddie Megaffin. Jake Blucher called me up this morning and he told me he offered you a thousand dollars to fight Joe Principe.'

Eddie sat down in a chair. He looked down at the floor, understanding why Arline had picked this particular afternoon.

'You would come out of that fight with seven hundred and fifty dollars.' Arline's voice was soft and inviting. 'I could go to Kansas . . .'

'Joe Principe will knock my ears off.'

Arline sighed. 'I am so anxious to see my mother. She is an old woman and soon she will die.'

'At this stage,' Eddie said slowly, 'I am not ready for Joe Principe. He is too strong and too smart for me.'

'Jake Blucher told me he thought you had a wonderful chance.'

'I have a wonderful chance to land in hospital,' Eddie said. 'That Joe Principe is made out of springs and cement. If you gave him a pair of horns it would be legal to kill him with a sword.'

'He is only a man with two fists just like you,' Arline said.

'Yeah.'

'You're always telling me how good you are.'

'In two years,' Eddie said, 'taking it very easy and careful, making sure I don't get knocked apart . . .'

'You could make the money easy!' Arline pointed her finger dramatically at him. 'You just don't want to. You don't want me to be happy. I see through you, Eddie Megaffin!'

'I just don't want to get beaten up,' Eddie said, shaking his head.

'A fine fighter!' Arline laughed. 'What kind of fighter are you, anyhow? A fighter is supposed to get beaten up, isn't he? That's his business, isn't it? You don't care for me. All you wanted was somebody to give you a kid and cook your goddamn steaks and lamb chops. In Brooklyn! I got to stay in a lousy little house day in and . . .'

'I'll take you to the movies tonight,' Eddie promised.

'I don't want to go to the movies. I want to go to Kansas City.' Arline threw herself face down on the bed and sobbed. 'I'm caught. I'm caught! You don't love me! You won't let me go to people who love me! Mama! Mama!'

Eddie closed his eyes in pain. 'I love you,' he said, meaning it. 'I swear to God.'

'You say it.' Her voice was smothered in the pillow. 'But you don't prove it! Prove it! I never knew a young man could be so stingy. Prove it . . . ' The words trailed off in sorrow.

Eddie went over and bent down to kiss her. She shook her shoulders to send him away and cried like a heartbroken child. From the next room, where the baby had been sleeping, came the sound of his wailing.

Eddie walked over to the window and looked out at the peaceful Brooklyn Street, at the trees and the little boys and girls skating.

'O.K..' he said. 'I'll call Blucher.'

Arline stopped crying. The baby still wailed in the next room.

'I'll try to raise him to twelve hundred,' Eddie said. 'You can go to Kansas City. You happy?'

Arline sat up and nodded. 'I'll write Mama right away,' she said.

'Take the kid out for a walk, will you?' Eddie said, as Arline started repairing her face before the mirror. 'I want to take a little nap.'

'Sure,' Arline said, 'sure, Eddie.'

Eddie took off his shoes and lay down on the bed to start storing up his energy.

The Lament of Madam Rechevsky

The telephone rang and rang through the silken room, tumbled with sleep, lit here and there by the morning sunlight that broke through the hangings in little bright patches. Helen sighed and wriggled in the bed, and, still with her eyes closed, reached out and picked up the phone. The ringing stopped and Helen sighed in relief and wearily put the phone to her ear.

The sound of weeping, deep and bitter, welled along the wires. 'Hello, Momma,' Helen said, still with her eyes closed.

'Helen,' Madam Rechevsky said. 'How are you, Helen?'

'Fine Momma.' Helen stretched desperately under the covers, 'What time is it?'

'Nine o'clock.' Helen winced, closed her eyes more tightly. 'Momma, darling,' she said gently, 'why must you call so early?'

'When I was your age,' Madam Rechevsky said, weeping, 'I was up at six in the morning. Working my fingers to the bone. A woman thirty-eight shouldn't spend her whole life sleeping.'

'Why do you always say thirty-eight?' Helen protested. 'Thirty-six. Why can't you remember – thirty-six!'

'On the subject, Helen, darling,' Madam Rechevsky said coldly, through her tears, 'I am absolutely definite.'

Helen finally opened her eyes, slowly, with effort, looked wearily up at the sun-streaked ceiling. 'Why're you crying, Momma?'

There was a pause over the wires, then the weeping started afresh, on a new high pitch, deep, despairing, full of sorrow.

'Tell me, Momma,' Helen said.

'I must go to Poppa's grave. You must come right downtown and take me to Poppa's grave.'

Helen sighed. 'Momma. I have three different places I have to be today.'

'My own child!' Madam Rechevsky whispered. 'My own

147

daughter! Refuses to take her mother to the grave of her own father.'

'Tomorrow,' Helen pleaded. 'Can't you make it tomorrow?'

'Today!' Madam Rechevsky's voice reached across Manhattan high and tragic, as in the old days, when she strode on the stage and discovered that her stepmother was wearing her dead mother's jewels. 'I woke up this morning and a voice spoke to me. "Go to Abraham's grave! Immediately! Go to the grave of your husband!"'

'Momma,' Helen said gently. 'Poppa's been dead fifteen years. How much difference can one day make to him?'

'Never mind,' Madam Rechevsky said, with magnificent, resounding resignation. 'Forgive me if I have troubled you on this trifling matter. Go. Go to your appointments. Go to the beauty parlour. Go to the cocktail parties. I will take the subway to your dead father's grave.'

Helen closed her eyes. 'I'll pick you up in an hour, Momma.'

'Yes,' said Madam Rechevsky decisively. 'And please don't wear that red hat. For your father's sake.'

'I won't wear the red hat.' Helen lay back and wearily put the phone back on its pedestal.

'This is a fine car to be going to a cemetery in,' Madam Rechevsky was saying as they drove out through Brooklyn. She sat up straight as a little girl in school, savagely denying her seventy-three years with every line of her smart seal coat, every expert touch of rouge, every move of her silken legs. She looked around her contemptuously at the red-leather and chromium of Helen's roadster. 'A sports model. A great man lies buried, his relatives come to visit him in a cream-coloured convertible automobile.'

'It's the only car I have, Momma.' Helen delicately twisted the wheel in her eloquent, finely gloved hands. 'And I'm lucky they haven't taken it away from me by now.'

'I told you that was the wrong man for you, in the first place, didn't I?' Madam Rechevsky peered coldly at her daughter, her deep grey eyes flashing and brilliant, rimmed beautifully in mascara, with a touch of purple. 'Many years ago I warned you against him, didn't I?'

'Yes, Momma.'

'And now – now you are lucky when you collect alimony six months out of twelve.' Madame Rechevsky laughed bitterly. 'Nobody ever listened to me, not my own children. Now they suffer.'

'Yes, Momma.'

'And the theatre.' Madam Rechevsky waved her hands fiercely. 'Why aren't you on the stage this season?'

Helen shrugged. 'The right part hasn't come along this season.'

'The right part!' Madam Rechevsky laughed coldly. 'In my day we did seven plays a year, right part or no right part.'

'Momma, darling . . . ' Helen shook her head. 'It's different now. This isn't the Yiddish Theatre and this isn't 1900.'

'That was a better theatre,' Madam Rechevsky said loudly. 'And that was a better time.'

'Yes, Momma.'

'Work!' Madam Rechevsky hit her thighs emphatically with her two hands. 'We worked! The actor acted, the writer wrote, the audience came! Now – movies! Pah!'

'Yes, Momma.'

'Even so, you're lazy.' Madam Rechevsky looked at herself in her handbag mirror to make sure that the violence of her opinions had not disarranged her face. 'You sit back and wait for alimony and even so it doesn't come. Also . . . ' She examined her daughter critically. 'The way you dress is very extreme.' She squinted to sharpen the image. 'But you make a striking impression. I won't deny that. Every one of my daughters makes a striking impression.' Madam Rechevsky shook her head. 'But nothing like me, when I was a little younger . . . ' She sat back and rode in silence. 'Nothing like me . . . ' she murmured. 'Nothing like me, at all . . . '

Helen walked briskly beside her mother through the marble-crowded cemetery, their feet making a busy scuffle along the well-kept gravel walks. Madam Rechevsky clutched a dozen yellow chrysanthemums in her hands and on her face was a look of anticipation, almost pleasure, as they approached the grave.

'Perhaps . . . ' A bearded old man in holy black, all very clean and pink-faced, came up to them and touched Madam Rechevsky's arm. 'Perhaps you would like me to make a prayer for the dead, lady?'

'Go away!' Madam Rechevsky pulled her arm away impatiently. 'Abraham Rechevsky does not need professional prayers!'

The old man bowed gently, spoke softly. 'For Abraham Rechevsky I will pray for nothing.'

Madam Rechevsky stopped, looked at the man for a moment. Her cold grey eyes smiled a little. 'Give the old man a dollar, Helen,' she said and touched the man's arm with royal condescension.

Helen dug in her bag and produced a dollar and the old man bowed gravely again.

Helen hurried after her mother.

'See,' Madam Rechevsky was muttering as she charged along. 'See. Dead fifteen years and still he is famous, all over the world. I bet that old man hasn't offered to pray for anyone free for twenty-five years.' She turned on Helen. 'And yet you didn't want to come!' She strode on, muttering, 'All over the world.'

'Don't walk so fast, Momma,' Helen protested. 'Your heart . . . '

'Don't worry about my heart,' Madam Rechevsky stopped, put her arm out sharply to stop her daughter. 'We are in sight. You stay here. I want to go to the grave alone.' She spoke without looking at Helen, her eyes on the massive grey granite tombstone thirty yards away, with her husband's name on it and underneath his, space for her own. She spoke very softly. 'Turn around, Helen, darling. I want this to be private. I'll call you when I'm ready for you.'

She walked slowly towards the tombstone, holding the chrysanthemums before her like a gigantic bride's bouquet. Helen sat on a marble bench near the grave of a man named Axelrod, and turned her head.

Madam Rechevsky approached her husband's grave. Her face was composed, the lips set, the chin high, out of the smart seal collar. She knelt gracefully, placed the chrysanthemums in a compact spray of yellow on the cold earth against the granite. She patted the flowers lightly with one hand to make a pattern more pleasing to the eye, and stood up. She stood without speaking, looking at the even, dead, winterbrown grass that spread across the grave.

Slowly, still looking at the faded grass, she took off first one glove, then the other, and absently stuffed them into a pocket, leaving her white and brilliantly manicured hands bare.

Then she spoke.

'Abraham!' she cried, her voice ringing and imperious and fiercely intimate. 'Abraham!' the proud, useful voice echoed and re-echoed among the marble on the small rolling hills of the cemetery. 'Abraham, listen to me!'

She took a deep breath, and disregarding the formal stone, spoke directly to the earth beneath her. 'You've got to help me, Abraham. Trouble, trouble . . . I'm old and I'm poor and you've left me alone for fifteen years.' The resonance and volume had gone from her voice, and she spoke quietly, with the little touch of impatience that comes to women's voices when they are complaining to their husbands. 'Money. All your life you never made less than fifteen hundred dollars a week and now they bother me for rent.' Her lips curled contemptuously as she thought of the miserable men who came to her door on the first of each month. 'You rode in carriages, Abraham. You always owned at least four horses. Wherever you went everybody always said, "There goes Abraham Rechevsky!" When you sat down to eat, fifty people always sat down with you. You drank wine with breakfast, dinner and supper, and fifty people always drank it with you. You had five daughters by me and God knows how many by other women and every one of them was dressed from Paris from the day she could walk. You had six sons and each one of them had a private tutor from Harvard College. You ate in the best restaurants in New York, London, Paris, Budapest, Vienna, Berlin, Warsaw, Rio de Janeiro. You ate more good food than any other man that ever lived. You had two overcoats at one time lined with mink. You gave diamonds and rubies and strings of pearls to enough women to make up three ballet companies! Sometimes you were paying railroad fare for five women at one time crossing the country after you, on tour. You ate and you drank and you always had a baby daughter in your lap till the day you died, and you lived like a king of the earth, in all respects.' Madam Rechevsky shook her head at the grave. 'And I? Your wife? Where is the rent?'

Madam Rechevsky paced deliberately to the foot of the grave and addressed herself even more directly to her husband. 'A king, to the day you died, with a specialist from Vienna and three trained nurses and four consulting doctors for an old man, seventy-seven, who had exhausted himself completely with eating and drinking and making love. Buried . . . buried like a king. Three blocks long. The line behind your coffin was three blocks long on Second Avenue at the funeral, thousands of grown men and women crying into their hand-kerchiefs in broad daylight. And I? Your wife? Forgotten! Money spent, theatre gone, husband dead, no insurance . . .

Only one thing left – children.'

Madam Rechevsky smiled coldly at her husband. 'And the children – like their father. Selfish. Thinking of themselves. Silly. Doing crazy things. Getting mixed up with ridiculous people. Disastrous. The whole world is disastrous, and your children have led disastrous lives. Alimony, movies, trouble with girls, never any money, never . . . Relatives are dying in Germany. Five hundred dollars would have saved them. No five hundred dollars. And I am getting older day by day and the ones that can help won't, and the ones that want to help, can't. Three times a week the dressmaker calls me with old bills. Disastrous! Why should it happen to me?'

Once more, for a moment, Madam Rechevsky's voice went high and clear and echoed among the small graveyard hills. 'Why should it happen to me? I worked for you like a slave. I got up at five o'clock in the morning. I sewed the costumes. I rented the theatres. I fought with the authors about the plays. I picked the parts for you. I taught you how to act, Abraham. The Great Actor, they said, the Hamlet of the Yiddish Theatre, people knew your name from South Africa to San Francisco, the women tore off their gowns in your dressing-room. You were an amateur before I taught you; on every line you tried to blow down the back of the theatre. I worked on you like a sculptor on a statue. I made you an artist. And in between . . . ' Madam Rechevsky shrugged ironically. 'In between I took care of the books, I hired the ushers, I played opposite you better than any leading lady you ever had, I gave you a child every two years and fed all the others other women gave you the rest of the time. With my own hands I polished the apples they sold during intermission!'

Madam Rechevsky slumped a little inside her fashionable seal coat, her voice sank to a whisper. 'I loved you better than you deserved and you left me alone for fifteen years and I'm getting older and now they bother me for rent . . . ' She sat down on the cold earth, on the dead winter grass covering the grave. 'Abraham,' she whispered, 'you've got to help me. Please help me. One thing . . . One thing I can say for you – whenever I was in trouble, I could turn to you. Always. Help me, Abraham.'

She was silent a moment, her bare hands outspread on the grass. Then she shrugged, stood up, her face more relaxed, confident, at peace, than it had been in months. She turned away from the grave and called.

'Helen, darling,' she called. 'You can come here now.'

Helen left the marble bench on the plot of the man named Axelrod and walked slowly towards her father's grave.

Night, Birth and Opinion

'Tents!' Lubbock was saying, gloomily swishing his beer a-round in his glass, his voice echoing hoarsely in the empty shadows of Cody's bar, dark and almost deserted now, deep in the heel of the winter night. 'Yuh join the Army, yuh sit in a tent and freeze yer tail all winter. I'm a civilised man. I'm used to living in steam-heated apartments.'

He looked around him challengingly. He was a big man, with huge longshoreman's hands and a long neat scar down one side of his face. The other two men at the bar looked carefully into their beer.

'National defence,' the bartender said. The bartender was a pale little man in a vest and apron, with pale, hairy arms and a long, nervous nose. 'Everybody has to make certain sacrifices.'

'The trouble with this country,' Lubbock said loudly, 'is there are too goddamn many patriots walking the streets.'

'Don't say anything against patriotism,' said the man nearest Lubbock. 'Not in my presence.'

Lubbock looked consideringly at him. 'What's *your* name?' he asked.

'Dominic di Calco,' the man said clearly, showing that he was not to be bullied, 'I don't see anything wrong with being a patriot.'

'He doesn't see anything wrong with being a patriot,' Lubbock said. 'An Italian patriot.'

'They need you, said Sweeney, the man on the other side of Lubbock. 'They need you bad – in Greece.'

The others laughed. Sweeney looked around him proudly, his little creased red face beery and complacent.

'I'm an American citizen,' Di Calco shouted. 'After you boys get through laughing.'

'You know what I'd like to see?' Sweeney waved his arms, laughing. 'I'd like to see the Italian Army try to invade Red Hook.'

'I'm not in favour of Mussolini,' Di Calco shouted. 'But keep yer trap shut about the Italian Army!'

'Three Irishmen,' Sweeney said. 'It would take three Irishmen about a half-hour. The Italians're wonderful when they fight other Italians.'

'Would you like to step outside, whatever yer name is?' Di Calco asked quietly.

'Boys!' the bartender spread his hands pacifically, 'Remember, we're in America.'

'Remember,' Di Calco said, 'I offered you satisfaction, whatever yer name is.'

'My name is Sweeney!' Sweeney shouted. 'I got two cousins in the Royal Air Force!'

'That's a hot one,' Lubbock said. 'A man by the name of Sweeney with two cousins in the English Army. Yuh can just about imagine' – Lubbock spoke reasonably to the bartender – 'what type of Irishman yuh could get to fight in the English Army.'

'What do you want?' the bartender asked. 'You want to disagree with every patron of this saloon?'

'That must be some family, the Sweeneys.' Lubbock went over and clapped Sweeney on the back.

'They're fightin' for you and me,' Sweeney said coldly. 'They're fightin' to preserve our way of life.'

'I agree,' said Di Calco.

'Yeah,' said the bartender.

Lubbock turned on the bartender. 'What's *your* name?'

'Cody,' said the bartender. 'William Cody.'

Lubbock glared at him. 'You kidding me?'

'I swear to God,' said the bartender.

'They got a statue in Wyoming. Buffalo Bill. Any relation?' Lubbock asked.

'It's pure coincidence,' the bartender said.

'Beer, Buffalo Bill,' Lubbock said. He watched the bartender draw the beer and place it before him. 'From the very hand,' Lubbock marvelled. 'A man with a statue in Wyoming. No wonder you're so patriotic. If I had a statue in Wyoming, I'd be patriotic too.'

'Pure coincidence,' protested the bartender.

Lubbock drank half his glass of beer, leaned back, spoke quietly and reflectively. 'I just love to think of two Sweeneys in England protecting my way of life. I just love it. I feel safer already.' He smacked the bar savagely. 'Tents! We'll be

155

sitting in tents in the middle of winter!'

'What do you want?' Di Calco said. 'You want Hitler to come over here and clean up?'

'I hate him; I hate the bastard,' Lubbock said. 'I'm a Dutchman myself, but I hate the Germans.'

'Give the Dutchman a beer,' Sweeney said. 'On me.'

'I hate the Germans,' Lubbock went on, 'and I hate the English and I hate the French and I hate the Americans . . . '

'Who do you like?' the bartender asked.

'The Italians. You can't get them to fight. They're civilised human beings. A man comes up to them with a gun, they run like antelopes. I admire that.'

Di Calco tapped warningly on the bar. 'I'm not going to stand here and have the Italian Army insulted.'

Lubbock ignored him. 'The whole world should be full of Italians. That's my programme. My name is Lubbock, boys. I come from a long line of Dutchmen, but I hate them all. If the British're defending my way of life, they can stop right now. My way of life stinks.'

'Boys,' the bartender said. 'Talk about something else, boys.'

'The truth is,' Sweeney said, 'I wouldn't mind if there was a war. I make eleven dollars a week. Any change would be an improvement.'

'This is the war of the Hotel Pee-yeah,' Lubbock said.

'What do you mean by that?' Di Calco looked at him suspiciously, sensing a new insult to the Italian Army.

'On Fifth Avenue and Sixtieth Street. They tea-dance,' Lubbock scowled. 'They tea-dance for the Empiuh.'

'What's objectionable about *that*?' the bartender asked.

'Yuh ever see the people that go into the Hotel Pee-yeah?' Lubbock leaned over the bar and scowled at the bartender. 'The little fat rabbits in the mink coats?'

'The best people,' the bartender said defiantly.

'Yeah,' Lubbock smiled mirthlessly. 'If they're for anything, it must be wrong.'

'I'm speaking carefully,' Di Calco said in measured tones. 'I don't want to be misconstrued, but to a neutral ear you sound like a Communist.'

Lubbock laughed, drained his beer. 'I hate the Communists,' he said. 'They are busy slitting their own throats seven days a week. Another beer, Buffalo Bill.'

'I wish you wouldn't call me Buffalo Bill.' The bartender filled Lubbock's glass. 'You start something like that, you can

156

wind up making life intolerable.' He flipped the head off the glass and pushed it in front of Lubbock.

'A statue in Wyoming . . . ' Lubbock shook his head wonderingly. 'Today they tea-dance for the Empiuh, tomorrow we get shot for the Empiuh.'

'It don't necessarily follow.' Sweeney moved closer, earnestly.

'Mr Sweeney, of the flying Sweeneys.' Lubbock patted him gently on the wrist. 'The reader of the *New York Times.* I'll put a lily on yer grave in the Balkans.'

'It may be necessary,' Di Calco said. 'It may be necessary to supply soldiers; it may be necessary for Sweeney to get shot.'

'Don't make it so personal,' Sweeney said angrily.

'Before we get through, Mr Sweeney.' Lubbock put his arm confidentially around him, 'this war is going to be very personal to you and me. It will be very personal to the rabbits from the Hotel Pee-yeah.'

'Why can't you leave the Hotel Pierre out of this discussion?' the bartender complained.

'The snow will fall,' Lubbock shouted, 'and we'll be sitting in tents!' He turned on Di Calco. 'The Italian patriot. I'd like to ask yuh a question.'

'Always remember,' Di Calco said coldly, 'that I'm an American citizen.'

'How will you feel, George Washington, sitting behind a machine-gun with Wops running at you?'

'I'll do my duty,' Di Calco said doggedly. 'And don't use the term "Wop".'

'What do you mean running *at* him?' Sweeney roared. 'The Italian Army don't run at anything but the rear.'

'Remember,' Di Calco shouted at Sweeney, 'I have a standing invitation to meet you outside.'

'Boys.' the bartender cried. 'Talk about other matters. Please . . . '

'One war after another,' Lubbock marvelled. 'One after another, and they get poor sons of bitches like you into tents in the wintertime, and yuh never catch on.'

'I'm overlooking the language.' Sweeney took a step back and spoke dispassionately, like a debater. 'But I'd like to hear your solution. Since you're so clear on the subject.'

'I don't want to overlook the language,' Di Calco said hotly.

'Let him talk.' Sweeney waved his hand majestically. 'Let's hear everybody's point of view. Let the Dutchman talk.'

'Well . . .' Lubbock started.

'Don't be insulting,' the bartender said. 'It's late and I'm ready to close up the bar, anyway, so don't insult the patrons.'

Lubbock rinsed his mouth with beer, let it slide slowly down his throat. 'Don't yuh ever clean the pipes?' he asked the bartender. 'Yuh know, that's the most important thing about beer – the pipes.'

'He's got a comment on everything!' Di Calco said angrily. 'This country's full of them!'

'They are dividing up the world,' Lubbock said. 'I got eighty-five cents to my name. No matter which way they finish dividing, I'll be lucky to still have eighty-five cents when it's all over.'

'That's not the way to approach the problem,' said Sweeney. 'Your eighty-five cents.'

'Will I get Greece?' Lubbock pointed his huge finger threateningly at Sweeney. 'Will Di Calco get China?'

'Who wants China?' Di Calco asked triumphantly.

'We get one thing,' Lubbock said soberly. 'You and me and Sweeney and Buffalo Bill . . .'

'Please,' said the bartender.

'We get trouble. The working man gets trouble.' Lubbock sighed and looked sadly up at the ceiling, and the other men silently drank their beer. 'Military strategists agree,' Lubbock said, his tongue going proudly over the phrase, 'that it takes four men to attack a position defended by one man.'

'What's that got to do with it?' Sweeney demanded.

'This war is going to be fought in Europe, in Africa, in Asia,' Lubbock chanted. 'It is not going to be fought in William Cody's Bar.'

'Sorry I can't oblige you,' the bartender said sarcastically.

'I've studied the situation,' Lubbock said, 'and I've decided that there's going to be four times as many Americans killed as anybody else. It stands to reason. They're not going to attack us here, are they? We're going to take the offensive. Four to one!' He banged the bar with savage certainty. 'Us four poor dumb yokels'll get it just to put one lousy Dutchman out of the way. Military strategy guarantees!'

'Don't yell so loud,' the bartender said nervously. 'The people upstairs don't like me.'

'The worst thing is,' Lubbock shouted, glaring wildly around him, 'the worst thing is I look around and I see the world full

158

of poor dumb stupid bastards like Sweeney and Di Calco and William Cody!'

'The language,' Di Calco snarled. 'Watch the language.'

'Hitler has to be beaten!' Sweeney yelled. 'That's a fundamental fact.'

'Hitler has to be beaten!' Lubbock's voice sank to a significant, harsh whisper. 'Why does Hitler have to be beaten? Because poor ignorant bastards like you put him there in the first place and left him there in the second place and went out to shoot him down in the third place and in the meantime just drank yer beer and argued in bars!'

'Don't accuse me,' said Sweeney. 'I didn't put Hitler any place.'

'Sweeneys all over the world!' Lubbock shouted. 'And now I got to get shot for it. I got to sit in tents in the wintertime!' Suddenly he grabbed Sweeney by the collar with one hand. 'Say . . . ' Sweeney gasped. Lubbock's other hand shot out, grasped Di Calco by his collar. Lubbock drew the two men close to his face and stared with terrible loathing at them. 'I would like to mash yer stupid thick heads,' he whispered.

'Now, lissen,' Di Calco gasped.

'Boys,' said the bartender, reaching for the sawed-off baseball bat he kept under the counter.

'If I get shot it's your fault!' Lubbock shook the two men fiercely. 'I oughta kill yuh. I feel like killin' every dump slob walkin' the streets . . . '

Di Calco reached back for a beer bottle and Sweeney grabbed the big hand at his throat and the bartender lifted the sawed-off baseball bat. The door swung open and a girl stepped through it and looked blankly at them.

'Go right ahead,' she said, the expression on her face not surprised or worried or amused. 'Don't let me interrupt.'

'Boys . . . ' the bartender said and put the baseball bat away. Lubbock gave Sweeney and Di Calco a last little push and released them and turned back to his beer.

'People like you,' Sweeney murmured, outraged, 'people like you they ought to commit to asylums.'

Di Calco straightened his tie and tried to smile gallantly through his rage at the girl, who was still standing by the open door, hatless, her dirty blonde hair falling straight down to her shoulders. She was a thin girl, with the bones showing plainly in her face, and her hands skinny and rough coming out of the sleeves of the light old grey coat she was wearing.

Her face was very tired, as though she had been working too long, too many nights.

'Would you like to close the door, miss?' the bartender asked. 'It's getting awfully cold.'

The girl wearily closed the door and stood against it for a moment, wearily surveying the four men.

'I need some help,' she said.

'Now, miss . . . ' the bartender started.

'Oh, shut up!' she snapped at him. Her voice was flat and worn. 'I'm not bumming anything. My sister's just had a kid and she's laying in a stinking little hospital and she was bleeding all day and they gave her two transfusions and that's all they got and they just told me maybe she's dyin'. I been walkin' past this saloon for the last half hour watchin' you four guys talkin', gettin' up nerve to come in. She needs blood. Any you guys got some blood you don't need?' The girl smiled a little.

The men carefully avoided looking at each other.

'We're busted,' the girl said, her tone as flat as ever. 'The kid came out seven months and her husband's a sailor; he's on his way to Portugal and there's nobody in this whole goddamn, freezin' town I can turn to.' She shrugged. 'My blood's the wrong type.' She took a step nearer the bar. 'She's only nineteen years old, my sister. She had to go marry a sailor . . . ' Lubbock turned and looked at her.

'All right,' Lubbock said. 'I'll go with yuh.'

'Me, too,' said Di Calco.

Sweeney opened his mouth, closed it, opened it again. 'I hate hospitals,' he said. 'But I'll come along.'

Lubbock turned and looked slowly at the bartender.

'It's late, anyway,' the bartender said, nervously drying the bar with a towel. 'I might as well come along, just in case . . . My type blood might . . . Yes.' He nodded vigorously, and started taking off his apron.

Lubbock reached over the bar and brought up a bottle of rye and a glass and silently poured it and pushed it in front of the girl. The girl took it without smiling and drained it in one gulp.

They all sat in the dreary hospital clinic room with the old dead light of the hospital on them and all the weary sorrowful smells of the hospital swelling around them. They sat without talking, waiting for the interne to come and tell them which one of them had the right type of blood for the transfusion. Lubbock sat with his hands between his knees, occasionally glancing sharply at Sweeney and Di Calco and Cody, all of them nervously squirming on their benches. Only the girl walked slowly back and forth down the middle of the room, smoking a cigarette, the smoke curling slowly over her lank, blonde hair.

The door opened and the interne came in and touched Lubbock on the arm. 'You're elected,' he said.

Lubbock took a deep breath and stood up. He looked around him, at Di Calco, at Sweeney, at Cody, triumphantly, smiled at the girl, and followed the interne out of the room.

When he was through, when the blood had poured out of his veins, slowly and delicately, into the veins of the pale, quiet girl on the table next to him, Lubbock got up and bent over her and whispered, 'You're going to be all right', and she smiled weakly at him.

Then he put on his coat and went back into the clinic room. The others were still there. They stood there, scowling at him in the blue hospital light. He smiled widely at them.

'Everything all right?' Di Calco asked solemnly.

'Everything's fine,' Lubbock said cheerfully. 'My blood is singing in her system like whisky.'

Di Calco looked at Sweeney, Sweeney at Cody, each with doubt and hesitancy in his eye.

'Say Dutchman,' Sweeney said loudly, 'we'll buy you a drink. What d'yuh say?'

They waited, tense, almost ready for attack.

Lubbock looked consideringly at them. Cody put up the collar of his coat.

'Sure,' Lubbock said, putting his arm around the girl. 'It'll be an honour.'

They walked out through the hospital doors together.

It Happened in Rochester

There were four girls sitting on the wooden benches of the agency's front room. They had on big hats and they talked fast and kept their gloves on and made believe they were very happy and high-spirited and every time one of the office doors opened and a man ran from one room to another through the front office the girls would spring up and cry gaily, 'Jules, oh, Jules, darling', or 'Harry, now Harry, darling', and Jules or Harry would grunt and wave and disappear and the girls would sit down slowly, not so gay, and wouldn't sound happy or high-spirited for five minutes after that.

I sat between two of the girls, trying to look old, keeping my hat on, flipping through the script of *It Happened in Rochester* and making notes in pencil on the margins to show the girls I was not an actor hanging around for a job.

The girl at the switchboard said, 'Mr McCleary', and I stood up. 'In the back office, Mr McCleary.'

The girls watched me coldly as I went through the little swinging gate and towards the back office, holding *It Happened in Rochester* negligently under my arm.

There was a little blond man in the back office. He looked like a boy for the first five minutes, clean and red cheeked, with all his teeth, and bright eyes.

'My name is Sundstrom,' he said, shaking hands with me. 'And this is Mrs Sundstrom.'

I looked at Mrs Sundstrom. She was a round, tall woman who had been Sundstrom's assistant in his juggling act, handing him the Indian Clubs and plates and clapping her hands and throwing him a handkerchief after each trick. She smiled at me, a nice, fat, middle-aged woman with good false teeth, who kept her hand always lightly touching her husband's sleeve. When I looked back at Sundstrom I saw that he wasn't a boy at all, but this woman's husband, slim, with a boy's direct, simple appearance, but forty-five years old.

'Sit down, Mr McCleary,' Sundstrom said.

I sat down, finally unhappily taking my hat off.

'Isn't he young to be a director?' Miss Sundstrom said, taking a good look at me with my hat off. She smiled at me, but there was doubt in her eye.

'I'm twenty-seven,' I said, lying for four years. 'I got a young look. When I die I'll have a young look.'

Both of them laughed, gently.

'In the theatre, dear,' Sundstrom said, 'age doesn't make any difference. Talent is the thing in the theatre. Wouldn't you say so, Mr McCleary?'

'Yes,' I said.

'Still,' said Mrs Sundstrom, 'a play like *It Happened in Rochester*, it's full of emotion, it takes an advanced understanding of human nature, very advanced. With all due respect, Mr McCleary.'

I couldn't say that I had an advanced understanding of human nature, so I kept quiet.

'Mr McCleary is very well recommended, dear,' Sundstrom said. 'He's the best one left.' He turned to me, speaking seriously. 'We tried many other directors, Mr McCleary. The best. All the best. Older men. Some were busy and others didn't like the script.'

'They didn't understand the play,' Mrs Sundstrom said. 'They want yelling and shooting and movie stars. A simple, honest play like *It Happened in Rochester* is beyond them.'

'It's a true story,' Mr Sundstrom said. 'It happened to me and I wrote it. I waited twenty years to write this play. It's an absolutely true story. The girl is a young woman I knew in Rochester. That was before I met Mrs Sundstrom.' He smiled at her and patted her hand in apology for ever having known another woman.

'That story is absolutely typical,' Mrs Sundstrom said. 'It shows how some women are. People will flock to see it.'

I looked at the blue covers of *It Happened in Rochester* and fiddled with my hat. 'Where's the money coming from?' I asked.

'I'm backing it,' Sundstrom said. 'My own money. Mrs Sundstrom and I worked steadily for twenty years. From one end of the country to another. When vaudeville was good. We made as high as three-fifty a week. We retired comfortably. We bought a house in New Jersey.'

'You must visit us,' Mrs Sundstrom said. 'Come on a Sunday for the whole day.'

'Yes,' I said. 'Why don't you try a regular producer with the play? Why risk your money?' I asked, trying, then, in the first fifteen minutes, to save them.

'We've tried other producers,' Sundstrom said.

'They're like the directors,' Mrs Sundstrom said. 'They don't understand real-life drama.'

'Maybe,' I said, 'maybe they know what the public wants. Maybe you oughtn't to take a chance. This'll cost about twelve thousand dollars.'

'The public will flock to it,' Mrs Sundstrom said.

'I am willing to take the chance,' Sundstrom said, smiling kindly at me. 'I have faith in this play. It's an absolutely true story.'

'What is your opinion of the play?' Mrs Sundstrom asked, suspicion for the first time in her voice.

I thought of all the offices I waited in for jobs, and all the 'No's', and all the years going past without plays to stage or actors to direct. I thought of my bank account, which read, 'Thirty-seven dollars and ninety cents.' I looked at the Sundstroms, happy and confident, determined to do the play with me or without me.

I nodded soberly. 'It has the ring of an absolutely true story,' I said.

The Sundstroms beamed at each other and shook my hand and we agreed to start rehearsals in two weeks and Mrs Sundstrom asked, 'What's your first name?'

'Robert,' I said.

'Very nice.' She smiled. 'It's so silly to call a young boy like you Mr McCleary.'

We shook hands again and I put on my hat and went down and bought a drink.

I cast the play in the little back office. The office belonged to the Lazarus Agency for Actors and Artists, and Jules Lazarus, out of pity or gambler's hope, loaned the Sundstroms the little office and a telephone and the firm's secretary. I sat behind the desk and talked to the actors and actresses and the Sundstroms sat behind me quietly, smiling. Mrs Sundstrom's hand on her husband's sleeve, trusting me, approving delightedly of every choice I made. From time to time members of their families would come in and silently stand in front of the window and watch and listen. Then they would go out into the hall and confer in whispers with the Sundstroms. Then they'd come back with a grave look of deliberation and take up their old places. I never found out what they said to each other out in the halls because they never questioned any decision I made.

'Young,' I heard Mrs Sundstrom saying to her mother one afternoon, 'but definitely talented.'

All the Sundstrom relatives who came to stand in front of the window in the Lazarus Agency's back office looked somehow as though they'd never been in New York before.

In the two weeks that I took to cast the play I carefully avoided reading *It Happened in Rochester*. By the time the cast assembled on the stage of the theatre for the first rehearsal I had worked myself into a condition of hope.

The Sundstroms and their relatives, now about fifteen in number, came in and sat themselves down along the rear of the dark auditorium as I gave out the sides to the actors.

'Ladies and gentlemen,' I said to the actors, 'this is a simple, true play, and I would like it to be played simply and truly. Act One, Scene One . . .'

By the time the first act was over the actors were suppressing giggles. In the first act the good but simple hero met and fell in love with the pretty but bad heroine. The pretty heroine told three different men in the first act that she loved them and spent a great deal of her time buying new dresses. The hero at the first act curtain was building dreams of a cottage in the country and children and raises in salary.

I called a recess after the first act, and all the actors fled the stage without looking at me. I sat at the director's table, with my back to the Sundstroms and their families out in the theatre. I counted the steam pipes along the back wall.

The man who was playing the hero came back for his pipe, passed close to my table, whispered as he passed, 'Lemons, mister? Any lemons today, Mr McCleary?'

He was a good friend of mine.

'Shut up!' I said.

He bowed soberly, got his pipe, smiled like a juvenile at the Sundstroms out in the theatre. They all smiled back.

He passed me on the way out, tamping down his pipe, 'Turkeys, mister. Are you interested in turkeys today, Mr Belasco?'

I sat there, rubbing my eyes, feeling as though I was going to have a headache in five minutes. I thought hard about my rent and my chances of getting anything else for the season. I got up and jumped down from the stage and walked up the aisle toward the fifteen Sundstroms. I didn't know what I was going to say, but I was going to say something.

They were all smiling widely at me as I came toward them. Sundstrom had an automatic pencil with a little light in it and a notebook for suggestions. He hadn't opened the notebook yet.

He patted my shoulder as I stopped next to his seat. 'We think it's wonderful,' he said, smiling happily, thinking about his words, planned for twenty years, being spoken that afternoon on the stage. 'My whole family and Mrs Sundstrom's whole family think it's wonderful.'

And all the fifteen Sundstroms leaned over so I could see them and nodded and smiled at me.

'That's good,' I said. 'Have you any suggestions?'

Sundstrom patted my shoulder again. 'We think it's wonderful,' he said.

I went back and started the cast on Act Two, Scene One.

For the next three weeks Sundstrom arrived promptly, with his notebook and automatic pencil and the light in it, for every rehearsal. Always, too, Mrs Sundstrom sat next to him in the last row of the theatre. The number of relatives varied, with the biggest collection of them coming in for the Sunday rehearsals when they were free of whatever work they did during the week.

The actors had given up by now and were just mumbling through their lines and looking for other parts during lunch hour. Sundstrom sat with the notebook. Occasionally he would draw a careful six-pointed star on the first page and then close the book with a decisive snap.

My headache had lasted for two and a half weeks now and I lived on coffee and aspirin, watching through half-closed eyes the weary rambling of the actors around the stage.

'Elspeth,' the hero was saying, 'I do not think that it is necessary for you to talk in that manner.'

'What manner do you mean?' Elspeth asked. She always sat down on this line as though she had been out for five nights steadily before it.

'You know what manner I mean,' the hero said.

'I do not understand you,' said Elspeth. She was chewing

166

gum. Suddenly I couldn't bear the fact that she was chewing gum.

'Please, for the love of God,' I shouted, 'throw that gum away!'

There was a hush in the theatre. It was the first time a voice had been raised in all three weeks.

'Well,' said the heroine coldly, 'there's no need to scream.'

She got up deliberately and walked all the way across the stage, chewing slowly. With a large sweeping gesture she stuck the gum on the gilt paint of the proscenium arch. Then she marched slowly and arrogantly back to her place and fell heavily into her chair.

'Move!' I stood up and yelled. 'You're supposed to be a young, passionate girl. You're supposed to dance around the stage! You're not supposed to act like a lead safe, darling! I want to see some signs of life! That goes for the whole damned company! We've been conducting a funeral around here for three weeks!'

There was silence for a moment, and then the heroine started to cry. She cried for five minutes with no signs of stopping, so I dismissed the company for the day.

'Tomorrow,' I said, 'we're going to put some life into this play. We're going to really try.'

They all went quietly off the stage, except for the heroine, who was still crying as loudly as ever.

'Now, Robert.' It was Sundstrom behind me, with Mrs Sundstrom right next to him. 'Was that absolutely necessary, Robert?'

I looked at them, standing there, puzzled, neatly dressed for Sunday, and I felt like crying, too.

'I wanted to make it move a little faster, Mr Sundstrom,' I said gently. 'It's been pretty dead up there.'

'We don't think so,' Sundstrom said, tapping his wrist with the notebook in which he had not entered one suggestion in three weeks. 'We think it's very nice.'

'My family thinks it's wonderful,' Mrs Sundstrom said. 'And they've been watching for three weeks now.'

'It's not wonderful,' I said, wanting to help them, to save them. 'I think you and I ought to sit down tonight, Mr Sundstrom, and map out a complete job of rewriting.'

'Now, Robert . . . ' Sundstrom began, his little-boy face wrinkling up.

'We start with the first act,' I said, talking fast, to get it over with, to make the last desperate attempt as easy and as quick as possible, 'and we go right through to the third act. We work mostly on the character of Elspeth. She's on the stage all the time, and we've got to make her talk like a human being . . . '

'But that's the way she talked,' Sundstrom said. I knew her for five years and that's the way she talked.'

'It's very natural talk,' Mrs Sundstrom said.

'It's terrible, Mr Sundstrom,' I said, being cruel, hoping to save him. 'If you leave it this way we're all completely sunk.'

'That's what you honestly think, Robert?' he asked.

'That's what I honestly think.' I sat down suddenly on the arm of one of the aisle chairs.

'I thought about this play for twenty years,' Sundstrom said, his hands going over his eyes, forty-five years old. 'It's the absolute truth.'

'I think we ought to talk it over with Momma and the boys,' Mrs Sundstrom said.

'You don't mind ?' Sundstrom asked me.

'No,' I said. 'I'll be across the street in the bar.'

I walked up the aisle, past the fifteen Sundstroms, who had been listening intently. They watched me silently as I went out.

I had three whiskies before Sundstrom came into the bar. He bought me another drink and put his hand on my shoulder before he said anything.

'They like it,' he said. 'The family. They think it will draw the public. They don't see anything wrong with it. I agree with them.'

'Sure,' I said, without knowing exactly what I was saying 'sure' to.

'I feel, Robert,' he went on, 'in the light of what you have just told me, that you are not quite in sympathy at this time with the play.'

I shook the ice in my glass.

'It's clear to me now,' he said, 'that you don't really understand this play. That's natural, Robert. You're a little young for such a play.'

'Sure,' I said.

'So if you don't mind, I'll relieve you of the responsibility of directing it.'

'Who'll direct it?' I asked.

'I will,' he said. 'After all, it happened to me. I ought to know how it happened.'

'Uhuh,' I said, remembering the notebook empty of all

notes. 'I'll give you back as much money as I have left.'

'Half,' Sundstrom said. 'We talked it over and we decided that you should get your pay. Is that fair?'

'Sure,' I said. 'Well I hope *It Happened in Rochester* wins the Pullitzer Prize.'

'Thank you, Robert. Come and visit us in New Jersey.'

'I will.' I waved to him and he went back to the theatre to his family and his wife's family and the leading lady who sat down like a lead safe and to the play he had thought of writing for twenty years.

I stayed at the bar.

The reviews were very bad. The *Times* said: '*It Happened in Rochester* opened last night at the Jackson Theatre. It was written, produced and directed by Leon Sundstrom.' That was all it said. It was the kindest review.

I didn't go to see it and I didn't see Sundstrom until two weeks later. He was walking along Broadway, very slowly, like an old man. He hadn't shaved and I noticed with surprise that his beard was grey. He had two advertising sandwich boards strapped on him.

'See *It Happened in Rochester*,' the boards read. 'It is an Absolutely True Story. Now Playing at the Jackson Theatre.'

He saw me and I had to stop.

'Hello, Robert,' he said, without smiling.

'Hello,' I said.

'Do you think this'll help, Robert?' he asked.

'What?'

'These signs. Will it bring people into the theatre? Will it help them understand that this is a real true story?'

'Of course,' I said.

'The critics didn't understand,' he said, shaking his head, the last trace of the little boy gone. 'They wrote about it as though it was impossible. I've written them. They won't believe that it actually happened to me. I could introduce them to the girl. She's married now and she has three children. In Rochester. Have you got a cigarette, Robert?'

I gave him a cigarette and lit it for him.

'I kept it running two weeks,' he said. 'Some people saw it. They liked it very much. They saw it was real life. Critics aren't real people. It cost me eight thousand dollars to keep it running two weeks. I sold my house and my car.' He sighed. 'I thought word would get around that it was a real life story.

169

I'm going to go back to juggling – if I can get a start. There's not much demand for jugglers these days and I'm not so steady any more. I would like to put enough aside so I could write another play.' He never smiled, not once. 'Could you lend me two or three cigarettes, Robert?'

I gave him my pack:

'Why don't you come and see the play?' he asked. 'I'll get you in for nothing.'

'Thanks.'

'That's all right. You better come tonight. It's closing tonight. I haven't got any more money to keep it going any more, and the family chipped in as much as they had.' He sighed. 'I guess I don't understand the theatre,' he said. 'Well, I like to keep moving. I like to give as many people as I can a look at this sign.'

'That's a good idea,' I said.

'It's not a bad sign, is it?'

'It's a very good sign.'

'It's the truth,' he said, and walked off, up Broadway, shifting the shoulder straps.

I haven't found another job yet.

During the cocktail hour, in Brownsville, the cab drivers gather in Lammanawitz's Bar and Grill and drink beer and talk about the world and watch the sun set slowly over the elevated tracks in the direction of Prospect Park.

'Mungo?' they say. 'Mungo? He got a fish for a arm. A mackerel. He will pitch Brooklyn right into the first division of the International League.'

'I saw the Mayor today. His Honour, himself. The Little Flower. What this country needs . . . '

'Pinky, I want you should trust me for a glass of beer.'

Pinky wiped the wet dull expanse of the bar. 'Look, Elias. It is against the law of the State of New York,' he said nervously, 'to sell intoxicating liquors on credit.'

'One glass of beer. Intoxicatin'!' Elias's lips curled. 'Who yuh think I am? Snow White?'

'Do you want me to lose my licence?' Pinky asked plaintively.

'I stay up night worryin' Pinky might lose his licence. My wife hears me cryin' in my sleep,' Elias said. 'One beer, J. P. Morgan.'

Regretfully, Pinky drew the beer, with a big head, and sighed as he marked it down in the book. 'The last one,' he said, 'positively the last one. As God is my witness.'

'Yeah,' Elias said. 'Keep yer mouth closed.' He drank the beer in one gulp, with his eyes shut. 'My God,' he said quietly, his eyes still shut, as he put the glass down. 'Fer a lousy dime,' he said to the room in general, 'yuh get somethin' like that! Fer a lousy dime! Brooklyn is a wonderful place.'

'Brooklyn stinks,' said another driver, down the bar. 'The borough of cemeteries. This is a first-class place for graveyards.'

'My friend Palangio,'' Elias said. 'Il Doochay Palangio. Yuh don't like Brooklyn, go back to Italy. They give yuh a gun,

171

yuh get shot in the behind in Africa.' The rest of the drivers laughed and Elias grinned at his own wit. 'I seen in the movies. Go back t' Italy, wit' the fat girls. Who'll buy me a beer?'

Complete silence fell over the bar, like taps over an Army camp.

'My friends,' Elias said bitterly.

'Brooklyn is a wonderful place,' Palangio said.

'All day long,' Elias said, reflectively rubbing his broken nose, 'I push a hack. Eleven hours on the street. I now have the sum of three dollars and fifty cents in my pocket.'

Pinky came right over. 'Now, Elias,' he said, 'there is the small matter of one beer. If I'd knew you had the money . . .'

Elias impatiently brushed Pinky's hand off the bar. 'There is somebody callin' for a beer down there, Pinky,' he said. 'Attend yer business.'

'I think,' Pinky grumbled, retreating, 'that a man oughta pay his rightful debts.'

'He thinks. Pinky thinks,' Elias announced. But his heart was not with Pinky. He turned his back to the bar and leaned on his frayed elbows and looked sadly up at the ceiling. 'Three dollars and fifty cents,' he said softly. 'An' I can't buy a beer.'

'Whatsamata?' Palangio asked. 'Yuh got a lock on yuh pocket?'

'Two dollars an' seventy-fi' cents to the Company,' Elias said. 'An' seventy-fi' cents to my lousy wife so she don't make me sleep in the park. The lousy Company. Every day for a year I give 'em two dollars an' seventy-fi cents an' then I own the hack. After a year yuh might as well sell that crate to Japan to put in bombs. Th' only way yuh can get it to move is t' drop it. I signed a contract. I need a nurse. Who wants t' buy me a beer?'

'I signed th' same contract,' Palangio said. A look of pain came over his dark face. 'It got seven months more to go. Nobody shoulda learned me how to write my name.'

'If you slobs would only join th' union,' said a little Irishman across from the beer spigots.

'Geary,' Elias said. 'The Irish hero. Tell us how you fought th' English in the battle of Belfast.'

'O.K., O.K.,' Geary said, pushing his cap back excitably from his red hair. 'You guys wanna push a hack sixteen hours a day for beans, don' let me stop yuh.'

'Join a union, get yer hair parted down the middle by the cops,' Elias said. 'That is my experience.'

'O.K., boys.' Geary pushed his beer a little to make it foam. 'Property-owners . Can't pay for a glass a beer at five o'clock in th' afternoon. What's the use a' talkin' t' yuh? Lemme have a beer, Pinky.'

'Geary, you're a red,' Elias said. 'A red bastidd.'

'A Communist,' Palangio said.

'I want a beer,' Geary said loudly.

'Times're bad,' Elias said. 'That's what's th' trouble.'

'Sure.' Geary drained half his new glass. 'Sure.'

'Back in 1928,' Elias said, 'I averaged sixty bucks a week.'

'On New Year's Eve, 1927,' Palangio murmured, 'I made thirty-six dollars and forty cents.'

'Money was flowin',' Elias remembered.

Palangio sighed, rubbing his beard bristles with the back of his hand. 'I wore silk shirts. With stripes. They cost five bucks apiece. I had four girls in 1928. My God!'

'This ain't 1928,' Geary said.

'Th' smart guy,' Elias said. 'He's tellin' us somethin'. This ain't 1928, he says. Join th' union, we get 1928 back.'

'Why the hell should I waste my time?' Geary asked himself in disgust. He drank in silence.

'Pinky!' Palangio called. 'Pinky! Two beers for me and my friend Elias.'

Elias moved, with a wide smile, up the bar, next to Palangio. 'We are brothers in misery, Angelo,' he said. 'Me and th' Wop. We both signed th' contract.'

They drank together and sighed together.

'I had th' biggest pigeon flight in Brownsville,' Elias said softly. 'One hundred and twelve pairs of pedigreed pigeons. I'd send 'em up like fireworks, every afternoon. You oughta've seen 'em wheelin' aroun' an' aroun' over th' roofs. I'm a pigeon-fancier.' He finished his glass. 'I got fifteen pigeons left. Every time I bring home less than seventy-five cents, my wife cooks one for supper. A pedigreed pigeon. My lousy wife.'

'Two beers,' Palangio said. He and Elias drank with grave satisfaction.

'Now,' said Elias, 'if only I didn't have to go home to my lousy wife. I married her in 1929. A lot of things've changed since 1929.' He sighed. 'What's a woman?' he asked. 'A woman is a trap.'

'You shoulda seen what I seen today,' Palangio said. 'My third fare. On Eastern Parkway. I watched her walk all th' way acrost Nostrand Avenue, while I was waitin' on the light.

173

A hundred-and-thirty pound girl. Blonde. Swingin' her hips like orchester music. With one of those little straw hats on top of her head, with the vegetables on it. You never saw nothin' like it. I held on to the wheel like I was drownin'. Talkin' about traps! She went to the St George Hotel.'

Elias shook his head. 'The tragedy of my life,' he said, 'is I was married young.'

'Two beers,' Palangio said.

'Angelo Palangio,' Elias said, 'yer name reminds me of music.'

'A guy met her in front of the St George. A big fat guy. Smilin' like he just seen Santa Claus. A big fat guy. Some guys...'

'Some guys...' Elias mourned. '*I* gotta go home to Annie. She yells at me from six to twelve, regular. Who's goin' to pay the grocer? Who's goin' to pay the gas company?' He looked steadily at his beer for a moment and downed it. 'I'm a man who married at the age a' eighteen.'

'We need somethin' to drink,' Palangio said.

'Buy us two whiskies,' Elias said. 'What the hell good is beer?'

'Two Calverts,' Palangio called. 'The best for me and my friend Elias Pinsker.'

'Two gentlemen,' Elias said, 'who both signed th' contract.'

'Two dumb slobs,' said Geary.

'Th' union man,' Elias lifted his glass. 'To th' union!' He downed the whisky straight. 'Th' hero of th' Irish Army.'

'Pinky,' Palangio shouted. 'Fill 'em up to the top.'

'Angelo Palangio,' Elias murmured gratefully.

Palangio soberly counted the money out for the drinks. 'Now,' he said, 'the Company can jump in Flushing Bay. I am down to two bucks even.'

'Nice,' Geary said sarcastically. 'Smart. You don't pay 'em one day, they take yer cab. After payin' them regular for five months. Buy another drink.'

Palangio slowly picked up his glass and let the whisky slide down his throat in a smooth amber stream. 'Don't talk like that, Geary,' he said. 'I don't want to hear nothin' about taxicabs. I am busy drinkin' with friends.'

'You dumb Wop,' Geary said.

'That is no way to talk,' Elias said, going over to Geary purposefully. He cocked his right hand and squinted at Geary. Geary backed off, his hands up. 'I don't like to hear people

174

call my friend a dumb Wop,' Elias said.

'Get back,' Geary shouted, 'before I brain yuh.'

Pinky ran up excitably. 'Lissen, boys,' he screamed, 'do you want I should lose my licence?'

'We are all friends,' Palangio said. 'Shake hands. Everybody shake hands. Everybody have a drink. I hereby treat everybody to a drink.'

Elias lumbered back to Palangio's side. 'I am sorry if I made a commotion. Some people can't talk like gentlemen.'

'Everybody have a drink,' Palangio insisted.

Elias took out three dollar bills and laid them deliberately on the bar. 'Pass the bottle around. This is on Elias Pinsker.'

'Put yer money away, Elias.' Geary pushed his cap around on his head with anger. 'Who yuh think yuh are? Walter Chrysler?'

'The entertainment this afternoon is on me,' Elias said inexorably. 'There was a time I would stand drinks for twenty-five men. With a laugh, an' pass cigars out after it. Pass the bottle around, Pinky!'

The whisky flowed.

'Elias and me,' Palangio said. 'We are high-class spenders.'

'You guys oughta be fed by hand,' Geary said. 'Wards of the Guvment.'

'A man is entitled to some relaxation,' Elias said. 'Where's that bottle?'

'This is nice,' Palangio said. 'This is very nice.'

'This is like the good old days,' Elias said.

'I hate to go home.' Palangio sighed. 'I ain't even got a radio home.'

'Pinky!' Elias called. 'Turn on the radio for Angelo Palangio.'

'One room,' Palangio said. 'As big as a toilet. That is where I live.'

The radio played. It was soft and sweet and a rich male voice sang, 'I Married an Angel'.

'When I get home,' Elias remembered, 'Annie will kill a pedigreed pigeon for supper. My lousy wife. An' after supper I push the hack five more hours and I go home and Annie yells some more and I get up tomorrow and push the hack some more.' He poured himself another drink. 'That is a life for a dog,' he said. 'For a Airedale.'

'In Italy,' Palangio said, 'they got donkeys don't work as hard as us.'

'If the donkeys were as bad as you,' Geary yelled, 'they'd have sense enough to organise.'

'I want to be a executive at a desk.' Elias leaned both elbows on the bar and held his chin in his huge gnarled hands. 'A long distance away from Brownsville. Wit' two thousand pigeons. In California. An' I should be a bachelor. Geary, can yuh organise *that*? Hey, Geary?'

'You're a workin' man,' Geary said, 'an' you're goin' to be a workin' man all yer life.'

'Geary,' Elias said. 'You red bastidd, Geary.'

'All my life,' Palangio wept, 'I am goin' to push a hack up an' down Brooklyn, fifteen, sixteen hours a day an' pay th' Company forever an' go home and sleep in a room no bigger'n a toilet. Without a radio. Jesus!'

'We are victims of circumstance,' Elias said.

'All my life,' Palangio cried, 'tied to that crate!'

Elias pounded the bar once with his fist. 'Th' hell with it! Palangio!' he said. 'Get into that goddamn wagon of yours.'

'What do yuh want me to do?' Palangio asked in wonder.

'We'll fix 'em,' Elias shouted. 'We'll fix those hacks. We'll fix that Company! Get into yer cab, Angelo. I'll drive mine, we'll have a chicken fight.'

'You drunken slobs!' Geary yelled. 'Yuh can't do that!'

'Yeah,' Palangio said eagerly, thinking it over. 'Yeah. We'll show 'em. Two dollars and seventy-fi' cents a day for life. Yeah. We'll fix em. Come on, Elias!'

Elias and Palangio walked gravely out to their cars. Everybody else followed them.

'Look what they're doin'!' Geary screamed. 'Not a brain between the both of them! What good'll it do to ruin the cabs?'

'Shut up,' Elias said, getting into his cab. 'We oughta done this five months ago. Hey, Angelo,' he called, leaning out of his cab. 'Are yuh ready? Hey, Il Doochay!'

'Contact!' Angelo shouted, starting his motor. 'Boom! Boom!'

The two cars spurted at each other, in second, head-on. As they hit, glass broke and a fender flew off and the cars skidded wildly and the metal noise echoed and re-echoed like artillery fire off the buildings.

Elias stuck his head out of his cab. 'Are yuh hurt?' he called. 'Hey, Il Doochay!'

'Contact!' Palangio called from behind his broken windshield. 'The Dawn Patrol!'

'I can't watch this,' Geary moaned. 'Two workin' men.' He went back into Lammanawitz's Bar and Grill.

The two cabs slammed together again and people came running from all directions.

'How're yuh?' Elias asked, wiping the blood off his face.

'Onward!' Palangio stuck his hand out in salute. 'Sons of Italy!'

Again and again the cabs tore into each other.

'Knights of the Round Table,' Palangio announced.

'Knights of Lammanawitz's Round Table,' Elias agreed, pulling at the choke to get the wheezing motor to turn over once more.

For the last time they came together. Both cars flew off the ground at the impact and Elias's toppled on its side and slid with a harsh grating noise to the curb. One of the front wheels from Palangio's cab rolled calmly and decisively towards Pitkin Avenue. Elias crawled out of his cab before anyone could reach him. He stood up, swaying, covered with blood, pulling loose ends of his torn sweater. He shook hands with Palangio and looked around him with satisfaction at the torn fenders and broken glass and scattered headlights and twisted steel. 'Th' lousy Company,' he said. 'That does it. I am now goin' to inform 'em of th' accident.'

He and Palangio entered the Bar and Grill, followed by a hundred men, women, and children. Elias dialled the number deliberately.

'Hullo,' he said, 'hullo, Charlie! Lissen, Charlie, if yuh send a wreckin' car down to Lammanawitz's Bar and Grill, yuh will find two of yer automobiles. Yuh lousy Charlie.' He hung up carefully.

'All right, Palangio,' he said.

'Yuh bet,' Palangio answered.

'Now we oughta go to the movies,' Elias said.

'That's right,' Palangio nodded seriously.

'Yuh oughta be shot,' Geary shouted.

'They're playin' Simone Simon,' Elias announced to the crowd. 'Let's go see Simone Simon.'

Walking steadily, arm in arm, like two gentlemen, Elias and Angelo Palangio went down the street, through the lengthening shadows, towards Simone Simon.

The Passion of Lance-Corporal Hawkins

Lance-corporal Alfred Hawkins stood on the Haifa dock, his fingers wet on the long nightstick in his hands, the unaccustomed helmet heavy on his head, watching a naval launch slowly bring in the two-masted schooner *Hope*, its decks and tattered rigging swarming with people, who looked like clustered dark bees, so far away, and not like people at all. Please, Lord, Hawkins prayed to himself, standing at ease with his platoon, warm in the yellow Mediterranean sun, please, Lord, keep me from hitting any of them.

'Don't take any nonsense from the buggers,' Lieutenant Madox said, standing in front of the platoon. 'Whack 'em a couple of times and they'll behave like bloody gentlemen.' He turned and peered at the shabby schooner slowly approaching the dock, and Hawkins was sure that the look on the Lieutenant's thick red face was one of pleasurable anticipation. Hawkins looked at the other men of the platoon. Except for Hogan, you couldn't tell anything from their faces. In London once, during the war, Hawkins had overheard an American Air Force major saying, 'The British would watch Hitler hanging or their daughters marrying into the Royal Family or their own legs being chopped off at the knee and not change expression by one twitch of the eyebrow. You can't beat an army like that.' The American had been drunk, of course, but, looking around him now, and remembering other times, too – like the day outside Caen and the day on the Rhine and the day his company went into the concentration camp at Belsen – Hawkins could understand what the American had been talking about. In ten or fifteen minutes, the men around him might be in the middle of a very mean fight on board the schooner, against clubs and knives, perhaps, and maybe even home-made bombs, and except for Hogan, again, all of them looked as though they were merely lined up for a routine roll call outside their barracks in the morning. And Hogan, of course, was an Irishman, and not the same thing at all. He was a small, thin boy, with a tough, broken-nosed, handsome face, and now he was fidgeting uneasily, his jaw rigid with excitement, pushing his helmet back and forth on his head, shifting his nightstick, breathing loudly enough to be heard over all the small noises of the harbour and the platoon around him.

They were singing now on the schooner. The rising and falling, chanting, foreign melody came thinly and defiantly across the oily green water. Hawkins could understand several words of Hebrew, but he could not make out what the song was about. It sounded wild and somehow menacing, as though it should not be sung in sunshine and in the mornings or by women's voices, but late at night, in the desert, by lawless and desperate men. Esther had translated two or three Hebrew songs for Hawkins in the last few weeks, and he had noticed that the words 'freedom' and 'justice' figured in them prominently, but those words did not seem to fit with the flat, dangerous, hoarse music hammering across the harbour from the slowly moving old boat.

Hawkins wished they wouldn't sing. It made it harder if they sang and you knew they were singing about freedom or justice. After all, they were singing to him, and to the other men around him, and what did they expect him to do?

Hawkins closed his eyes, as though by shutting out the sight of the dark-clustered boats inexorably being pushed to the dock, and the clubs, and the transport waiting to take them to the stockade on Cyprus, he could somehow also shut out the sound of the rough, challenging voices of the Jews.

He closed his eyes, his youthful, almost childish face, sweating under the hot helmet, painfully composed, painfully disclosing nothing to the Lieutenant or the men around him or to the eyes of the fugitives he was expected to punish. He closed his eyes. He was uncomfortable in his wool battledress and the tight canvas belting, and he was sorry he was in Palestine, sorry he was in the Army, sorry he was an Englishman, sorry he was alive. This was not what he had expected when he had re-enlisted, six months after the war was over. He didn't know exactly what he had expected. He had just known he did not want to live in Southampton, in the foggy weather, among the torn and ruined buildings; in the same house with his father, who had had his arm torn off during a raid in 1941; in the same house with his sister, whose husband had been killed at

179

Bari in 1943; in the same house in which he had lived for such a short while with Nancy, who had later divorced him and married an American sergeant in the port battalion – and that was a soft job for a soldier, wasn't it, during a war. He had just known that after four years in the Army, ever since he was seventeen, he did not want to start looking for a job as a longshoreman on the battered wharves, he did not want to stand in a queue collecting the unemployment dole, he did not want the bitter weather of unheated winter England after glimpses of Africa and summer France. And the only thing he had known was soldiering. They had made it a little more attractive – they had raised the pay and promised many rather vague benefits – and, if the truth must be told, the only time anyone had ever really taken care of him was in the Army. It was certain no one was really going to take care of you as a civilian, Socialist government or no Socialist government. Though he had voted for them, of course. He had read all the pamphlets and he knew what he was doing, a common soldier in the Army of the King, the son of a working man, the grandson of a working man, the great-grandson of a working man. That was another thing about the Army. It had given him the chance to read for the first time in his life. Especially the two periods he'd been in the hospital, first with the bullet in his hip and then with the piece of shrapnel he'd picked up twelve days before the end of the war. The hospital library had had a complete set of H. G. Wells, and he had slowly and studiously gone through it all, soberly agreeing with the energetic arguments of the old man. By the time he'd got out of the hospital, he had become a confirmed Socialist, believing that education could change the world, and that violence was a hangover from primitive times, and that year by year the human race was certain to improve. He opened his eyes for a moment and looked at the schooner. It was much closer now, and he could smell it, too. There were perhaps three hundred people jammed on to it, men and women, and they had obviously not had the most complete sanitation facilities. He wished H. G. Wells were on the dock in the uniform of an infantry lance-corporal today; it would be interesting to see what he would do.

It had been so much simpler during the war. There were the Germans across the fields, or up on a hill two miles away, and you shot at them and they shot you. They had bombed your home and torn the arm off your father's shoulder and killed your brother-in-law, and there were no further decisions to be made about them. And all the men around you felt exactly as you did, no matter who they were. But now . . . There was Lieutenant Madox, who hated all Jews and was delighted with this duty on the dock this morning. Of course, Lieutenant Madox hated everybody, except Englishmen, and if he had been in India or Malaya or France, he would have looked forward to cracking Indian or Malayan or French skulls with equal pleasure. But he happened to be in Palestine, and he happened to be looking forward to hitting Jews. Then there was Private Fleming, a quiet, capable man of thirty-five. Private Fleming was a Communist. Communists, Hawkins knew, did not think much of Zionism, but certainly they didn't believe in braining Jews, and yet there was Private Fleming, an excellent soldier, standing quietly at ease, ready to do his duty, gripping his nightstick like all the others. And there was Hogan, who was one of Hawkins's best friends, with whom he drank beer in Jerusalem and Tel Aviv, and who was a Catholic, like Hawkins, and went to Mass on Sunday morning with him, and whose father had been killed by the British in the trouble in Dublin in 1916. Hogan often went out with him and Esther, too. Esther would bring a friend and they would swim on the beach at Tel Aviv and go to the movies at night when they played musical pictures. Hogan hated the Jews, though, because his second cousin, who was in the Sixth Airborne, had got his foot blown off by a Jewish mine on the Rehovoth Road two months before. What would H. G. Wells have made of the Dublin orphan on the sunny dock this morning, tense with pent-up fury as he glared at the naval launch slowly pushing the tattered, dark, chanting refugees toward him?

And, supposing H. G. Wells had been a Jew, and were standing on the deck of the *Hope* this morning, after the years of murder in Germany, after the displaced persons' camps, after the illegal journey across Europe and the crooked voyage down the Mediterranean, what clever, hopeful statement would he make then, waiting there like an old bull in the knacker's yard, waiting for the clubs and the Cyprian wire?

An Arab labourer walked by, rolling a wheelbarrow. He put the wheelbarrow down in front of the platoon, his long, skinny arms dark mahogany, dangling out of his tattered shirt. He had a little black scraggly beard, and he didn't smell so good, either. He grinned at the soldiers. His teeth were not all there, but when he smiled, he looked childlike and ingratiating, and some of the men smiled back at him. The Arab looked

181

over his shoulder at the approaching boat, grinned more widely, and moved his finger across his Adam's apple in the gesture of throat-slitting.

'Get out of here, you filthy old rascal,' Lieutenant Madox said, smiling broadly. 'Go ahead. Out of the way. We'll have no international incidents on this dock.'

The Arab bobbed his head, the grin fixed on his face, and made the throat-cutting gesture again, like a child who repeats a trick that he sees has pleased his elders. Then he bent and picked up the handles of the wheelbarrow again and trundled it off, giggling to himself.

Hawkins didn't remember what H. G. Wells had had to say about the Arabs. He was sure there must have been something on the subject, because there was something on every subject in the old man's books, but he couldn't remember. The Arabs Hawkins had to admit, were much more pleasant to have around than the Jews. For one thing, they did what you told them. For another thing, they weren't likely to get you off in a corner and engage you in a loud political argument. Esther lived in the same house with a family by the name of Freedman, who were German refugees and whose two sons had been in the Jewish Brigade during the war. The two boys lay in wait for Hawkins when he came to call for Esther and battered him with questions like 'Why doesn't Britain live up to the Balfour Declaration?' and 'Why does Britain allow the Grand Mufti of Jerusalem, who worked with the Nazis during the war, to come back to lead the Arabs from Cairo?' It was very queer, sitting in the small white living-room of the apartment house, with your rifle leaning against the wall (from time to time, Division Headquarters ordered that all troops be armed when they left the barracks), drinking tea and eating little sweet cookies that Mrs Freedman kept pressing on you, debating politely with the two fierce young veterans, who were probably members of the Jewish underground and had probably blown up a sergeant-major in the morning.

'It's not fair,' he had said to Esther after one such session, when he had finally managed to get her away from the house. 'They talk as though I was personally responsible.'

Esther had glanced at him obliquely, then looked away. 'Maybe,' she said softly, 'maybe that's what they think about every British soldier.'

'Is that what you think?'

Esther had shaken her head and gripped his arm more firmly.

'No,' she had said gravely, her low, soft voice solemn and warm. 'No. I do not think of you as a British soldier.' They had been walking along the quiet, white street, in the clear, foreign evening air – his boots making a hob-nailed clatter on the pavement and his rifle sling pulling at his shoulder and the girl beside him in a thin white dress with a blue sweater over it, her hair blowing gently, soft and pale brown, in the stirring wind.

'Listen to them sing,' Hogan said, his voice nervous and angry. 'The murderin' heathen! They'll sing a different tune an hour from now, they will!'

Hawkins opened his eyes. The ship was much closer now, and the songs clamoured across the water from the packed ship, with the soprano of the women shrill and glittering over the menacing bass of the men's voices. Hogan, Hawkins remembered, also sang songs in another language – in Gaelic – the words 'freedom' and 'justice' figured prominently in them, too. They were songs Hogan's grandfather had taught him in memory of his dead father, shot through the throat on a Dublin pavement by men in the same uniform that Hogan was wearing now so far away, seventy-five miles north of Jerusalem.

Hawkins closed his eyes again. It would do no good to watch the boat come nearer, foot by foot. There would be time enough to look later. He thought of Esther. He had arranged to meet her that night in Tel Aviv and take her to a movie if he got off duty early. He had not known what the duty would be, though, and he doubted if he would tell her later on. Matters were complicated enough with Esther as it was. She looked so cheerful and agreeable, so pretty and young, like the very nicest kind of girl you might meet by a lucky accident at home, but there had been the terrible times when she had suddenly broken down, for no apparent reason, and wept in his arms, wildly and inconsolably, clutching him as though to make certain again and again that he was there and alive. She was a German girl, whose mother and father had been killed in Munich, and whose husband had been caught by the British near Haifa unloading illegal immigrants in 1939. He had been put into a camp, where he had caught typhus and died. The authorities had permitted Esther to visit her husband the day he died, and once Esther had told Hawkins about it, although most of the time they avoided talking about things like that. The husband, who was twenty-four years old and had been a robust, laughing young man (Hawkins had seen

183

his picture), had been wasted by the disease to ninety pounds and was screaming in his delirium when Esther finally saw him. He did not recognise his wife at all when she came into the room, and that, somehow, was Esther's bitterest memory – the screaming, skeleton-like boy turning his head senselessly to the wall in the bare, barred room. Then, after that, all through the war, Esther had been kept under house arrest and had not been permitted to go out into the streets from sunset to dawn. When Hawkins had first known her, she had been quiet, almost fearful, and perhaps it was because she had matched his own shyness and fearfulness so well that he had begun to love her.

For the past several months, whenever Hawkins was waiting somewhere, and closed his eyes, as he was doing now, he had had a recurrent daydream. It was winter in the dream, a cold, windy night, and he and Esther were sitting before a warm fire in their own house. He could never decide whether the house was in England, in a quiet village, or on a farm in Palestine, cupped in the small, old hills, among the orange orchards. They were reading, and occasionally they looked up from their books and smiled at each other, not having to talk, in the firelight. After a time, there was a knock on the door and guests began to come in, not many of them, just good friends. Hogan, with his wild hair plastered down politely. Fleming, with the schoolteacher wife from Leeds he talked about so often. Robinson, who had been in Hawkins's platoon in Africa – it was always hard to remember, especially in a daydream, that Robinson was dead, buried in the small, windy cemetery near Constantine. They talked quietly in the warm room, and Hawkins opened up the tall bottles of heavy beer, and after a while Hogan sang, in his hoarse, accurate boy's voice, the sad, thrilling songs his grandfather had taught him in his father's honour, songs whose words no one understood, but whose melodies made you somehow melancholy and proud.

Hawkins blinked and refused himself the pleasure of taking the daydream through to its quiet ending. It was ridiculous to allow himself to moon like that, and it only made it worse when he finally opened his eyes and looked around him. There he was, on the dock, in the hot, bare sun, with the nightstick, waiting for Lieutenant Madox to order him to fight. And in the hills behind him, among the orange groves, people were hiding rifles and knives and machine-guns to murder each other in the long winter nights. And in England, from all the

184

letters he got from his family, they were preparing to starve and freeze to celebrate their victory in the war. He was sorry he was not older. Perhaps if he were thirty or forty or fifty, he could understand it better. During the war they had been warm, during the war they had been fed, during the war the Russians had loved them, the Americans had admired them, the French had kissed them when they came into a town; wherever they had gone, they had been heroes and saviours. He remembered the day that the election returns came out. He was still in Germany, in Hamburg, and an American sergeant had come over to him and said, very solemnly, 'Soldier, my name is McCarthy. I'm a paid-up C.I.O. member from Indianapolis. I decided I wanted to tell some Englishman how wonderful I think they are, and you're the first one I've come across since I made the decision. You've shown the whole world how civilised human beings should behave.' The American had been drunk, of course (was it possible that Americans appreciated other people only when they had ten drinks under their belts?), but he had shaken Hawkins's hand sternly and clapped him on the back, and Hawkins had walked away grinning and feeling proud because he had voted for Attlee and the others who were going to prove that a country could be run for the benefit of the working man without violence or disaster. He was glad the American wasn't around to see him standing on the dock today with helmet and nightstick, in this land of widows and orphans, in this land where there were no whole families, only survivors, in this land where everyone – every girl on the street, every child in a schoolroom, every farmer ploughing a furrow – had a story like Esther's, memories like Esther's, nightmares like Esther's where the memory of the furnace flickered across every face, the knocking of the midnight arrest broke into every dream, where agony was so commonplace that no one even remarked it. What a puzzling, sad thing it was to be an Englishman today Hawkins thought, staring at the boat, which was so close now. If he was in England, he was caught between cold and hunger, in Palestine between Jew and Arab, in India between Hindu and Moslem, in the East Indies between Dutchmen and Javanese, and no friends anywhere, no approval anywhere, just the helmet and the nightstick, the barbed wire and the Lieutenant, the songs in the strange languages hurled at your head like hand-grenades. You could read all the pamphlets, vote all the elections, pray all the Sundays, and each day it became worse, each day made you more of a villain, each day your uniform was cursed on the streets of more cities, in more languages. He closed his eyes.

'Hawkins!'

Hawkins jumped and straightened up. Lieutenant Madox was standing in front of him. 'Damn you, Hawkins!' Madox was saying. 'Will you keep your bloody eyes open! Get over here!'

'Yes, sir,' said Hawkins. He gripped his club and moved to where two sailors were swinging a gangplank up to the railing of the boat. The boat was tied to the dock now, and a terrible stillness had settled over the people on it.

'Spread out, spread out,' Madox was shouting to the platoon. 'Don't let anyone jump on to the dock. Make 'em all come down the gangplank.'

The smell was awful now, and in the silence the Jews stared down at the Lieutenant and the men of the platoon with cold, devouring hatred. Over a loudspeaker came a cool, pleasant voice.

'Ladies and gentlemen,' the voice said, and it sounded like at least a colonel in the Guards, 'we wish to do this in as orderly a fashion as possible. You will please come down the gangplank in twos and march to your right and go aboard the vessel moored directly behind your boat. You are going to be transferred to Cyprus, where you will be taken care of in British Army camps. Your sick will be treated and you will be given every consideration possible. Now, if you please, start leaving your vessel.'

The voice halted in a mechanical crackle. No one moved.

'All right,' Madox said. 'Let's get on board.'

Slowly and deliberately, the men of the platoon started up the gangplank. Hawkins was right behind the Lieutenant, with Hogan at his side. For a moment, at the top of the gangplank, he stopped. He looked down at the deck of the schooner. There was a blur of eyes, dark, staring, wild; a confusion of gaunt, ravaged faces; a wavering mass of tattered clothing such as might have been recovered from the corpses of a dug-up graveyard. Hawkins tottered momentarily, feeling, dizzily, this has happened to me before. Then he remembered. Belsen, he thought – wherever you turn, it is Belsen. In Belsen, he remembered, there had been the smell, too, and the same eyes, the same clothes, and there had been the old man (although later Hawkins had found out the man was only thirty) who had

186

opened a door of one of the huts and come slowly out, holding his hands in front of him, his hands like claws, his face twisted skull-like and horrible in what Hawkins had later realised the man had meant as a glorious smile of greeting but which at the moment had seemed weird and threatening. Then, just as he had reached Hawkins, he had dropped to the ground, and when Hawkins had bent over him, he had died. But no one had approached Hawkins; there was no expression here that might later be deciphered into a smile. On the other side of the deck, there were the women, and standing, facing the gangplank, were the young men, and then Hawkins knew there was going to be a fight. Crazily, he thought: I'll bet there are some of these people here who will recognise me from Belsen. What will they think of me?

'Come on!' Madox was shouting furiously. 'Come on, Hawkins, get in there!'

Slowly, with dreamy obedience, Hawkins moved towards the first line of men. I am not going to hit them, he thought as he walked through the stinking, unreal silence. No matter what, I am not going to hit them. Then he saw Hogan swing and there was the flat, awful noise of the stick hitting a shoulder. Then the screams began, and the shouting, which closed around you in a savage, wild, echoing vault of sound, and the bodies slamming into you, and the spurt of someone's blood, hot and slippery, in your face, and the confused flailing of arms and the black gleam of wood flashing against the yellow sky and a form dropping with a scream out of the rigging. Hawkins tried to keep his arms over his head, so that he wouldn't be pinned in helplessly, but hands grabbed at his club, and stabbed into his face, and he had to move his arms furiously to keep the club from being torn away. Then, suddenly, there was a pair of hands at his throat and he was staring into a dark, grimacing face, the eyes, just six inches from his, pitiless, mad, as the powerful fingers pressed and pressed. Hawkins tried to pull away, but there was no escaping the hands. Oh, God, Hawkins thought, feeling the blood pounding in his head, oh, God, he is going to kill me. No, he wanted to say, you don't understand. I am not doing anything. I was at Belsen. I was one of the people at Belsen. But the hands gripped firmer and firmer, the eyes stared coldly and triumphantly close to his own, as though the man who was choking him were finally taking vengeance for the Ghetto in Poland, the death of his children, the locked cars, the whips, the furnaces, the graves of Europe. Hawkins felt his eyes clouding, his throat being torn, his knees slowly crumpling, as he pressed back and back, with the screams and the wet smashing of blows all around him. With his waning strength, he wrenched away. Then he hit the man. The man did not let go. Hawkins hit him again, across the face, and the man's face disappeared in a fuzz of blood, but still the fingers gripped, as strong as ever. Then, again and again, with all the desperate strength in his arms and body, Hawkins lashed out at the man who was trying to strangle him. The man's face seemed to crumble in a red, dissolving tissue, his jaw hanging queer and sideways in a broken leer, only his eyes, steadfast and full of hatred, still glaring into Hawkins's own. There was a last, convulsive spasm of the fingers at Hawkins's throat; then the man slowly and silently slid slowly down and away. Hawkins stared at him, then fell on top of him, and something crashed across his head, and when he opened his eyes again, he was lying on the dock and everything was very quiet, except for the weeping of women, soft and far away.

Hawkins sat up. The fight was over. Now they were taking the women down the gangplank, and that was where the weeping was coming from – from the raddled bundles of living rags being carried by troopers on to the soil of Palestine and back on to the other ship, thirty-five feet away Hawkins felt his throat. It was terribly sore, and blood was still oozing from a cut under his ear. He felt sick and light-headed. He turned his head away from the women. He did not want to look at them. Lying next to him on the dock, very quiet, face downward, was a man. He had on an American Army shirt and a pair of Royal Air Force pants. He was bare-footed and his feet were terribly cut and swollen, black with blood. Slowly, Hawkins took the man's shoulder and rolled him over. The eyes were still open. The face was smashed, the jaw leering and dislocated, the teeth broken and red at the roots. But the eyes were open and they were the eyes of the man who had tried to kill Hawkins on board the schooner *Hope*.

Hawkins stood up. It was hard to walk, but he moved slowly over to the gate in the barbed wire at the other end of the dock. Madox was there, sweating but looking pleased.

'Very well done, Hawkins,' Madox said. 'I watched you. Are you hurt?'

'A little sir,' Hawkins said, surprised at the croaking, strange noise that came from his throat. 'Not too bad.'

'Good,' said Madox. 'It's just about finished here. We'll be going back to camp in a minute.' He looked solicitously at Hawkins's torn throat. 'You're in rather bad shape. You'd better not go with the others in the lorry. I'll take you with me in my jeep.'

'Yes, sir,' said Hawkins flatly. He walked slowly over to where the jeep was parked and laboriously climbed into the back. He leaned against the canvas. He closed his eyes, thinking of nothing.

Ten minutes later, Madox and his driver got into the jeep, and the jeep rolled slowly through the gate. Hawkins did not look back purposely, but he could not help seeing the dock, the two boats, the old, silent, broken, deserted schooner, and the full transport, beginning to work up steam for the voyage to Cyprus. They were singing again on board the transport, but softer now, and wearily, and Hawkins thought, I must get Esther to translate that song for me. And on the dock, with the Arab labourer, still holding his wheelbarrow, standing curiously over him, lay the dead man, flat and alone. Hawkins closed his eyes as the jeep spurted away from the waterfront.

I wonder, he was thinking, slowly and painfully, because his head did not seem familiar or normal to him any more. I wonder if I can get off tonight to go into Tel Aviv to take Esther to the movies. Then there was the explosion, and even as he felt himself slamming through the air, Hawkins thought, They must have got hold of some Army mines. Then he hit. He moved with crawling, broken slowness, feeling everything slippery and sliding all around him, thinking with dull persistence, I must tell them, they mustn't do this to me, they don't understand, I was at Belsen. Then he lay still.

Widows' Meeting

The noise of the plane came fitfully from the dark, foggy sky. Emily Clemens stood on the edge of the field, lightly holding her daughter Peggy's arm, listening to the muffled, searching, ebbing and flowing roar in the night mist that swirled in from the wintry Pacific. Occasionally a door was opened in the operations room of the terminal and a figure came silently out, gliding through the fog in a weak glow of neon light, like a nurse coming out of an operating-room, quiet, sad, and abstracted.

Emily was seventy years old and she felt tired. In the plane that had come out of New York and was now circling blindly through the dangerous soft grey stuff between the mountains and the sea was her other daughter, whom she had not seen in eleven years.

It had been a very bad day for Emily. There had been the bitter argument with Peggy at breakfast in the sunny dining-room of the peeling stucco house which they had shared for the past three years. Then the slow hours of nervous anticipation. Now, this was almost too much to bear. The engines whined and coughed hesitantly in the wet darkness. Emily could feel the mist condensing in fine, sharp drops on her skin. She wanted to sit down some place, but it did not seem like the proper thing to do, to sit comfortably while your daughter wandered overhead in danger of her life. Unreasonably, Emily felt that if she stood, and accepted the ache in her legs and back and the piercing dizziness at the base of her skull, it would somehow make her daughter's safety more certain.

She looked sidelong at Peggy. Peggy's face was reserved and distant, outlined softly by the neon edge of the wet light. Peggy had on a scarf and had her hands plunged into the pockets of her loose, schoolgirlish coat, and looked younger by far than her fifty years.

'Do you think,' Emily asked hesitantly, 'do you think they'll be all right?'

'I don't know, Mother,' Peggy said. Her voice was calm and terribly cool. 'You heard what the man said. They expect a break in the fog within the next thirty minutes.'

'Yes,' Emily said. She sighed. At least, she reflected, at least Peggy should sound worried. No matter what she'd thought about her sister for the last ten years. Peggy had acted so well about everything during the war; she had been so reasonable and sane when Lawrence, her husband, had died; she had been so stolidly brave when she'd heard that Bud had been killed in Germany, and Bud, after all, had been her only child. Peggy had acted so well that it had come as a shock when she had showed such violence about Irene. It was almost as though she didn't care whether Irene lived or died, arrived or didn't arrive, crashed or not. It was one thing to have a family quarrel, but to carry it to such lengths, for so many years, with so many deaths along the way, leaving them three lone women out of the whole gay, hopeful family . . . It was the new type of woman, Emily thought resentfully, the modern woman, who had shaken off so many claims of convention and order and had lost some of the capacity to forgive and to love that her mother had had.

The plane creaked painfully through the sky very close by. You could almost sense the effort of the engines, the straining eyes of the pilot, the rain-stained, sweating windshield a dim glow of light in the unrelenting obscurity. And back in the passenger compartment, strapped into her seat in case of a crash, Irene, after all these years.

Emily closed her eyes and remembered her two daughters in better days.

There was only one year between them, and they had been almost like twins – always together, always playing side by side, wearing each other's clothes, scolding each other's dolls in the sunny back-yard in the sunny time before the other war, when they all had lived in the big house in Los Angeles and Mr Clemens had been alive. The girls had been so pretty – both of them blonde and slender, with large, grave, dark eyes; each of them given to looking at the other and going off into spasms of secretive, little girl laughter, private, dear, unapproachable by the outside, adult world.

'I am going to sit back,' Mr Clemens would tell them, tilted on the porch in the fragrant California night, peering down

191

at the two small girls at his feet. 'I am going to sit back and take it easy and preserve myself until you ripen. Then you are both going to marry Eastern millionaires with railroad stock, because you are going to be so beautiful that no one will be able to resist you, and I'll throw up my job with the oil company and live off the fat of the land. I'll live for six months of the year with Irene and her husband on his yacht off the summer colony of Newport, Rhode Island, eating lobster and clam chowder out of silver bowls. Then I'll go and live with Peggy and her husband on his hunting preserve in Georgia, chasing the fox and the pheasant all the day and drinking fine wines all the night.'

Her eyes closed, the sound of the aeroplane engines dwindling in the misted distance, Emily could almost hear her husband's low voice in the homely garden so many years ago, could almost hear the high, shrill laughter of the girls and their 'Daddy, Daddy, you *are* a fool!'

There was a five-storey factory building, now, where the garden had been. And Mr Clemens had died in 1914, and the girls' marriages had not been exactly as he had prophesied. They had been pretty enough and there had been a flood of young men, of astonishing variety in looks, fortune, and talents, passing through the apartment in New York to which Emily and the girls had moved after Mr Clemens died. Peggy and Irene had handled the young men with charming mercilessness, trading them off to each other, giggling icily, late at night in the bedroom they shared, over the lame and pathetic pretensions of first one suitor, then another. They had almost invariably gone out together in those days, sternly insisting on a kind of double courtship from their stricken lovers, and it had seemed to Emily then that her two daughters far preferred each other's company to that of any of the young men they fleetingly favoured.

Coldly, and with cynical girlish precision, they had worked out contrasting and complementary personalities for themselves, so that if a young man escaped one, he would be taken by the other; if he slipped the flame, he would succumb to the ice. Irene, who had been the taller and more handsome of the two, had played the role of the independent, dashing young woman, outspoken, sardonic, intellectual. Peggy, smaller and softer, had been all sliding smiles and oblique glances, and Emily had overheard them roaring, in the privacy of their room, over their campaigns, like pirates adding up the season's haul and recalling the season's saltiest stratagems.

Emily, who had been a simple girl, rather afraid of men, would shake her head and, half in earnest half mockingly, say, over breakfast the next morning, in the confusion of newspapers and toast and coffee and lace and satin. 'There's a reckoning coming, my dears, there's a reckoning coming. There's a man waiting for each of you, and he'll make you pay up, and double and triple, for all your clever tricks.'

There had been a man, of course, and Emily had been right, but what she hadn't foreseen was that it would be the same one for both her daughters.

Emily blinked and looked around her strangely and tried to remember what she had come here for, what she was doing standing in the cold mist near midnight, with the ebbing noise of a plane overhead. Then she remembered, but it took an effort. Old age, she thought – everything gets jumbled. The images and memories slide in one on top of another, like a doubly exposed film, and something that happened thirty years ago is much brighter and more intense than something that happened yesterday, and dead men speak in more lively tones than the substantial people all around you, and your daughter at the age of twenty seems more real and more familiar than the cold-faced woman standing beside you holding your arm.

She was sitting in the living-room in the apartment in New York City. 1915, was it? 1916? She was sewing a blouse for Irene. It was a wet night and the rain was snapping at the windows and the curtains were shaking a little. She looked at the curtains and said to Irene, 'Next week they have to be washed'. Irene didn't answer. She was lying stretched out on the couch, staring up at the ceiling.

The door opened and Peggy came in with a man. They were both glistening with rain, and Peggy was laughing as she shook her head to get the water out of her hair. 'This is Reinhold Weigen, Mother,' Peggy said. 'He's a German. He's a journalist and he likes the opera. He'll sing Wagner for you if you're not careful. Reinhold, my sister Irene.'

He was a very polite man. He was rather small and a little chubby. He did not look like the dark agent of disaster. He bowed and he kissed Emily's hand, and bowed and kissed Irene's hand. By this time Irene was sitting up and looking curiously at him.

'Ah,' the German said. 'What a delightful family.' He wore

old-fashioned clothes, and there was something old-fashioned about the way he spoke. He had practically no accent.

'Tea,' Peggy said. 'We're dying for a cup of tea. Sit here, Reinhold,' she said, 'and charm my mother and sister and I'll be right back with a gallon.'

Peggy went into the kitchen, and Irene stood up and went over to the brocade chair under the lamp and sat there, her skirt flaring out, catching the light. 'I don't suppose,' Irene said, her voice low and suddenly melodious, 'our opera sounds like much to somebody like you, Mr Weigen – somebody who's heard it in Europe.'

'Oh,' said Reinhold gallantly, 'quite the opposite. I find it excellent. Excellent. Do you go often?'

'Occasionally,' Irene smiled. 'It's difficult to get American men to take you there.'

'Do you like the opera?'

'I adore it,' Irene said, and Emily looked at her in surprise, because Irene hadn't gone more than two or three times since she'd come to New York. 'I can't get enough of it.'

'Ah,' said Reinhold, beaming gravely. 'Perhaps you would do me the honour of attending with me?'

'I'd adore it,' Irene said.

Weigen took a deep breath. 'They are singing *Siegfried* Friday night,' he said. 'Is that agreeable?'

'Wonderful,' said Irene. 'I can hardly wait till Friday night.' They looked at each other, and Emily, sitting in the easy chair near the window with her sewing, thought: Poor Peggy, she needn't come out with that tea at all; it won't do her any good, any good in the world.

Emily blinked again. She was with the girls in their bedroom, with the pink satin ruffling on the dressing-table. Peggy was sitting white-lipped and silent on the bed, and Irene was talking, loudly and harshly. 'I'm going to marry him. If they'd let me, I'd go down to Georgia now and marry him right there in the prison cell I don't care what people say. I don't care if he's a German agent or an Egyptian agent or any kind of an agent. They have no right to put a man like that in jail, war or no war. I don't care about the war. We ought to lose it! We're barbarians, we don't know how to treat civilised human beings, it would be the best thing for us if we *did* lose.'

The door of the operations room opened and a man came out, bareheaded. He stood there, holding the door open with one hand, looking sadly and reflectively up at the swirling

194

sky, from which came the even, heavy sound of the engines. He shook his head and went back inside. The door closed, muffled and dull in the fog.

Weddings, Emily thought. An old woman had so many weddings to remember, so many brides, so many flowers, so many guests . . . Irene in white satin in the church on Twenty-fourth Street that had been torn down later on. The triumphant challenging look she gave the guests, not at all like a polite, joyous bride. Reinhold, thin and pale from the jail, but composed and happy. Peggy very pretty in yellow tulle as bridesmaid, but with slight dark smudges under her eyes, as though she hadn't been sleeping for the past few nights.

Then Peggy's wedding, six months later. Lawrence, very handsome, so tall, with an angular, long, honest face. Irene hadn't been there, because she was in Germany by then. But she had sent a long cable, and at the wedding party Peggy had opened it first among the messages, because she knew who it was from, and handed it to Lawrence. 'From my sister,' Peggy had said. 'She sends us her blessings. She's going to have a baby and she urges us to do likewise. She also wants me to send a picture of you. She says my descriptions are useless. No man could look like that.' Lawrence had grinned and stuffed the cable in his pocket, and it had lain around the house in one of those cardboard files, with all the other telegrams and letters, for years, until a new maid had thrown them out.

The plane passed overhead again in its slow, blind circle of the field, and Emily sighed as she listened to the fateful engines. If Peggy had been a little more knowing or crafty about the German all those years ago, if Irene had not been so certain and shrewd, would it have been Peggy circling in the mist tonight and Irene standing waiting, tight-lipped and frozen, beside her? Or if Peggy just hadn't brought the man home . . . Or if Irene had been out that night . . . You tried so hard to be sensible about your daughters, to protect them, guide them, mould the stubborn clay of circumstance, and at the age of seventy there you were, standing, exhausted, on a closed-in field, like a bankrupt gambler, afflicted by accident, pushing the last, pathetic bet out to the croupier's rake on the chequered board.

Among the faces that you remembered, and the rooms where you had been happy or where terrible things had happened to you, among the confused images that tumbled in an old woman's brain, there were the letters. You remembered how they looked – the foreign postmark; Irene's racing, large handwriting; the heavy grey envelopes; even the slight smell of Irene's perfume that somehow managed to survive the long crossing of the ocean. 'This is Hans.' (How curious it was to have a grandson called Hans in a family whose men had always been called John and Peter and Luke and Thomas.) 'It is true that he looks a little like Bismarck, but we expect that by the time he is three, he will give up the resemblance.' And 'Reinhold is not doing so well, but nobody is doing very well in this poor country and we do not mind at all. Hans now has seven teeth and we are going to stop counting when he reaches ten.' And 'Dietrich weighed ten pounds when he was born and it was a minor scandal, in this hungry country, like being caught hoarding food or taking bribes. I insisted upon calling him Dietrich Jonathan, after Papa, and all of Reinhold's very Prussian relatives raised their eyebrows, but I didn't budge an inch, and I suppose they went home and said to each other, "That is what you must expect if you insist upon marrying an American".' And 'Please send me some new pictures of Bud. He must be off that bear rug by now. If we don't get some new pictures here, his German cousins will be terribly surprised when they finally see him and find out that he is not always naked and lying on his belly.'

But the cousins never met. When Irene wrote, in 1936, that she and Reinhold were coming over for three months on a wonderful assignment that Reinhold had got from his paper, she had added that she couldn't take the boys out of school. Peggy had redecorated the guest-room in her house (the wall-paper with the large, full-blown red roses, and the new blue rug). And she had taught Bud to say, in German, 'Good morning, Aunt Irene and Uncle Reinhold', and 'How is the health of my cousins? I hope it is good.' Bud, who was very proud of his accomplishment in the field of languages, and who was twelve then, had gone on independently to learn '*Auf Wiedersehen*' and 'My father is very fond of the beer of Munich'. Emily smiled, even now, in the midnight mist, remembering Bud standing in a worn sweat-shirt and an old pair of long white ducks in the middle of the living-room, grinning, slowly and proudly announcing that his father was very fond of the beer of Munich.

It was hard to remember the day they arrived. Nineteen thirty-six was so far away and so many things had happened. The handsome big German boat – was it the *Europa*? – with its soaring prow that seemed to jut over the street from its berth on the North River. The band playing. (What was is playing in 1936? A German song, but she didn't remember it, although later, in newsreels, she heard it during pictures of German Army parades.) The cold biting in off the ice-filled river. Bud, delighted with the ship, shuffling around in a new blue coat that already seemed too short in the sleeves. Lawrence holding Peggy's arm, smiling, but pale, because even then his health was beginning to fail. Peggy grave, but with her eyes shining, searching the gangplank and the railings for the first glimpse of her sister. Then a tall, beautiful woman coming down the gangplank in a fur coat, a woman with a flashing, barely familiar face. Emily remembered thinking: That woman must be very wealthy. And then, the sudden realisation that it was her daughter and the fumbling through her handbag to find her glasses to make sure. And the man beside Irene looking rather small and dumpy, and comfortably fat, and when he took his hat off, Emily realised that is was Reinhold and that he had grown bald.

The gaps that opened up in your memory as you reached seventy . . . You remembered that there had been a great deal of excitement and everybody was kissing everybody else and everybody was talking and laughing at once, but what, exactly, it was like – what it was, exactly, that Peggy said to Reinhold, and how she looked when she said it, and if there was any indication there of any old pain or regret – you couldn't remember at all. And then the next thing you remembered was the party.

It was a big dinner party, or at least big for Peggy and Lawrence, in their basement dining-room, which led out into a small back garden. You remember that somehow you'd found out that Reinhold had been doing very well recently in Germany, and that he was very highly thought of and had moved to Berlin, and he and Irene had a large house in the country, where their sons were staying now, as well as an apartment in Berlin, and you were quite proud of him, fat and bald as he was, as he sat beaming, pleasant, deferential, his clothes still somehow old-fashioned, at the dark table, among all Lawrence's and Peggy's friends.

Then Irene's voice had cut across the mild confusion of the general conversation, saying, 'Hitler? Of course I believe in Hitler.' And the whole room had fallen silent, and Emily had watched Mr Rosen, Lawrence's partner, slowly and care-

fully put his fork down on his plate, as though it weighed a
great deal and were terribly fragile. 'I think it's impudent,'
Irene's voice had gone on, 'for your Mr Roosevelt to make
speeches complaining about what's happening in Germany.
How would you like it if Herr Hitler made speeches complaining about the internal affairs of America?'

'Darling,' Reinhold had said smoothly, 'I think we ought
not talk about politics at dinner. It is bad for the digestion.'

'Nonsense,' Irene had said. 'This gentleman on my right'
– she gestured towards Henry Connolly, who was one of
Lawrence's oldest friends – 'has been making a political speech
for a half-hour, and I think we ought to straighten him out.
He's been saying we need a revolution in Germany, that if we
don't get the Nazis out, the world will have to destroy us, that
we are barbarians – the whole silly bill of fare.' Irene had
looked challengingly around the table, and Emily had thought
anxiously: Perhaps she has had too much to drink; women
really should not drink when they go out. 'I've been reading the
papers ever since I got here,' Irene had said loudly, 'and I've
been listening to people talk, and I must confess it makes me
sick. You don't know what's happening. You swallow all that
Communist propaganda about us without trying to find out
the truth at all. I've been living there and you haven't, and I
tell you that if Hitler hadn't come along –'

'Darling,' Reinhold had said, 'please talk on another subject.'

'I will not,' Irene had said. 'You were sent here to convince
the Americans. This is just as good a place to begin as any.'
She spoke once more to all the guests. 'I tell you that if Hitler
hadn't come along, we'd have all been destroyed by the Jews
and the Communists.'

'Lawrence' – Mr Rosen had stood up quietly – 'I'm afraid
Carol and I will have to go now.' Then Carol Rosen had got
up, too, and Emily remembered the pale wash of fright on
her face. Lawrence had taken a deep breath and got up slowly
and wearily from his chair and followed the Rosens out into
the hall. There had been a mumble of voices from the hall,
but Emily had been unable to hear what they were saying there,
because Irene had continued loudly, 'I suppose Mr Rosen is a
Jew. I'm sorry if I've hurt his feelings, but if he's so tender,
he oughtn't to go out in company where he can hear a few of
the facts of life.'

Then Lawrence had come back. He stopped behind
Irene's chair, looking exhausted and drained, and had said

quietly, 'I'm afraid there's no use pretending this is a party any more. I imagine you're all as anxious to go home as I am for you to go. Peggy darling' – he had turned to his wife – 'may I speak to you alone for a moment?'

'Of course,' Peggy had said. She had stood up and gone out with Lawrence, and Emily had heard their slow footsteps mounting the stairs.

'Irene,' Emily had said sorrowfully, 'why can't you keep quiet about things like this? It's not for women to make speeches, one way or another.'

'Oh, Mother,' Irene had said. Don't be any sillier than you have to be. Go read your grandchild a bedtime story and leave the grown-ups alone. She had stared coldly around at the other guests. 'I'm sorry if I've made an ugly scene, but I couldn't help it. I've been in America three days and I am thoroughly disgusted with it and hope I never have to see it again. I suppose you all think more or less the way your friend Lawrence does. It's no wonder Europeans laugh at you. You don't know any more about what's really happening in the world than a Sioux Indian in the middle of the Dakota prairie. In Berlin I spend most of my time defending you people, telling my friends it's just that you're a little slow, that you're really intelligent, progressive people. I'm going to go back to Berlin and apologise.'

The other guests stood up and said good-night politely to Emily and left. Reinhold was sitting slumped in his chair, reflectively moving his coffee cup around in its saucer.

Emily had stared, puzzled, at her daughter. It was hard to understand what had provoked her to such violence. Emily hadn't even voted since 1924, and politics to her was something you left to the Irish.

'I certainly am glad my sons aren't growing up in this idiotic country,' Irene said.

The door opened and Peggy came in. She looked nervous, but in control of herself, and Emily knew that it was going to be bad.

'Irene,' Peggy said, 'I'd like to talk to you.'

'Now girls,' Emily said anxiously. 'Don't say anything you're going to regret later.'

'I know what she's going to say,' Irene said. 'Her woolly-headed husband has been lecturing her and she's going to tell us that she wants us to leave.'

'Exactly,' Peggy cried. 'Tonight, if possible.'

'Peggy!' Emily cried. 'Irene!'

'Delighted,' said Irene. 'Reinhold . . .'

Reinhold stood up, trying to hold his belly in. 'It is necessary for civilised human beings,' he began loudly, 'to consider a question like this impersonally, in abstract terms, if you understand, in its historical perspec –'

'Get out of here,' Peggy said evenly.

'Peggy,' said Emily faintly. 'Irene.'

Irene had swept out of the room and Reinhold had stopped at the door to bow stiffly before he followed his wife.

And now Peggy was standing coldly beside Emily, with the noise of the doubtful plane in their ears, far away from New York. And Lawrence was dead, and Reinhold was dead, killed by the Eighth Air Force in Berlin, his body unrecovered even now from the ruins of the apartment house. And not so far from where his uncle lay, Bud was dead, at the Saar River, which he had tried to cross but had not managed; and Irene's two sons were dead in Russia, and what rivers had they failed to cross? And the letters from Irene finally had been so sad, so broken – widowed, sonless, bereft in a shattered country. ('I said goodbye to Reinhold at eleven in the morning and the bombers came over at one and I never saw him again.' And 'Dietrich was only seventeen-years old, but they took him, anyway. They told me they would only put him in the anti-aircraft, but they put him in the infantry just the same, and what chance did he have? His comrades said he died very bravely, and they are all dead now themselves.' And 'Of course, our lovely home in Berlin is no more, but luckily there is still the country place. And, thanks to God, it is in the American zone, and I cannot tell you the thrill and the way the tears came to my eyes when I saw those blessed American faces and heard the first American say, "Ma'am, I come from Milwaukee, Wisconsin". The Americans have been very kind to me and even went so far as to put a guard of three men in my house when they heard that I was an American citizen. A guard is absolutely essential, because there are wild bands of released prisoners from the concentration camps, who roam the country and kill and rob and burn and have no more mercy in their hearts than so many tigers. Most of my money is in the Russian zone and I have been to Berlin three times to try to negotiate with them to get some of it back from the banks, but they are very cunning and they do not wish to co-operate at all. So your money order, sent through the very charming Lieutenant Wilson, who has been extraordinarily good to me, was most welcome. I can tell you how anxious I am to see my native land again and settle down with you, as in the old days, and forget the horrible things that have happened.')

That was what the fight with Peggy at breakfast had been about. 'I will not have that woman living in the same house with me,' she had repeated stubbornly over and over again when Emily had pleaded with her.

'What is Irene going to do?' Emily had asked. 'She's over fifty. We're the only flesh and blood she has in the whole world, the only ones she can turn to.'

Peggy had suddenly begun to weep. Every time I look at her,' she'd said, 'I'll think of Bud, drowning in that river. Why should I have to put up with anything like that? Flesh and blood? What sort of flesh and blood is that?'

'Peggy, darling,' Emily had said. 'She's changed, she's changed. You can see from her letters. That's all behind her. You've got to forgive her, you have to . . . ' Then she'd begun to weep, too, thinking of all the wrong, tragic, hopeless things that lay behind her, thinking of the graves and the hatred and the ended hopes. The sight of her mother crying, the old, worn, faded face gripped in rigid grief, had softened Peggy.

She had put her arms about Emily, comforting her. 'There. There,' she had said. 'All right. Don't cry. All right. She can come here. If she's changed, she can come here.'

And after breakfast, pretending that she had to go to town to do some shopping, Emily had gone to church and had sat stiffly in the empty building, with the mild, religious sunlight sifting in through the coloured windows, and had prayed that Irene had changed. Emily knew she was not going to go on much longer, and for that little time she wanted to live in the small, secure atmosphere of love, in the same house with her two ageing daughters, who had started out so brightly, with such promise of full, gay lives, and had ended, somehow, so badly, so lonely, bereaved, poor, plagued by the dead.

The lights of the field went on, watery and weak in the fog. The noise of the plane suddenly became much stronger, and then Emily saw it's lights tentatively sliding out of the veiled sky. The plane side-slipped, almost stalled, roared unnervingly, then hit the ground hard. It jarred up into the air, then crashed down again. It skidded; one wing touched the strip; then it righted itself and went in a crazy half-circle before it ground to a halt in front of them.

The engines stopped and the propellers turned more and more slowly, throwing moisture off their surfaces in pale, lighted arcs. Emily sighed.

'All right, Mother,' Peggy said. 'She's safe.'

'I think I must sit down now,' Emily said. Peggy led her along the fence to a bench near the gate through which the passengers would come, and Emily sat down heavily, feeling her knees trembling under her thick wool dress.

The attendants wheeled the steps over to the plane. The door was opened and the passengers slowly started to come out.

'Disgraceful!' one of the women getting off the plane was saying.

'Absolutely disgraceful. It's a wonder we weren't all killed.'

A stream of eight or nine people moved slowly towards the gate. There were three women and five or six men. Emily stared anxiously at them, searching for Irene. One of the women was very young and was carrying a child in her arms. That could not be Irene. The two other women were much older. They were both about Irene's size, and as they came into the light, Emily stood up and moved swiftly over to the gate, with Peggy holding her arm, to scan them more closely. Neither of the faces was known to her. She turned to Peggy. 'Do you see her?' she asked.

Peggy shook her head slowly. One of the women, quite well dressed, came toward them, smiling, and Emily half-started to smile, thinking: Oh, dear Lord, this is Irene and I don't recognise her, my own daughter! But the woman went right past her and was swept into the arms of a large young man who was standing behind them and who said, 'My God, Mother, don't do that to me again!'

The other woman who had come off the plane was standing in the full glare of the light at the gate. She was obviously at least sixty, dowdy, poorly dressed, in a frayed coat with a beaver collar. She had a fat, wrinkled, commanding face, very red from the cold.

'Peggy,' Emily said nervously, 'don't you think you ought to go ask the stewardess if . . . '

'Wait a minute,' Peggy said. 'I think perhaps that woman . . . '

'Disgusting,' the dowdy woman was saying to the man who was standing next to her. 'A sickening performance. Risking all our lives like that. What a country! I can tell you, it would never have happened in Germany! America! We had fog-dispellers on every field as long ago as 1937. Disgusting!'

Emily felt Peggy's hand tightening on her arm. The dowdy woman looked around her disdainfully once more, her eyes passing over Peggy's face without stopping. 'They must be waiting for me over there,' she said to the man, pointing towards the dim headlights of the cars on the parking lot. She started to walk away, toward the parking lot, a heavy, aged, slow-moving figure gradually being lost in the dark mist. Emily wanted Peggy to call out before the woman wandered out of sight.

'Peggy,' she said, speaking with difficulty, her tongue almost uncontrollable between her teeth, 'I think that's your sister Irene.'

'I know,' Peggy said. 'I know it is.'

Then Emily knew that Peggy would never call out. 'Irene,' Emily said weakly. Then, more strongly, 'Irene! We're over here.' The dim figure in the fog stopped and turned, then started slowly towards them, growing more real and more familiar with each step. 'Over here, Irene,' Emily said, weeping. 'Welcome home.'

Welcome to the City

As he drew nearer to it, Enders looked up at his hotel through the black drizzle of the city that filled the streets with rain and soot and despair. A small red neon sign blossomed over the hotel entrance, spelling out CIRCUS HOTEL, REASONABLE, turning the drizzle falling profoundly around it into blood.

Enders sighed, shivered inside his raincoat, and walked slowly up the five steps to the entrance and went in. His nostrils curled, as they did each time he opened the door of the hotel, and his nose was hit by the ancient odour of ammonia and lysol and old linoleum and old beds and people who must depend on two bathrooms to the floor and over the other odours the odour of age and sin, all at reasonable rates.

Wysocki was at the desk, in his grey suit with the markings of all the cafeteria soup in the city on it, and the pale face shaven down to a point where at any moment you half-expected to see the bone exposed, gleaming and green. Wysocki stood against the desk with the thirty-watt bulb shining down on his thinning hair and his navy-blue shirt and the solid orange tie, bright as hope in the dark hotel lobby, gravely reading the next morning's *Mirror*, his pale, hairy hands spread importantly, with delicate possessiveness, on the desk in front of him.

Josephine was sitting in one of the three lobby chairs, facing Wysocki. She wore a purple tailored suit with a ruffled waist, and open-toed red shoes, even though the streets outside were as damp and penetratingly cold as any marsh, and Enders could see the high red polish under her stockings, on her toenails. She sat there, not reading, not talking, her face carved out of powder and rouge under the blonde hair whose last surge of life had been strangled from it a dozen years before by peroxide and small-town hairdressers and curling irons that could have been used to primp the hair of General Sherman's granite horse.

'The English,' Wysocki was saying, without looking up from his paper. 'I wouldn't let them conduct a war for me for one million dollars in gilt-edged securities. Debaters and herring-fishermen,' he said. 'That's what they are.'

'I thought Jews ate herring,' Josephine said. Her voice scraped in the lobby, as though the Circus Hotel itself had suddenly broken into speech in its own voice, lysol and ammonia and rotting ancient wood finally put into sound.

'Jews eat herring,' Wysocki said. 'And the English eat herring.'

Enders sighed again and walked up to the desk. In the chair near the stairway, he noticed, a girl was sitting, a pretty girl in a handsome green coat trimmed with lynx. He watched her obliquely as he talked to Wysocki, noticed that her legs were good and the expression cool, dignified, somehow hauntingly familiar.

'Hello, Wysocki,' Enders said.

'Mr Enders,' Wysocki looked up pleasantly from the newspaper. 'So you decided to come in out of the rain to your cosy little nest.'

'Yes,' said Enders, watching the girl.

'Did you know,' Josephine asked, 'that the English eat herring?'

'Yes,' Enders said, digging into his mind for the face the girl reminded him of.

'That's what Wysocki said.' Josephine shrugged. 'I was living in happy ignorance.'

Enders leaned over so that he could whisper into Wysocki's ear. 'Who is she?' Enders asked.

Wysocki peered at the girl in the green coat, his eyes sly and guilty, as a thief might peer at a window at Tiffany's through which he intended to heave a brick later in the evening. 'Zelinka,' Wysocki whispered. 'Her name's Bertha Zelinka. She checked in this afternoon. You could do worse, couldn't you?' He chuckled soundlessly, his bone-shaven face creasing without mirth, green and gleaming under the thirty-watt bulb.

'I've seen her some place,' Enders whispered, looking at the girl over his shoulder. She sat remote, cold, her legs crossed beautifully under the green coat, looking under heavy lids at the scarred and battered clock over Wysocki's head. 'I know that face,' Enders said. 'But from where?'

'She looks like Greta Garbo,' Wysocki said. 'That's where you know her from.'

Enders stared at the girl in the green coat. She did look like Greta Garbo, the long pale face, the long eyes, the wide, firm mouth, the whole thing a mirror of passion and pain and deep, Northern melancholy and bony, stubborn beauty. Suddenly Enders realised that he was a stranger in a strange city, a thousand miles from home, that it was raining out, that he had no girl, and that no one in this huge and wrangling seven-million town had ever said anything more tender to him than, 'Pass the mustard'. And here, before him, solid as his hand, in a green coat with a lynx collar, sat a tall, melancholy girl who looked enough like Greta Garbo, pain and passion and beauty and understanding all mixed on the bony, pale face, to be her twin sister. His voice charged at his throat, leaping to say the first tender word in this rat-eaten, roach-claimed hotel lobby.

'Enders!' His name was spoken gaily, warmly. He turned from looking at Bertha Zelinka, wrenching his soul. 'Mr Enders, I was waiting for your appearance.' It was Bishop, the owner of the hotel, a little fat, grey-faced man with wet moustaches. He was rubbing his hands jovially now. 'You were just the person I wanted to see tonight,' he said.

'Thanks,' said Enders.

'Wait!' Bishop's voice trilled. 'Don't move an inch from the spot! I have a treat in store for you.'

He darted back of the desk through the door into his office. Enders turned and looked at Bertha Zelinka, sitting there as calmly, as remotely, as Garbo herself.

'Observe!' Bishop darted out again from his office. 'Look!' He held his hand high above his head. From it dangled a dead wet chicken. 'See what I've saved for you. I am willing to give you this chicken for sixty cents, Mr Enders.'

Enders looked politely at the chicken, hanging sadly in death from Bishop's proud hand.

'Thanks, Mr Bishop,' Enders said. 'But I have no place to cook a chicken.'

'Take it to your home.' Bishop whirled the chicken lovingly, giving it a spruce and electric appearance of life, the wings spreading, the feathers ruffling. 'Your mother would be delighted with this bird.'

'My mother's in Davenport, Iowa,' Enders said.

'You must have some relatives in the city.' Bishop pushed it lovingly under his nose, spreading the limp wings for inspection. 'They'll receive you with open arms with this chicken. This is a guaranteed Plymouth Rock chicken. Birds like this are exhibited in poultry shows from coast to coast. Sixty cents, Mr Enders,' Bishop said winningly. 'Can you go wrong for sixty cents?'

Enders shook his head. 'I have no relatives in the city,' he said. 'Thanks a lot, but I can't use it.'

Bishop looked at him coldly. He shrugged. 'I could've sold this chicken five times already,' he said, 'but I was saving it for you because you looked so pale. You gained my sympathy.' He shrugged again, and holding the Plymouth Rock by the neck, he went into his office.

'Well,' said Enders loudly, looking squarely at Bertha Zelinka. 'I guess I'll turn in for the night.'

'Want some company, Baby?' Josephine asked, in her voice the first note of hope she had allowed to sound there all evening.

'No, thank you,' Enders said, embarrassedly, glad that Miss Zelinka wasn't looking at him at the moment.

'You certainly are a great ladies' man,' Josephine said, her voice rasping through the lobby. 'Don't you know you'll go crazy, you go so long without a woman? You been here two weeks, you haven't had a woman all that time. They face that problem in Sing Sing, the convicts climb on the walls.'

Enders looked uneasily at Miss Zelinka. He didn't want a girl who looked like Greta Garbo to hear him mixed up in that kind of a conversation. 'Good-night,' he said, and walked past Miss Zelinka, down the hallway to his own room, which was on the ground floor, at the bottom of an airwell, three dollars a week. He looked back regretfully. Miss Zelinka's legs were visible, jutting out, like a promise of poetry and flowers, past the grime and gloom of the hallway. Sadly he opened the door and went into his room, took off his hat and coat and fell on the bed. He could hear Josephine talking, as though the walls, the vermin, the old and wailing plumbing, the very rats hurrying on their gloomy errands between the floors, had at last found a voice.

'The papers are full of boys like him,' Josephine was saying. 'Turning the gas on and stuffing their heads into the oven. What a night! What a stinking whore of a night! They'll find plenty of bodies in the river tomorrow morning.'

'Josephine,' Wysocki's voice floated down the hallway. 'You

ought to learn to talk with more cheerfulness. You're ruining your business, Josephine. The wholesale butchers from Tenth Avenue, the slaughterhouse workers, your whole regular clientele,. they're all avoiding you. Should I tell you why?'

'Tell me why,' Josephine said.

'Because you're gloomy! Wysocki said. 'Because you depress them with your talk. People like a woman to be cheerful. You can't expect to succeed in your line if you walk around like the last day of the world is beginning in two and three-quarter hours, Bulova watch time.

'The butchers from Tenth Avenue!' Josephine snarled. 'Who wants them? I give them to you as a gift.' .

Enders lay on the bed, regretting that a proud and beautiful woman like Bertha Zelinka had to sit in one of the three chairs of the lobby of the Circus Hotel on a rainy night and listen to a conversation like that. He put on the light and picked up the book he was reading. .

> *I was neither at the hot gates*
> *Nor fought in the warm rain*
> *Nor knee deep in the salt marsh, heaving a cutlass,*
> *Bitten by flies, fought . . .*

'What a night!' Josephine's voice scraped down the hallway. 'The river will be stuffed with bodies in the morning.'

Enders put down T. S. Eliot. It was hard to read T. S. Eliot in the Circus Hotel without a deep feeling of irony. Enders got up and looked around the doorpost, down the hall. The proud, poetic legs were still there, lean, muscular, beautifully shaped, aristocratic, stemming down into slim ankles and narrow feet. Enders leaned dreamily against the doorpost, regarding Miss Zelinka's legs. Music played from a well-known orchestra in a night club lit by orange lamps, where no dish cost less than a dollar seventy-five, even tomato juice, and he danced with Bertha Zelinka, both of them dressed beautifully, shiningly, and he made those deep, long eyes, charged with Northern melancholy, crinkle with laughter, and later grow sober and reflective as he talked swiftly of culture, of art, of poetry. 'Nor fought in the warm rain.' in the phrase of T. S. Eliot, a favourite of mine,. 'nor knee deep in the salt marsh . . . '

He walked quickly down the hallway, looking neither to right nor left until he stopped at the desk. 'Have there been any telephone calls for me today?' he asked Wysocki, carefully avoiding looking at Miss Zelinka.

'No,' said Wysocki. 'Not a thing.'

Enders turned and stared fully at Miss Zelinka, trying, with the deep intensity of his glance, to get her to look at him, smile at him . . .

'Heads like yours, my friend,' Josephine said, 'they find in ovens.'

Miss Zelinka sat passionless, expressionless, heedless, looking at a point twenty-five feet over Wysocki's shoulder, patiently, but coolly, in the attitude of a woman who is expecting a Lincoln to drive up at any moment and a uniformed chauffeur to spring from it and lead her fastidiously to the heavy, upholstered door, rich with heavy hardware.

Enders walked slowly back to his room. He tried to read some more. 'April is the cruellest month . . . ' He thumbed through the book. 'Here,' said she, is your card, the drowned Phoenician Sailor . . . ' Enders put the book down. He couldn't read tonight. He went to the door and looked out. The legs, silk and skin and firm muscle, were still there. Enders took a deep breath and walked back towards the desk.

'Look,' said Josephine, 'the shuttle's back.'

'I forgot to ask.' He looked straight at Wysocki. 'Is there any mail for me?'

'No mail,' said Wysocki.

'I'll tell you frankly, friend,' Josephine said. 'You should've stayed in Davenport, Iowa. That's my honest opinion. New York City will break you like a peanut shell.'

'Nobody asked for your opinion,' Wysocki said, noticing Enders peering uneasily at Miss Zelinka to see what impression Josephine's advice had made on her. 'He's a nice boy, he's educated, he's going to go a long way. Leave him alone.'

'I'm only giving him my honest opinion,' Josephine said. 'I've been in New York a dozen years. I see them begin and I see them wind up in the river.'

'Will you, for Christ's sake, stop talking about the river?' Wysocki slammed his hand on the desk.

Gratefully, Enders noticed that Miss Zelinka was listening to the conversation, that her head tilted just a little, a shade went across her disdainful, beautiful eyes.

'I come from Fall River,' Josephine said. 'I should've stayed there. At least when you're dead in Fall River they bury you. Here they leave you walk around until your friends notice it. Why did I ever leave Fall River? I was attracted by the glamour of the Great White Way.' She waved her red-and-white umbrella ironically, in salute to the city.

Enders noticed that a hint, a twitch of a smile, played at the corner of Miss Zelinka's mouth. He was glad that she'd heard Wysocki say he was educated, he was going to go a long way.

'If you'd like,' he heard his voice boom out suddenly in the direction of Miss Zelinka, 'if you'd like, if you're waiting for someone, you can wait in my room. It's not so noisy there.'

'No, thank you,' Miss Zelinka said, speaking curiously, her lips together, not showing her teeth. Her voice, behind the closed, beautiful lips, was deep and hoarse and moving, and Enders felt it grip at his throat like a cool, firm hand. He turned to Wysocki, determined now that he was not going back to his room.

'I was curious,' he said. 'Where did Bishop get that chicken he wants to sell me?'

Wysocki looked behind him carefully. 'Don't buy those chickens, Enders,' he said in a low voice. 'I advise you as a good friend. Bishop picks them up on Tenth Avenue, alongside the railroad tracks.'

'What're they doing there?' Enders asked.

'The trains bring them in from the farms, from the country,' Wysocki said. 'The one's that died on the trip for one reason or another, the trainmen throw them off the cars and they're piled up alongside the tracks and Bishop picks out the ones that looks as though they died most peaceful and he tries to sell them.' Wysocki slid back to the office door, listened guiltily for a moment for Bishop, like a spy in the movies. 'I advise you not to buy them. They're not the most nourishing articles of food in the world.'

Enders smiled. Bishop ought to be in Wall Street,' he said. 'With talent like that.'

Miss Zelinka laughed. Feeling twice as tall as had felt a moment before, Enders noticed that Miss Zelinka was laughing, quietly, and without opening her mouth, but true laughter. He laughed with her and their eyes met in friendly, understanding amusement.

'May I buy you a cup of coffee?' hurled out of his throat, at Miss Zelinka's head, like a hand grenade.

The light of thought, consideration, appeared in the large grey eyes, while Enders waited. Then Miss Zelinka smiled.

'All right,' she said. She stood up, five feet six inches tall, graceful as a duchess.

'I'll be right back,' Enders said, quickly. 'Just have to get my coat.'

He fled lightly down the hall toward his room.

'That's what keeps me poor,' Josephine said. 'Girls like that. What a night, what a dirty whore of a night!'

'I'm a dancer,' Bertha Zelinka was saying two hours later, her coat off, in Enders's room as she drank the whisky straight in one of the two water tumblers the room boasted. 'Speciality dancing.' She put the whisky down, suddenly sank beautifully to the floor in a split. 'I'm as supple as a cat.'

'I see,' Enders said, his eyes furious with admiration for Miss Zelinka, full-breasted, flat-bellied, steel-thighed, supple as a cat, spread magnificently on the dirty carpet. It was more pleasant to look at her body, now that he had seen her eating, mouth opened to reveal the poor, poverty-stricken, ruined teeth jagged and sorrowful in her mouth. 'That looks very hard to do.'

'My name's been in lights,' Miss Zelinka said from the floor. 'Please pass the whisky. From one end of the country to another. I've stopped show after show. I've got an uncanny sense of timing.' She stood up, after taking another draught of her whisky, closing her eyes with a kind of harsh rapture as the Four Roses went down past the miserable teeth, down inside the powerful, long white throat. 'I'm an actress, too, you know, Mr Enders.'

'I'm an actor,' Enders said shyly, feeling the whisky beat in his blood, keeping his eyes fiercely and wonderingly on Miss Zelinka. 'That's why I'm in New York. I'm an actor.'

'You ought to be a good actor,' Miss Zelinka said. 'You got the face for it. It's refined.' She poured herself another drink, watching the amber liquor pour into her glass with a brooding, intense expression in her face. 'I had my name in lights from coast to coast. Don't you believe it?'

'I believe it,' Enders said sincerely, noting that half the bottle was already gone.

'That's why I'm here now,' she said. She walked beautifully around the small, flaky-walled room, her hands running sorrowfully over the warped bureau, the painted bedstead. 'That's why I'm here now.' Her voice was faraway and echoing, hoarse with whisky and regret. 'I'm very much in demand, you know. I've stopped shows for ten minutes at a time. They wouldn't let me get off the stage. Musicals that cost one hun-

211

dred and fifty thousand to ring the curtain up. That's why I'm
here now,' she said mysteriously, and drained her glass. She
threw herself on the bed next to Enders, stared moodily
through almost closed eyes, at the stained and beaten ceiling.
'The Shuberts're putting on a musical. They want me for it.
Rehearsals are on Fifty-second Street, so I thought I'd move
close by for the time being.' She sat up, silently reached for
the bottle, poured with the fixed expression, brooding and
infatuate, which she reserved for the distillers' product. Enders,
too full for words, sitting on the same bed with a woman who
looked like Greta Garbo, who had stopped musical shows with
speciality dancing from coast to coast, who got drunk with
the assured yet ferocious grace of a young society matron,
watched her every move, with hope, admiration, growing passion.

'You might ask,' Miss Zelinka said, 'what is a person like
myself doing in a rat-hole like this.' She waited, but Enders
merely gulped silently at his whisky. She chuckled and patted
his hand. 'You're a nice boy. Iowa, you said? You come from
Iowa?'

'Iowa.'

'Corn,' Miss Zelinka said. 'That's what they grow in Iowa.'
She nodded, having placed Iowa and Enders firmly in her
mind. 'I passed through Iowa on my way to Hollywood.' Half
the whisky in her glass disappeared.

'Have you acted in pictures?' Enders asked, impressed, sitting on the same bed with a woman who had been in Hollywood.

Miss Zelinka laughed moodily. 'Hollywood!' She finished
her drink. 'Don't look for my footprints in front of Grauman's
Chinese.' She reached fluently for the bottle.

'It seems to me,' Enders said seriously, breathing deeply
because Miss Zelinka was leaning across him for the moment.
'It seems to me you'd do very well. You're beautiful and you've
got a wonderful voice.'

Miss Zelinka laughed again. 'Look at me,' she said.

Enders looked at her.

'Do I remind you of anybody?' Miss Zelinka asked.

Enders nodded.

Miss Zelinka drank moodily. 'I look like Greta Garbo,' she
said. 'Nobody could deny that. I'm not being vain when I tell
you when I photograph you couldn't tell me apart from the
Swede.' She sipped her whisky, ran it lovingly around in her

mouth, swallowed slowly. 'A woman who looks like Greta
Garbo in Hollywood is like the fifth leg on a racehorse. Do you
understand what I mean?'

Enders nodded sympathetically.

'It's my private curse,' Miss Zelinka said, tears looming in
her eyes like mist over the ocean. She jumped up, shaking her
head, walked lightly and dramatically around the room. 'I have
no complaints,' she said. 'I've done very well. I live in a two-
room suite on the twentieth floor of an hotel on Seventy-fifth
Street. Overlooking the park. All my trunks and bags are up
there. I just took a few things with me, until the rehearsals are
over. Seventy-fifth Street, on the East Side, is too far away;
when you're rehearsing a musical comedy, you got to be on tap
twenty-four hours a day for the Shuberts. A very luxurious
two-room suite in the Hotel Chalmers. It's very exclusive, but
it's too far from Fifty-second Street.' She poured some more
whisky for herself, and Enders noticed that the bottle was
almost empty. 'Oh, yes,' she said, crooning to the glass in her
hand, 'I've done very well. I've danced all over the country. In
the most exclusive night-spots, I was the featured entertainment. I'm very greatly in demand.' She sat down, close to him,
her body moving gently and rhythmically as she spoke.
'Seattle, Chicago, Los Angeles, Detroit.' She gulped her whisky
and her eyes clouded with a final, deep, vague mist and her
voice suddenly got very throaty and hoarse. 'Miami, Florida.'
She sat absolutely still and the cloud dissolved into tears and
the tears coursed slowly down her face.

'What's the matter?' Enders asked anxiously. 'Did I do
something?'

Miss Zelinka threw the empty tumbler against the opposite
wall. It broke heavily and sullenly, scattered over the carpet.
She threw herself back on the bed, wept. 'Miami, Florida,' she
sobbed. 'Miami, Florida . . .'

Enders patted her shoulder consolingly.

'I danced in The Golden Horn in Miami, Florida,' she cried.
'It was a Turkish night club. Very exclusive.'

'Why're you crying, darling?' Enders asked, feeling sorry
for her, but elated, too, because he had said 'darling'.

'Every time I think of Miami, Florida,' Miss Zelinka said, 'I
cry.'

'Can I do anything to help?' Enders held her hand softly.

'It was January, 1936,' Miss Zelinka's voice throbbed with
old, hopeless, broken tragedy, forlorn as the story of a siege of

213

a lost and ruined village. 'I was dressed in Turkish garments: a brassiere, and veils around my legs and nothing around the middle. At the end of the dance I had to do a back-bend. I leaned back and touched the floor with my hands, with my hair falling down to the floor. There was a bald man. There was a convention of the Metal-Trades Union in Miami, Florida. He had on a badge. The whole night club was full of them.' The tears and the anguish pulled at her face. 'I'll remember that bald son of a bitch until the day I die. There was no music at that part of the dance. Drums and tambourines. He leaned over and put an olive in my navel and sprinkled it with salt.' Miss Zelinka rolled suddenly over on her face and, clutching the bedspread, her shoulders heaving, burrowed into the greyish cotton. 'It was a cartoon. He saw it in a cartoon in a magazine. It's funny in a magazine, but wait until it happens to you! The humiliation,' she wept. 'Every time I think of the humiliation I want to die. Miami, Florida.'

Enders watched the bedspread stain with tears, mascara and rouge. With genuine sympathy, he put his arm around her. 'I want to be treated with respect,' Miss Zelinka wailed. 'I was brought up in a good family, why shouldn't I be treated with respect? That fat, bald man, with the badge from the Metal-Trades Union Convention. He leaned over and put the olive in my navel like an egg in an egg cup and sprinkled salt like he was starting breakfast and everybody laughed and laughed, including the orchestra . . . ' Her voice went wailing up the air well, lost, despairing, full of an ancient and irreparable sorrow.

She sat up and threw her arms around Enders, digging her grief-torn head into his shoulder, clutching him with strong hands, both of them rocking back and forth like Jews praying, on the enamelled bed that squeaked and wailed in the little room.

'Hold me tight,' she wept, 'hold me tight. I haven't got a two-room suite on East Seventy-fifth Street. I got no trunks in the Hotel Chalmers. Hold me tight.' Her hands dug into him and her tears and rouge and mascara stained his coat. 'The Shuberts aren't giving me a job. Why do I lie, why do I always lie?' She lifted her head, kissed his throat fiercely. He shook at the soft, violent pressure, at the wetness of her lips and the tragic and exhilarating trickle of her tears under his chin, knowing that he was going to have this woman, this Bertha Zelinka. Lonely, far from home on a rainy night, the city was pulling him in, making a place in its wild and ludicrous life for him. As he kissed her, this woman who looked like Greta Garbo, the century's dream of passion and tragedy and beauty, this woman whom he had met in a rat-tenanted lobby off Colombus Circle, among whores thinking of death and a Pole in an orange tie checking in each night's transients, age and sin, at reasonable rates, Enders felt suddenly at home, accounted for. The city had produced for him a great beauty, supple as a cat, full of lies and whisky and ancient, shadowy victories, a woman with magnificent, proud legs and deep, storm eyes who wept bitterly behind the frail, warped door because once, in 1936, a bald man from a Metal-Trades Union had put an olive in her navel. Enders held Bertha Zelinka's head in his two hands, looked intently at the bony, drunken, beautiful, tear-stained face. Bertha Zelinka peered longingly and sadly at him through half-closed classic lids, her mouth hanging softly open in passion and promise, her poor jagged teeth showing behind the long, heart-breaking lips. He kissed her, feeling deep within him, that in its own way, in this rainy night, the city had put out its hand in greeting, had called, in its own voice, wry and ironic, 'Welcome Citizen.'

Gratefully, near tears, hating himself, his hands shaking exultantly, Enders bent to his knees and took the scraped, year-worn shoes, swollen with the streets' rain, from the long and handsome feet of Bertha Zelinka.

Gunners' Passage

'In Brazil,' Whitejack was saying, 'the problem was girls. American girls.'

They were lying on the comfortable cots with the mosquito netting looped gracefully over their heads and the barracks quiet and empty except for the two of them and shaded and cool when you remembered that outside the full sun of Africa stared down.

'Three months in the jungle, on rice and monkey meat.' Whitejack lit a large, long, nickel cigar and puffed deeply, squinting up at the tin roof. 'When we got to Rio we felt we deserved an American girl. So the Lieutenant and Johnny and myself, we got the telephone directory of the American Embassy, and we went down the list, calling up likely names – secretaries, typists, interpreters, filing clerks . . . ' Whitejack grinned up at the ceiling. He had a large, sunburned, rough face, that was broken into good looks by the white teeth of his smile, and his speech was Southern, but not the kind of Southern that puts a Northener's teeth on edge.

'It was the Lieutenant's idea, and by the time we got to the Q's he was ready to give up but we hit pay dirt on the S's.' Slowly he blew out a long draught of cigar smoke. 'Uh-uh,' he said, closing his eyes reflectively. 'Two months and eleven days of honey and molasses. Three tender and affectionate American girls as loving as the day is long, with their own flat. Beer in the icebox from Sunday to Sunday, steaks big enough to saddle a mule with, and nothing to do, just lie on the beach in the afternoon and go swimmin' when the mood seized yuh. On *per diem*.'

'How were the girls?' Stais asked. 'Pretty?'

'Well, Sergeant.' Whitejack paused and pursed his lips with thoughtful honesty. 'To tell you the truth, Sergeant, the girls the Lieutenant and Johnny Moffat had were as smart and pretty as chipmunks. Mine . . . ' Once more he paused. 'Ordinarily, my girl would find herself hard put to collect a man in the middle of a full division of infantry soldiers. She was small and runty and she had less curves than a rifle barrel, and she wore glasses. But from the first time she looked at me, I could see she wasn't interested in Johnny or the Lieutenant. She looked at me and behind her glasses her eyes were soft and hopeful and appealing.' Whitejack flicked the cigar ash off into the little tin can on his bare chest he was using as an ash-tray. 'Sometimes,' he said slowly, 'a man feels mighty small if he just thinks of himself and turns down an appeal like that. Let me tell you something, Sergeant. I was in Rio two months and eleven days and I didn't even look at another woman. All those dark-brown women walkin' along the beach three-quarters out of their bathing suits, just wavin' it in front of your face . . . I didn't look at them. This runty, skinny little thing with glasses was the most lovin' and satisfactory and decent little person a man could possibly conceive of, and a man'd just have to be hog-greedy with sex to have winked an eye at another woman.' Whitejack doused his cigar, took his ash-tray off his chest, rolled over on his belly, adjusted the towel properly over his bare buttocks. 'Now,' he said, 'I'm going to get myself a little sleep . . .'

In a moment Whitejack was snoring gently, his tough mountaineer's face tucked childishly into the crook of his arm. Outside the barracks the native boy hummed low and wild to himself as he ironed a pair of suntan trousers on the shady side of the building. From the field, two hundred yards away, again and again came the sliding roar of engines climbing or descending the afternoon sky.

Stais closed his eyes wearily. Ever since he'd got into Accra he had done nothing but sleep and lie on his cot, day-dreaming, listening to Whitejack talk.

'Hi,' Whitejack had said, as Stais had come slowly into the barracks two days before, 'which way you going?'

'Home,' Stais had said, smiling wearily as he did every time he said it. 'Going home. Which way you going?'

'Not home.' Whitejack had grinned a little. 'Not home at all.'

Stais liked to listen to Whitejack. Whitejack talked about America, about the woods of the Blue Ridge Mountains where he had been in the forestry service, about his mother's cooking and how he had owned great dogs which had been extraordinary at finding a trail and holding it, about how they had

217

tried hunting deer in the hills from the medium bomber, no good because of the swirling winds rising from the gorges, about pleasant indiscriminate week-end parties in the woods with his friend Johnny Moffat and the girls from the mill in the next town . . . Stais had been away from America for nineteen months now and Whitejack's talk made his native country seem present and pleasantly real to him.

'There was a man in my town by the name of Thomas Wolfe,' Whitejack had said irrelevantly that morning. 'He was a great big feller and he went away to New York to be an author. Maybe you heard of him?'

'Yes,' said Stais. 'I read two books of his.'

'Well, I read that book of his,' said Whitejack, 'and the people in town were yellin' to lynch him for a while, but I read that book and he got that town down fair and proper, and when they brought him back dead I came down from the hills and I went to his funeral. There were a lot of important people from New York and over to Chapel Hill down for the funeral and it was a hot day, too, and I'd never met the feller, but I felt it was only right to go to his funeral after readin' his book. And the whole town was there, very quiet, although just five years before they were yellin' to lynch him, and it was a sad and impressive sight and I'm glad I went.'

And another time, the slow, deep voice rolling between sleep and dreams in the shaded heat . . . 'My mother takes a quail and bones it, then she scoops out a great big sweet potato and lays some bacon on it, then she puts the quail in and cooks it slow for three hours, bastin' it with butter all the time . . . You got to try that some time . . .'

'Yes,' said Stais, 'I will.'

Stais did not have a high priority number and there seemed to be a flood of colonels surging towards America, taking all the seats on the C-54's setting out westward, so he'd had to wait. It hadn't been bad. Just to lie down, stretched full-out, unbothered, these days, was holiday enough after Greece, and anyway he didn't want to arrive home, in front of his mother, until he'd stopped looking like a tired old man. And the barracks had been empty and quiet and the chow good at the transient mess and you could get Coca-Cola and chocolate milk at the PX. The rest of the enlisted men in Whitejack's crew were young and ambitious and were out swimming all day and going to the movies or playing poker in another barracks all night, and Whitejack's talk was smooth and amusing in the periods between sleep and dreams. Whitejack was an aerial photographer and gunner in a mapping-and-survey squadron and he'd been in Alaska and Brazil and back to the States and now was on his way to India, full of conversation. He was in a Mitchell squadron and the whole squadron was supposed to be on its way together, but two of the Mitchells had crashed and burned on the take-off at Natal, as Whitejack's plane had circled the field, waiting to form up. The rest of the squadron had been held at Natal and Whitejack's plane had been sent on to Accra across the ocean, by itself.

Vaguely and slowly, lying on the warm cot, with the wild song the Negro boy outside the window, Stais thought of the two Mitchells burning between sea and jungle three thousand miles away, and other planes burning elsewhere, and what it was going to be like sitting down in the armchair in his own house and looking across the room at his mother, and the pretty Viennese girl in Jerusalem, and the DC-3 coming down slowly, like an angel in the dusk to the rough secret pasture in the Peloponnesian hills . . .

He fell asleep. His bones knit gently into dreams on the soft cot, with the sheets, in the quiet barracks, and he was over Athens again, with the ruins pale and shining on the hills, and the fighters boring in, and Lathrop saying, over the intercom, as they persisted in to a hundred, fifty-yards, twisting, swiftly and shiftily in the bright Greek sky. 'They grounded all the students today. They have the instructors up this afternoon . . . And, suddenly, and wildly, fifty feet over the Ploesti, with Liberators going down into the filth in dozens, flaming . . . Then swimming off the white beach at Benghazi with the dead boys playing in the mild, tideless swell, then the parachute pulling at every muscle in his body, then the green and forest blue of Minnesota woods and his father, fat and small, sleeping on pine needles on his Sunday off, then Athens again, Athens . . .

'I don't know what's come over the Lieutenant,' a new voice was saying as Stais came out of his dream. 'He passes us on the field and he just don't seem to see us.'

Stais opened his eyes. Novak, a farm boy from Oklahoma, was sitting on the edge of Whitejack's bed, talking. 'It has all the guys real worried.' He had a high, shy, rather girlish voice. 'I used to think they never came better than the Lieutenant . . . Now . . . ' Novak shrugged. 'If he does see you, he snaps at you like he was the General George Patton.'

'Maybe,' Whitejack said, 'maybe seeing Lieutenant Brogan

go down in Natal . . . He and Brogan were friends since they were ten years old. Like as if I saw Johnny Moffat go down . . . '

'It's not that.' Novak went over to his own cot and got out his writing pad. 'It began back in Miami four weeks ago. Didn't you notice it?'

'I noticed it,' Whitejack said slowly.

'You ought to ask him about it.' Novak stared writing a letter. 'You and him are good friends. After all, going into combat now, it's bad, the Lieutenant just lookin' through us when he passes us on the field. You don't think he's drunk all the time, do you?'

'He's not drunk.'

'You ought to ask him.'

'Maybe I will.' Whitejack sat up, tying the towel around his lean middle. 'Maybe I will.' He looked forlornly down at his stomach. 'Since I got into the Army, I've turned pig-fat. On the day I took the oath, I was twenty-eight and one-half inches around the waist. Today I'm thirty-two and three-quarters, if I'm an inch. The Army . . . Maybe I shouldn't've joined. I was in a reserved profession, and I was the sole support of an ailing mother.'

'Why did you join?' Stais asked.

'Oh,' Whitejack smiled at him, 'you're awake. Feeling any better, Sergeant?'

'Feeling fine, thanks. Why did you join?'

'Well . . . ' Whitejack rubbed the side of his jaw. 'Well . . . I waited and I waited. I sat up in my cabin in the hills and I tried to avoid listenin' to the radio, and I waited and I waited, and finally I went downtown to my mother and I said "Ma'am, I just can't wait any longer," and I joined up.'

'When was that?' Stais asked.

'Eight days . . . ' Whitejack lay down again, plumping the pillow under his head. 'Eight days after Pearl Harbour.'

'Sergeant,' Novak said, 'Sergeant Stais, you don't mind if I tell my girl you're a Greek, do you?'

'No,' Stais said gravely. 'I don't mind. You know, I was born in Minnesota.'

'I know,' said Novak, writing industriously. 'But your parents came from Greece. My girl'll be very interested, your parents coming from Greece and you bombing Greece and being shot down there.'

'What do you mean, your girl?' Whitejack asked. 'I thought

220

you said she was going around with a Technical Sergeant in Flushing, Long Island.'

'That's true,' Novak said apologetically. 'But I still like to think of her as my girl.'

'It's the ones that stay at home,' said Whitejack darkly, 'that get all the stripes and all the girls. My motto is: Don't write to a girl once you get out of pillow-case distance from her.'

'I like to write to this girl in Flushing, Long Island,' Novak said, his voice shy but stubborn. Then to Stais, 'How many days were you in the hills before the Greek farmers found you?'

'Fourteen,' said Stais.

'And how many of you were wounded?'

'Three. Out of seven. The others were dead.'

'Maybe,' Whitejack said, 'he doesn't like to talk about it, Charley.'

'Oh, I'm sorry.' Novak looked up, his young, unlined face crossed with concern.

'That's all right,' Stais said. 'I don't mind.'

'Did you tell them you were a Greek too?' Novak asked.

'When one finally showed up who could speak English.'

'That must be funny,' Novak said reflectively. 'Being a Greek, bombing Greece, not speaking the language . . . Can I tell my girl they had a radio and they radioed to Cairo . . . ?'

'It's the girl of a Technical Sergeant in Flushing, Long Island,' Whitejack chanted. Why don't you look facts in the face?'

'I prefer it this way,' Novak said with dignity.

'I guess you can tell about the radio,' Stais said. 'It was pretty long ago. Three days later, the DC-3 came down through a break in the clouds. It'd been raining all the time and it just stopped for about thirty minutes at dusk and that plane came down throwin' water fifteen feet in the air . . . We cheered, but we couldn't get up from where we were sitting, any of us, because we were too weak to stand.'

'I got to write that to my girl,' Novak said. 'Too weak to stand.'

'Then it started to rain again and the field was hip-deep in mud and when we all got into the DC-3, we couldn't get it started.' Stais spoke calmly and thoughtfully, as though he were alone, reciting to himself. 'We were just bogged down in that Greek mud. Then the pilot got out – he was a captain – and he looked around, with the rain coming down and all those farmers just standing there, sympathising with him, and nothing anyone could do and he just cursed for ten minutes. He was from San Francisco and he really knew how to curse. Then everybody started breaking branches off the trees in the woods around that pasture, even two of us who couldn't stand one hour before, and we just covered that big DC-3 complete with branches and waited for the rain to stop. We just sat in the woods and prayed no German patrols would come out in weather like that. In those three days I learned five words of Greek.'

'What are they?' Novak asked.

'*Vouno*,' Stais said. 'That means mountain. *Vrohi:* Rains. *Theos:* God. *Avrion:* Tomorrow. And *Yassov:* That means farewell.'

'*Yassov*,' Novak said. 'Farewell.'

'Then the sun came out and the field started to steam and nobody said anything. We just sat there, watching the water dry off the grass, then the puddles started to go here and there, then the mud to cake a little. Then we got into the DC-3 and the Greeks pushed and hauled for a while and we broke loose and got out. And those farmers just standing below waving at us, as though they were seeing us off at Grand Central Station. Ten miles farther on we went right over a German camp. They fired at us a couple of times, but they didn't come anywhere close. The best moment of my whole life was getting into that hospital bed in Cairo, Egypt. I just stood there and looked at it for a whole minute, looking at the sheets. Then I got in very slow.'

'Did you ever find out what happened to those Greeks?' Novak asked.

'No,' said Stais. 'I guess they're still there, waiting for us to come back some day.'

There was silence, broken only be the slow scratching of Novak's pen. Stais thought of the thin, dark mountain faces of the men he had last seen, fading away, waving, standing in the scrub and short silver grass of the hill pasture near the Aegean Sea. They had been cheerful and anxious to please, and there was a look on their faces that made you feel they expected to die.

'How many missions were you on?' Novak asked.

'Twenty-one and a half,' Stais said. He smiled. 'I count the last one as half.'

'How old are you?' Novak was obviously keeping the Technical Sergeant's girl carefully posted on all points of interest.

'Nineteen.'

'You look older,' said Whitejack.

'Yes,' said Stais.

'A lot older.'

'Yes.'

'Did you shoot down any planes?' Novak peered at him shyly, his red face uncertain and embarrassed, like a little boy asking a doubtful question about girls. 'Personally?'

'Two,' Stais said. 'Personally.'

'What did you feel?'

'Why don't you leave him alone?' Whitejack said. 'He's too tired to keep his eyes open, as it is.'

'I felt – relieved,' Stais said. He tried to think of what he'd really felt when the tracers went in and the Focke-Wolfe started to smoke like a crazy smudge-pot and the German pilot fought wildly for half a second with the cowling and then didn't fight wildly any more. There was no way of telling these men, no way of remembering, in words, himself. 'You'll find out,' he said. 'Soon enough. The sky's full of Germans.'

'Japs,' Whitejack said. 'We're going to India.'

'The sky's full of Japs.'

There was silence once more, with the echo of the word 'Japs' rustling thinly in the long, quiet room, over the empty rows of cots. Stais felt the old waving dizziness starting behind his eyes that the doctor in Cairo had said came from shock or starvation or exposure or all of these things, and lay back, still keeping his eyes open, as it became worse and waved more violently when he closed his eyes.

'One more question,' Novak said. 'Are – are guys afraid?'

'You'll be afraid,' Stais said.

'Do you want to send that back to your girl in Flushing?' Whitejack asked sardonically.

'No,' said Novak quietly. 'I wanted that for myself.'

'If you want to sleep,' said Whitejack, 'I'll shut this farmer up.'

'Oh, no,' said Stais. 'I'm pleased to talk.'

'If you're not careful,' Whitejack said, he'll talk about his girl in Flushing.'

'I'd be pleased to hear it,' said Stais.

'It's only natural I should want to talk about her,' Novak said defensively. 'She was the best girl I ever knew in my whole life. I'd've married her if I could.'

'My motto,' said Whitejack, 'is never marry a girl who goes to bed with you the first time out. The chances are she isn't pure. The second time – that, of course, is different.' He winked at Stais.

'I was in Flushing, Long Island, taking a five-weeks' course in aerial cameras,' Novak said, 'and I was living at the Y.M.C.A. . . .'

'This is where I leave.' Whitejack got off the bed and put on his pants.

'The Y.M.C.A. was very nice. There was bathrooms for every two rooms, and the food was very good,' said Novak, talking earnestly to Stais, 'but I must confess I was lonely in Flushing, Long Island . . .'

'I will be back,' Whitejack was buttoning up his shirt, 'for the ninth instalment.'

'As long as you're going out,' Novak said to him, 'I wish you'd talk to the Lieutenant. It really makes me feel queer passing him, and him just looking through me like I was a window-pane.'

'Maybe I'll talk to the Lieutenant. And leave the Sergeant alone. Remember he's a tired man who's been to the war and he needs his rest.' Whitejack went out.

Novak stared after him. 'There's something wrong with him, too,' he said. 'Just lying on his back here for ten days, reading and sleeping. He never did that before. He was the liveliest man in the United States Air Force. Seeing those two planes go down . . . It's a funny thing, you fly with fellers all over the world, over America, Brazil, Alaska; you watch them shoot porpoises and sharks in gunnery practice over the Gulf Stream, you get drunk with them, go to their weddings, talk to them over the radio with their planes maybe a hundred feet away, in the air – and after all that flying, in one minute, for no reason, two planes go down. Fourteen fellers you've been livin' with for over a year . . . ' Novak shook his head. 'There was a particular friend of Whitejack's in one of those planes. Frank Sloan. Just before we left Miami, they had a big fight. Frank went off and married a girl that Whitejack's been going with off and on for a year, every time we hit Miami. Whitejack told him he was crazy, half the squadron had slept with the lady, and that was true, too, and just to teach him a lesson he'd sleep with her himself after they'd been married. And he did, too . . . ' Novak sighed. 'A lot of funny things happen in the Army, when fellers've been together a long time and get to know each other real well. And then, one minute, the Mitchell goes down. I guess Whitejack must've felt sort of queer, watching Frankie burn.' Novak had put his writing pad down and now he screwed the top on his fountain-pen. 'The truth is,' he said, 'I don't feel so solid myself. That's why I like to talk. Especially to you . . . You've been through it. You're young, but you've been through it. But if it's any bother to you, I'll keep quiet . . . '

'No,' said Stais, still lying back, abstractedly wondering whether the waving would get worse or better, 'not at all.'

'This girl in Flushing, Long Island,' Novak said slowly. 'It's easy for Whitejack to make fun of me. The girls fall all over themselves chasing after him; he has no real conception of what it's like to be a man like me. Not very good-looking. Not much money. Not an officer. Not humorous. Shy.'

Stais couldn't help grinning. 'You're going to have a tough time in India.'

'I know,' Novak said. 'I have resigned myself to not having a girl until the armistice. How did you do with the girls in the Middle East?' he asked politely.

'There was a nice Viennese girl in Jerusalem,' Stais said dreamily. 'But otherwise zero. You have to be very good unless you're an officer in the Middle East.'

'That's what I heard,' Novak said sorrowfully. 'Well, it won't be so different to me from Oklahoma. That was the nice thing about this girl in Flushing, Long Island. She saw me come into the jewellery store where she worked and . . . I was in my fatigues and I was with a very smooth feller who made a date with her for that night. But she smiled at me, and I knew if I had the guts I could ask her for a date, too. But of course I didn't. But then later that night I was sitting in my room in the Y.M.C.A. and my phone rang. It was this girl. The other feller had stood her up, she said, and would I take her out.' Novak smiled dimly, thinking of that tremulous moment of glory in the small hotel room far away. 'I got my fatigues off in one minute and shaved and showered and I picked her up. We went to Coney Island. It was the first time in my entire life I had ever seen Coney Island. It took three and a half weeks for me to finish my course and I went out with that girl every single night. Nothing like that ever happened to me before in my life – a girl who just wanted to see me every night of the week. Then the night before I was due to leave to join my squadron she told me she had got permission to take the afternoon off and she would like to see me off if I let her. I called at the jewellery shop at noon and her boss shook my hand and she had a package under her arm and we got into the subway and we rode to New York City. Then we went into a cafeteria and had a wonderful lunch and she saw me off and gave me the package. It was Schrafft's candy, and she was crying at the gate there, crying for me, and she said she would like me to write, no matter what . . . ' Novak paused and Stais could tell that the scene at the gate, the hurrying crowds, the package of Schrafft's chocolates, the weeping young girl, were as clear as the afternoon sunlight to Novak there on the coast of Africa. 'So I keep writing,' Novak said. 'She's written me she has a Technical Sergeant now, but I keep writing. I haven't seen her in a year and a half, and what's a girl to do? Do you blame her?'

'No,' said Stais. 'I don't blame her.'

'I hope I haven't bored you,' Novak said.

'Not at all.' Stais smiled at him. Suddenly the dizziness had gone and he could close his eyes. As he drifted down into that weird and ever-present pool of sleep in which he half-lived these days, he heard Novak say, 'Now I have to write my mother.'

Outside, the Negro boy sang and the planes grumbled down from the Atlantic and laboriously set out across the Sahara Desert.

Dreams again. Arabs, bundled in rags, driving camels along the perimeter of the field, outlined against the parked Liberators and waiting bombs, two Mitchells still burning on the shores of Brazil and Frank Sloan burning there and circling above him, Whitejack, who had told him he'd sleep with his wife and had, the hills around Jerusalem, gnarled, rocky, dusty, with the powdered green of olive groves set on slopes here and there, clinging against the desert wind. Mitchells slamming along the gorges of the Blue Ridge Mountains, bucking in the updraughts, their guns going, hunting deer, the Mediterranean, bluer than anything in America, below them on the way home from Italy, coming down below oxygen level, with the boys singing dirty songs over the intercom and leave in Alexandria ahead of them. The girl from Flushing, Long Island, quietly going hand in hand with Novak to Coney Island on a summer's night . . .

It was Whitejack who awakened him. He woke slowly. It was dark outside and the electric light was shining in his eyes and Whitejack was standing over him, shaking him gently.

'I thought you'd like to know,' Whitejack was saying, 'your name's on the bulletin board. You're leaving tonight.'

'Thanks,' Stais said, dimly grateful at being shaken out of the broken and somehow sorrowful dreams.

'I took the liberty of initialling it for you, opposite your name,' Whitejack said. 'Save you a trip up to the field.'

'Thanks,' said Stais. 'Very kind of you.'

'Also,' said Whitejack, 'there's fried chicken for chow.'

Stais pondered over the fried chicken. He was a little hungry, but the effort of getting up and putting on his shoes and walking the hundred yards to the mess-hall had to be weighed in the balance. 'Thanks. I'll just lie right here,' he said. 'Any news of your boys?' he asked.

'Yes,' said Whitejack. 'The squadron came in.'

'That's good.'

'All except one plane,' Whitejack sat down on the end of Stais's cot. His voice was soft and expressionless, under the bright electric light. 'Johnny Moffat's plane.'

In all the months that Stais had been in the Air Force, on fields to which planes had failed to return, he had learned that there was nothing to say. He was only nineteen years old, but he had learned that. So he lay quiet.

'They got separated in clouds on the way out of Ascension, and they never picked them up again. There's still a chance,' Whitejack said, 'that they'll drop in any minute.' He looked at his watch. 'Still a chance for another hour and forty minutes...'

There was still nothing to say, so Stais lay silent.

'Johnny Moffat,' said Whitejack, 'at one time looked as though he was going to marry my sister. In a way, it's a good thing he didn't. It'd be a little hard, being brothers-in-law, on some of the parties the Air Force goes on in one place and another.' Whitejack fell silent, looked down at his belly. Deliberately, he let his belt out a notch. He pulled it to, with a severe little click. 'That fried chicken was mighty good,' he said. 'You sure you want to pass it up?'

'I'm saving my appetite,' Stais said, 'for my mother's cooking.'

'My sister,' said Whitejack, 'was passing fond of Johnny, and I have a feeling when he gets home from the war and settles down, she's going to snag him. She came to me right before I left and she asked me if I would let her have ten acres on the north side of my property and three acres of timber

227

to build their house. I said it was O.K. with me.' He was silent again, thinking of the rolling ten acres of upland meadow in North Carolina and the three tall acres of standing timber, oak and pine, from which it would be possible to build a strong country house. 'There's nobody in the whole world I'd rather have living on my property than Johnny Moffat. I've known him for twenty years and I've had six fist fights with him and won them all, and been alone with him in the woods for two months at a time, and I still say that . . . ' He got up and went over to his own cot, then turned and came back. 'By the way,' he said softly, 'this is between you and me, Sergeant.'

'Sure,' said Stais.

'My sister said she'd murder me for my hide and taller if I ever let Johnny know what was in store for him.' He grinned a little. 'Women're very confident in certain fields,' he said. 'And I never did tell Johnny, not even when I was so drunk I was singing "Casey Jones" naked in the middle of the city of Tampa at three o'clock in the morning.' He went over to his musette bag and got out a cigar and thoughtfully lit it. 'You'd be surprised,' he said, 'how fond you become of nickel cigars in the Army.'

'I tried smoking,' said Stais. 'I think I'll wait until I get a little older.'

Whitejack sat heavily on his own cot. 'Do you think they'll send you out to fight again?' he asked.

Stais stared up at the ceiling. 'I wouldn't be surprised,' he said. 'There's nothing really wrong with me. I'm just tired.'

Whitejack nodded, smoking slowly. 'By the way,' he said, 'you heard us talking about the Lieutenant, didn't you?'

'Yes.'

'I went out to the field and had a little conversation with him. He's just been sittin' there all day and most of the night since we got here, outside the Operations Room, just lookin' and starin' across at the planes comin' in. Him and me, we've been good friends for a long time and I asked him pointblank. I said, "Freddie," I said, "there's a question the boy's're askin' themselves these days about you.' And he said, "What's the matter?" And I said, "The boys're asking if you've turned bad. You pass 'em and you don't even look at them as though you recognise 'em. What is it, you turn G.I. after a year?" I said. He looked at me and then he looked at the ground and he didn't say anything for maybe a minute. Then he said, "I beg your pardon, Arnold. It never occurred to me." Then he told me what was

228

on his mind.' Whitejack looked at his watch, almost automatically, then lifted his head again. 'Ever since we got the order to go overseas he's been worrying. About the waistgunner and his navigator.'

'What's he worrying about?' For a moment a crazy list of all the thousand things you can worry about in the crew of one aeroplane flashed through Stais's head.

'They're not fighting men,' Whitejack said slowly. 'They're both good fellers, you wouldn't want better, but the Lieutenant's been watchin' 'em for a long time on the ground, in the air, at their guns, and he's convinced they won't measure. And he feels he's responsible for taking the Mitchell in and getting it out with as many of us alive as possible and he feels the waist-gunner and the navigator're dangerous to have in the plane. And he's makin' up his mind to put in a request for two new men when we get to India, and he can't bear to think of what it'll do to the gunner and the navigator when they find out he's asked to have 'em grounded, and that's why he just sits there outside Operations, not even seein' us when we go by . . . ' Whitejack sighed. 'He's twenty-two years old, the Lieutenant. It's a strain, something like that, for a man twenty-two years old. If you see Novak, you won't tell him anything, will you?'

'No,' said Stais.

'I suppose things like this come up all the time in any army.'

'All the time,' said Stais.

Whitejack looked at his watch. Outside there was the growing and lapsing roar of engines that had been the constant sound of both their lives for so many months.

'Ah,' said Whitejack, 'they should've put me in the infantry. I can hit a rabbit at three hundred yards with a rifle; they put me in the Air Force and give me a camera . . . Well, Sergeant, I think it's about time you were movin'.'

Slowly, Stais got up. He put on his shoes and put his shaving kit into his musette bag and slung it over his shoulder.

'You ready?' asked Whitejack.

'Yes,' said Stais.

'That all the baggage you got – that little musette bag?'

'Yes,' said Stais. 'I was listed as missing, presumed dead, and they sent all my stuff into the supply room and all my personal belongings home to my mother.'

Stais looked around the barracks. It shone in the harsh Army light of barracks at night all over the world, by now

229

familiar, homelike, to all the men who passed through them. He had left nothing.

They walked out into the soft, engine-filled night. A beacon flashed nervously across the sky, dimming the enormous pale twinkle of Southern stars for a moment. They walked slowly, stepping cautiously over the ditches dug for the flood rains of the African West Coast.

As they passed the Operations Room, Stais saw a young lieutenant slumped down in a wobbly old wicker chair, staring out across the field.

'They come yet?' Whitejack asked.

'No,' said the Lieutenant, without looking up.

Stais went into the building and into the room where they had the rubber raft and the patented radio and the cloth painted blue on one side and yellow on the other. A fat middle-aged A.T.C. captain wearily told them about ditching procedure. There were more than thirty people in the room, all passengers on Stais's plane. There were two small, yellow Chinese who were going to be airsick and five bouncing fat Red Cross women, and three sergeants with a lot of Air Force medals, trying not to seem excited about going home, and two colonels in the Engineers, looking too old for this war. Stais only half listened as the fat captain explained how to inflate the raft, what strings to pull, what levers to move, where to find the waterproofed Bible . . .

Whitejack was standing outside when Stais started for his plane. He gave Stais a slip of paper. 'It's my home address,' he said. 'After the war, just come down some time in October and I'll take you hunting.'

'Thank you very much,' said Stais gravely. Over Whitejack's shoulder he saw the Lieutenant, still slumped in the wicker chair, still staring fixedly and unrelievedly out across the dark field.

Whitejack walked over to the great plane with Stais, along the oil-spattered concrete of the runway, among the Chinese and loud Red Cross women and the sergeants. They stopped, without a word, at the steps going up to the doorway of the plane and the other passengers filed past them.

They stood there, silently, with the two days of random conversation behind them and Brazil and Athens behind them, and five hundred flights behind them, and Jerusalem and Miami behind them, and the girls from Vienna and the American Embassy and Flushing, Long Island, behind them, and the Greek mountaineers behind them and Thomas Wolfe's funeral, and friends burning like torches, and dogs under treed raccoons in the Blue Ridge Mountains behind them, and a desperate twenty-two-year-old Lieutenant painfully staring across a dusty airfield for ten days behind them, and the Mediterranean and the hospital bed in Cairo and Johnny Moffat wandering that night over the Southern Atlantic, with ten acres of meadow and three acres of timber for his house, and Whitejack's sister waiting for him, all behind them. And, ahead of Stais, home and a mother who had presumed him dead and wept over his personal belongings, and ahead of Whitejack the cold, bitter mountains of India and China and the tearing dead sound of the fifties and the sky full of Japs . . .

'All right, Sergeant,' the voice of the Lieutenant checking the passengers. 'Get on.'

Stais waved, a little broken wave, at Whitejack standing there. 'See you,' he said, 'in North Carolina.'

'Some October.' Whitejack smiled a little in the light of the floodlamps.

The door closed and Stais sat down in the seat in front of the two Chinese.

'I think these planes are absolutely charming,' one of the Red Cross women was saying loudly. 'Don't you?'

The engines started and the big plane began to roll. Stais looked out of the window. A plane was landing. It came slowly into the light of the runway lamps and set down heavily, bumping wearily. Stais stared. It was a Mitchell. Stais sighed to himself. As the big C-54 wheeled at the head of the runway, then started clumsily down, Stais put the slip of paper with Arnold Whitejack written on it, and the address, in scrawling childlike handwriting, into his pocket. And as he saw the Mitchell pull to a stop near the Operations Room, he felt for the moment a little less guilty for going home.

Mixed Doubles

As Jane Collins walked out on to the court behind her husband, she felt once more the private, strong thrill of pride that had moved her again and again in the time she had known him. Jane and Stewart had been married six years, but even so, as she watched him stride before her in that curious upright, individual, half-proud, half-comic walk, like a Prussian drill sergeant on his Sunday off, Jane felt the same mixture of amusement and delight in him that had touched her so strongly when they first met. Stewart was tall and broad and his face was moody and good-humoured and original, and Jane felt that even at a distance of five hundred yards and surrounded by a crowd of people, she could pick him out unerringly. Now, in well-cut white trousers and a long-sleeved Oxford shirt, he seemed elegant and a little old-fashioned among the other players, and he looked graceful and debonair as he hit the first few shots in the preliminary rallying.

Jane was sensibly dressed, in shorts and tennis shirt, and her hair was imprisoned in a bandanna, so that it wouldn't get into her eyes. She knew that the shorts made her look a little dumpy and that the handkerchief around her head gave her a rather skinned and severe appearance, and she had a slight twinge of female regret when she looked across the net and saw Eleanor Burns soft and attractive in a prettily cut tennis dress and with a red ribbon in her hair, but she fought it down and concentrated on keeping her eye on the ball as Mr Croker, Eleanor's partner, sliced it back methodically at her.

Mr Croker, a vague, round, serious little man, was a neighbour of the Collinses' hosts. His shorts were too tight for him, and Jane knew, from having watched him on previous occasions, that his face would get more serious and more purple as the afternoon wore on, but he played a steady, dependable game and he was useful when the other guests were too lazy or had drunk too much at lunch to play in the afternoon.

Two large oak trees shaded part of the court, and the balls flashed back and forth, in light and shadow, making guitar-like chords as they hit the rackets, and on the small terrace above the court, where the other guests were lounging, there was the watery music of ice in glasses and the bright flash of summer colours as people moved about.

How pleasant this was, Jane thought – to get away from the city on a week-end, to this cool, tree-shaded spot, to slip all the stiff bonds of business and city living and run swiftly on the springy surface of the court, feeling the country wind against her bare skin, feeling youth in her legs, feeling, for this short Sunday hour at least, free of desks and doors and weekday concrete.

Stewart hit a tremendous overhead smash, whipping all the strength of his long body into it, and the ball struck the ground at Eleanor's feet and slammed high in the air. He grinned. 'I'm ready,' he said.

'You're not going to do that to me in the game, are you?' Eleanor asked.

'I certainly am,' Stewart said. 'No mercy for women. The ancient motto of the Collins family.'

They tossed for service, and Stewart won. He served and aced Eleanor with a twisting, ferocious shot that spun off at a sharp angle.

'Jane, darling,' he said, grinning, as he walked to the other side, 'we're going to be sensational today.'

They won the first set with no trouble. Stewart played very well. He moved around the court swiftly and easily, hitting the ball hard in loose, well-coached strokes, with an almost exaggerated grace. Again and again, the people watching applauded or called out after one of his shots, and he waved his racket, smiling at them, and said, 'Oh, we're murderous today.' He kept humming between shots – a tuneless, happy composition of his own – like a little boy who is completely satisfied with himself, and Jane couldn't help smiling and adoring him as he light-heartedly dominated the game and the spectators and the afternoon, brown and dashing and handsome in his white clothes, with the sun flooding around him like a spotlight on an actor in the middle of the stage.

Occasionally, when Stewart missed a shot, he would stand, betrayed and tragic, and stare up at the sky and ask with mock despair, 'Collins, why don't you just go home?' And then he would turn to Jane and say, 'Jane, darling, forgive me. Your husband's just no good.'

And even as she smiled at him and said, 'You're so right,' she could sense the other women, up on the terrace, looking down at him, their eyes speculative and veiled and lit with invitation as they watched.

Jane played her usual game, steady, unheroic, getting almost everything back quite sharply, keeping the ball in play until Stewart could get his racket on it and kill it. They were a good team. Jane let Stewart poach on her territory for spectacular kills, and twice Stewart patted her approvingly on the behind after she had made difficult saves, and there were appreciative chuckles from the spectators at the small domestic vulgarity.

Stewart made the last point of the set on a slamming deep backhand that passed Eleanor at the net. Eleanor shook her head and said, 'Collins, you're an impossible man,' and Croker said stolidly, 'Splendid. Splendid,' and Stewart said, grinning, 'Something I've been saving for this point, old man.'

They walked off and sat down on a bench in the shade between sets, and Croker and Jane had to wipe their faces with towels and Croker's alarming purple died a little from his cheeks.

'That overhead!' Eleanor said to Stewart. 'It's absolutely frightening. When I see you winding up, I'm just tempted to throw away my poor little racket and run for my life.'

Jane lifted her head and glanced swiftly at Stewart to see how he was taking it. He was taking it badly, smiling a little too widely at Eleanor, being boyish and charming. 'It's nothing,' he said. 'Something I picked up on Omaha Beach.'

That, too, Jane thought bitterly. Foxhole time, too. She ducked her head into her towel to keep from saying something wifely. This is the last time, she thought, feeling the towel sticky against her sweaty forehead, the last time I am coming to any of these week-end things, always loaded with unattached or semi-attached man-hungry, half-naked, honey-mouthed girls. She composed her face, so that when she looked up from the towel she would look like a nice, serene woman who merely was interested in the next set of tennis.

Eleanor, who had wide green eyes, was staring soberly and unambiguously over the head of her racket at Stewart, and Stewart, fascinated, as always, and a little embarrassed, was staring back. Oh, God, Jane thought, the long stare, too.

'Well,' she said briskly, 'I'm ready for one more set.'

'What do you say,' Stewart asked, 'we divide up differently

234

this time? Might make it more even. Croker and you, Jane, and the young lady and me.'

'Oh,' said Eleanor, 'I'd be a terrible drag to you, Stewart. And besides, I'm sure your wife loves playing on your side.'

'Not at all,' Jane said stiffly. The young lady! How obvious could a man be?

'No,' said Croker surprisingly. 'Let's stay the way we are.' Jane wanted to kiss the round purple face, a bleak, thankful kiss. 'I think we'll do better this time. I've been sort of figuring out what to do with you, Collins.'

Stewart looked at him briefly and unpleasantly, then smiled charmingly. 'Anything you say, old man. I just thought . . . '

'I'm sure we'll do better,' Croker said firmly. He stood up. 'Come on, Eleanor.'

Eleanor stood up, lithe and graceful in her short dress, which whipped around her brown legs in the summer wind. Never again, Jane thought, will I wear shorts. Dresses like that, even if they cost fifty dollars apiece, and soft false bosoms to put in them, too, and no bandanna, even if I'm blinded on each shot.

Stewart watched Eleanor follow Croker on to the court, and Jane could have brained him for the buried, measuring glint in his eye.

'Let's go,' Stewart said, and under his breath, as they walked to their positions on the base-line, he added, 'Let's really show the old idiot this time, Jane.'

'Yes, dear,' Jane said, and pulled her bandanna straight and tight around her hair.

The first three games were ludicrously one-sided. Stewart stormed the net, made sizzling, malicious shots to Croker's feet, and purposely made him run, so that he panted pitifully and grew more purple than ever, and from time to time muttered to Jane. 'Ridiculous old windbag,' and 'I thought he had me figured out,' and 'Don't let up, Janie, don't let up.'

Jane played as usual steady, undeviating, as predictably and sensibly as she always played. She was serving in the fourth game and was at 40-15 when Stewart dropped a shot just over the net, grinning as Croker galloped heavily in and barely got his racket on it. Croker's return wobbled over Stewart's head and landed three inches beyond the base-line.

'Nice shot,' she heard Stewart say. 'Just in.'

She looked at him in surprise. He was nodding his head emphatically at Croker.

235

Eleanor was at the net on the other side, looking at Stewart. 'It looked out to me,' she said.

'Not at all,' Stewart said. 'Beautiful shot. Serve them up, Janie.'

Oh, Lord, Jane thought, now he's being sporting.

Jane made an error on the next point and Croker made a placement for advantage and Stewart hit into the net for the last point, and it was Croker's and Eleanor's game. Stewart came back to receive the service, not humming any more, his face irritable and dark.

Croker suddenly began to play very well, making sharp, sliding, slicing shots that again and again forced Stewart and Jane into errors. As they played, even as she swung at the ball, Jane kept remembering the shot that Stewart had called in, that had become the turning point of the set. He had not been able to resist the gallant gesture, especially when Eleanor had been standing so close, watching it all. It was just like Stewart. Jane shook her head determinedly, trying to concentrate on the game. This was no time to start dissecting her husband. They had had a lovely week-end till now and Stewart had been wonderful, gay and funny and loving, and criticism could at least be reserved for weekdays, when everything else was dreary, too. But it *was* just like Stewart. It was awful how everything he did was all of a piece. His whole life was crowded with gestures. Hitting his boss that time in the boss's own office with three secretaries watching, because the boss had bawled him out. Giving up his R.O.T.C. commission and going into the Army as a private in 1942. Giving five thousand dollars, just about the last of their savings, to Harry Mather, for Mather's business, just because they had been to school together, when everyone knew Mather had become a hopeless drunk and none of his other friends would chip in. To an outsider, all these might seem the acts of a generous and rather noble character, but to a wife, caught in the consequences . . .

'Damn these pants,' Stewart was muttering after hitting a ball into the net. 'I keep tripping over them all the time.'

'You ought to wear shorts, like everyone else,' Jane said.

'I will. Buy me some this week,' Stewart said, taking time out and rolling his cuffs up slowly and obviously. Jane had bought him three pairs of shorts a month before, but he always pretended he couldn't find them, and wore the long trousers. His legs are surprisingly skinny, Jane thought, hating herself for thinking it, and they're hairy, and his vanity won't let him . . . She started to go for a ball, then stopped when she saw Stewart going for it.'

He hit it out to the backstop. 'Janie, darling,' he said, 'at least stay out of my way.'

'Sorry,' she said. Stewie, darling, she thought, Stewie, be careful. Don't lay it on. You're not really like this. I know you're not. Even for a moment, don't make it look as though you are.

Stewart ended the next rally by hitting the ball into the net. He stared unhappily at the ground. 'The least they might do,' he said in a low voice to Jane, 'is roll the court if they invite people to play on it.'

Please, Stewie, Jane begged within herself, don't do it. The alibis. The time he forgot to sign the lease for the apartment and they were put out and he blamed it on the lawyer, and the time he lost the job in Chicago and it was because he had gone to the wrong college, and the time . . . By a rigorous act of will, Jane froze her eyes on the ball, kept her mind blank as she hit it back methodically again and again.

Eleanor and Croker kept winning points. Croker had begun to chop every ball, spinning soft, deceptive shots that landed in mid-court and hardly bounced before they fell a second time. The only way that Jane could return them was to hit them carefully, softly, just getting them back. But Stewart kept going in on them furiously, taking his full, beautiful swing, sending the ball whistling into the net or over the court into the backstop. He looked as pretty and expert as ever as he played, but he lost point after point.

'What a way to play tennis,' he grumbled, with his back to his opponents. 'Why doesn't he play ping-pong or jacks?'

'You can't slam those dinky little shots like that,' Jane said. 'You have to get them back soft.'

'You play your game,' Stewart said, 'and I'll play mine.'

'Sorry,' Jane said. Oh, Stewart, she mourned within her.

Stewart went after two more of Croker's soft chops, each time whipping his backhand around in his usual, slightly exaggerated, beautiful stroke, and each time knocking the ball into the net.

I can't help it, Jane thought. That *is* the way he is. Form above everything. If he were hanging over a cliff, he'd let himself fall to the rocks below rather than risk being ungraceful climbing to safety to save his life. He always has to pick up the check in bars and restaurants, no matter whom he is with or how many guests there are at the table, always with the same lordly, laughing, slightly derisive manner, even if we are down to our last fifty dollars. And when they had people in to dinner, there had to be two maids to wait on table, and French wines, and there always had to be those special bottles of brandy that cost as much as a vacation in the country. And he became so cold and remote when Jane argued with him about it, reminding him they were not rich and there was no sense in pretending they were. And his shoes. She blinked her eyes painfully, getting a sudden vision, there in the sun and shadow, of the long row of exquisite shoes, at seventy dollars a pair, that he insisted upon having made to his order. How ridiculous, she thought, to allow yourself to be unnerved at your husband's taste in shoes, and she loyally reminded herself how much a part of his attraction it had been in the beginning that he was always so beautifully dressed and so easy and graceful and careless of money.

The score was 4–3 in favour of Eleanor and Croker. Stewart's shots suddenly began to work again, and he and Jane took the next game with ease. Stewart's grin came back then, and he cheerfully reassured Jane. 'Now we're going to take them.' But after winning the first two points of the next game he had a wild streak and missed the base-line by a few inches three times in a row, and they eventually lost the game.

I will make no deductions from this, Jane told herself stonily as she went up to the net for Stewart's serve. Anybody is liable to miss a few shots like that – anybody. And yet, how like Stewart! Just when it was most important to be steady and dependable . . . The time she'd been so sick and the maid had quit, and Jane lay, broken and miserable, in bed for three weeks, with no one to take care of her except Stewart . . . He had been charming and thoughtful for the first week, fixing her meals, reading to her, sitting at her side for hours on end, cheerful and obliging, making her illness gently tolerable. And then he had suddenly grown nervous and abrupt, made vague excuses to leave her alone, and vanished for hours at a time, only to come back and hastily attend to her for a few moments and vanish again, leaving her there in the rumpled bed, staring, lonely and shaken, at the ceiling as dusk faded into night and night into morning. She had been sure there was another girl then and she had resolved that when she was well and able to move around again, she would come to some decision with him, but as unpredictably as his absences had begun, they stopped. Once more he was tender and helpful, once more he sat at her side and nursed her and cheered her, and out of gratitude and love she had remained quiet and pushed her doubts deep to the back of her mind. And here they were again, in the middle of a holiday afternoon, foolishly, in this most unlikely place, during this mild, pointless game, with half a dozen people lazily watching, laughing and friendly, over their drinks.

She looked at him a few moments later, handsome and dear and familiar at her side, and he grinned back at her, and she was ashamed of herself for the thoughts that had been flooding through her brain. It was that silly girl on the other side of the net who had started it all, she thought. That practised, obvious, almost automatic technique of flattering the male sex. That meaningless, rather pitiful flirtatiousness. It was foolish to allow it to throw her into the bitter waters of reflection. Marriage, after all, was an up-and-down affair and in many ways a fragile and devious thing, and was not to be examined too closely. Marriage was not a bank statement or a foreign policy or an X-ray photograph in a doctor's hand. You took it and lived through it, and maybe, a long time later – perhaps the day before you died – you totalled up the accounts, if you were of that turn of mind, but not before. And if you were a reasonable, sensible, mature woman, you certainly didn't do your additions and subtractions on a tennis court every time your husband hit a ball into the net. Jane smiled at herself and shook her head.

'Nice shot,' she said warmly to Stewart as he swept a fore-hand across court, past Croker, for a point.

But it was still set point. Croker placed himself to receive Stewart's service, tense and determined and a little funny-looking, with his purple face and his serious round body a little too tight under his clothes. The spectators had fallen silent, and the wind had died, and there was a sense of stillness and expectancy as Stewart reared up and served.

Jane was at the net and she heard the sharp twang of Stewart's racket hitting the ball behind her and the rifle-like report as it hit the tape and fell away. He had just missed his first service.

Jane didn't dare look around. She could feel Stewart walking into place, in that stiff-backed, pleasant way of his, and feel him shuffling around nervously, and she couldn't look back. Please, she thought, please get this one in. Helplessly, she

239

thought of all the times when, just at the crucial moment, he had failed. Oh, God, this is silly, she thought. I mustn't do this. The time he had old man's Sawyer's account practically in his hands and he got drunk. On the sporting pages, they called it coming through in the clutch. There were some players who did and some players who didn't, and after a while you got to know which was which. If you looked at it coldly, you had to admit that until now Stewart had been one of those who didn't. The time her father died, just after her sister had run off with the vocalist in that band, and if there had been a man around, taking hold of things, her father's partner wouldn't't've been able to get away with most of the estate the way he did, and the vocalist could have been frightened off. One day's strength and determination, one day of making the right move at the right time . . . But after the funeral, Stewart had pulled out and gone to Seattle on what he had said was absolutely imperative business, but that had never amounted to anything anyway, and Jane's mother and sister, and Jane, too, were still paying for that day of failure.

She could sense Stewart winding up for his service behind her back. Somewhere in her spine she felt a sense of disaster. It was going to be a double fault. She knew it. No, she thought, I mustn't. He isn't really like that. He's so intelligent and talented and good, he can go so far. She must not make this terrible judgement on her husband just because of the way he played tennis. And yet, his tennis was so much like his life. Gifted, graceful, powerful, showy, flawed, erratic . . .

Please, she thought, make this one good. Childishly, she felt, If this one is good it will be a turning point, a symbol, his whole life will be different. She hated herself for her thoughts and stared blankly at Eleanor, self-consciously alert and desirable in her pretty dress.

Why the hell did she have to come here this Sunday? Jane thought despairingly.

She heard the crack of the racket behind her. The ball whistled past her, hit the tape, rolled undecidedly on top of the net for a moment, then fell back at her feet for a double fault and the set.

'Too bad.' She turned and smiled at Stewart, helplessly feeling herself beginning to wonder how she would manage to find the six weeks it would take in Reno. She shook her head, knowing that she wasn't going to Reno, but knowing too, that the word would pass through her thoughts again and again, more and more frequently, with growing insistence, as the days went by.

She walked off the court with Stewart, holding his hand.

'The shadows,' Stewart was saying. 'Late in the afternoon, like this. It's impossible to see the service line.'

'Yes, dear,' Jane said.

Little Henry Irving

The dice rolled like cavalry across the concrete floor of the academy basement.

'Eight's the point,' Eddie said, pulling at the high collar of his cadet's uniform. 'Eight, baby, come eight, oh, you eight.' He stood up with a grin, dusting the knife-creases at his knees. 'Read them,' he said.

The Custodian shook his head and sat down backward. 'I might just as well lay down and die. On Christmas. How can a man be as unlucky as me on Christmas?'

'Roll for the pot,' Eddie offered seductively.

'My better nature says no,' the Custodian said.

'Roll you for the pot.'

'If I lose I'm cleaned. I won't even be able to buy a pint of beer for my throat on Christmas.'

'O.K.,' Eddie said offhandedly, starting to rake in the silver, 'if you want to quit, losing . . .'

'Roll for the pot,' the Custodian said grimly. He put out his last dollar-twenty with the desperate calm of a man signing his will. 'Go ahead, Diamond Jim.'

Eddie cooed to the dice, held warmly and cosy in his hands, and rocked soothingly back and forth on his skinny knees. 'The moment has come,' he cried softly into his hands. 'Little sweethearts . . .'

'Roll!' the Custodian cried irritably. 'No poetry!'

'Four and three, five and two, six and one,' Eddie coaxed into his hands. 'That's all I ask.'

'Roll!' the Custodian yelled.

Delicately Eddie spun the dice along the cold hard floor. They stopped like lovers, nestling together against Fate. 'Do we read seven?' Eddie asked gently.

'On Christmas!' the Custodian said despairingly.

Eddie carefully counted and sorted his money. 'You put up a good fight,' he said comfortingly to the Custodian.

'Yeah,' the Custodian muttered. 'Oh, yeah. A kid like you. Say, how old *are* you anyway, a million?'

'I am thirteen years old,' Eddie said, pocketing the last coins. 'But I come from New York.'

'You ought to be home with your family. On Christmas. A kid like you. I wish to hell you was home with yer family!'

'In Connecticut,' Eddie said, pulling his skimpy uniform jacket down, 'nobody knows anything about crap. I'm telling you for your own good.'

'You ought to be home with yer family,' the Custodian insisted.

A veil of tears came suddenly over Eddie's large dark eyes. 'My Pop told me he don't want to see me for a year.'

'What'd ye do?' the Custodian asked. 'Win his pants from him last Christmas?'

Eddie blew his nose and the tears left his eyes. 'I hit my sister with a lamp. A bridge lamp.' His mouth tightened in retrospect. 'I would do it again. Her name's Diana. She's fifteen years old.'

'That's nice,' the Custodian said. 'You're a fine little boy, all around.'

'It took four stitches. She cried for five hours. *Diana!* She said I mighta ruined her beauty.'

'Well, it wouldn't do her beauty no good, hitting her with a bridge lamp,' the Custodian said reasonably.

'She's going to be an actress. A stage actress.'

'That's nice for a girl,' the Custodian said.

'Aaah,' Eddie snorted. 'What's nice about it? She takes lessons from dancing teachers and French teachers and English teachers and horseback teachers and music teachers and Pop is always kissin' her and callin' her his little Bernhardt. She stinks.'

'That's no way to talk about yer sister,' the Custodian said sternly. 'I won't listen to a little boy talkin' like that about his sister.'

'Aaah, shut up!' Eddie said bitterly. 'Little Bernhardt. Pop's an actor, too. The whole damn family's actors. Except me,' he said with sombre satisfaction.

'You're a crap-player,' the Custodian said. 'You got nothing to worry about.'

'Little Bernhardt. Pop takes her with him all over the country. Detroit, Dallas, St Louis, Hollywood.'

'Hollywood!'

'Me they send to Military Academy.'

'Military Academy is good for young minds,' the Custodian said loyally.

'Aaah,' Eddie said. 'Little Bernhardt. I would like to step on her face.'

'That's no way to talk.'

'She goes in three times a week to see my Pop act. My Pop can act better than anybody since Sir Henry Irving.'

'Who says so?' the Custodian wanted to know.

'My Pop,' Eddie said. 'He's a Polack, my Pop. He's got feeling. Real feeling. Everybody says my Pop's got feeling. You oughta see him act.'

'I only go to the movies,' the Custodian said.

'He's actin' in *The Merchant of Venice*. With a long white beard, you'd never know it was my Pop. When he talks people laugh and cry in the audience. You can hear my Pop's voice for five blocks, I bet.'

'That's the kind of actin' I like,' the Custodian said.

Eddie threw out his arm in a tragic, pleading gesture. 'Hath not a Jew eyes?' he demanded in tones of thunder. 'Hath not a Jew hands, organs, dimensions, senses, affections, passions? Like that, that's the way my Pop does it.' He sat down slowly on an upturned box. 'It's the most beautiful thing in the world, the way my Pop does it,' he said softly.

'You shouldn't've hit yer sister with a bridge lamp,' the Custodian said morally. 'Then you could've been seein' him act tonight.'

'He smacked me for fifteen minutes, my Pop. He weighs two hundred and fifteen pounds an' he's built like Lou Gehrig, my Pop, like a truck horse, an' he was swingin' from his heels, but I didn't cry an' I didn't tell him why I hit her with a bridge lamp, I didn't cry one tear. I showed him. His little Bernhardt.' Eddie got up with determination. 'What the hell, I might just as well spend Christmas in a Military Academy as any place else.' He started out into the bleak December afternoon.

'Lissen, Eddie,' the Custodian said hurriedly, before Eddie could get through the door, 'I wanna ask you a question.'

'What?' Eddie asked coldly, sensing what was coming.

'It's Christmas Eve,' the Custodian said, preparation in his voice.

'All right,' Eddie said. 'It's Christmas Eve.'

'I'm an old man.' The Custodian brushed his white moustache pitifully. 'I'm an old man without kith or kin.'

'All right,' Eddie said.

'Usually on Christmas, Eddie, I buy myself a little pint of something, applejack usually, and I warm my old heart in a corner to forget that I'm deserted by the world. When you get older, you'll know what I mean.'

'Yeah,' Eddie said.

'This year,' the Custodian shifted uneasily, 'this year you happen to've won all my money. Now, I was wonderin', if you would . . .'

'No,' Eddie said, starting out.

'On Christmas Eve, for an old man, Eddie.'

'You lost,' Eddie said without heat. 'I won. O.K.'

He left and the Custodian settled down in his carpet-seated rocker next to the furnace. The Custodian rocked mournfully back and forth and shook his head as he watched Eddie go up the cellar steps out into the grey afternoon.

Eddie shambled aimlessly around the winter-bare school grounds. 'Military School! Aaah!' he said to himself. He should be home in New York City, blazing with lights, green and red and white lights, filled with people hurrying happily through the streets with packages done up in coloured ribbon, and Santa Clauses ringing their little bells on the street corners for the Salvation Army and the thousand movie houses gaping invitingly along the sidewalks. He should go watch Pop act tonight and go to dinner with him afterward on Second Avenue, and eat duck and potato pancakes and drink spiced wine and go home and listen to Pop sing German songs at the top of his voice, accompanying himself on the piano loudly, until the neighbours complained to the police.

He sighed. Here he was, stuck at a Military Academy in Connecticut, because he was a bad boy. Ever since his sixth birthday he'd been known as a bad boy. He'd had a party on his sixth birthday and he'd had a fine time, with cake, candy, ice cream and bicycles, until his sister Diana had come into the middle of the room and done a scene from *As You Like It* that her English teacher had coached her in. 'All the world's a stage,' she'd piped in her imitation Boston accent that the English teacher gave her, 'and all the men and women in't merely playahs . . . ' At the end of it everybody shouted 'Bravo!' and Pop grabbed her and swung her up and cried on her blonde hair and said over and over again, 'Little Bernhardt, my little Bernhardt!'

Eddie had thrown a plate of ice cream at her and it had spattered all over Pop, and Diana had cried for two hours and he'd been spanked and sent to bed.

'I hate Connecticut,' he said to a leafless elm leaning coldly over the dirty snow on the side of the walk.

Since then he had thrown Diana off the porch, tearing ligaments in her arm; he had run away in a rowboat off the coast of New Jersey and had had to be rescued by the Coast Guard at ten o'clock at night; he had played truant from seven different private and public schools; he had been caught coming out of burlesque houses with older friends; he had disobeyed his father on every possible occasion, and had been beaten three times to the month, standing there proud and stubborn, conscious in those moments at least, as Pop stood over him angry and terrible, that, actor or no actor, he was getting some attention, some evidence of paternal love.

He leaned against a tree and closed his eyes. He was in his Pop's dressing-room at the theatre and Pop was in his silk bathrobe with pieces of beard stuck here and there over his face and his hair grey with powder. Beautiful women with furs came in, talking and laughing in their womanly musical voices and Pop said, 'This is my son, Eddie. He is a little Henry Irving,' and the women cried wtih delight and took him in their arms, among the scented furs and kissed him, their lips cool from the winter outside on his warm red face. And Pop beamed and patted his behind kindly and said, 'Eddie, you do not have to go to Military School any longer and you don't have to spend Christmas with your aunt in Duluth, either. You are going to spend Christmas in New York alone with me. Go to the box-office and get a ticket for tonight's performance, Row A, centre. 'Hath not a Jew eyes? Hath not a Jew hands, organs . . . ' Yes, Pop, yes, Pop, yes . . . '

Eddie blinked his eyes and looked around him at the mean wood walls of the Academy. Prison, prison. 'I wish you'd burn,' he said with utter hate to the peeling paint and the dead ivy and the ramshackle bell tower. 'Burn! *Burn!*'

Abruptly he became quiet. His eyes narrowed and the cast of thought came over his face beneath the stiff short visor of his military cap. He regarded the dreary buildings intently, his lips moving silently over deep, unmentionable thoughts, the expression on his face a hunter's expression, marking down prey for the kill far off in the tangled jungle.

If the school burned down he couldn't sleep in the December woods, could he, they would have to send him home, wouldn't they, and if he was rescued from the burning building Pop would be so grateful that his son was not dead that . . . The school would have to burn down completely and they would never send him back and fire burns from the bottom up and the bottom was the cellar and the only person there was the Custodian sitting lonely there, longing for his Christmas bottle . . .

With a sharp involuntary sigh, Eddie wheeled swiftly and walked towards the cellar entrance, to seize the moment.

'Lissen,' he said to the Custodian, rocking mournfully back and forth next to the furnace. 'Lissen, I feel sorry for yuh.'

'Yeah,' the Custodian said hopelessly. 'I can see it.'

'I swear. An old man like you. All alone on Christmas Eve. Nothin' to comfort yuh. That's terrible.'

'Yeah,' the Custodian agreed. 'Yeah.'

'Not even a single drink to warm yuh up.'

'Not a drink. On Christmas!' The Custodian rocked bitterly back and forth. 'I might as well lay down and die.'

'I got a change of heart,' Eddie said deliberately. 'How much does a bottle of applejack cost?'

'Well,' the Custodian said craftily, 'there's applejack and applejack.'

'The cheapest applejack,' Eddie said sternly. 'Who do you think I am?'

'You can get a first-rate bottle of applejack for ninety-five cents, Eddie,' the Custodian said in haste. 'I would take that kindly. That's a thoughtful deed for an old man in the holiday season.'

Eddie slowly assorted ninety-five cents out in his pocket. 'Understand,' he said, 'this ain't a usual thing.'

'Of course not, Eddie,' the Custodian said quickly. 'I wouldn't expect . . .'

'I won it honest,' Eddie insisted.

'Sure, Eddie.'

'But on Christmas . . .'

'Sure, just on Christmas . . .' The Custodian was on the edge of his rocker now, leaning forward, his mouth open, his tongue licking at the corners of his lips.

Eddie put out his hand with the coins in it. 'Ninety-five cents,' he said. 'Take it or leave it.'

The Custodian's hand trembled as he took the money. 'You got a good heart, Eddie,' he said simply. 'You don't look it, but you got a good heart.'

'I would go get it for you myself,' Eddie said, 'only I got to write my father a letter.'

'That's all right, Eddie, my boy, perfectly all right. I'll take a little walk into town myself.' The Custodian laughed nervously. 'The clear air. Pick me up. Thank you, Eddie, you're one of the best.'

'Well,' Eddie said, starting out. 'Merry Christmas.'

'Merry Christmas,' the Custodian said heartily. 'Merry Christmas, my boy, *and* a happy New Year.'

And he sang 'I saw three ships go sailing by, go sailing by', as Eddie went up the cellar steps.

Five hours later Eddie walked down Forty-fifth Street, in New York City, without an overcoat, shivering in the cold, but happy. He marched across from the Grand Central Station through the good-natured holiday crowds, reciting gaily to the lights, the neon signs, the blue-coated policemen, 'If you prick us, do we not bleed? If you tickle us, do we not laugh? If you poison us, do we not die?' He crossed Sixth Avenue, turned into the stage-entrance alley of the theatre over which the huge sign read in electric bulbs, *The Merchant of Venice* by William Shakespeare. 'And if you wrong us, shall we not revenge?' he shouted thickly at the alley walls, as he opened the stage door and ran upstairs to his father's dressing-room.

The door was open and his father was sitting at his make-up table, applying grease and false hair carefully, close to the mirror. Eddie sidled in softly.

'Pop,' he said, standing at the door. Then again, 'Pop.'

'Uh.' His father touched up an eyebrow with a comb, making it bush out.

'Pop,' Eddie said. 'It's me.'

His father soberly put down the grease-stick, the small comb, the false hair, and turned around.

'Eddie,' he said.

'Merry Christmas, Pop,' Eddie said, smiling nervously.

'What're you doing here, Eddie?' His father looked him straight and seriously in the eye.

'I'm home, Pop,' Eddie said quickly. 'I'm home for Christmas.'

'I am paying that money-grabbing military academy forty-five dollars extra to keep you there and you tell me you are home for Christmas!' The great voice boomed out with the passion and depth that made audiences of fifteen hundred souls shiver in their seats. 'A telephone! I want a telephone! Frederick!' he called for his dresser. 'Frederick, by God Almighty, a telephone!'

'But, Pop . . . ' Eddie said.

'I will talk to those miserable toy soldiers, those uniformed schoolma'ams! Frederick, in the name of God!'

'Pop, Pop,' Eddie wailed. 'You can't call them.'

His father stood up to his six-foot-three magnificence in his red-silk dressing-gown and looked down on Eddie, one eye-brow high with mockery on the huge domed forehead. 'I can't call them, my son says. Little snot-nose tells me what to do and what not to do.'

'You can't call, Pop,' Eddie yelled, 'because there's nothing to talk to. See?'

'Oh,' his father said with searing irony, 'the school has dis-appeared. Poof! and off it goes. The Arabian Nights. In Con-necticut.'

'That's why I'm here, Pop,' Eddie pleaded rapidly. 'There ain't no more school. It burned. It burned right down to the ground. This afternoon. Look, even my overcoat. Look, I don't have an overcoat.'

His father stood silent, regarding him soberly through the deep-set cold grey eyes under the famous grey brows. One of the famous long thick fingers beat slowly, like the pendulum of doom, on the dressing-table, as he listened to his son, stand-ing there, chapped by exposure, in his tight uniform, talking fast, shifting from one foot to another.

'See, Pop, it burned down, I swear to God, you can ask any-one, I was lying on my bed writing a letter and the firemen got me, you can ask them, and there wasn't no place for them to put me and they gave me money for the train and . . . I'll stay here with you, Pop, eh, Pop, for Christmas, what do you say, Pop?' Pleading, pleading . . . His voice broke off under his father's steady, unrelenting stare. He stood silent, pleading with his face, his eyes, the twist of his mouth, with his cold, chapped hands. His father moved majestically over to him, raised his hand and slapped him across the face.

Eddie stood there, his face quivering, but no tears. 'Pop,' he said, controlling his voice as best he could. 'Pop, what're you hitting me for? It ain't my fault. The school burned down, Pop.'

'If the school burned down,' his father said in measured tones, 'and you were there, it was your fault. Frederick,' he said to his dresser, who was standing in the doorway, 'put Eddie on the next train to his aunt in Duluth.' And he turned, immutable as Fate, back to his dressing-table and once more carefully started applying false hair to the famous face.

In the train to Duluth an hour later, Eddie sat watching the Hudson River fly past, crying at last.

The Captain was getting more and more remote every moment. He kept stuffing papers into a heavy saddle-leather bag, whistling tunelessly under his breath. From time to time he looked out over the windy plain, swirling with dust in the late afternoon sun. He would peer thoughtfully into the eye-burning distance, then shake himself a little and resume his packing, a little more quickly each time. He never looked at Lieutenant Dumestre.

Lieutenant Dumestre sat on the edge of the desk, very neat in his expensive uniform. He was a tall, fairish man, who looked too young to be in his lieutenant's uniform, too young to be so serious, too young to be in a war.

He never took his eyes off the Captain. The Captain was a round, solid man, who had been very jovial when they had met in Algiers and had paid for the wine and had sighed gallantly over all the pretty women in the café. There was nothing jovial or gallant about the Captain now, as he prepared in a business-like way to disappear, each moment seeming more and more remote.

'Do you expect to come back, sir?' Lieutenant Dumestre finally asked, because the silence in the orderly room broken only by the low bumble of the Captain's humming was at last too much to bear.

The Captain stopped his packing and looked thoughtfully out over the plain again, as though there, in the dust and scrub, some answer to a profound although somewhat vague question was to be found. He stood silently, even forgetting to hum.

'Do you expect to come back, sir?' the Lieutenant asked loudly.

The Captain at last turned and looked at the Lieutenant. His eyes were very cool and you would never have thought from looking at him in this moment that he had ever bought a bottle of wine for a lieutenant in his life. 'Come back?' the Captain said. He turned away and sturdily buckled his bag. 'Who can tell?'

'What do I do with the Americans?' The Lieutenant's voice, he noticed angrily, was much higher than it should have been. At Saint Cyr they had been after him all the time to pitch his voice lower. 'An order given in the soprano register, mister, is not calculated to drive troops to impossible glories.' 'What happens when the Americans arrive?'

The Captain was putting his helmet on very carefully in front of a mirror. 'That is just what I hope to discover,' he said.

'In the meantime?'

'In the meantime your orders are to resist. Naturally.'

The Lieutenant peered out over the plain, hoping painfully that over the rim of the horizon the Americans would appear before the Captain could leave on his personal retreat. But the only movement to be seen was a corporal hurrying to the battery observation post.

'They'll arrive tomorrow morning, at the latest,' the Lieutenant said.

'Quite possibly.' The Captain picked up his bag decisively, marched out and into the command car. The Lieutenant followed him and saluted. The Captain saluted and the car started and the Captain drove down the road.

The Lieutenant plodded slowly up the road towards the forward gun, thinking of the Captain, in the command car, speeding over a macadam road to Algiers, where there would be other men to make the decisions, other men to say, 'We will move to the left, we will move to the right . . . ' and the Captain would have to make no decisions himself. No matter how things turned out, he would not be committed and would be a fine fellow with whichever side turned up on top, and would jovially buy wine for his new lieutenants at the second-best restaurant in town . . .

The Lieutenant made his way to the aimless little mud house they used as an observation post and climbed the ladder and stood under the umbrella next to the red-eyed little corporal and peered through his glasses at the plain. He looked until his eyes ached, but aside from the blowing dust there was nothing.

The men who served the forward gun had rigged up a tarpaulin to one side and lay under it, out of the wind. Usually they slept all the afternoon, but today no one was sleeping.

Sergeant Fourier even went so far as to get up and look out across the plain.

'Anything?' Labat asked.

The Sergeant squinted anxiously. 'Nothing.'

'Waiting; everything is waiting,' Labat said. He was a long, ugly man, with a big nose and large ears. He was from Paris and excitable and given to throwing his arms around in rage and was a great patriot of the French Republic. 'In a war you wait for everything! Even the Americans! At last, I thought, things will finally move. The Americans are famous for their briskness . . . We're still waiting . . . '

'Only a day,' said Boullard. Boullard was a big, quiet man, over forty, with a wrinkled, brown, farmer's face. 'They'll be here soon enough.'

'I can't wait,' Labat said. He stood up and peered out. 'For a year I sat in the Maginot Line. Now for two years I sit here. I am finally impatient. A day is too much.'

'Shut up,' Boullard said calmly. 'You'll get us all nervous.'

Labat lay down and put his hands behind his head and looked up at the tarpaulin angrily. Sergeant Fourier came back and sat down.

'More of the same,' Sergeant Fourier said. 'More nothing.'

'It must be worse for Americans,' Corporal Millet said. He was a man who, although he was nearly thirty-five, was still plagued by pimples. His face had raging red blots on it all the time and he suffered meanly under his affliction, taking his misfortune out on the work details in his charge. 'It must be unbearable for Americans.'

'Why?' Labat asked angrily. 'What's wrong with the Americans?'

'They are not a military people,' Corporal Millet said. He had a lawyer's voice, smooth and reasonable and superior, and on bad days it made men want to kill Corporal Millet. 'They are used to sitting back and pushing buttons.'

'Corporal,' Labat said calmly, 'you are perhaps the biggest idiot in the French Army of 1942.'

'The jokes,' Corporal Millet said. 'We can do without the jokes. It is a fact that war is harder on some races than on others. The Americans must be suffering the tortures of the damned.'

'I repeat,' Labot said. 'The biggest.'

Corporal Millet was a devotee of Vichy, and Labat enjoyed making him angry.

253

'Push buttons,' Boullard said reflectively. 'I could use a few push buttons at the moment.'

'See,' Corporal Millet gestured to Boullard. 'Boullard agrees.'

'See,' Boullard said. 'Boullard does not agree.'

There was silence for a moment, while the men thought of the wind and the ugliness of the men around them and the possibility of dying tomorrow.

'This war,' the sergeant said. 'This disease of war.'

'Somebody talk about a woman,' Private Jouvet said. 'I'm tired of the war. I am in the mood for breasts and hips.' Private Jouvet was twenty years old and made a desperate effort to keep on an equal footing with these sun-stricken veterans of bed and battle.

'It can't be,' Labat said, 'that the Americans will appear and we will be asked to shoot at them. It's impossible.'

'In the French Army,' Boullard said, 'nothing is impossible.'

'Why not?' Corporal Millet asked in his bland voice. 'An invasion of French soil . . . '

'I am very tired of those two words,' Boullard said. 'French soil.'

Labat opened his canteen and took a mouthful. He closed the canteen over the precious water and then thought that perhaps he would be shot by morning, and said, 'Hell,' and opened the canteen and took another mouthful.

'The problem is,' Private Jouvet said, 'are the Americans to be regarded as friends, enemies or tourists?'

'What a war!' Sergeant Fourier sighed. He had just married three months before, a masseuse with a good clientele in Algiers, and he was by and large as comfortable as a sergeant could hope to be in this foul year. 'What a disease of a war!'

'Layfayette,' Boullard said, 'we are here.'

'We will be given our orders,' Corporal Millet said loudly.

'That's what we're afraid of,' said Labat.

'After all,' said Corporal Millet, tenderly touching his current most blazing pimple, 'we are soldiers. We have officers. They have their instructions.'

'Please, Corporal,' said Labat. 'Quiet. Such official sentiments have a tendency to make me throw up.'

'The Americans.' Sergeant Fourier sighed again. 'Things were going as well as could be expected. This wasn't good, but a man could bear it. They are crazy with anxiety to make a landing some place . . . They have all Europe to make a landing on. No! They must choose Africa! We will all be dead.'

'Be more cheerful,' Boullard said, 'or kindly keep quiet.'

The men sat silently for a moment, everyone heavy and gloomy because the word 'death' had finally been mentioned.

'It will be a ridiculous thing,' Labat said. 'To be killed by an American.' Labat had fought at Sedan and made his way bitterly down the length of France, cursing the politicians, cursing the officers, cursing the Germans and English and Italians and Americans. At last he had stowed away aboard a freighter to Algiers and without losing a day had joined up all over again and had since then sat, full of pent-up vengeance, in the gloom of Africa, waiting to fight the Germans once more.

'I refuse,' Labat said. 'I refuse to be killed by an American.'

'You will be told what your orders are,' Corporal Millet said, 'and you will follow them.'

Labat stared gloomily and dangerously at Corporal Millet. His face, which was ugly but usually pleasant enough, now was harsh and his eyes were squinted balefully. 'Corporal,' he said, 'Corporal of the pimples, do you know what our orders are?'

'No.'

'Does anybody know?' Labat looked around, his face still flushed and glowering, angry at Corporal Millet and the Government of France and his position in the world that afternoon.

Sergeant Fourier cleared his throat professionally. 'The Lieutenant. He must know. The Captain's gone . . . '

'What a wonderful thing,' Boullard said, 'to be a captain . . .'

'Let us ask the Lieutenant,' Labat said.

'Sergeant Fourier, we make you a committee of one.'

Sergeant Fourier looked around him uneasily, pulling in his round little belly nervously, uncomfortable at the thought of any action that would make him conspicuous, endanger his pleasant anonymous future with the masseuse in Algiers. 'Why me?' he asked.

'Highest non-commissioned officer present,' Labat chanted. 'Channels of communication with the commissioned personnel.'

'I haven't said two words to him,' Sergeant Fourier protested. 'After all, he just got here five days ago. And he's reserved . . . All he's said to me in five days is, "Make sure the men do not smoke in the open at night".'

'Enough,' Labat said cheerfully. 'It's obvious he likes you.'

'Don't joke,' Boullard said sharply. 'We have no more time to joke.'

'I'm only joking,' Labat said soberly, 'because I am willing to slit my throat.'

He got up and went to the edge of the tarpaulin and stood there, his back to the men, watching across the enigmatic plain for the first fateful dust cloud.

'What sort of man is this Lieutenant Dumestre?' Boullard asked.

'It's hard to tell,' Sergeant Fourier said with the caution born of three years in an army where a hasty approval of a man, before all the facts of courage, sense and rectitude were in, might one day cause your death. 'He's very quiet. Stiff . . . '

'A bad sign,' said Boullard.

'Very rich in the uniform department.'

'Another bad sign.'

'It doesn't pay to be too hurried,' Sergeant Fourier protested.

'It's the Americans,' Boullard said. 'They're in a hurry, not me. Well, there's only one thing to be done.' He rubbed his cheek absently with the back of his hand, like a man determining whether or not he needs a shave. The other men watched him silently, anxious and curious about a definite plan that might have finally bloomed on this last nervous afternoon. 'One thing,' Boullard repeated. 'We kill him.'

Lieutenant Dumestre stood in the observation post and felt the headache coming on like an express train. Every afternoon the boredom and misery of the day accumulated in his brain-pan and punished him for still living. He stared painfully over the darkening plain, which was silently enveloping itself in blue and purple folds, intangible and deceptive, in which the shapes of men and machines might be capriciously and dangerously lost . . .

Lieutenant Dumestre shook his head and closed his eyes, measuring gloomily the exact extent of the pain in his skull.

How do you do it? he asked himself. How does a first lieutenant hand a battery over to an advancing army, without orders? How does a first lieutenant save his life in a situation like this? In the distance there is a puff of dust and soon the first shell dropping somewhere near you, and all around you doubtful and uncertain men whom you do not know but who, for the lack of a better word, are under your command. Why had he left his post in Algiers? In this one, crazy, fateful week, his transfer had to be granted, this transfer to dilemma, this transfer to death . . . In the days of Napoleon it was said that every French private had a marshal's baton in his knapsack. Today every French soldier had in his knapsack a fatal and insoluble conundrum.

Lieutenant Dumestre had asked to be transferred from Algiers because he had been spending too much money there. It was as simple as that. The bills came in, the monthly reckonings were made, the deductions for the money sent home to his mother and father, who were lean and ailing in Paris, and it became clear that on a lieutenant's salary you could not save money in a gay town, especially if you had been rich all your life and your family rich before you and certain habits of eating and drinking and generosity ingrained in you, war or no war . . .

So, it was too expensive. Algiers. So, the desert would prove to be even more expensive.

. . . Back in Algiers he knew the men of his battery had mimicked him behind his back – his slow, painful way of delivering orders, full of agonised pauses, as he tried to remember to keep his voice down, tried not to sound like a young idiot imposing callously on these veterans of a war that had passed him by . . . They had mimicked him, but he knew them and even felt they liked him, and if he were with them now in this tragedy of a situation he would be able to go to them, talk to them, draw strength and resolution, one way or another from the men who would have to bear the burden of living and dying with him.

But here he was, on the one important day of the last two years, with a group of sullen and bearded strangers, who regarded him only with steady and cool hostility, a newcomer and an officer in an army where newcomers were automatically suspect and officers automatically hated . . .

Lieutenant Dumestre walked slowly out toward the west across the dusty scrub. The sun had set and the wind had died and the walking, he felt might help somehow. Perhaps, he thought, smiling a little to himself, there will be an American patrol and I am unavoidably captured and there's an end to the problem . . . It's like a child, he thought, hoping that by morning he will have a sore throat so he does not have to go to school and take his examination in arithmetic. What an arithmetic was being imposed upon him now! What a savage and pitiless calculation! He looked towards the last blur of the horizon beyond which the Americans were marching. How simple it was to be an American! In their arithmetic there was an answer to all problems. How merry and dashing a lieutenant in the artillery in the American army must feel tonight, marching beside men whom he could trust, who trusted him, who all believed the same thing, who knew an enemy when they saw one, whose parents were well-fed and healthy, in no one's power, three thousand sweet miles from the battlefields . . .

What a tragic thing to be a Frenchman this year! Hamlet, sword out, killing Polonius and uncle in blind unprofitable lunges . . . Frenchmen, Hamlets of the world . . .

Lieutenant Dumestre stopped and sat down like a little boy on the dark earth and put his head in his hands and wept. He stopped suddenly and bit his lips and neglected to dry the tears from his cheeks. Nonsense, he thought, a grown man . . . There must be an answer to this, too. After all, I am not the only Frenchman afloat on this continent. The thing is, the men. If I knew what they wanted . . . If there was only some way to be present, without being seen. Armies have surrendered before. Detachments have surrendered before. Officers have appeared under a flag of truce and offered their services to their official enemies. The Captain was in Algiers, there was no one to stop him. 'Dear sir, is there anyone here who speaks French? Dear sir, Lieutenant Dumestre, Battery C, wishes to state that he desires to join forces with the American Army in North Africa and put himself under the flag of the United States for the duration against the common enemy . . . ' There must be a technique to surrender, just the way there was a technique for everything else in the Army. His mother and father would have to look out for themselves. Now, if only the men . . .

Lieutenant Dumestre slapped his thigh briskly as he stood up. At last he had reached a decision. He had faced the arithmetic and at least he knew what answer he wanted. There only remained going in frankly to the men and putting the situation up to them, in words of one syllable, simply . . . He started back towards the forward gun, walking more swiftly than he had walked for a week.

'Men,' he would say, remembering to keep his voice pitched low, 'this is the way it is. You may or may not know it, but tomorrow an American army will appear.' You never knew how much the men knew, what rumours had reached them, what facts confirmed, what punishments and discharges and prophecies and movements were peddled at the latrine or over a morning cigarette. 'I am under orders to resist,' he would say. 'Personally, I do not believe we are bound by those orders, as I believe all Frenchman to be on the side for which the Americans are now fighting.' Perhaps that was too heroic, but it was impossible to fight a war without sounding from time to time a little heroic. 'I intend to go out under a flag of truce and give over the guns of this battery.' Now the question of dissenters. 'Anyone who does not wish to join me in this action is free to leave towards the rear . . . ' No, they'd go back and talk and by morning a troop of cavalry would come up and Lieutenant Dumestre would be finished in thirty minutes. Keep them with him? How do that? Supposing they were all Vichy men? After all, they were being paid by Vichy and there were thousands of Frenchmen in Africa who had staked their lives on a German victory. They'd shoot him in cold blood.

Once more he cursed the trick that had landed him at this moment among two hundred strangers. In his old company he would have been able to take Sergeant Goubille aside and talk honestly and get an honest answer. Sergeant Goubille was forty-five years old and there was something fatherly and tolerant of young officers in his bearing, and a man like that would be worth a man's life on this harsh and doubtful plain tonight. Well, there was no Sergeant Goubille at hand . . . Perhaps that Breton, that farmer, Boullard. He was an older man and he looked honest and pleasant.

He took a deep breath and walked swiftly, not knowing exactly what he would do but knowing he had to do something, towards the forward gun . . .

Under the tarpaulin, Boullard was talking, his voice low and harsh, all the kindly countryman's lines somehow vanished from the set, desperate face. 'There will be a token resistance,' he was saying to the men, who were all sitting up, looking at the ground most of the time, looking up only occasionally at Boullard with a kind of deep embarrassment. 'In a token resistance there are token deaths.' He looked around him calmly from face to face, his thought plain in his eyes. 'A token corpse feeds as many worms as any other . . . '

Jouvet, the young one, was the only one who could not manage to sit still. He rubbed his heels back and forth, making marks in the sand, and studying them intensely.

Kill the pretty lieutenant,' Boullard said, 'and we have our own lives in our hands. We dispose of them as we see fit.'

'Let us look at it from the political angle,' Labat said. 'Politically, we are fried if the Germans win . . .'

'Perhaps,' Sergeant Fourier said uneasily, his voice full of the nagging pain of having to make a decision. 'Perhaps we ought to wait and see what happens.'

'We will wait and see ourselves buried,' Boullard said.

'At least,' said Labat, 'we ought to talk to the lieutenant. Sound him out.'

'I was on the Meuse,' said Boullard. 'I know better than to talk to a lieutenant. I'll take the responsibility. If you're all afraid . . . ' He looked around him with savage, peasant contempt. 'There's a lot of men still to be killed in this war. I don't mind making it one more or less, personally . . . '

'We have to talk to him first,' Labat said stubbornly.

'Why?' Boullard asked loudly.

'Maybe he's with us. Maybe he wants to fight with the Americans, too . . . '

Boullard laughed harshly. Then he spat. 'I'm surrounded by children,' he said. 'If he's still an officer in the French Army after two years, he is not fond of the Americans. I am. At this moment, I am crazy about Americans. If there is any hope for anybody in this stinking war, it is in the Americans. I'm forty-four years old and I've fought in two wars. The third one, I want to pick my own side . . . '

'Still,' Labat said, his voice low and persistent, 'still, we ought to talk to him.'

'For myself,' Corporal Millet said briskly, standing up, 'I am on duty at the observa – '

He let his hands fall gently to his sides as Boullard brought his rifle up and touched his chest lightly with the bayonet.

'You are on duty here, Corporal.' Boullard moved the bayonet tenderly on a breast button. 'There is a question before the house that must be decided by a full membership.'

Corporal Millet sat down carefully.

'I don't care,' Labat was saying, grinning at Corporal Millet, 'what you do to the fighting corporal, but nothing happens to the Lieutenant until we talk to him.' He patted Boullard's shoulder in a small, reassuring gesture. Boullard slowly took his eyes off Millet and the Corporal sighed.

Boullard looked around him searchingly at the men caught in this hour on this desert with him. Sergeant Fourier, haunted by dreams of a pension and his masseuse and still troubled by some obscure, painful sense of patriotism and honour, refused

260

to look at him. Jouvet faced at the age of twenty with the ancient, tangled threads of a bloody and complex century, looked ready to weep. Labat was smiling but stubborn. Corporal Millet was sweating, and was making a great effort to look like a man who did not intend to rush to the nearest officer and announce a mutiny.

'All right,' Boullard said wearily, 'if that's what you want. Although I tell you, two words too many and we are all against a wall, looking at a firing squad.'

Jouvet fumbled with his handkerchief quickly and Boullard looked at him curiously and impersonally.

'It is not necessary to commit ourselves,' said Labat. His long, workman's arms waved in argument. 'We approach the subject, we skirt it, we take soundings like a boat coming into harbour . . . '

'Better!' Sergeant Fourier said loudly, happy at all deferment. 'Excellent! Much better!'

Boullard stared at him coldly and Sergeant Fourier became quiet and nervously took out a pack of cigarettes.

'It's possible,' Labat was saying, convincing Boullard, 'to judge a man without a direct question . . . '

'Possibly,' Boullard said with no enthusiasm. 'Possibly.'

'I'll do the talking,' Labat said. 'I'm used to things like this. I have talked at union meetings for seven years and nothing could be more delicate . . . ' He looked around him anxiously, hoping for a little laughter to take some of the deadly tension away, but only little Jouvet, who was always polite, smiled nervously because he realised Labat had meant it as a little joke.

'All right,' Boullard said. He fingered his rifle gently and let it dip almost imperceptibly towards Corporal Millet. 'I will judge. And you . . . ' The rifle dipped very clearly toward Corporal Millet. 'You will not open your mouth. Is that clear?'

Corporal Millet sat up stiffly at attention, feeling sorrowfully within him that his honour demanded some show of resistance and that his life would not be worth a great deal if he was incorporated in the army of the United States. He looked at Boullard's huge crushing hands, calm on the rifle. 'It is your affair,' he said faintly. 'I wash my hands of it.'

Boullard laughed.

Sergeant Fourier lighted his cigarette, gift of his plump wife the masseuse, eating her dinner comfortably, all unknowing, in the curtainy little apartment in Algiers with three exposures,

He sighed and stood up and walked between Boullard and the limp Corporal Millet and stood at the edge of the tarpaulin in the full darkness, pulling with small comfort at his cigarette, while behind him, under the tarpaulin, there was no sound from the waiting men.

Lieutenant Dumestre made his way slowly across the rough black ground towards the gun position, turning over in his mind his possible opening sentences to the gun crew. 'Men,' he could say, 'I am going to be absolutely honest with you. I am putting a white flag up beside this gun and I am delivering this battery over to . . . ' Or he could say, 'There is a possibility that tomorrow morning American troops will appear. Hold your fire until I give the word . . . while silently swearing to himself that the word would never be given. There was much to be said for this method, as it was indefinite and seemed less dangerous and didn't tip his hand until the last moment, when it would probably be too late for anyone to do anything about it. Of course there was always the possibility that he could stand up in front of the men and pour his heart out to them, remind them in ringing words of their country's shame, call upon them with blood and passion to forget themselves, forget their families in France, remember only honour and final victory . . . ' He could see himself, pale and fluent, in the dim light of the moon, roaring, whispering, his voice singing in the quiet air, the men listening entranced, the tears starting down their cheeks . . . He shook himself, smiled wryly at the dream, remembering his harsh, slow way of speaking, plain, indefinite, without the power to move men to the nearest café, much less throw themselves grandly and thoughtlessly upon a doubtful and possibly fatal cause . . .

Oh, Lord, he thought I am the wrong man for this, the wrong man, the wrong man . . .

He turned the corner of the tarpaulin, seeing the watchful, hateful shape of the gun outlined stubbornly against the starlit sky.

Sergeant Fourier was smoking pensively in the open and the other men were sitting, strangely quiet, under cover. When Sergeant Fourier saw him he started guiltily and threw his cigarette away as unostentatiously as possible. He stood at attention and saluted and with his right heel tried to douse the glowing speck in the dirt. Somehow, the sight of the small man with the comfortable little pot belly trying to pretend, like a

262

vaudeville comedian, that he hadn't been smoking, irritated Lieutenant Dumestre, who all morning and all afternoon had been grappling bitterly with war and fratricide and tragic, bloody policy . . .

He returned the Sergeant's salute curtly. 'What's wrong with you?' he asked sharply, his high voice making all the men in the tarpaulin turn their heads coldly and automatically to watch him. 'You know there's to be no smoking.'

'Please, sir,' Sergeant Fourier said stupidly, 'I was not smoking.'

'You were smoking,' Lieutenant Dumestre said, weeping inside because inside he knew how ridiculous this charge and counter-charge was.

'I was not smoking, sir,' Sergeant Fourier stood very straight and formal and stupid with the problem of the evening, almost happy to have a simple little idiotic argument to worry about at least for ten minutes . . .

'You've been told, you've been told!' Lieutenant Dumestre shrieked in his highest voice, mourning deep within himself for that womanly timbre, for his military insistence upon form and truth at this unmilitary hour, but somehow unable, with the Captain's departure and the imminence, potent and desperate, of the Americans over the horizon, to stop the high noise of his tongue. 'At any moment we may be bombed. A cigarette glows like a lighthouse in a black desert at ten thousand feet! Why don't you draw a map of the gun position and publish it in the morning newspapers?' He saw Labat look at Boullard and shrug coldly and turn away with an air of dangerous significance and something within him clutched at his throat, but now there was no stopping that high, silly tongue, freed for a moment from the locked agony and doubt of the day's decision making. Here at least was familiar ground. Troops disobeying orders. Troops endangering security of the post or station. Troops slightly insubordinate, lying . . . His weary, ragged mind, terribly grateful to be relieved of its unaccustomed task of painful exploration, relapsed into the formal, years-long grooves of Saint Cyr, of countless garrisons, countless lectures . . . 'There will be double security tonight, two-hour watches for everyone,' the voice still high, but with the three-thousand-year-old bite of military command. 'An extra half day's ammunition will be drawn up from the battery dump by three this morning.' He saw the men's faces bleakly collapse and also something else in them, although he couldn't tell in the rush of his commands what it was. Even as he spoke he hated himself for what he was doing, knowing that a better man would have ignored the cigarette or joked about it . . . He hated Sergeant Fourier, standing there, pained and stupid and impassive, but in a way he was grateful to him, because he had given him the opportunity at this late hour once more for postponement.

He turned on his heel and strode away. Later, perhaps at midnight, he would come back, he told himself, and finally get this question of the Americans settled. He pulled his shoulders high in disgust as the sound of his own voice squalling about the cigarette sounded in his ears, but there was nothing to be done about it and he walked without looking back. Midnight, he thought, midnight is still time . . .

Back under the tarpaulin, Boullard looked around him at the men. Their faces were grave, but except for Millet, there was consent in all of them.

Boullard walked out from under the tarpaulin with his rifle.

Midnight, Lieutenant Dumestre was thinking, when the bullet struck, midnight is still time . . .

They buried him quickly without marking the grave and sat down in front of the gun to wait for the army of the Americans.

The Indian in Depth of Night

The city lay around Central Park in a deep hush, the four-o'clock-in-the-morning sky mild with stars and a frail, softly rising mist. Now and then a car went secretly by, with a sigh of tyres and wind and a sudden small flare of headlights. The birds were still, and the trolley cars and buses; the taxicabs waited silently at scattered corners; the drunks were lying by this time in the doorways; the bums bedded for the night, the lights of the tall, choked buildings out, save for a window here and there lit in lust or illness. There was no wind, and the smell of earth, heavy and surprising in the concrete city, rose with the mist.

O'Malley walked slowly from east to west on the rolling footpaths of the park, free now of nurses and children and policemen and scholars and old men retired heartbrokenly from business. The paths were free now of everything but the soft night and the mist and the country smell of spring earth and the endless and complex memory of all the feet that had trod and worn the paths in the green park in the palm of the city's hand.

O'Malley walked slowly, carrying his head with the exaggerated and conscious care of a man who feels he has drunk one whisky past absolute clarity. He breathed deeply of that rare and fragrant early morning air which seemed to O'Malley to have been made especially by God, in assurance of His mercy and benign tolerance, to follow whisky.

O'Malley looked around him at the city slumbering magnificently past the trees of the park and was glad to know his home was there, his work, his future. He walked slowly from east to west, breathing in the quiet air, holding his head carefully, but comfortably.

'Pardon me.' A man slipped out in front of him. 'Have you got a light?'

O'Malley stopped and struck a match. He held the match to

the man's cigarette, noticing the touch of rouge on the cheeks, the long, carefully waved hair, the white trembling hands cupping the match, the slight smear of rouge on the man's lips.

'Thanks.' The man lifted his head, looked sidewise, but challengingly, at O'Malley. O'Malley put the matches away and started to move westward, holding his head in gentle balance.

'Lovely night,' said the man hurriedly. His voice was shrill and girlish and came from high in his throat, all breath, nervous, almost hysterical. 'I adore walking in the park at this time on a night like this. Breathe,' he said. 'Just breathe the air.'

O'Malley breathed the air.

'All alone?' the man asked nervously.

'Uhuh,' O'Malley said.

'You're not lonesome?' The man's hands pulled at each other as he talked. 'You're not afraid to walk alone through the park at this hour?'

'No,' O'Malley said, ready, with the drinks and the sweetness of the air, and the feeling of living in and, in a way, owning the great city of New York, to pass on a kind word to every living thing. 'I never get lonesome and I like to walk through the park when it's empty and dark like this.'

The man nodded unhappily. 'Are you sure you don't want company?' he asked desperately, looking up at O'Malley with that sidewise and challenging look, like the look of a frightened but determined woman at a man she had decided to catch.

'I'm sure,' O'Malley said gently. 'I'm sorry.' And he left the man with the carefully waved hair standing next to a tree with the little light of the cigarette gleaming in his hand and walked slowly on. He walked on, feeling sorry for the man, feeling good that he had enough of a fund of sympathy and human feeling so that he could sorrow, even slightly, over a man like that, rouged and roaming the park on a sinful and illicit errand, met for sixty seconds in the middle of the night.

'Say, Buddy,' another man, small, and even in the darkness, knobby and gnarled, stepped out from behind a tree. 'I want a dime.'

O'Malley dug dreamily in his pocket. There was nothing there. 'I haven't got a dime,' he said.

'I want a dime,' the man said. O'Malley saw that his face was dark and savage-looking, not a city face, grimy, hard, gleaming in the light of a distant lamp-post. The clothes the man wore were too large and improvised and torn, and he

266

continually lifted his arm to slide the sleeves back from his wrist, giving him a supplicant and religious look.

'I told you I haven't got a dime,' O'Malley said.

'Gimme a dime!' the little man said loudly. His voice was rough and hoarse, as though he had been shouting in noisy places for years on end.

O'Malley took out his wallet and opened it and showed it to the man. 'There's nothing there,' he said. 'Look.'

The man looked. He lifted his arms to free his wrists from his sleeves, looked uneasily over O'Malley's shoulder up at the lamp-post. O'Malley put his wallet away.

'Gimme a dollar,' the man said.

'I showed you my wallet,' O'Malley said. 'I haven't got a dollar. I haven't got anything. I'm busted.'

The man walked thoughtfully around O'Malley, walking lightly, on his toes, as though he expected to take O'Malley by surprise. 'I'll beat you up,' he said. 'No matter how big you are. I'm a prizefighter. I'm an Indian. I'm a Creek Indian. My name's Billy Elk. Gimme a dime!' He put out his hand as though he was absolutely confident now that he'd convinced O'Malley and the money would be dropped in his hand.

'I'm busted,' O'Malley said. 'Honest.'

Billy Elk circled O'Malley slowly, his large and ragged garments flapping around him. O'Malley stood there, gently willing, in the fragrance and loneliness and peace of the night, to befriend a penniless Creek Indian prizefighter astray far from home in Central Park.

Billy Elk's face creased in thought as he tiptoed around O'Malley. 'Give me the wallet,' he said suddenly. 'I can get a dollar for that.'

'It only cost seventy-five cents,' O'Malley said.

Billy Elk's face creased in thought again. Only half-consciously now, he walked lightly in a circle around O'Malley, who stood there dreamily, looking up at the towers of the city rearing dark and magnificent against the clear soft sky, with here and there the scattered lights, lust and illness, keeping the city from total sleep in the depths of the night.

Suddenly Billy Elk leaped at him, snatching from his outside breast pocket the fountain pen O'Malley carried there. Billy Elk covered it proudly and lovingly in his gnarled hands, half-bent over it, his dark and savage face lit now by wild satisfaction. 'I can get a dollar for this,' he said.

'It only cost twenty-five cents,' O'Malley said gently. 'In the five and ten.'

Billy Elk considered the pen in his hands. 'All right,' he said. 'I can get twenty-five.'

'Who'll give you twenty-five?' O'Malley asked.

Billy Elk backed up three steps to think about this. He sighed, came up to O'Malley and gave him the pen. O'Malley put the pen in his pocket, smiled in a pleasant, brotherly way at the Indian.

'Give me a dollar!' Billy Elk said harshly.

O'Malley smiled again and patted him on the shoulder. 'Good night,' he said, and started slowly home.

'If you don't give me the dollar,' Billy Elk shouted, keeping pace with him, talking up at him, 'I'll report you to the police.'

O'Malley stopped. 'For what?' he asked, smiling dreamily, pleased that the city and the night had produced, after the one Scotch too many, this wild and tiny creature.

'For talking to a fairy,' Billy Elk shouted. 'I saw you!'

'What did you see?' O'Malley asked mildly.

'I saw you with that fairy,' Billy Elk said. 'I'll take you to a policeman. Don't try to get away. I'm a prizefighter. Keep your hands in your pockets!'

'Take me to a policeman,' O'Malley said, feeling somehow that it was his duty, as one of the few citizens of the city awake and moving, to be pleasant, hospitable, at the service of visitors, beggars, lunatics, lost children and young girls fled from home.

They walked out of the park in silence. Billy Elk's face was cast in harsh, savage lines, his eyes glittered, his mouth was set. At the corner on Central Park West, a fat policeman was wearily talking to a cab-driver slouched in his seat. All the weight of the night hung over them, the deaths in the hospitals, the pain endured, the crimes committed in the dark hours, the hearts broken and the torture of men betrayed by women while the city slept, distilled and poured down in the bleak lamplight over the officer of the law and the tired man at the wheel of the old cab under the lamp-post.

O'Malley stopped ten yards away and Billy Elk strode up to the policeman, who was lamenting the fact that his wife had kidney trouble and that his daughter was free with the boys, although she was only in the third term of high school.

The policeman stopped talking when Billy Elk stopped in front of him, and looked at the Indian slowly, mournfully, expecting only trouble, the night's everlasting gift to him.

'Well?' he asked Billy Elk sadly.

Billy Elk looked fleetingly and wildly over his shoulder at O'Malley, then turned back to the policeman. 'Is there an Indian Reservation around here?' he asked loudly.

The policeman, grateful that no murder had turned up, no entry, rape, arson, assault, double-parking, committed, thought seriously for a full minute. 'No,' he said. 'I don't know of any Indian Reservation in these parts.'

'There's a place called Indian Point,' said the cab driver. 'It's up the river.'

Billy Elk nodded soberly, with ancient dignity, came back to O'Malley, and the policeman went on to tell the cab-driver that although his daughter was merely sixteen years old she was built in all respects like a full-blooded woman of thirty.

Billy Elk stood in front of O'Malley and smiled, his face suddenly broken by the flash of teeth and gleam of eye into warm childishness. 'See,' he said. 'I'm not such a bad guy.'

He waved and departed into the park, slipping silently and expertly among the trees, like Tecumseh's braves and the slippery, valiant red defenders of Kentucky's bloody ground.

O'Malley walked slowly home, breathing deeply the clear morning air, pleased to be in a city in which Indians roamed the streets and went to great lengths to prove their friendliness and goodness of heart.

They came out of the movie house and started slowly east-ward in the direction of Fifth Avenue. 'Hitler!' a newsboy called. 'Hitler!'

'That Fletcher,' Dora said, 'the one that played her father. Remember him?'

'Uh huh,' Paul said, holding her hand as they walked slowly up the dark street.

'He's got stones in his kidney.'

'That's the way he acts,' Paul said. 'Now I know how to describe the way that man acts – he acts like a man who has stones in his kidney.'

Dora laughed. 'I X-rayed him last winter. He's one of Dr Thayer's best patients. He's always got something wrong with him. He's going to try to pass the stones out of his kidney this summer.'

'Good luck, Fletcher, old man,' Paul said.

'I used to massage his shoulder. He had neuritis. He makes fifteen hundred dollars a week.'

'No wonder he has neuritis.'

'He asked me to come to his house for dinner.' Dora pulled her hand out of Paul's and slipped it up to his elbow and held on, hard. 'He likes me.'

'I bet he does.'

'What about you?'

'What about me what?' Paul asked.

'Do you like me?'

They stopped at Rockefeller Plaza and leaned over the marble wall and looked down at the fountain and the statue and the people sitting out at the tables, drinking, and the waiters standing around, listening to the sound of the fountain.

'I can't stand you,' Paul said. He kissed her hair.

'That's what I thought,' Dora said. They both laughed.

They looked down at the Plaza, at the thin trees with the

light-green leaves rustling in the wind that came down between the buildings. There were pansies, yellow and tight, along the borders of the small pools with the bronze sea statues, and hydrangeas, and little full trees, all shaking in the wind and the diffuse, clear light of the flood lamps above. Couples strolled slowly down from Fifth Avenue, talking amiably in low, calm, week-end voices, appreciating the Rockefeller frivolity and extravagance which had carved a place for hydrangeas and water and saplings and spring and sea-gods riding bronze dolphins out of these austere buildings, out of the bleak side of Business.

Paul and Dora walked up the promenade, looking in the windows. They stopped at a window filled with men's sports clothes – gaberdine slacks and bright-coloured shirts with short sleeves and brilliant handkerchiefs to tie around the throat.

'I have visions,' Paul said, 'of sitting in my garden, with two Great Danes, dressed like that, like a Hollywood actor in the country.'

'Have you got a garden?' Dora asked.

'No.'

'Those're nice pants,' Dora said.

They went on to the next window. 'On the other hand,' Paul said, 'there are days when I want to look like that. A derby hat and a stiff blue shirt with a pleated bosom and a little starched white collar and a five-dollar neat little necktie and a Burberry overcoat. Leave the office at five o'clock every day to go to a cocktail party.'

'You go to a cocktail party almost every afternoon anyway,' Dora said. 'Without a derby hat.'

'A different kind of cocktail party,' Paul said. He started her across Fifth Avenue. 'The kind attended by men with starched blue pleated bosoms. Some day.'

'Oh, Lord,' Dora said as they ran to escape a bus, 'look at those dresses.'

They stood in front of Saks.

'Fifth Avenue,' Paul said. 'Street of dreams.'

'It's nice to know things like that exist,' Dora murmured, looking into the stage-lit window at the yellow dress and the sign that said 'Tropical Nights in Manhattan' and the little carved-stone fish that for some reason was in the same window. 'Even if you can't have them.'

'Uptown?' Paul asked. 'Or to my house?'

'I feel like walking.' Dora looked up at Paul and grinned.

'For the moment.' She squeezed his arm. 'Only for the moment. Uptown.'

They started uptown.

'I love those models,' Paul said. 'Each and every one of them. They're superior, yet warm; inviting, yet polite. Their breasts are always tipped at the correct angle for the season.'

'Sure,' Dora said, 'papier-mâché. It's easy with papier-mâché. Look. Aluminium suitcases. Travel by air.'

'They look like my mother's kitchen pots.'

'Wouldn't you like to own a few of them?'

'Yes.' Paul peered at them. 'Fly away. Buy luggage and depart. Leave for the ends of the earth.'

'They got a little case just for books. A whole separate little travelling bookcase.'

'That's just what I need,' Paul said, 'for my trips on the Fifth Avenue bus every morning.'

They passed St Patrick's, dark and huge, with the moon sailing over it.

'Do you think God walks up Fifth Avenue?' Paul asked.

'Sure,' said Dora. 'Why not?'

'We are princes of the earth,' Paul said. 'All over the world men slave to bring riches to these few blocks for us to look at and say "Yes, very nice" or "Take it away; it stinks". I feel very important when I walk up Fifth Avenue.'

They stopped at the window of the Hamburg-American Line. Little dolls in native costumes danced endlessly around a pole while other dolls in native costume looked on. All the dolls had wide smiles on their faces. 'Harvest Festival in Buckeburg, Germany,' a small sign said.

A private policeman turned the corner and stood and watched them. They moved to the next window.

' "A suggestion to passengers to promote carefree travel," ' Paul read off a booklet. 'Also, Hapag-Lloyd announces a twenty per cent reduction for all educators on sabbatical leave. They are "Masters in the Art of Travel", they say.'

'I used to want to go to see Germany,' Dora said. 'I know a lot of Germans and they're nice.'

'I'll be there soon,' Paul said as they passed the private policeman.

'You're going to visit it?'

'Uh huh. At the expense of the Government. In a well-tailored khaki uniform. I'm going to see glamorous Europe, seat of culture, at last. From a bombing plane. To our left we have the Stork Club, seat of culture for East Fifty-third Street. Look at the pretty girls. A lot of them have breasts at the correct angle, too. See how nature mimics art. New York is a wonderful city.'

Dora didn't say anything. She hung on to him tightly as they went down the street. They turned at the corner and walked down Madison Avenue. After a while they stopped at a shop that had photographs and radios in the window. 'That's what I want.' Paul pointed at a machine. 'A Capehart. It plays two symphonies at a time. You just lie on your back and out come Brahms and Beethoven and Prokofieff. That's the way life should be. Lie on your back and be surrounded by great music, automatically.'

Dora looked at the phonograph, all mahogany and doors and machinery. 'Do you really think there's going to be a war?' she said.

'Sure. They're warming up the pitchers now. They're waiting to see if the other side has right-handed or left-handed batters before they nominate their starting pitchers.'

They continued walking downtown.

'But it's in Europe,' Dora said. 'Do you think we'll get into it?'

'Sure. Read the papers.' He glanced at the window they were passing. 'Look at those nice tables. Informal luncheons on your terrace. Metal and glass for outdoor feeding. That would be nice, eating out on a terrace off those wonderful coloured plates, rich food with green salads. With a view of mountains and a lake, and inside, the phonograph.'

'That sounds good,' Dora said quietly.

'I could get an extra speaker,' Paul said, 'and wire it out to the terrace, so we could listen as we ate. I like Mozart with dinner.' He laughed and drew her to a bookstore window.

'I always get sad,' Dora said, 'when I look in a bookshop window and see all the books I'm never going to have time to read.'

Paul kissed her. 'What did you think the first time you saw me?' he asked.

'What did *you* think?'

'I thought, "I must get that girl!" '

Dora laughed, close to him.

'What did you think?' Paul asked.

'I thought' – she giggled – 'I thought, "I must get that man!" '

'Isn't New York marvellous?' Paul said. 'Where did you say you come from?'

'Seattle,' Dora said. 'Seattle, Washington.'

'Here we are on Madison Avenue, holding hands, shopping for the future . . .

'Even if there was a war,' Dora said after a while, 'why would you have to get mixed up in it? Why would the United States have to get mixed up in it?'

'They got into the last one, didn't they?' Paul said. 'They'll get into this one.'

'They were gypped the last time,' Dora said. 'The guys who were killed were gypped.'

'That's right,' said Paul. 'They were killed for six-per cent interest on bonds, for oil wells, for spheres of influence. I wish I had a sphere of influence.'

'Still,' said Dora, 'you'd enlist this time?'

'Yep. The first day. I'd walk right up to the recruiting office and say, "Paul Triplett, twenty-six years old, hard as nails, good eyes, good teeth, good feet; give me a gun. Put me in a plane, so I can do a lot of damage.'

They walked a whole block in silence.

'Don't you think you'd be gypped this time, too?' Dora said. 'Don't you think they'd have you fighting for bonds and oil wells all over again?'

'Uh huh.'

'And even so, you'd sign up?'

'The first day.'

Dora pulled her hand away from him. 'Do you *like* the idea of killing people?'

'I hate the idea,' Paul said slowly. 'I don't want to hurt anybody. I think the idea of war is ridiculous. I want to live in a world in which everybody sits on a terrace and eats off a metal-and-glass table off coloured plates and the phonograph inside turns Mozart over automatically and the music is piped out to an extra loudspeaker on the terrace. Only Hitler isn't interested in that kind of world. He's interested in another kind of world. I couldn't stand to live in his kind of world, German or home-made.'

'You wouldn't kill Hitler,' Dora said. 'You'd just kill young boys like yourself.'

'That's right.'

'Do you like that?'

'I'm really not interested in killing Hitler, either,' Paul said.

'I want to kill the idea he represents for so many people. In years to come I'll cry over the young boys I've killed and maybe if they kill me, they'll cry over me.'

'They're probably just like you.' They were walking fast now.

'Sure,' Paul said. 'I'm sure they'd love to go to bed with you tonight. I bet they'd love to walk along the fountains with the bronze statues in Rockefeller Plaza, holding hands with you on a spring Saturday evening and looking at the sports clothes in the windows. I bet a lot of them like Mozart, too, but still I'll kill them. Gladly.'

'Gladly?'

'Yes, gladly.' Paul wiped his eyes with his hands, suddenly tired. 'Gladly today. I'll weep for them in years to come. Today they're guns aimed at me and the world I want. Their bodies protect an idea I have to kill to live. Hey!' He stretched out his hand and caught hers. 'What's the sense talking about things like this tonight?'

'But it's all a big fraud,' Dora cried. 'You're being used and you know it.'

'That's right,' Paul said. 'It's all a big fraud, the whole business. Even so, I got to fight. I'll be gypped, but by a little bit I'll do something for my side, for Mozart on a terrace at dinner. What the hell, it's not even heroism. I'll be dragged in, whatever I say.'

'That's too bad,' Dora said softly, walking by herself. 'It's too bad.'

'Sure,' Paul said. 'Some day maybe it'll be better. Maybe some day the world'll be run for people who like Mozart. Not today.'

They stopped. They were in front of a little art store. There was a reproduction of the Renoir painting of a boating party on the river. There was the woman kissing the Pekingese, and the man in his underwear with a straw hat and his red beard, solid as earth, and the wit with his cocked derby hat whispering to the woman with her hands to her ears, and there was the great still life in the foreground, of wine and bottles and glasses and grapes and food.

'I saw it in Washington,' Paul said. 'They had it in Washington. You can't tell why it's a great picture from the print. There's an air of pink immortality hanging over it. They got it in New York now and I go look at it three times a week. It's settled, happy, solid. It's a picture of a summertime that vanished a long time ago.' Paul kissed her hand. 'It's getting late, darling, the hours're dwindling. Let's go home.'

They got into a cab and went downtown to his apartment.

The Priest

The priest walked leisurely across the Besancon Bridge. The Doubs flowed swiftly past, springlike and ruffled and green, carrying with it a bright mountain breeze through the sunny valley. The priest was round and small and his dark, tanned face was rosy and cheerful in the pleasant morning as he walked with little steps next to the stone balustrade, keeping off the side as a tank marked with the black cross rumbled past a wagonload of cabbages into town. Two young blond paratroopers, with their caps off, were leaning on the balustrade, staring quietly into the rushing water, their hair blowing in the wind, and the priest stopped next to them and stood by their side looking east to the mountains.

'Very pretty morning,' the priest said, smiling.

'Excuse us, Father,' one of the paratroopers said, haltingly, 'we do not speak French. We speak only German.'

The priest shrugged, smiled, patted one of the boys in a fatherly gesture on the shoulder. '*Guten tag,*' he said, moving off.

'*Auf Wiedersehen,* Father,' the boy said, standing up straight. He was almost a foot taller than the priest and he seemed very young, seventeen, eighteen perhaps, standing there with his hair blowing over his unlined, rather pale face.

The priest moved on, his small, scuffed, dusty shoes making a little mincing pattern under the swinging, worn folds of his cassock. He walked slowly along the busy street, pleased with the morning traffic, nodding agreeably at the housewives with their net shopping bags stuffed with vegetables. He stopped in front of one of the shops which was used as an art gallery, and looked at a local painter's water-colour of the Besançon cathedral, his dark, round face grave with judgement.

In the same window, by the same artist, there were three plump, long-legged nudes lying in abandoned positions on rugs and sofas, and the priest glanced rather hastily at the pink and fleshy confections. A little grin played around the corners of his mouth as he turned away from the window and continued up the street.

He crossed the cobbled square at the end of the street, and, holding the skirts of his cassock, skipped nimbly and good-naturedly to dodge a large German Army truck that was rumbling through. A little out of breath, and smiling, he walked to a table on the open terrace of the large café that stood under the new foliage of the trees along one side of the square. The man sitting at the table stood up as he approached.

'Good morning, Father,' he said, holding a chair for the priest, and smiling with pleasure.

'Good morning, my son.' The priest sat down, smiling at him, but sighing, too, as a fat man does at sudden changes of position.

The man seated himself beside the priest, so that they both could look out over the square and enjoy the fresh bustle of the spring morning. He was a large, slender man, with weary, dark eyes and a sharp mouth, and he was dressed in faded workman's clothes, with old, washed oil and grease stains evident here and there in the worn cloth.

'I hope,' said the priest, 'I didn't keep you waiting long.'

'I just arrived,' the man said.

The waiter trotted to their table. 'Messieurs,' he said.

'White wine for me,' said the priest.

'Two,' said the other man.

The waiter trotted off.

The man in workman's clothes surveyed the priest fondly, but with amusement. 'Solomon,' he said. 'you're getting fatter every week.'

The priest sighed. 'Flesh is the curse of man. I live on cabbage and skimmed milk and I walk a hundred kilometres a week up and down mountain roads and I grow more and more like a pincushion. Still, Maurice, in a way, it has its points. Everyone expects a priest to be fat.'

'That's true,' said Maurice.

The waiter came back with the two glasses of white wine and the saucers. 'Messieurs,' he said, serving them. He trotted off.

The priest looked after him absently, noticing that there was no one at the nearby tables. 'All right, Maurice,' he said.

Maurice sipped his wine. 'In Marcel Artois's barn, in the hayloft . . .'

'Yes,' said the priest.

'On the road to Epinal.'

'I know the house.' The priest sipped his drink, nodding absently, his eyes squinted a little, looking out over the square.

'Two Sten guns with a thousand rounds of ammunition . . .'

'Well,' said the priest.

'Three Enfield rifles with two hundred and fifty rounds of ammunition. A Luger and six grenades. How many men does Philip have with him?'

'Ten.'

'Does that include you?'

'That includes me.' The priest nodded.

'The difficulty with the child,' Maurice said loudly, as two German lieutenants passed, 'is that he refuses to recognise the authority of his mother.'

'I will come by Wednesday afternoon,' the priest said clearly, 'and attempt to reason with him.'

'There will be a gasoline convoy passing the crossroad two miles north of Epinal around eleven o'clock tomorrow night,' said Maurice. 'Ordinarily, the convoys are lightly guarded in this area, and there is brush right down to the roadside, and they stop at the crossroads for a minute or two to wait for stragglers. Tell Philip I suggest that that is the most profitable place . . .'

'I'll tell him,' said the priest.

'However, he understands,' Maurice said, 'that it is his business and I am merely offering suggestions.'

'I'll tell him,' said the priest.

'Messieurs?' The waiter was standing over them, questioning.

'Nothing more for me, thank you,' said the priest.

Maurice put down the money for the drinks and the waiter cleared away the glasses and the saucers.

'Gasoline trucks,' said Maurice, 'make a very satisfactory target. They have a tendency to blow up.'

'Philip will be pleased.' The priest nodded again, with a trace of amusement in his dark eyes.

'Tell Philip I pray that God smiles upon your enterprise,' said Maurice, very seriously.

The priest smiled a little. 'I will pass on yours and God's good wishes . . .'

Maurice turned and stared soberly at the priest for the first time. 'Solomon,' he said softly, 'I think you are taking too much of a risk.'

The priest grinned. 'Again,' he said, 'the old song . . . '

'But to pretend to be a priest!' Maurice shook his head. You're always on the verge of being discovered. Any *curé* with his eyes half-open . . . Any sudden or unexpected situation . . . '

The priest looked around him, his eyes crinkled. 'I know this will offend your deep religious sensibilities, Maurice,' he said, 'but it is amazing how little people expect of the servants of the Church. And priests're always rambling around, poking their noses into other people's business. They make perfect messengers for the Underground. If we could really get the holy men of France into the movement, we would have a system of intelligence better than any telephone network ; . . '

'The Church has its own spiritual problems,' Maurice said bleakly.

'Forgive me.' The priest stretched out his hand and touched Maurice's arm. 'I mean no offence.'

'It still strikes me as dangerous,' Maurice said.

The priest shook his head. 'Look at me,' he said.

Maurice stared at him. 'Well?'

'In every magazine,' the priest said, 'on every wall, there are pictures of criminals against Germany who look just like me – Jews, swarthy, with thick lips, and hooked noses . . . Why, Maurice,' the priest said, grinning, 'I could make a fortune as a photographer's model in Berlin.'

Maurice chuckled. 'I must admit . . . '

'But dressed like this . . . ' The priest shrugged. 'A priest is expected to look like anything at all in the world. Anyway, I've got away with it for three years now. I couldn't conduct Mass, but I tell my beads in public, and I carry a breviary and read a little Latin, and I got a smattering of the sacraments from Father Morand before they killed him, and my papers look more authentic than a monastery full of Benedictine brothers, and the cassock is very handy when it comes to hiding my pistol.'

Maurice stood up, smiling. 'You always win this argument. Still, it gives me a chill every time I see you pass a church.'

'I promise to defrock myself,' the priest said, 'ten minutes after the Germans're out of France.'

'Well,' said Maurice, 'I must get back to work.' They shook hands. 'Good-bye, Father.'

'I promise,' Solomon said gravely, 'to do nothing to disgrace the cloth. God be with you, my son.'

Solomon sat at the table in the playful, sunny wind, watching Maurice cross the square. Maurice had a square, upright way of walking, and, knowing him, Solomon felt that by his walk Maurice betrayed himself to all the world — honest, righteous, devoid of subservience or fear. Each time, after their meetings, when they said good-bye, Solomon was moved by worriment and sorrow for his friend, and a bitter sense that they would not meet again. The trick was, in their business, to feel nothing, no affection, no sympathy, no regrets for the dead and dying. But fighting beside men in this obscure war, with your lives on the tips of each other's tongues a hundred times a day, with your life dependent every moment on their rectitude and sacrifice, you found yourself loving the good ones better than a wife or a son, and then the trick, of course, did not work . . .

Maurice disappeared around a corner and Solomon sighed and stood up heavily, pulling his cassock down.

He stared back across the terrace, but at that moment a canvas-covered Army truck drove up and the soldiers jumped out and the young lieutenant said loudly, 'Nobody will move, if you please. All the patrons of this establishment will come with me, if you please . . .'

Solomon looked at the corner to make sure that Maurice had disappeared and then sat down, sighing like a fat man, waiting for the Germans to reach him.

The interior of the truck was dark and crowded with some twenty patrons of the café. An odour of fear hung over the twenty heads and people attempted to remain frigid and remote from neighbours pressing on all sides.

'This is a formidable nuisance,' one gentleman said in a loud voice, looking angrily at the impassive guard at the rear of the truck. 'I have a very important business engagement at one o'clock. And I have a pass signed personally by General Meister himself, who is a personal acquaintance of mine.'

'I have a personal request,' a voice cut into the semi-gloom under the canvas from near the front of the truck. 'Please keep personally quiet.'

'I will remember that voice,' said the personal acquaintance of General Meister threateningly.

The priest wriggled a little on his bench and his two neighbours looked at him sourly.

'Excuse me,' he said apologetically. 'A fat man finds it

281

difficult to be comfortable in his clothes . . . ' He put his hands under his cassock, through the side slits and pulled at his belt.

'What's the matter?' a man across the aisle muttered. 'The priest wearing a corset?'

Two or three of the men tittered a little sourly.

'Excuse me again,' the priest said, lifting himself a little from the narrow wooden bench, under which there were some tow chains loosely stowed.

'Only the priests,' said his neighbour loudly, 'still remain uncomfortably fat in France.'

Solomon sat back once more, sighing, a tiny smile on his lips in the darkness. Below him, hidden by the chains, lay the small pistol he had contrived to loosen from his belt and drop there.

'What did you have for dinner last night, Father?' his neighbour asked unpleasantly. 'A whole stuffed duck?'

'God be with you, my son,' Solomon said serenely as the truck rattled into the courtyard of Gestapo headquarters.

Solomon was sleeping when they came to his cell and opened the door. It was near dawn and dark and cold, and he woke shivering when the two S.S. men drew back the bolt and shone the beam of the electric lantern in his face, where he lay on the wooden bench that served the cell as a bed.

'You,' one of the jailers said. 'Get up.'

Solomon sat up, rubbing the ruffled thin hair on the top of his head, still half-caught in the sharp darkness in the vague, delicious dream he'd been having in which he had been eating a large dinner in a warm, sunny café in Marseilles. A warm, peppery soup and lobster with a tomato sauce . . .

'Well,' he said, blinking, struggling with the old, familiar cold knot of fear at the sight of the black uniforms, 'well gentlemen . . . '

'Get up.'

Solomon stood up.

'Are you dressed?' The man with the lantern played it up and down the ragged cassock.

'Yes.' Solomon swallowed and he felt himself shiver, thin waves of cold trembling from his groin upwards, finally tightening the skin on his forehead and around his ears in little spasms.

'This way,' said the man with the flashlight.

Between the two S.S. men, Solomon walked out of the cell

282

and down the stone corridor, his knees hurting as though the act of walking was a shocking and unnatural activity. Too bad, too bad, Solomon thought, licking the corner of his lips dryly, as he followed the dark figure along the dim stone. He had thought that he was going to get away with it. His papers had been in perfect order, excellently forged, and they had searched him only perfunctorily and questioned him hardly at all, and had even been slightly apologetic, or as apologetic as you could ever expect a German to be. When he had dropped off to his cold sleep he had really thought they would release him in the morning. Well, he thought wryly, there are several different kinds of release.

The S.S. men stopped in front of a door.

'There's a man in there,' the German with the lantern said, 'who's going to be shot in a few minutes. He wants the last rites of the Church. Ordinarily, we are not so agreeable, but' – with a small grin in the weak light – 'since we had the Church so handy this evening, we saw no harm in letting him make his soul comfortable. I, myself, am a Catholic, and I understand that a man, before he . . . At any rate, you have fifteen minutes.'

He swung the door open and put his lantern down on the floor inside the cell. Solomon walked slowly in and stood still as the door closed behind him.

The lantern diffused a thin pale light along the floor, leaving the corners and walls of the cell in heavy darkness. A man was standing with his back to the door, his head lost in the shadows in the bare room. He turned when the sound of the Germans at the door had ceased.

'Father,' he said softly, but mechanically, as though he had rehearsed the speech, 'I am very glad you came. I have lived by the Church all my life and I believe in the life everlasting and I wish to make my peace with God in accordance with the sacraments before facing judgement . . . ' The voice was bruised and muffled in the shadowy room, as though it came from a throat and lips that had been sorely torn and battered, but Solomon recognised it.

'We have fifteen minutes, my son,' he said, trying to control the sorrow in his throat. He stepped forward so that Maurice could see his face.

Maurice slowly lifted his eyes to look at Solomon. His lips were puffed and cut and three teeth were missing, with the blood still coming from the sockets. He held his hands stiffly in front of him. They were torn and swollen and covered with blood from the places at the fingertips where his nails had been torn out.

'The Germans told me,' Maurice said evenly, 'that I was lucky to be killed on just this night, being a good Catholic. They happened to have a priest here and they were releasing him in the morning. Shall we begin, Father?'

'Are you sure . . . ' Solomon could not keep his voice from trembling.

'Yes, Father,' said Maurice, staring at the door of the cell, behind which the Germans might or might not be listening.

Solomon sat on the small three-legged stool in the centre of the room and, stiffly, with the pale light making his ruined face look clotted and grotesque, Maurice kneeled before him.

The jail was absolutely quiet and Solomon could hear the breath whistling brokenly through Maurice's smashed nose. Solomon closed his eyes, trying to remember some scraps of what Father Morand had taught him before the Germans killed him.

'Son, I will hear your confession now,' he said, surprised at the clarity and steadiness of his own voice.

Maurice bowed his head at Solomon's knee. 'Forgive me, Father,' he said evenly, 'for my sins . . . ' Then, in the quiet night, he confessed. He confessed to the sin of doubt, the sins of anger and murder, the sins of envy and desire, the sin of despair. Kneeling rigidly, his wounded hands resting for support on Solomon's knees, staining the old cloth with the slow, dark blood, he spoke soberly and clearly, his voice swelling occasionally in the stone room, loud enough to be heard through the open grating of the oak door, if anyone were listening there . . .

As the voice went on, Solomon remembered another man he had talked with, played another game with, before death. It was when he was a boy of fourteen and a neighbour was dying and too weak to leave the house, and Solomon had gone every afternoon and played chess with the dying man in the sickroom. The man had once been fat and red of face, but now his skin was yellow and old and hung in loose folds from his bones. He was an avid player and loved to win, and occasionally cheated, moving pieces surreptitiously and taking back moves, falling back to his pillows in exhausted triumph after the game was over. Solomon had played with him on the day of his death, and at the funeral had watched with dry eyes as the coffin was lowered, the mourners and the cold earth, and stone crosses of the cemetery somehow mixed in his mind with bishops taking pawns and black wooden knights held in a yellow hand advancing over red squares. Ever since then, death and chess had lain in troubled confusion in his mind, funerals and ivory, flowers and squares, tears and pawns tumbled in a box mingling in obscure, painful symbols in his brain. As he regarded his friend, kneeling before him, he felt as though he were betraying him in this double game of priest and chessman, and he wrenched at his will to focus all his pity and affection on the dying man. He put his hand out humbly and touched the bloody fingers of his friend. The Jews did it differently, he thought. They went into death hot and guilty, as to a roaring battle in a dark, bloody, doubtful abyss, with intercession to their wrathy, fitful God not to be hoped for. He thought of the times he had seen Maurice coldly skirt death, and the times he had seen him wash his child's face, and of the times he had seen Maurice kill, with a rather abstracted, calm, regretful air, and of the times he had seen him walk side by side with his wife, dressed for Sunday, on the road to church.

As the voice went on in the cold stone room, Solomon thought of the times he had looked at Maurice's slender, strained face, and known deep in his heart that he was going to die before their business came to an end. You felt that about yourself from time to time, and often about others, and you took a drink, or you got into an argument, and tried to forget it, but he had been sure of Maurice. Solomon was not a religious man, and he doubted that God would condemn Maurice because he had been shriven by a Jew, but he looked closely at Maurice to see if the orthodox Catholic soul, so obedient to the ordered sacraments and hierarchy, was suffering at the deception. But Maurice's face and voice were calm and clear, as though he were being granted absolution for all his earthly deeds by the Bishop of Rome, himself.

Finally, the droning, broken voice stopped in the cold cell. Somewhere down the corridor there was the chilly clank of steel and a young German voice singing the mournful words of 'Lili Marlene', the sorrowing, sentimental melody hanging cloyingly on the stale, condemned, frozen air. Solomon stared at the austere, destroyed face of his friend. If there were only some way of giving him one word to carry with him to the final wall, one word to tell him, you are loved, you will not be forgotten, we do not believe the shallow coffin and the quick limepit are the end, we will mention your name later in the century . . . His hands groped in a small, lost gesture before him, but there was the sound of steps outside the door, and the fiddling with the lock.

He blindly ruffled the pages of his breviary and read a scrap of Latin for the absolution, and as the door swung open, made vague, wandering motions with his hands, from some dim memory of another deathbed.

Maurice stood up as the Germans came in. 'I am very happy, Father,' he said courteously as the Germans bound his hands, 'that you were here tonight. I hope it has not interfered too much with your business in these parts.'

Solomon stared at the Germans, knowing that Maurice was telling him he had not broken, that he had told the Germans nothing, that no plans were invalidated by his death.

'It has not interfered, son,' he said. He stood up and followed them out to the corridor and watched Maurice walk away between the Germans, the familiar walk unchanged by the prison, or the cords on his wrist, or the knowledge that the wall was waiting. Maurice walked away, as he had walked away from the terrace of the café, the lean shoulders set square and upright, betraying himself to all the world.

A third guard came up to Solomon, touched his elbow. 'This way, Father,' he said, and led him back to his cell. He was sitting there, waiting for his deliverance when he heard the small muffled sound, like a door closing sharply far away, from the other side of the prison.

Medal from Jerusalem

'The question that haunts me,' Schneider was saying in his high, soft voice, 'is my jazz, is it real jazz or is it merely European jazz?' He was leaning against the bar of the Patio restaurant between Tel Aviv and Jaffa, which used to be the old German Consulate, and speaking to Lieutenant Mitchell Gunnison in short, gaspy bursts of talk, smiling a little sadly and a little archly at Mitchell, and occasionally touching his sleeve lightly with the tips of his fingers. 'I mean,' he said, 'I know it's good enough for Palestine, but in America what would they say about a pianist like me?'

'Well,' said Gunnison gravely, 'I'd say they'd think it was real jazz. He was young and he spoke slowly and he seemed to think very hard before he answered a question.

'You don't know,' Schneider said, sighing, 'how you've encouraged me. I listen to the records, of course, but they're old, and you never know what actually is going on in America and, after all, we all know where *is* no other jazz, no place, and with a war like this, and God knows how long it's going to last, a musician gets out of touch. And once you are out of touch, you might as well die. Just die.'

'You have nothing to worry about,' Mitchell said. 'You'll be a sensation in America.'

'If I ever get there.' Schneider smiled sadly and shrugged a little. 'Anyway, you must come tomorrow. I'm working on a new arrangement with the drummer. A rhumba, Viennese style. It's ridiculous, but I think you'll like it.'

'I'm sorry,' Mitchell said. 'I won't be here tomorrow.'

'Then next night,' said Schneider.

'I won't be here then, either,' Mitchell said. 'I'm going tomorrow. Leave's up.'

There was a little silence and Schneider looked down at the bar and flicked his beer glass with his fingernail, making a frail musical sound in the dark oak bar-room. 'Some more fighting?' Schneider asked.

'A little more fighting'' Mitchell nodded soberly.

'You fly, no doubt,' said Schneider. 'I have no wish to intrude on military information, but the wings on the chest . . . '

'I'm a navigator.' Mitchell smiled at him.

'It must be an interesting profession. Measuring the distance between one star and another star.' Schneider finished his beer slowly. 'Well, *sholom aleichem* . . . That's good luck. Or, to be more exact, peace be with you.'

'Thank you,' Mitchell said.

'Hebrew,' said Schneider. 'I'm ashamed to talk Hebrew to anybody who knows it. The accent, they tell me, is frightful. But you don't mind, do you?'

'No,' said Mitchell. He turned to the bartender. 'Mr Abrams,' he said, 'another beer please, for Mr Schneider.'

'No, no.' Schneider waved his hands in protest. 'The artist should not drink before the performance. After . . . Another matter . . . Ah,' he said, bowing elaborately, '*Fräulein*, we are enchanted.'

Mitchell turned around. Ruth was standing there, looking a little hurried and out of breath, but smiling, and as pretty as ever in a light cotton dress, with her skin burned dark by the sun and her eyes full of welcome and pleasure at seeing him.

'I was afraid,' she said, coming over to him and taking his hand, 'I wasn't going to leave,' Mitchell said. 'Not until they closed the doors on me and threw me out.'

'I am delighted,' Ruth laughed and squeezed his arm. 'I am so absolutely delighted.'

'My presence,' Schneider said, bowing, 'I no longer consider necessary. A hundred thanks for the beer, Lieutenant. Now I play or Mr Abrams will start complaining he is not getting his money's worth out of me. Listen, carefully, if it is not too much of a bore, to my version of "*Stardust*".'

'We'll listen very carefully,' Mitchell said.

Schneider went outside to the *patio*, and a moment later preliminary erratic runs and fragments of melody came floating into the bar as he warmed up for the night's work.

'So.' Ruth faced him, looking at him with an expression that was half ownership, half amusement. 'So. What have we been doing all day?'

'Well,' Mitchell started, 'we . . . '

'You are the most beautiful lieutenant in the American Army,' Ruth said, grinning.

'Well, we went swimming,' Mitchell said, pleased and embarrassed, pretending she'd said nothing. 'And we hung around on the beach. And we flew a couple of bar-room missions. Gin and grapefruit juice.'

'Isn't Palestinian grapefruit wonderful?' Ruth asked loyally.

'Sensational,' Mitchell said. 'Nothing like it in America.'

'You're such a liar.' Ruth leaned over and kissed him lightly.

'There was an Eighth Air Force pilot down from England,' Mitchell said, 'and he told us how tough it was over Wilhelmshaven and we told the lies about Ploesti, and then it was time to shave and come to see you.'

'What did you think while you were shaving? Were you sad because you had to leave your interesting friends and see me?'

'Broken-hearted,' Mitchell said.

'You've got such a nice, skinny face,' Ruth touched the line of his jaw. 'You're as pretty as an English lieutenant. I'm not fond of the English, but they have the prettiest lieutenants of any army.'

'We send our pretty ones to the Pacific,' said Mitchell. 'Guadalcanal. We preserve them for American womanhood.'

Ruth signalled Mr Abrams for a drink. 'I was in Jerusalem today. I told my boss I was sick and went there. It's so bad – we never got to see Jerusalem together.'

'Some other time,' Mitchell said. 'I'll come back and we'll see Jerusalem.'

'Don't lie to me,' Ruth said, seriously. 'Please don't lie. You won't come back. You won't see me again. Absolutely no lies, please.'

Mitchell felt very young. He felt there was something to be said, and an older man would know how to say it, but he felt dumb and bereaved and clumsy, and it must have showed on his face as he peered at his glass, because Ruth laughed and touched his lips with her fingers and said, 'You have such a tragic face for an American. Where do you come from in America?'

'Vermont,' Mitchell said.

'Has everybody got a face like yours in Vermont?'

'Everybody.'

'I will visit there,' Ruth drained her glass, 'at some later date.'

'I'll give you my address,' Mitchell said.

'Of course,' said Ruth politely. 'You must write it down some time.'

They went out into the *patio* and sat down at a table on the old flagstones under a palm tree, with blue blackout lights shining dimly over the uniforms and pale dresses, and the moon riding over the Mediterranean and causing flickering shadows over the dancers who now claimed the spot where the German Consul had lived well in days gone by. Mitchell ordered champagne because it was his last night. It was Syrian champagne, but not bad, and to both of them it gave an air of festivity and importance to the evening, as it rocked in its silver bucket of ice. Eric, the waiter with the limp, ceremoniously took Ruth's ration tickets, and Schneider, seated with the drummer across the *patio*, with the drum dimly lit from inside by an orange light of which Schneider was very proud, played 'Summertime' because he had decided that was the song Mitchell liked best. The old song, played trickily and well in the soft, echoing *patio*, somehow sounded, by some ineradicable stamp in Schneider's blood, like Carolina and Vienna and the Balkans, with here and there chords of an old Hebrew chant, quite just and indigenous here between the heavy stone walls on the edge of the Sinai Desert.

'I'm jealous of him,' said Ruth, speaking over the edge of her glass.

'Who?'

'Schneider.'

'Why?' Mitchell asked.

'Because of the way he looks at you. He's crazy about you. Has he asked you to come to tea with him and his mother?'

'Yes,' said Mitchell, trying not to smile.

'I'll tear his eyes out,' Ruth said. 'I'm jealous of anybody who looks at you that way. The girls back in Vermont and those Red Cross girls.'

'You have nothing to worry about,' Mitchell said. 'Nobody looks at me that way. Not even Schneider or you.'

'That's the nicest thing about you,' Ruth said. 'You don't know anything. I'm so used to men who know just how many steps out of bed each look a woman gives them measures. I must visit America after the war . . .'

'Where will you really go?' Mitchell asked. 'Back to Berlin?'

'No.' Ruth stared reflectively down at her plate. 'No, not back to Berlin. Never back to Berlin. The Germans have made clear their feelings about me. A little thing like a war will not

290

change them. The lamb does not go back to the slaughterhouse. Anyway, I have nobody there. There was a young man . . . ' She leaned over and picked up the bottle and absently poured for Mitchell and herself. 'I don't know what happened to him. Stalingrad, maybe, Alamein . . . who knows?'

Four men came into the *patio* and walked through the brief illumination of the blue lights. Three of them were Arabs in European dress, and the fourth was a man in the uniform of the American Army with the civilian technical adviser patch on his shoulder. They stopped at the table. The three Arabs bowed a little, ceremoniously to Ruth, and the American said, 'I thought you were sick.'

'This is Mr Carver,' Ruth said to Mitchell with a wave to the American. 'He's my boss.'

'Hi, Lieutenant,' said Carver. He was a big, fat man, with a weary, puffy, intelligent face. He turned back to Ruth. 'I thought you were sick,' he repeated in a pleasant, loud slightly drunken voice.

'I was sick,' Ruth said, cheerfully. 'I had a miraculous recovery.'

'The American Army,' Carver said, 'expects every civilian worker to do her duty.'

'Tomorrow,' said Ruth. 'Now please go away with your friends. The lieutenant and I are having an intimate talk.'

'Lieutenant . . . ' It was one of the Arabs, the shortest of the three, a slight, dark man, with a round face and liquid, veiled eyes. 'My name is Ali Khazen. Permit me to introduce myself, as no one here seems to remember his manners well enough to do so.'

Mitchell stood up. 'Mitchell Gunnison,' he said, putting out his hand.

'Forgive me,' Carver said. 'I'm suffering from drink. This is Sayed Taif . . . ' He indicated the tallest of the Arabs, a middle-aged man with a severe, handsome, tight-lipped face. Mitchell shook hands with him.

'He doesn't like Americans,' Carver said loudly. 'He's the leading journalist of the local Arab world and he writes for thirty-five papers in the United States and he doesn't like Americans.'

'What was that?' Taif asked politely, inclining his head in a reserved, small gesture.

'Also, he's deaf,' said Carver. 'Most useful equipment for any journalist.'

Nobody bothered to introduce the third Arab, who stood a little to one side, watching Taif with a fierce, admiring stare, like a boxer dog at his master's feet.

'Why don't you all go away and eat your dinner?' Ruth said.

'Lieutenant,' Carver said, ignoring her, 'take the advice of a veteran of the Middle East. Do not become involved with Palestine.'

'He's not becoming involved with Palestine,' Ruth said. 'He's becoming involved with me.'

'Beware Palestine.' Carver weaved a little as he spoke. 'The human race is doomed in Palestine. For thousands of years. They chop down the forests, burn down the cities, wipe out the inhabitants. This is no place for an American.'

'You drink too much, Mr Carver,' Ruth said.

'Nevertheless' – Carver shook his big head heavily – 'it is no accident that they picked this place to crucify Christ. You couldn't pick a better place to crucify Christ if you scoured the maps of the world for five hundred years. I'm a Quaker myself, from the city of Philadelphia, Pennsylvania, and all I see here is the blood of bleeding humanity. When this war is over I'm going back to Philadelphia and wait until I pick up the morning newspaper and read that everybody in Palestine has exterminated everybody else in Palestine the night before.' He walked unsteadily over to Ruth's chair and bent over and peered intently into her face. 'Beautiful girl,' he said, 'beautiful, forlorn girl.' He straightened up. 'Gunnison, I admonish you, as an officer and gentleman, do not harm one hair on this beautiful girl's head.'

'Every hair,' Mitchell said, gravely, 'is safe with me.'

'If you must drink,' Ruth said to Carver sharply, 'why don't you do it with Americans? Why do you have to go around with bandits and murderers like these?' She waved her hand towards the Arabs. The journalist smiled, his handsome face frosty and amused in the wavering light.

'Impartiality,' Carver boomed. 'American impartiality. We are famous for it. We are nobody's friend and nobody's enemy. We merely build airfields and pipelines. Impartially. Tomorrow I lunch with the President of the Jewish Agency.'

Ruth turned to the journalist. 'Taif,' she said loudly, 'I read your last piece.'

'Ah, yes,' he said, his voice a little dead and without timbre. 'Did you like it?'

'You'll be responsible for the death of thousands of Jews,' said Ruth.

'Ah, thank you,' he said. He smiled. 'It is my fondest hope.' He turned to Mitchell. 'Naturally, Lieutenant,' he said, our charming little Ruth is biased in the matter. It is necessary to give the Arab side of the proposition.' He began to speak more seriously, with a severe, oratorical emphasis, like an evangelical preacher. 'The world is dazzled by the Jewish accomplishment in Palestine. Fine, clean cities, with plumbing. Industries. Where once was desert, now the rose and the olive bloom. Etcetera.'

'Taif, old boy' – Carver pulled at his arm – 'let's eat and you can lecture the lieutenant some other time.'

'No, if you please.' The journalist pulled his arm politely away from Carver's hand. 'I welcome the opportunity to talk to our American friends. You see, my good Lieutenant, you may be very pleased with the factory and the plumbing, and perhaps even, from one point of view, they may be good things. But they have nothing to do with the Arab. Perhaps the Arab prefers the desert as it was. The Arab has his own culture . . . '

'When I hear the word "culture",' Carver said, 'I reach for my pistol. What famous American said that?'

'To Americans and Europeans,' the journalist went on, in his singsong, dead voice, 'the culture of the Arab perhaps seems backward and dreadful. But forgive us, the Arab prefers it. The virtues which are particularly Arab are kept alive by primitive living. They die among the plumbing.'

'Now,' said Ruth, 'we have heard a new one. Kill the Jew because he brings the shower-bath.'

The journalist smiled indulgently at Ruth, as at a clever child. 'Personally,' he said, 'I have nothing against the Jews. I swear that I do not wish to harm a single Jew living in Palestine today. But I will fight to the death to keep even one more Jew from entering the country. This is an Arab state, and it must remain an Arab state.'

'Gunnison,' Carver said, 'aren't you glad you came?'

'Six million Jews have died in Europe,' Ruth said, her voice harsh and passionate, and surprising to Mitchell. 'Where do you want the survivors to go?' She and the journalist had forgotten the rest of them and were locked with each other across the table.

The journalist shrugged and looked for a moment up above the palm fronds at the dark sky. 'That,' he said, 'is a question for the world to decide. Why must the poor Arab have the whole decision? We've taken in much more than our share. If the rest of the world really wants to see the Jewish race survive, let them take them in. America, Britain, Russia . . . I do not notice those large countries taking in great masses of Jews.'

'There are no great masses,' Ruth said. 'There is only a handful.'

Taif shrugged. 'Even so. The truth may be, perhaps,' he paused, a little doubtfully, reminding Mitchell of an old Latin teacher in a class in Cicero, shrewdly hesitating for effect, before telling the class whether the word in question was in the ablative or dative absolute, 'the truth may be that the rest of the world really wants to see the Jewish race die out.' He turned and smiled warmly at Mitchell. 'It is an interesting supposition, Lieutenant. It might be most interesting to examine it before talking any more about Palestine.' He walked over to Ruth and leaned over and kissed her fleetingly on the forehead. 'Good-night, little Ruth,' he said, and went to a table across the *patio*, with the silent, adoring Arab behind him.

'If I see you with that man once more,' Ruth spoke to the man who had introduced himself to Mitchell, and who had remained standing at their table, 'I'll never talk to you again.'

The Arab looked swiftly at Mitchell, a veiled, probing flick of the eyes, and said something to Ruth in Arabic.

'No,' said Ruth, her voice clipped and sharp. 'Definitely no.'

The Arab bowed slightly, put out his hand to Mitchell and, as they shook hands, said, 'Very pleasant meeting you, Lieutenant,' and went off to join his friends at their table.

'*The dansants* in old Tel Aviv,' said Carver. 'Bring the kiddies. Good-night.' He waddled over to the other table.

'Ruth,' Mitchell started to talk.

'Lieutenant Gunnison . . . ' It was the soft, apologetic voice of Schneider at his elbow. 'I am so anxious for your opinion. What did you think of "Stardust"?'

Mitchell turned slowly from staring at Ruth, who was sitting tense and upright in her chair. 'Great, Schneider,' Mitchell said. 'I thought it was sensational.'

Schneider beamed with pleasure. You are too kind,' he said. 'I will play you "Summertime" once more.'

'Thanks a lot,' said Mitchell. He put out his hand and covered Ruth's, lying on the table. 'You all right?' he asked.

She smiled up at him. 'Sure,' she said. 'I am an admirer of

abstract political discussions.' Her face grew serious. 'Do you want to know what Khazen asked when he spoke to me in Arabic?'

'Not if you don't want to tell me.'

'I want to tell you.' Ruth absently caressed his fingers. 'He asked me if I would meet him later.'

'Yes,' said Mitchell.

'I told him no.'

'I heard you.' Mitchell grinned at her. 'They probably heard you in Cairo.'

'I didn't want you to feel disturbed or doubtful,' Ruth said, 'your last night.'

'I feel fine,' Mitchell said.

'I've been going with him for four years.' She played for a moment with the food on the plate that the waiter had put before her. 'When I came here in the beginning I was frightened and lonely and he was very decent. He's a contractor for the Americans and British and he's made a fortune during the war. But when Rommel was outside Alexandria he and his friends used to celebrate in secret. I can't stand him any more. I tell him when I take up with other men. But he hangs on. Ah, finally, I suppose he'll get me to marry him. I'm not strong enough any more.' She looked up at Mitchell and tried to smile. 'Don't be shocked, darling,' she said. 'Americans can't understand how tired the human race can get.' She stood up suddenly. 'Let's dance.'

They went on to the floor and Schneider broke into 'Summertime' when he saw them and smiled fondly at them as they danced. She danced very well, lightly and passionately, and Mitchell knew as he danced that he was going to remember this for a long time, at odd moments, swinging away from targets with the flak falling off behind him, and later, if he made it, in the snowy hills of his home state, the light, soft pressure of the bright cotton dress, the dark, curved, delicate face below his, the hushed sound of their feet on the old floor under the palms, the clever, rich music of the piano under the small blue lights strung out from the stone building. There were a million things that crowded his throat that he wanted to tell her, and there was no way of saying them. He kissed her cheek as the music ended, and she glanced up at him, and smiled and said, 'There, that's better,' and they were laughing by the time they got back to their table.

He paid the bill and they went out, saying good-night to

Schneider, not looking back at the table where Carver and the three Arabs sat, but hearing Carver's deep voice rolling through the music and the darkness, calling, 'Does anyone want an airfield? I'll build it for him. Does anyone want a crown of thorns? I'll build it for him.'

There was an old carriage waiting outside the restaurant, its driver dozing and its lights dimmed, and they climbed in and sat close together as the driver clucked to the horse and they rattled slowly towards town. The breeze had gone down, as it did at nine o'clock every night, and there was a small, warm breath of salt off the Mediterranean and every once in a while a jeep rushed past in a whistle of American wind, with its slits of cat's-eye lights cutting a darting, frail, skidding pattern in the darkness, making the creakings and rustlings of the old carriage older and dearer and more private as they sat there holding on to each other in silence.

'They got off a block from where Ruth lived because the people from whom she rented her room were intensely moral and did not approve of their boarder going out with soldiers. They walked past the corner where the Italian bombers had killed a hundred and thirty people on a Friday morning the year before, and turned into Ruth's street. From a darkened window came the sound of someone practising the third movement of the Brahms violin concerto, and Mitchell couldn't help smiling and realising that one of his strongest memories of Tel Aviv would be the strains of Tchaikovsky and Brahms and Beethoven coming through the opened windows on every street of the town, as the furiously cultured inhabitants practised runs and cadenzas with never-ending zeal.

All the houses were blacked out, but there was a tiny sliver of light along one of the windows in the third-floor apartment in which Ruth lived, and they stopped in dismay when they saw it.

'She's up,' Ruth said.

'Doesn't she ever sleep?' Mitchell asked angrily.

Ruth giggled and kissed him. 'She can't stay up for ever,' Ruth said. 'We'll take a little walk and by the time we get back she'll be asleep.'

Mitchell took her arm and they walked slowly down towards the sea. Soldiers and whores and fat, placid couples strolled on the concrete walk along the beach, and the Mediterranean heaved gently under the moon and broke in small white rolls of foam against the beach, with a steady, foreign grumble, not like the roar of the Atlantic on the cold northern beaches of home. From a café a hundred yards away came the sound of a string quartet playing a Strauss waltz as though Vienna had never been taken, the waltz never lost to the enemy.

Mitchell and Ruth went down the steps to the beach. A weaving British lance-corporal, coming up the steps with a girl, stiffened and saluted rigidly, his hand quivering with respect for authority, and Mitchell saluted back, and Ruth giggled.

'What're you laughing at?' Mitchell asked, when they had passed the lance-corporal.

'I laugh,' Ruth said, 'every time I see you salute.'

'Why?'

'I don't know why. I just laugh. Forgive me.' She took off her shoes and walked barefoot in the sand up to the water's edge. The sea swept softly in from Gibraltar and Tunis and Cyrene and Alexandria and lapped at her toes.

The Mediterranean,' Ruth said. 'I hate the Mediterranean.'

'What's the matter with it?' Mitchell stared out at the flickering silver path of the moon over the water.

'I was on it,' Ruth said, 'for thirty-three days. In the hold of a Greek steamer that used to carry cement. Maybe I oughtn't to tell you things like that. You're a tired boy who's been sent here to have a good time so he can go back and fight well . . . '

'You tell me anything you want to tell me,' Mitchell said. 'I'll fight all right.'

'Should I tell you about Berlin, too? Do you want to hear about Berlin? Ruth's voice was hard and cold, and somehow a little sardonic, not at all like her voice as he had heard it in the whole week he had known her. The meeting with the journalist at the restaurant had started something stirring within her, something that he hadn't seen before, and he felt that before he left he should see that side of her too.

'Tell me about Berlin,' Mitchell said.

'I worked for a newspaper,' Ruth said, her toes digging lightly in the sand, 'even after the Nazis came in, and I was in love with the man who wrote the economics column and he was in love with me . . . '

'Economics?' Mitchell was puzzled.

'The stock exchange. The prophecies and excuses.'

'Oh,' said Mitchell, trying to picture what a man who wrote stock exchange tips in Berlin in 1934 would look like.

'He was very gay,' Ruth said. 'Very young, but elegant, with chequered vests and he wore a monocle and he lost all his money at the races. His name was Joachim. He used to take me to the races and to the cafés and it used to drive my mother crazy, because if they ever found out I was a Jewish girl out with a Gentile man, they would have sentenced me to death for polluting the blood stream of the German nation. They'd have sent him to a concentration camp, too, but he was always easy and laughing, and he said, 'The important thing is to be brave,' and we were never questioned, and I went to every night club in Berlin, even nights that Goering and Goebbels were in the same room.

'My father was taken to a concentration camp and we decided it was time for me to leave, and Joachim got together all the money he could lay his hands on and gave it to me and I went to Vienna. I was supposed to go to Palestine, if I could, and send for my mother, and for my father, too, if he ever got out of the concentration camp. There was an office in Vienna, and it was filled with refugees from all over Germany, and we collected money to buy transportation and bribe the nations of the world to let some of us in. I slept in the bath-tub and talked to sailors and thieves and murderers and crooked shipowners, and finally we got a Greek steamer that was supposed to put in at Genoa and pick us up if we managed to get there. We gave the man 75,000 dollars in cash in advance because that's the only way he would do it, and somehow we got the Austrian Government and the Italian Government to look the other way, at a price, and they piled us into freight cars, eight hundred of us, and locked us in, men, women and children, lying one on top of another, and the trip took a week and a day to Genoa, and when we got there the ship never arrived. The Greek took the 75,000 dollars and disappeared. There are all kinds of Greeks, and I have nothing against them, but this was a bad one. Then the Italian Government sent us back to Vienna and six people committed suicide because they couldn't bear it, and we started it all over again.'

Mitchell stared out at the dark line of the sea where it blended in the western distance with the purple of the sky. He tried to think of what it would have been like for his sister and mother if they had been locked into freight cars at Rutland and forced to travel for eight days up to Quebec, say, to wait for an illegal ship to an unknown country. His mother was tall and white-haired and unruffled and pleasant, and his sister was cool and pretty and had some irritating superior mannerisms that she had picked up when she had been foolishly sent for a year to a fancy girls' finishing school in Maryland.

'Let's start home,' Ruth said. 'If my landlady's still up, we'll shoot her.'

They turned their backs on the quiet, white churn of the waves and walked, hand in hand, across the heavy sand of the beach towards the black pile of the buildings of the city.

'Well,' Mitchell said, 'I want to hear the rest of it.'

'No, you don't,' Ruth said. 'Forgive me for telling you so much. It's too dreary.'

'I want to hear,' Mitchell said. In the week he had known Ruth, she had been gay and light-hearted, and had helped him to forget the planes spinning out of control and the dying men lying in their frozen blood on the tangled wires and broken aluminium of the Liberator floors, and now he felt as though he owed it to himself and to Ruth to take back with him some of her agony, too, not only the laughter and the tender jokes and the self-effacing merriment. Suddenly, to-night, she had become terribly dear to him, and he felt responsible to her in a way he had never felt responsible to a girl before.

'Tell me,' he said.

Ruth shrugged. 'Back in Vienna,' she said, 'we did it all over again. It took two months and the police caught a lot of us, and it meant hiding and running most of the time, but we collected the money again, and we found ourselves another Greek, and this time he turned out to be honest. Or at least as honest as people were to Jews without passports in those days in Europe. We got down to Genoa in only five days this time, and we boarded the steamer at night and they locked the hatch doors on us after we had paid every cent of the money in advance, and we set sail before dawn. The steamer had been built in 1887.' They were at the edge of the beach now, and Ruth leaned on Mitchell's shoulder as she put on her shoes. 'Nobody can have any idea,' Ruth said as they went up the steps to the concrete walk above, 'of what dirt is like until he has been locked into the hold of a fifty-year-old Greek ship with 700 people for over a month. People died every day, and the ship captain would let a rabbi and three other people up on deck at night to perform the burial service and dump the body overboard. The only thing we got to eat was biscuit and canned beef, and there were always worms in everything, even the water we got to drink, and everybody got sores all over their bodies, and the old people got too weak to move and the children wept all day, and the relatives of the people who died screamed a good deal of the time, and it is impossible to tell anyone who was not on the boat what it smelled like, in the middle of the summer in the Mediterranean, with a ventilating system that had been installed in Salonika in 1903.'

They turned off the beach walk and climbed slowly up the hill towards the centre of the town, past the clean, white, very modernistic apartment houses with gardens and fountains and balconies that faced the sea.

'We were supposed to be let off in Turkey,' Ruth went on, her voice almost without inflection and emotion, as though she were reciting from a ledger the business accounts of an importing firm for the year 1850. 'And we had given the Greek money to pay off every officer of the port, but something went wrong and we had to put out to sea again, and we started toward Palestine, although the British had patrols along every mile of coastline. But there was no place else to go. People started to get hallucinations about food, and the sailors would sell a sandwich or a lemon for twenty dollars or a bowl of soup for a gold candlestick. And three of the girls couldn't stand it any more and allowed themselves to be taken up every night to be used by the sailors in exchange for regular meals. It was hard to blame them, but they were cursed by the older people as they walked through the crowd each night towards the ladder, and once a Polish woman with two small daughters knocked one of the girls down with an iron pin and tried to stab her with a kitchen knife she had in her bag.'

They turned into Ruth's street and looked up at the window just in time to see the thin edge of light under the blind disappear. They stood and leaned against a stucco fence in front of a plain, shining white house with cactus plants and a fig tree in the front yard.

'We were on that ship for thirty-five days,' Ruth said, 'and we came to the coast of Palestine between Haifa and Rehovoth, at night, and maybe someone had been bribed, and maybe it was just lucky, but people were waiting for us in row-boats and in eight hours we were all off. There was one woman, who looked as strong as anyone, a solid, sensible-looking woman, and she seemed cheerful and healthy when she got into the little boat with me, but she suddenly died ten feet off the coast, when the water was so shallow a child could have stepped out and walked ashore. Luckily it was a dark night, and there were no patrols, and we were taken in cars to a movie theatre in a little town near Haifa and put inside. The theatre had been playing Betty Grable in *Campus Confessions*, a musical picture, and there were signs with her in tights and ostrich plumes all over it, and the management had written all over the posters, "Closed This Week for Repairs".'

'I saw the picture,' Mitchell said. He had seen it one night in Cambridge, and he remembered how some of the boys in the audience had whistled when Miss Grable had kissed the leading man.

'We were all told to keep absolutely quiet,' Ruth said, 'because the British had patrols going through every town. They must have known something, because that week three men high up in the police force were suspended and investigated. It wasn't so hard to keep the older people quiet, but it was awful with the children, and one man really proposed that a little girl who kept crying all day be strangled for the good of the others. We sat there for a week, whispering, making a noise like thousands of mice in a cupboard, and each night cars would come and some people would be taken away to a collective farm somewhere in the hills. Finally, my turn came and I stayed on that farm for two years, working on the fields and teaching children how to read and write German.

'After two years, the British gave you papers, if you managed to dodge them all that time, and I got my papers and started to work for a canning factory outside Tel Aviv. My father was let out of concentration camp in 1938, but his ship was turned back at Haifa, and he was put back in concentration camp in Germany, and for all I know he's still there now, although he's probably dead.'

'Joachim wrote me, and my mother, from Berlin. They became good friends once I was gone, and he brought her food, and on Friday nights would come and watch her light the candles. My mother wrote me he told her he had a girl, but he was dissatisfied, he guessed he'd gotten the taste for Jewish girls.' Ruth smiled slightly, thinking of the boy with the chequered vest and the monocle many years ago, and Mitchell wondered if he had dropped a bomb near the market-analyser somewhere in Africa, or in Sicily or Italy.

'He helped my mother get out of Germany,' Ruth went on, staring up at the window of her home, which was now secure and dark. 'She came out in a Portugese boat, and I heard she was coming and I was on the shore at Haifa Harbour when it came in. But the British wouldn't let it dock, and after six days they insisted that it turn back, and there were thousands of people on the shore, relatives and friends of the people on the boat, and the worst sound I've ever heard in the world was the sound those people on the shore made when the boat turned around and started to steam towards the Haifa breakwater. But the boat never got out of the harbour.' Ruth paused and licked her lips, and spoke very matter-of-factly. 'There was an explosion. We saw the puff of dirty black smoke first, then a long time later we heard the noise, and the people on shore were screaming and laughing and crying. Then there was fire and the boat started to go down, and everybody grabbed at any kind of boat they could find and started out towards the steamer, and there were people who couldn't find boats who just jumped into the water, clothes and all, and started to swim, and nobody ever found out how many people drowned that way, because bodies were washed in to shore for three weeks afterwards. My mother was drowned and five hundred other people on the boat, but 700 were saved, and then the British had to let them in, and I suppose that's what the people who set the bomb figured would happen. Some people would die, but some would be saved. If the boat went back to Europe, everybody would be killed. Of course, they bungled it somewhat, and they didn't figure on the fire, and they thought the boat would sink more slowly and only a few people would be killed, but even so it was a pretty fair bargain.' Ruth lit a cigarette calmly and held the light for Mitchell. 'My mother was washed up a week later, and at least her grave is in Palestine. I couldn't tell my father she was dead, so when I wrote to him in concentration camp, I forged letters from my mother, because I had a lot of her letters and I learned how to make good copies. Even now, through the Red Cross, I write him notes in my mother's handwriting, and if he's alive he thinks my mother is living on a farm with a family near Rehovoth.'

Ruth pulled at her cigarette and inhaled deeply and in the increased glow Mitchell looked at her and thought again, as he'd thought so many times before, that it was a wonderful and terrible thing that the human race covered its scars so completely, so that Ruth, standing there, with the torture and smuggling and burning and drowning and hiding and dying behind her, looked, with her lipstick and fluffy, cleverly combed hair, and soft, fragile, print dress, like any one of a thousand girls at a dance in America, with nothing more behind them than a weekly allowance from Father, and two proms a season at New Haven or Cambridge.

'Ah,' Ruth said, throwing her cigarette away, 'she must be asleep by now. Come.' She smiled at him, dry-eyed and pleasant, and took his hands and they walked quietly up through the dim hallways to the apartment in which she lived. She opened the door silently and waved him in, her finger to her lips, and when they were safely in her room, with the door locked behind them, she giggled like a child who has pulled some sly trick on the grown-up world, then kissed him hungrily in the dark room and whispered, 'Mitchell, Mitchell,' making the name somehow foreign and tender by the way she said it.

He held her tight, but she pulled away. 'Not yet, Lieutenant,' she said grinning, 'not yet.' She put on a light and went over to a chest of drawers in a corner and started to rummage under some scarves. 'I have something for you. Sit down and wait, like a polite boy.'

Mitchell sat on the low daybed, blinking in the light. The room was small and painted white and very clean. There was a large piece of Egyptian batik in red and dark green on the wall over the bed and there were three photographs on a dressing table. Mitchell looked at the photographs – a round, smiling woman, with a healthy, simple face, Ruth's mother, the picture taken long before the morning when the ship went down in Haifa Harbour. The other two photographs were of men. There was a man who looked like Ruth, obviously her father, a studious, humorous, rather weak face, with frail, delicate bones and shy, childish eyes. And there was the young man in the chequered vest, slender and laughing and proud of himself, with the monocle in his eye like a burlesque of a German general or a British actor.

'Here.' Ruth came over to him and sat down beside him. She had a soft chamois bag, and there was a little rich clinking as she put it in his hand. 'To take with you,' she said.

Mitchell slowly opened the bag. A heavy silver medal on a chain, glittering dully in the lamplight, fell into his hand. Ruth was crouched on her knees on the couch beside him, looking anxiously at his face to see if her present would meet with favour. Mitchell turned it over. It was a Saint Christopher, old and irregular, of heavy silver, with the saint awkward and angular and archaic and very religious in the loving workmanship of a silversmith who had died a long time before.

'It's for voyages,' Ruth said, hurriedly. 'For a navigator, I thought, it might be quite – quite useful . . . ' She smiled uncertainly at him. 'Of course,' she said, it is not in my religion, but I don't think it would do any harm to give it to you. That's why I went to Jerusalem. Something like this, something holy, might have a tendency to be more effective if it comes from Jerusalem, don't you think?'

'Of course,' Mitchell said. 'It's bound to be.'

'Will you wear it?' Ruth glanced quickly and shyly at him, sitting there, dangling the medal on its chain.

'All the time,' Mitchell said. 'Day and night, every mission, every jeep-ride, year in, year out.'

'May I put it on for you?'

Mitchell opened his collar and gave the medal to Ruth. She stood up and he bowed his head and she slipped it on, then leaned over and kissed the back of his neck where the chain lay against the flesh.

She stepped back. 'Now,' she said matter of factly. 'There we are.' She went over to the lamp. 'We don't need this any more.' She put the light out and went over to the window and threw back the blackout blinds, and a faint breeze carrying salt and the scent of gardens came into the room. She stood at the window, looking out, and Mitchell got up and crossed over to her, feeling the unfamiliar cool jewellery of the medal dangling against his chest. He stood behind her, silently, holding her lightly, looking out over the city. The white buildings shone in the heavy moonlight machined and modern and Biblical all at once, and from the west came the faint sound of the sea. Mitchell wanted to tell her that he would remember her, remember everything about her, her drowned mother and imprisoned father, her old, courageous lover, drinking champagne with her at the Nazi cafés; he wanted to tell her that he would remember the dealings with the Greek sailor and the hold of the ship that had been built in 1887 and the dying Jews buying a lemon with a gold candlestick; he wanted to tell her that flying over the Germans in Europe or watching the first snow fall at Stowe he would remember the small boat grating on the sand in the darkness outside Rehovoth and the week in the closed movie theatre with the British patrols outside; he wanted to tell her that the terror and courage would not be forgotten, but he didn't know how to say it, and besides, being honest with himself, he knew it would be difficult to remember, and finally, back in Vermont, it would blur and cloud over and seem unreal as a story in a child's book, read many years ago and now almost forgotten. He held her more tightly, but he said nothing.

'There he is,' Ruth said, her voice casual and unimpressed. 'See him standing down there next to the house with the picket gate . . . '

Mitchell looked over Ruth's shoulder. Down on the street, thirty yards from the entrance of Ruth's house, was a small dark figure, almost completely lost in shadow.

'Ali Khazen,' Ruth said. 'He comes and waits outside my window. Ah . . . ' she sighed, 'I suppose finally he'll kill me.'

She turned away from the window and led him back to the couch across the strip of moonlight that divided the room. She looked up at him gravely, then suddenly pushed him gently down to the couch and fell beside him, holding on to him. She held him and kissed his cheek and chuckled a little. 'Now, Lieutenant,' she said, 'tell me about Vermont.'

20

Lemkau, Pogran & Blaufox

The machine operators, the cutters, the boys from the shipping room had departed for the night. One light burned in the partitioned-off showroom of Lemkau, Pogran & Blaufox, Knit Goods, Girdles, Brassières, Corsets of All Descriptions. It was quiet as only a factory can be quiet twenty minutes after the machines have stopped, the girls gone, and the lights been extinguished. Through the soft new dark, outside the windows, came the distant sounds of taxis and people hurrying home to dinner. A low wail rose from the elevator shafts as the elevators dropped towards the ground floor.

In the showroom. Lemkau and Pogran sat, not looking at each other and not talking. They heard the elevator doors and a lively skipping step approaching along the hall. The door swung open and Maurice Blaufox bustled in, singing softly, 'I didn't know what time it was.' He stopped when he saw them. His hands went up in cordial surprise as he stood there, fresh from the barber, his face pink and well conditioned, his pince-nez swinging smartly on a black ribbon, his spats immaculate. 'Lemkau! Pogran!' he cried. 'My partners. You don't work hard enough all day, you got to work at night, too!' He laughed heartily: 'You can't make money day and night boys. You got to live from time to time.' He slapped them on the back, one with each hand. He was only five feet five inches tall but standing next to his partners, Maurice Blaufox was a large man, full of juice and confidence.

'We were not making money,' Pogran said.

'In a manner of speaking,' Lemkau said, 'we were waiting for you, Maurice.'

'Ah!' Blaufox threw up his hands. 'I have overdrawn my expense account. Give me a lecture, boys,' he said good-naturedly. 'Sometimes the money slips through the fingers with a buyer on the hook.'

'It is not the expense account,' Pogran said.

Blaufox lit a cigar. 'Some day I will take you boys out for the night on the expense account. Dinner in Longchamps, a musical comedy with speculator's tickets, a night club.' He laughed. 'All on the firm's money. Just like you were a buyer. Wouldn't that be nice?'

'That would be very nice,' Pogran said.

'Thank you very much,' said Lemkau.

'So, boys,' Blaufox asked waving the cigar, 'so what is it?'

Lemkau ran his hand over his bald head, ruffling the few grey hairs still clinging there. 'Maurice,' he began in a stiff voice. 'It is this way . . . ' He stopped.

'Anything you want to say to me,' Blaufox said kindly, 'I will listen to. Anything my friends have on their mind.'

'Maurice,' Pogran broke in, much louder than he expected, 'it is about that girl, that woman, that lady from the French Follies.'

Blaufox's face settled into hard lines under the barber's finish, and he put away his cigar. 'Excuse me,' he said, starting towards the door. 'I have an appointment.'

'Maurice,' Lemkau cried, following him, 'please don't take that attitude! What is the use of taking an attitude like that?'

'Listen to us,' Pogran held Blaufox's elbow. 'Five minutes of your time. We are all friends, we can listen to each other.'

Blaufox stopped, his hand on the door. He said nothing, but he didn't move.

'We have seen cheques,' Pogran said, 'made out to her, signed by Maurice Blaufox. We saw you in the Chesterfield Restaurant with her. We found out the telephone number you leave on rainy afternoons is the Hotel Lowrie on Twenty-third Street. We saw you go in and come out with Anna Gerenson.'

'My partners,' Blaufox said bitterly. 'The Secret Police. Dick Tracy and his friends.'

'We don't hold it against you,' Lemkau said. 'Not one little tiny bit.'

'On the contrary,' Pogran said. 'Quite on the contrary.'

'So,' Blaufox said. 'Assuming, for the sake of argument, it is true. So?'

'She is a fine-looking woman,' Lemkau said. He sighed.

'A first-class figure of a woman,' Pogran said.

'All my life,' said Lemkau, 'I have dreamed of a woman like that.'

The expression on Blaufox's face changed. A slight hint of satisfaction, of complacency, crept over his lips. 'She is not a bad-looking girl,' he said. 'She is really an actress, you know, not just a show-girl. Only there are no parts for her. The theatre is dying; there are six thousand actresses out of work.'

'Yes,' said Pogran and Lemkau.

'She has to make a living, don't she?' Blaufox asked. 'The French Follies is merely temporary.'

'Yes,' said his partner. 'Yes, yes.'

'The truth is' – Blaufox sat down and crossed his neat legs – 'the whole truth is I contribute to the support of her apartment. I won't hide it from you, because, after all, we have been partners for sixteen years. Why should we hide things from each other?'

'Oh,' Lemkau sighed, 'oh, the life a salesman leads.'

'I do not keep her on the expense account,' Blaufox said. 'Please understand that from the beginning.'

There was quiet in the showroom. The faraway noise of New York on a winter evening sifted through the windows.

'I am not doing anything wrong,' Blaufox continued in a troubled voice. 'I still love my wife. But she is a sick woman, Bertha. She's fat, she has upset glands. I take care of her, hand and foot. I would die for Bertha. I spend a fortune of money on her. But' – he flicked the cigar that he had put down on the showroom table off into a waste-basket – 'the fact is she is away six months of the year for her health. Arizona in the winter for her asthma. New Hampshire in the summer for her hay fever. A man gets lonely. He can't spend all his time with buyers.'

'We are not blaming you.' Lemkau went over and patted Blaufox on the shoulder. 'Believe me.'

Blaufox tilted his head and examined his partners closely for the first time that evening. 'What is the reason,' he asked, 'for bringing this subject up?'

Lemkau looked at Pogran, who in turn looked down at the carpet and shuffled his feet uneasily.

'Kindly talk up,' Blaufox said. 'We have gone so far, let us go further.'

'You are a lucky man,' Lemkau said.

Blaufox shrugged.

'In your way, Maurice,' said Lemkau. 'Other people are lonely, too.'

'Poor Lemkau.' Blaufox shook his head. 'A man should not live alone in a hotel room. I have told you that three thousand times.'

'Maurice . . . ' Lemkau stopped and looked despairingly at Pogran.

'Maurice,' Pogran said. 'I will get to the hilt of the matter. You have a girl. She is a fine girl. We admire her. It would be a great pleasure to us if from time to time we could all go out together. A purely social evening. Say, every other Thursday. It would break up the month.' He talked hurriedly, his hands in his pockets, his eyes fixed on the third button of Blaufox's vest. 'Dinner in a nice sea-food restaurant, three friends, and a handsome woman.'

'Oh,' said Blaufox.

'It would be pleasant,' Lemkau said, 'to make the acquaintance of a person we would not normally make the acquaintance of. A lady of the theatrical profession, for example, who – oh, my God!' he said, and dropped, shaking, into a chair.

They sat in silence, looking out of the window.

'Never mind,' Lemkau said after a time. 'I did not really expect – I am a little, funny-looking man, and she wouldn't want to be seen with me.'

'You are not so funny-looking, Lemkau,' Blaufox said loyally.

'Don't tell me lies. I am little and I look like a rabbit. Where is my hat?' Lemkau reached absently towards the hat-rack. 'It was a wild idea from the beginning,' he said to Pogran. 'Blaufox is tall, he is merry, he knows what to say to women, he makes jokes and drinks cocktails. Me? He shrugged, and put on his hat.

'I wish I had your talent,' Blaufox said. 'There is not another knit-goods designer in the whole country like Adolph Lemkau. An artist!'

Lemkau laughed. 'An artist. The artist goes home by himself. Pogran, you coming down with me?'

Pogran took his hat off the rack.

'Wait a minute,' Blaufox said. 'I tell you what. We will go and talk to the lady. We will let her decide whether or not she wants to have dinner with us.'

'That is fair,' Pogran said. 'That is altogether equitable.'

They marched out together, forgetting to lock the showroom door.

'Rest assured,' Pogran said solemnly in the elevator, 'that all expenses will be divided three ways.'

'The firm,' Lemkau suggested. 'Why can't we put it on the books of the firm?'

They all nodded in agreement and took a taxi to the Lowrie Hotel.

Pogran and Lemgau waited downstairs in the lobby after Blaufox had left them to go up to Anna Gerenson's room. They sat, flanked by palms, making believe they were calm, blushing when the clerk looked at them.

'It is no go,' Lemkau said after a while. 'I have that feeling in my bones. Frankly . . . '

Blaufox came out of the elevator and walked towards them with dignity. 'Kindly follow me,' he said, and they got into the elevator. 'She wants to look at you,' he said.

Lemkau's mouth dropped. 'What is the use?' he asked as they got out on the eighth floor.

Anna shook hands with them gravely and said, 'Please be seated, gentlemen.'

They sat, looking at the floor.

'Mr Blaufox has told me about you gentlemen,' Anna said. She looked at Lemkau. 'Mr Blaufox told me you was afraid you was so awful-looking I wouldn't want to be seen with you. I don't think you're awful looking at all.'

Lemkau beamed at her. 'Thank you, Miss Gerenson,' he said. 'Very kind of you indeed.'

She turned to Pogran. 'Mr Blaufox tells me you're a family man, Mr Pogran.'

Pogran sighed. 'True,' he said. 'Absolutely true. A wife and three daughters.'

'He lives in a house on Albemarle Road in Brooklyn,' Blaufox said. 'A first-class property.'

'If the truth must be told, Miss Gerenson,' Pogran said, 'I am as alone as a cat in an alley. For the last sixteen years, Miss Gerenson, I have worked morning, noon and night . . . '

'He is the brains of the business,' Blaufox said. 'No exaggeration. A human dynamo.'

'In those sixteen years my wife has drifted apart from me.' Pogran looked at the ceiling and spoke with his head tilted back. 'She attends lectures, she is on committees, she reads new books. Frankly, she is ashamed of me, Miss Gerenson. Also, my daughters. They go to New York University.'

'That's a very nice school,' Anna said politely.

'When I stay in town at night to work,' Pogran said, 'my wife and daughters feel much better.'

Anna shook her head, reflecting. 'You are very nice guys,' she said at last. 'Gentlemen.' She smiled at them, showing her fine white teeth. 'What do you say, boys,' she said, 'we all have dinner together?'

They nodded briskly at each other, and Blaufox patted Anna's cheek, standing on his toes to do so. 'A celebration is in order!' He picked up the telephone and got the bar and said, 'Champagne. A nice medium-priced bottle of champagne with four glasses in Room 804.' He turned to his partners as he put the phone down. 'On the expense account,' he said, laughing.

They laughed with him their voices ringing out loud and cheerful in the room.

'Would you gentlemen object,' Anna asked, 'if I invited in two girl friends after dinner? Two very nice ladies.'

Lemkau and Pogran looked at each other. 'No,' said Pogran, 'we wouldn't object.'

They watched Anna as she picked up the phone and asked for a Chelsea number.

'Isn't this nice?' Lemkau asked Blaufox. 'Isn't this wonderful?'

The Man with One Arm

'I would like complete reports on these three people,' Captain Mikhailov was saying. He pushed a slip of paper across the desk to Garbrecht, and Garbrecht glanced at the names. 'They are interpreters at the American civil affairs headquarters. The Americans have a charming habit of hiring ex-Nazis almost exclusively for those jobs, and we have found it rewarding to inquire into the pasts of such gentlemen.' Mikhailov smiled. He was a short, stocky man with a round, shielded face, and pale, unsmiling eyes, and when he smiled it was like a flower painted unconvincingly on stone.

Garbrecht recognised two of the three names. Mikhailov was right. They were Nazis. It would take some thinking out, later, though, to decide whether to expose them to Mikhailov, or exactly how far to expose them. Garbrecht watched Mikhailov unlock a drawer in his desk and take out some American marks. Methodically, Mikhailov counted the notes out in his square machine-like hands. He locked the drawer and pushed the money across the desk to Garbrecht.

'There,' Mikhailov said, 'that will keep you until we see each other next week.'

'Yes, Captain,' Garbrecht said. He reached out and pulled the money towards him, leaving it on top of the desk. He took out his wallet, and, slowly, one by one put the notes into the wallet. He was still slow and clumsy with things like that, because he had not yet learned how to handle things deftly with his left hand, and his right hand and arm were buried behind the field hospital in the brewery fourteen hundred miles away. Mikhailov watched him impassively, without offering aid.

Garbrecht put his wallet away and stood up. His overcoat was thrown over a chair and he picked it up and struggled to get it over his shoulders.

'Till next week,' he said.

'Next week,' Mikhailov said.

Garbrecht did not salute. He opened the door and went out.

At least, he thought, with a nervous sensation of triumph, as he went down the grimy steps past the two plain-clothes men loitering in the dark hall, at least I didn't salute the bastard. That's the third week in a row I didn't salute him.

The plain-clothes men stared at him with a common, blank, threatening look. By now he knew them too well to be frightened by them. They looked that way at everything. When they looked at a horse or a child or a bunch of flowers, they threatened it. It was merely their comfortable professional adjustment to the world around them, like Mikhailov's smile. The Russians, Garbrecht thought as he went down the street, what a people to have in Berlin!

Garbrecht walked without looking about him. The landscape of the cities of Germany had become monotonous – rubble, broken statues, neatly swept lanes between piled cracked brick, looming blank single walls, shells of buildings, half-demolished houses in which dozens of families somehow lived. He moved briskly and energetically, like everyone else, swinging his one arm a little awkwardly to maintain his balance, but very little of what he saw around him made any impression on him. A solid numbness had taken possession of him when they cut off his arm. It was like the anaesthesia which they injected into your spine. You were conscious and you could see and hear and speak and you could understand what was being done to you, but all feeling was absent. Finally, Garbrecht knew, the anaesthesia would wear off, but for the present it was a most valuable defence.

'Lieutenant.' It was a woman's voice somewhere behind him, and Garbrecht did not look around. 'Oh, Lieutenant Garbrecht.'

He stopped and turned slowly. Nobody had called him lieutenant for more than a year now. A short, blonde woman in a grey cloth coat was hurrying towards him. He looked at her, puzzled. He had never seen her before, and he wondered if it were she who had called his name.

'Did you call me?' he asked as she stopped in front of him.

'Yes,' she said. She was thin, with a pale, rather pretty face. She did not smile. 'I followed you from Mikhailov's office.'

'I'm sure,' Garbrecht said, turning and staring away, 'that you have made some mistake.'

The woman fell in beside him, walking swiftly. She wore no stockings and her legs showed a little purple from the cold.

313

'Please,' she said, 'do not behave like an idiot.'

Then, in a flat, undemanding voice, she said several things to him that he had thought nobody alive remembered about him, and finally she called him by his correct name, and he knew that there was no escaping it now. He stopped in the middle of the ruined street and sighed, and said, after a long time, 'Very well. I will go with you.'

There was a smell of cooking in the room. Good cooking. A roast, probably, and a heavy, strong soup. It was the kind of smell that had seemed to vanish from Germany some time around 1942, and even with all the other things happening to him, Garbrecht could feel the saliva welling helplessly and tantalisingly up from the ducts under his tongue. It was a spacious room with a high ceiling that must have been at one time quite elegant. There was a bricked-up fireplace with a large, broken mirror over it. By some trick of fracture, the mirror reflected separate images in each of its broken parts, and it made Garbrecht feel that something shining and abnormal was hidden there.

The girl had ushered him without formality into the room and had told him to sit down and had disappeared. Garbrecht could feel his muscles slowly curling as he sat rigidly in the half-broken wooden chair, staring coldly at the battered desk, the surprising leather chair behind the desk, the strange mirror, the ten-inch high portrait of Lenin which was the only adornment on the wall. Lenin looked down at him from the wall, across the years, through the clumsy heroics of the lithographer, with a remote, ambiguous challenge glaring from the dark, wild eyes.

The door through which he had himself come was opened and a man entered. The man slammed the door behind him and walked swiftly across the room to the desk. Then he wheeled and faced Garbrecht.

'Well, well,' the man said, smiling, his voice hearty and welcoming, 'here you are. Here you are. Sorry to keep you waiting. Terribly sorry.' He beamed across the room, leaning forward hospitably from his position in front of the desk. He was a short, stocky man with a light, pink face, and pale, silky hair that he wore long, possibly in an attempt to hide what might be an increasing tendency to baldness. He looked like an amiable butcher's boy, growing a little old for his job, or the strong man in a tumbling act in a small-time circus, the one on the bottom that the others climbed on. Garbrecht stood up and peered at him, trying to remember if he had ever seen the man before.

'No, no,' the man said, waving his pudgy hands, 'no, we have never met. Do not trouble your brain. Sit down, sit down. Comfort first. Everything else after.' He leapt lightly across the room and almost pushed Garbrecht into his chair. 'It is a lesson I have learned from our friends, the Americans. How to slouch. Look what they've accomplished merely by spending most of their time on the base of their spines.' He laughed uproariously, as though the joke were too merry not to be enjoyed, and swept quickly across the room, with his almost leaping, light gait, and hurled himself into the large leather chair behind the desk. He continued beaming at Garbrecht.

'I want to say,' said Garbrecht, 'that I have no notion of why I was asked to come here. I merely came,' he said carefully, 'because the young lady made me curious, and I had an hour to spare, anyway, and ...'

'Enough, enough.' The man rocked solidly back and forth in the squeaking chair. 'You came. Sufficient. Delighted. Very pleased. Have a cigarette ...' With a sudden movement, he thrust out the brass cigarette box that lay on the desk.

'Not at the moment, thank you,' Garbrecht said, although his throat was quivering for one.

'Ah,' the fat man said, grinning. 'A rarity. Only German known to refuse a cigarette since the surrender. Still, no matter ...' He took a cigarette himself and lighted it deftly. 'First, introductions, Lieutenant. My name. Anton Seedorf. Captain Hermann Goering Division. I keep the title.' He grinned. 'A man saves what he can from a war.'

'I imagine,' Garbrecht said, 'you know my name.'

'Yes.' Seedorf seemed to bubble with some inward humour. 'Oh, yes, I certainly do. Yes, indeed. I've heard a great deal about you. Been most anxious to meet you. The arm,' he said, with sudden solemnity. 'Where was that?'

'Stalingrad.'

'Ah, Stalingrad,' Seedorf said heartily, as though he were speaking the name of a winter resort at which he had spent a marvellous holiday. 'A lot of good souls left there, weren't there, many good souls. A miscalculation. One of many. Vanity. The most terrible thing in the world, the vanity of a victorious army. A most interesting subject for historians – the role of vanity in military disasters. Don't you agree?' He peered eagerly at Garbrecht.

'Captain,' Garbrecht said coldly, 'I cannot remain here all afternoon.'

'Of course,' Seedorf said. 'Naturally. You're curious about why I invited you here. I understand.' He puffed swiftly on his cigarette, wreathing his pale head in smoke before the cracked mirror. He jumped up and perched himself on the desk, facing Garbrecht, boyishly. 'Well,' he said, heartily, 'it is past time for hiding anything. I know you. I know your very good record in the Party . . .'

Garbrecht felt the cold rising in his throat. It's going to be worse, he thought, worse than I expected.

' . . . promising career in the Army until the unfortunate accident at Stalingrad,' Seedorf was saying brightly, 'loyal, dependable, etcetera; there is really no need to go into it at this moment, is there?'

'No,' said Garbrecht, 'none at all.' He stood up. 'If it is all the same to you, I prefer not to be reminded of any of it. That is all past and, I hope, it will soon all be forgotten.'

Seedorf giggled. 'Now, now,' he said. 'There is no need to be so cautious with me. To a person like you or me,' he said, with a wide, genial gesture, 'it is never forgotten. To a person who has said the things we have said, who did the things we have done, for so many years, a paid Party official, a good soldier, a good German . . .'

'I am not interested any more,' Garbrecht said loudly but hopelessly, 'in being what you call a good German.'

'It is not a question,' Seedorf said, smiling widely and dousing his cigarette, 'of what you are interested in, Lieutenant. I beg your pardon. It is a question of what must be done. Simply that.'

'I am not going to do anything,' said Garbrecht.

'I beg your pardon once more.' Seedorf rocked happily back and forth on the edge of the desk. 'There are several little things that you can be very useful doing. I beg your pardon, you will do them. You work for the Russians, collecting information in the American zone. A useful fellow. You also work for the Americans, collecting information in the Russian zone.' Seedorf beamed at him. 'A prize!'

Garbrecht started to deny it, then shrugged wearily. There might be a way out, but denial certainly was not it.

'We, too, several of us, maybe more than several, could use

a little information.' Seedorf's voice had grown harder, and there was only an echo of jollity left in it, like the sound of laughter dying down a distant alley on a cold night. 'We are not as large an organisation at the moment as the Russians; we are not as well equipped for the time being as the Americans . . . but we are ever more . . . more . . . ' He chuckled as he thought of the word . . . 'curious. And more ambitious.'

There was silence in the room. Garbrecht stared heavily at the pale, fat head outlined against the broken mirror with its insane, multiplied reflections. If he were alone, Garbrecht knew he would bend his head and weep, as he did so often, without apparent reason, these days.

'Why don't you stop?' he asked heavily. 'What's the sense? How many times do you have to be beaten?'

Seedorf grinned. 'One more time, at least,' he said. 'Is that a good answer?'

'I won't do it,' Garbrecht said. 'I'll give the whole thing up. I don't want to get involved any more.'

'I beg your pardon,' said Seedorf happily, 'you will give up nothing. It is terrible for me to talk to a man who gave his arm for the Fatherland this way,' he said with a kind of glittering facsimile of pity, 'but I am afraid the Russians would be told your correct name and Party position from 1934 on, and they would be told of your affiliations with the Americans, and they would be told of your job as adjutant to the commanding officer of Maidanek concentration camp in the winter of 1944, when several thousand people died by orders with your name on them . . . '

Seedorf drummed his heels softly and cheerfully against the desk. 'They have just really begun on their war trials . . . and these new ones will not run ten months, Lieutenant. I beg your pardon, for talking this way, and I promise you from now on we will not mention any of these matters again.' He jumped up and came across the room in his swift, round walk. 'I know how you feel,' he said softly. 'Often, I feel the same way. Quit. Quit now, once and for all. But it is not possible to quit. In a little while you will see that and you will be very grateful.'

'What is it?' Garbrecht said. 'What is it that you want me to do?'

'Just a little thing,' Seedorf said. 'Nothing at all, really. Merely report here every week and tell me what you have told the Russians and the Americans and what they have told you. Fifteen minutes a week. That's all there is to it.'

'Fifteen minutes a week.' Garbrecht was surprised that he had actually laughed. 'That's all.'

'Exactly.' Seedorf laughed. 'It won't be so bad. There's always a meal to be had here, and cigarettes. It is almost like old times. There!' He stepped back, smiling widely. 'I am so happy it is settled.' He took Garbrecht's hand and shook it warmly with both his. 'Till next week,' he said.

Garbrecht looked heavily at him. Then he sighed. 'Till next week,' he said.

Seedorf held the door open for him when he went out. There was no one else in the corridor and no guards at the door, and he walked slowly down the creaking hall, through the rich smell of cooking, and on into the street and the gathering cold evening air.

He walked blankly through the broken brick wastes towards the American control post, staring straight ahead of him. Next week, he thought, I must ask him what the picture of Lenin is doing on the wall.

The office of Captain Peterson was very different from the bleak room in which Captain Mikhailov conducted his affairs. There was a clerk in the corner and an American flag on the wall, and the busy sound of American typewriters from the next room. There was a water-cooler and a warm radiator, and there was a picture of a pretty girl with a small blond child on Peterson's disordered desk. Garbrecht took his coat off and sat down in one of the comfortable looted plush chairs and waited for Peterson. The interviews with Peterson were much less of a strain than the ones with Mikhailov. Peterson was a large young man who spoke good German and, amazingly, fair Russian. He was good-natured and naïve, and Garbrecht was sure he believed Garbrecht's excellently forged papers and innocuous, false record, and Garbrecht's quiet, repeated insistence that he had been anti-Nazi from the beginning. Peterson was an enthusiast. He had been an enthusiast about the war, in which he had performed quite creditably, he was an enthusiast about Germany, its scenery, its art, its future, its people, whom he regarded as the first victims of Hitler. Mikhailov was different. He bleakly made no comment on the official soft tones issuing from Moscow on the subject of the German people, but Garbrecht knew that he regarded the Germans not as the first victims, but as the first accomplices.

Of late, Garbrecht had to admit, Peterson had not seemed

quite so enthusiastic. He had seemed rather baffled and sometimes hurt and weary. In the beginning, his *naïveté* had spread to cover the Russians in a rosy blanket, too. The assignments he gave to Garbrecht to execute in the Russian zone were so routine and so comparatively innocent, that if Garbrecht had had a conscience he would have hesitated at taking payment for their fulfilment.

Peterson was smiling broadly when he came in, looking like a schoolboy who has just been promoted to the first team on a football squad. He was a tall, heavy young man with an excited, swift manner of talking. 'Glad to see you, Garbrecht,' he said. 'I was afraid I was going to miss you. I've been busy as a bartender on Saturday night, hand-carrying orders all over the place, packing, saying good-bye . . . '

'Good-bye?' Garbrecht said, shaken by a small tremor of fear. 'Where are you going?'

'Home.' Peterson pulled out three drawers from his desk and started emptying them in a swift jumble. 'The United States of America.'

'But I thought,' Garbrecht said, 'that you had decided to stay. You said your wife and child were coming over and . . . '

'I know . . . ' Peterson threw a whole batch of mimeographed papers lightheartedly into the trash-basket. 'I changed my mind.' He stopped working on the drawers and looked soberly at Garbrecht. 'They're not coming here. I decided I didn't want my child to grow up in Europe.' He sat down heavily, staring over Garbrecht's head at the moulding around the ceiling. 'In fact,' he said, 'I don't think I want to hang around Europe any more myself. In the beginning I thought I could do a lot of good here. Now . . . ' He shrugged. 'They'd better try someone else. I'd better go back to America and clear my head for a while. It's simpler in a war. You know whom you're fighting and you have a general idea about where he is. Now . . . ' Once more the shrug.

'Maybe I'm too stupid for a job like this,' he continued. 'Or maybe I expected too much. I've been here a year, and everything seems to be getting worse and worse. I feel as though I'm sliding downhill all the time. Slowly, not very perceptibly . . . but downhill. Maybe Germany has always struck everybody the same way. Maybe that's why so many people have always committed suicide here. I'm going to get out of here before I wake up one morning and say to myself, "By God, they have the right idea." '

Suddenly he stood up, swinging his big feet in their heavy Army shoes down to the floor with a commanding crash. 'Come on,' he said. 'I'll take you in to see Major Dobelmeir. He's going to replace me.' Peterson opened the door for Garbrecht, and they went out into the anteroom with the four desks and the girls in uniform typing. Peterson led the way. 'I think the United States Army is going to begin to get its money's worth out of you now, Garbrecht,' Peterson said, without looking back. 'Dobelmeir is quite a different kettle of fish from that nice, simple young Captain Peterson.'

Garbrecht stared at the back of Peterson's head. So, he thought coldly, he wasn't so completely fooled by me, after all. Maybe it's good he's going.

But then Peterson opened the door to one of the rooms along the hall and they went in, and Garbrecht took one look at the major's leaf and the heavy, brooding, suspicious face, and he knew that he was wrong; it would have been much better if Peterson had stayed.

Peterson introduced them and the Major said, 'Sit down,' in flat, heavy-voiced German, and Peterson said, 'Good luck. I have to go now,' and left. The Major looked down at the papers on his desk and read them stolidly, for what seemed to Garbrecht like a very long time. Garbrecht felt the tension beginning again in his muscles, as it had in Seedorf's room. Everything, he thought, gets worse and worse, more and more complicated.

'Garbrecht,' the Major said without looking up, 'I have been reading your reports.' He did not say anything else, merely continued to read slowly and effortfully, his eyes covered, his heavy chin creasing in solid fat as he bent his head over the desk.

'Yes?' Garbrecht said finally, because he could no longer stand the silence.

For a moment, Dobelmeir did not answer. Then he said, 'They aren't worth ten marks, all of them together, to anybody. The United States Government ought to sue you for obtaining money on false pretences.'

'I am very sorry,' Garbrecht said hurriedly, 'I thought that that is what was wanted, and I . . .'

'Don't lie.' The Major finally lifted his head and stared fishily at him.

'My dear Major . . .'

'Keep quiet,' the Major said evenly. 'We now institute a new régime. You can do all right if you produce. If you don't, you can go find another job. Now we know where we stand.'

'Yes, sir,' said Garbrecht.

'I should not have to teach you your business at this late date,' the Major said. 'There is only one way in which an operation like this can pay for itself; only one rule to follow. All our agents must act as though the nation on which they are spying is an active enemy of the United States, as though the war has, in fact, begun. Otherwise the information you gather has no point, no focus, no measurable value. When you bring me information it must be information of an enemy who is probing our line for weak spots, who is building up various depots of supplies and troops and forces in specific places, who is choosing certain specific fields on which to fight the crucial battles. I am not interested in random, confusing gossip. I am only interested in indications of the disposition of the enemy's strength and indications of his aggressive intentions towards us. Is that clear?'

'Yes, sir,' said Garbrecht.

The Major picked up three sheets of clipped-together papers. 'This is your last report,' he said. He ripped the papers methodically in half and then once more in half and threw them on the floor. 'That is what I think of it.'

'Yes, sir,' said Garbrecht. He knew the sweat was streaming down into his collar and he knew that the Major must have noticed it and was probably sourly amused at it, but there was nothing he could do to stop it.

'This office has sent out its last chambermaid-gossip report,' the Major said. 'From now on, we will send out only useful military information, or nothing at all. I'm not paying you for the last two weeks' work. You haven't earned it. Get out of here. And don't come back until you have something to tell me.'

He bent down once more over the papers on his desk. Garbrecht stood up and slowly went out the door. He knew that the Major did not look up as he closed the door behind him.

Greta wasn't home, and he had to stand outside her door in the cold all evening because the janitress refused to recognise him and let him in. Greta did not get back till after midnight, and then she came up with an American officer in a closed car, and Garbrecht had to hide in the shadows across the street while the American kissed Greta clumsily again and again before going off. Garbrecht hurried across the broken pavement of the street to reach Greta before she retreated into the house.

Greta could speak English and worked for the Americans as a typist and filing clerk, and perhaps something else, not quite so official, in the evenings. Garbrecht did not inquire too closely. Greta was agreeable enough and permitted him to use her room when he was in the American zone, and she always seemed to have a store of canned food in her cupboard, gift of her various uniformed employers, and she was quite generous and warm-hearted about the entire arrangement. Greta had been an energetic patriot before the defeat, and Garbrecht had met her when she visited the hospital where he was lying with his arm freshly severed after the sombre journey back from Russia. Whether it was patriotism, pity, or perversity that had moved her, Garbrecht did not know, nor did he inquire too deeply; at any rate, Greta had remained a snug anchorage in the wild years that had passed, and he was fond of her.

'Hello,' he said as he came up behind her. She was struggling with the lock, and turned abruptly, as though frightened.

'Oh,' she said. 'I didn't think you'd be here tonight.'

'I'm sorry,' he said. 'I couldn't get in touch with you.'

She opened the door, and he went in with her. She unlocked the door of her own room, which was on the ground floor, and slammed it irritably behind her. Ah, he thought unhappily, things are bad here, too, tonight.'

He sighed. 'What is it?' he said.

'Nothing,' she said. She started to undress, methodically, and without any of the usual graceful secrecy she ordinarily managed even in the small drab room.

'Can I be of any help?' Garbrecht asked.

Greta stopped pulling off her stockings and looked thoughtfully at Garbrecht. Then she shook her head and yanked at the heel of the right stocking. 'You could,' she said, contemptuously. 'But you won't.'

Garbrecht squinted painfully at her. 'How do you know?' he asked.

'Because you're all the same,' Greta said coldly. 'Weak. Quiet. Disgusting.'

'What is it?' he asked. 'What would you want me to do?' He would have preferred it if Greta had refused to tell him, but he knew he had to ask.

Greta worked methodically on the other stocking. 'You

322

ought to get four or five of your friends, the ex-heroes of the German Army,' she said disdainfully, 'and march over to Freda Raush's house and tear her clothes off her back and shave her head and make her walk down the street that way.'

'What?' Garbrecht sat up incredulously. 'What are you talking about?'

'You were always yelling about honour,' Greta said loudly. 'Your honour, the Army's honour, Germany's honour.'

'What's that got to do with Freda Raush?'

'Honour is something Germans have only when they're winning, is that it?' Greta pulled her dress savagely over her shoulders. 'Disgusting.'

Garbrecht shook his head. 'I don't know what you're talking about,' he said. 'I thought Freda was a good friend of yours.'

'Even the French,' Greta said, disregarding him, 'were braver. They shaved their women's heads when they caught them . . .'

'All right, all right,' Garbrecht said wearily. 'What did Freda do?'

Greta looked wildly at him, her hair disarranged and tumbled around her full shoulders, her large, rather fat body shivering in cold anger in her sleazy slip. 'Tonight,' she said, 'she invited the lieutenant I was with and myself to her house . . .'

'Yes,' said Garbrecht, trying to concentrate very hard.

'She is living with an American captain.'

'Yes?' said Garbrecht, doubtfully. Half the girls Greta knew seemed to be living with American captains, and the other half were trying to. That certainly could not have infuriated Greta to this wild point of vengeance.

'Do you know what his name is?' Greta asked rhetorically. 'Rosenthal! A Jew. Freda!'

Garbrecht sighed, his breath making a hollow, sorrowful sound in the cold midnight room. He looked up at Greta, who was standing over him, her face set in quivering, tense lines. She was usually such a placid, rather stupid, and easy-going girl that moments like this came as a shocking surprise.

'You will have to find someone else,' Garbrecht said wearily, 'if you want to have Freda's head shaved. I am not in the running.'

'Of course,' Greta said icily. 'I knew you wouldn't be.'

'Frankly,' Garbrecht said, trying to be reasonable with her, 'I am a little tired of the whole question of the Jews. I think we ought to drop it, once and for all. It was all right for a while, but I think we've probably just about used it all up by now.'

'Ah,' Greta said, 'keep quiet. I should have known better than to expect anything from a cripple.'

They both were silent then. Greta continued undressing with contemptuous asexual familiarity, and Garbrecht slowly took his clothes off and got into bed, while Greta, in a black rayon night-gown that her American Lieutenant had got for her, put her hair up in curlers before the small, wavy mirror. Garbrecht looked at her reflection in the mirror and remembered the nervous, multiple reflections in the cracked mirror in Seedorf's office.

He closed his stinging eyes, feeling the lids trembling jumpily. He touched the folded, raw scar on his right shoulder. As long as he lived, he probably would never get over being shocked at the strange, brutal scar on his own body. And he would never get over being shocked when anybody called him a cripple. He would have to be more diplomatic with Greta. She was the only girl he was familiar with, and occasionally there was true warmth and blessed hours of forgetfulness in her bed. It would be ridiculous to lose that over a silly political discussion in which he had no real interest at all. Girls were hard to get these days. During the war it was better. You got a lot of girls out of pity. But pity went out at Rheims. And any German, even a whole, robust one, had a hard time competing with the cigarettes and chocolates and prestige of the victors. And for a man with one arm . . . It had been a miserable day, and this was a fitting, miserable climax to it.

Greta put out the light and got aggressively into bed, without touching him. Tentatively he put his hand out to her. She didn't move. 'I'm tired,' she said. 'I've had a long day. Good night.'

In a few moments she was asleep.

Garbrecht lay awake a long time, listening to Greta snore; a wavering, troubling reflection from a street light outside played on his lids from the small mirror across the room.

As he approached the house in which Seedorf kept his head-quarters, Garbrecht realised that he had begun to hurry his pace a little, that he was actually looking forward to the meeting. This was the fourth week that he had reported to the fat ex-Captain, and he smiled a little to himself as he reminded himself of how affectionately he had begun to regard Seedorf. Seedorf had not been at all demanding. He had listened with eager interest to each report of Garbrecht's meeting with Mikhailov and Dobelmeir, had chuckled delightedly here and there, slapping his leg in appreciation of one point or another, and had shrewdly and humorously invented plausible little stories, scraps of humour, to give first to the Russian, then to the American. Seedorf, who had never met either of them, seemed to understand them both far better than Garbrecht did, and Garbrecht had risen steadily in the favour of both Captain Mikhailov and Major Dobelmeir since he had given himself to Seedorf's coaching.

As Garbrecht opened the door of Seedorf's headquarters, he remembered with a little smile the sense of danger and apprehension with which he had first come there.

He did not have to wait long at all. Miss Renner, the blonde who had first talked to him on the street, opened the door to the ex-Captain's room almost immediately.

Seedorf was obviously in high spirits. He was beaming and moving up and down in front of his desk with little, mincing, almost dancing steps. 'Hello, hello,' he said warmly, as Garbrecht came into the room. 'Good of you to come.'

Garbrecht never could make out whether this was sly humour on Seedorf's part, or perfectly automatic good manners, this pretence that Garbrecht had any choice in the matter.

'Wonderful day,' Seedorf said. 'Absolutely wonderful day. Did you hear the news?'

'What news?' Garbrecht asked cautiously.

'The first bomb!' Seedorf clasped his hands delightedly. 'This afternoon at two-thirty the first bomb went off in Germany. Stuttgart! A solemn day. A day of remembrance! After 1918 it took twelve years before the Germans started any real opposition to the Allies. And now . . . less than a year and a half after the surrender . . . the first bomb! Delightful!' He beamed at Garbrecht. 'Aren't you pleased?' he asked.

'Very,' said Garbrecht diplomatically. He was not fond of bombs. Maybe for a man with two arms, bombs might have an attraction, but for him . . .

'Now we can really go to work.' Seedorf hurled himself forcefully into his leather chair behind the desk and stared piercingly out at Garbrecht. 'Until now, it hasn't meant very much. Really only developing an organisation. Trying out the parts. Seeing who could work and who couldn't. Instituting necessary discipline. Practice, more than anything else. Now the manoeuvres are over. Now we move on to the battlefield!'

Professional soldiers, Garbrecht thought bitterly, his new-found peace of mind already shaken, they couldn't get the jargon of their calling out of their thinking. Manoeuvres, battlefields . . . The only accomplishment they seemed to be able to recognise was the product of explosion, the only political means they really understood and relished, death.

'Lieutenant,' Seedorf said, 'we have been testing you, too. I am glad to say,' he said oratorically, 'we have decided that you are dependable. Now you really begin your mission. Next Tuesday at noon Miss Renner will meet you. She will take you to the home of a friend of ours. He will give you a package. You will carry it to an address that Miss Renner will give you at the time. I will not hide from you that you will be in a certain danger. The package you will carry will include a timing mechanism that will go into the first bomb to be exploded in the new war against the Allies in Berlin . . .'

Seedorf seemed to be far away and his voice distant and strange. It had been too good to be true, Garbrecht thought dazedly, the easy-going, undangerous, messenger-boy life that he had thought he was leading. Merely a sly, deadly game that Seedorf had been playing, testing him.

'Captain,' he whispered, 'Captain . . . I can't . . . I can't . . .'

'The beginning,' Seedorf said, ecstatically, as though he had not heard Garbrecht's interruption. 'Finally, there will be explosions day and night, all over the city, all over the country . . . The Americans will blame the Russians, the Russians will blame the Americans, they will become more and more frightened, more and more distrustful of each other. They will come to us secretly, bargain with us, bid for us against each other . . .'

It will never happen, Garbrecht said dazedly to himself, never. It is the same old thing. All during the war they told us that. The Americans would break with the British, the British with the Russians. And here they all were in what was left of Berlin: Cockneys, Tartars from Siberia, Negroes from Mississippi. Men like Seedorf were victims of their own propaganda, men who listened and finally believed their own hopes, their own lies. And, he, Garbrecht, next week, would be walking among the lounging American M.P.'s with the delicate, deadly machinery ticking under his arm, because of Seedorf's hallucination. Any other nation, Garbrecht thought, would be convinced. They'd look around at the ruin of their cities, at the ever-stretching cemeteries, at the marching enemy troops in the heart of their capital, and they'd say, 'No, it did not work.' But not the Germans. Goering was just dead in the Nuremberg jail, and here was this fat murderer with the jolly smile who even looked a bit like Goering, rubbing his hands and shouting, 'A day of remembrance! The first bomb has exploded!'

Garbrecht felt lost and exhausted and hopeless, sitting in the wooden chair, watching the fat man move nervously and jubilantly behind the desk, hearing the rough, good-natured voice saying, 'It took fourteen years last time, it won't take four years this time! Garbrecht, you'll be a full colonel in 1950, one arm and all.'

Garbrecht wanted to protest, say something, some word that would stop this careening, jovial, bloodthirsty, deluded lunatic, but he could get no sound out between his lips. Later on, perhaps, when he was alone, he might be able to figure some way out of this whirling trap. Not here, not in this tall, dark room, with the fat, shouting captain, the broken mirror, the sombre incongruous, brooding picture of Lenin, Seedorf's obscure, mocking joke, that hung on the cracked wall.

'In the meantime,' Seedorf was saying, 'you continue your regular work. By God!' he laughed, 'you will be the richest man in Berlin when they all get through paying you!' His voice changed. It became low and probing. 'Do you know two men called Kleiber and Machewski who work out of Mikhailov's office?' He peered shrewdly at Garbrecht.

'No,' said Garbrecht after a moment. He knew them. They were both on Mikhailov's pay-roll and they worked in the American zone, but there was no sense in telling that, yet, to Seedorf.

'No matter,' Seedorf laughed, after an almost imperceptible pause. 'You will give their names and this address to your American Major.' He took a piece of paper out from his pocket and put it down on the desk before him. 'You will tell the Major that they are Russian spies and that they can be found at this place.' He tapped the paper. 'It will be quite a haul for the Major,' Seedorf said ironically, 'and he will be sure to reward you handsomely. And he will have a very strong tendency after that to trust you with quite important matters.'

'Yes,' said Garbrecht.

'You're sure,' Seedorf said inquiringly, smiling a little at Garbrecht, 'you're sure you don't know these men?'

Then Garbrecht knew that Seedorf knew he was lying, but

it was too late to do anything about it.

'I don't know them,' he said.

'I could have sworn . . . ' Seedorf shrugged. 'No matter.' He got up from the desk, carrying the slip of paper, and came over to the chair where Garbrecht was sitting. 'Some day, my friend,' he said, putting his hand lightly on Garbrecht's shoulder, 'some day you will learn that you will have to trust me, too. As a matter of . . . ' He laughed. 'A matter of discipline.'

He handed Garbrecht the slip of paper and Garbrecht put it in his pocket and stood up. 'I trust you, sir,' he said flatly. 'I have to.'

Seedorf laughed uproariously. 'I like a good answer,' he shouted. 'I do like a good answer.' He put his arm around Garbrecht in a brotherly hug. 'Remember,' he said, 'my first and only lesson – the one principle in being a hired informer is to tell the man who is paying you exactly what he wishes to hear. Any information must fit into theories which he already holds. Then he will trust you, pay you well, regard you as a more and more valuable employee. However . . . ' and he laughed again, 'do not try to work this on me. I am different. I don't pay you . . . and therefore, I expect the truth. You will remember that?' He turned Garbrecht around quite roughly and peered into his eyes. He was not smiling now.

'Yes, sir,' said Garbrecht. 'I will remember it.'

'Good.' Seedorf pushed him towards the door. 'Now go downstairs and talk to Miss Renner. She will make all the arrangements.'

He pushed Garbrecht gently through the door and closed it sharply behind him. Garbrecht stared at the closed door for a moment, then walked slowly downstairs to Miss Renner.

Later, on the street, on his way to Mikhailov's office, he tried not to think of Seedorf's conversation, or the ingenious, deadly device that even now was waiting for him on the other side of the city.

He felt like stopping and leaning his head against the cold, cracked brick wall of a gutted house he was passing, to weep and weep in the twisting, cutting wind. After so much, after all the fighting, all the death, after the operating-room in the brewery at Stalingrad, a man should be entitled to something, some peace, some security. And, instead, this onrushing dilemma, this flirtation with next week's death, this life of being scraped agianst every rock of the jagged year by every tide that crashed through Germany. Even numbness was no longer possible.

He shuffled on dazedly, not seeing where he was going. He stumbled over a piece of pavement that jutted crazily up from the sidewalk. He put out his hand to try to steady himself, but it was too late, and he fell heavily into the gutter. His head smashed against the concrete, and he felt the hot laceration of broken stone on the palm of his hand.

He sat up and looked at his hand in the dim light. There was blood coming from the dirty, ripped wounds, and his head was pounding. He sat on the kerb, his head down, waiting for it to clear before he stood up. No escape, he thought, heavily, there never would be any escape. It was silly to hope for it. He stood up slowly, and continued on his way to Mikhailov's office.

Mikhailov was crouched over his desk, the light of a single lamp making him look froglike and ugly as he sat there, without looking up at Garbrecht. ' . . Tell the man who is paying you exactly what he wishes to hear . . . ' Garbrecht could almost hear Seedorf's mocking, hearty voice. Maybe Seedorf knew what he was talking about. Maybe the Russian was that foolish, maybe the American was that suspicious . . . Suddenly, Garbrecht knew what he was going to tell Mikhailov.

'Well?' Mikhailov said finally, still peering down at his desk. 'Anything important? Have you found out anything about that new man the Americans are using?'

Mikhailov had asked him to find out what he could about Dobelmeir last week, but Garbrecht had silently resolved to keep his mouth shut about the American. If he said too much, if he slipped once, Mikhailov would become suspicious, start prying, set someone on Garbrecht's trail. But now he spoke in a loud, even voice. 'Yes,' he said. 'He is a second generation German-American. He is a lawyer in Milwaukee in civilian life. He was under investigation early in the war because he was said to have contributed to the German-American Bund in 1939 and 1940.' Garbrecht saw Mikhailov slowly raise his head and look at him, his eyes beginning to glisten with undisguised interest. It's working, Garbrecht thought, it actually is working. 'The case was never pressed,' he went on calmly with his invention, 'and he was given a direct commission late in the war and sent to Germany on special orders. Several members of his family are still alive in the British zone, Hamburg, and a cousin of his was a U-boat commander in the German Navy and was sunk off the Azores in 1943.'

'Of course,' said Mikhailov, his voice triumphant and satisfied. 'Of course. Typical.' He did not say what it was typical of, but he looked at Garbrecht, with an expression that almost approached fondness.

'There are two things you might work on for the next few weeks,' Mikhailov said. 'We've asked everyone working out of this office to pick up what he can on this matter. We are quite sure that the Americans have shipped over a number of atomic bombs to Great Britain. We have reason to believe that they are being stored in Scotland, within easy distance of the airfield at Prestwick. There are flights in from Prestwick every day, and the crews are careless. I would like to find out if there are any preparations, even of the most preliminary kind, for basing a group of B-29's somewhere in that area. Skeleton repair shops, new fuel storage tanks, new radar warning stations, et cetera. Will you see if you can pick up anything?'

'Yes, sir,' said Garbrecht, knowing that for Mikhailov's purpose, he would make certain to pick up a great deal.

'Very good,' said Mikhailov. He unlocked the drawer in his desk and took out the money. 'You will find a little bonus here,' he said with his mechanical smile.

'Thank you, sir,' said Garbrecht, picking up the money.

'Till next week,' Mikhailov said.

'Till next week,' said Garbrecht. He saluted and Mikhailov returned the salute as Garbrecht went out the door.

Although it was dark and cold outside, and his head was still throbbing from his fall, Garbrecht walked lightly, grinning to himself, as he moved towards the American zone.

He didn't see Dobelmeir till next morning. 'You might be interested in these men,' he said, placing before the Major the slip of paper with the names of the men Seedorf had instructed him to denounce. 'They are paid agents for the Russians, and the address is written down there, too.'

Dobelmeir looked at the names, and a slow, delighted grin broke over his heavy face. 'Very, very interesting,' he said. 'Excellent.' His large hand went slowly over the crumpled paper, smoothing it out in a kind of dull caress. 'I've had some more inquiries for information about that Professor I asked you to check. Kittlinger. What did you find out?'

Garbrecht had found out, more by accident than anything

else, that the Professor, an ageing, obscure physics teacher in the Berlin Medical School, had been killed in a concentration camp in 1944, but he was sure that there was no record anywhere of his death. 'Professor Kittlinger,' Garbrecht said glibly, 'was working on nuclear fission from 1934 to the end of the war. Ten days after the Russians entered Berlin, he was arrested and sent to Moscow. No word has been heard since.'

'Of course,' Dobelmeir said flatly. 'Of course.'

The atom,' Garbrecht thought, with a slight touch of exhilaration, is a marvellous thing. It hangs over everything like a magic charm. Mention the atom, and they will solemnly believe any bit of nonsense you feed them. Perhaps, he thought, grinning inwardly, I will become a specialist. Garbrecht, Atomic Secrets Limited. An easy, rich, overflowing, simple field.

Dobelmeir was industriously scratching down the doubtful history of Professor Kittlinger, Atomic Experimenter. For the first time since he had begun working for the Americans, Garbrecht realised that he was actually enjoying himself.

'You might be interested,' he said calmly, 'in something I picked up last night.'

Dobelmeir looked up assiduously from his desk. 'Of course,' he said gently.

'It probably doesn't amount to anything, just drunken, irresponsible raving . . .'

'What is it?' Dobelmeir leaned forward keenly.

'Three days ago a General Bryansky, who is on the Russian General Staff . . .'

'I know, I know,' said Dobelmeir impatiently. 'I know who he is. He's been in Berlin for a week now.'

'Well,' said Garbrecht, deliberately playing with Dobelmeir's impatience, 'he made a speech before a small group of officers at the Officers' Club, and later on he got quite drunk, and there are rumours about certain things that he said . . . I really don't know whether I ought to report anything as vague as this, as I said, just a rumour . . .'

'Go ahead,' Dobelmeir said hungrily. 'Let me hear it.'

'He is reported to have said that there will be war in sixty days. The atomic bomb is meaningless, he said. The Russian army can march to the Channel from the Elbe in twenty-five days. Then let the Americans use the atomic bomb on them. They will be in Paris, in Brussels, in Amsterdam, and the

Americans won't dare touch them . . . Of course, I cannot vouch for this, but . . .'

'Of course he said it,' Dobelmeir said. 'Or if he didn't, some other of those murderers did.' He leaned back wearily. 'I'll put it in the report. Maybe it'll make somebody wake up in Washington. And don't worry about reporting rumours. Very often there's more to be learned from a rumour than from the most heavily documented evidence.'

'Yes, sir,' said Garbrecht.

'I don't know,' said Dobelmeir, 'whether you heard about the bombing in Stuttgart yesterday.'

'Yes, sir. I did.'

'I have my own theory about it. There are going to be more, too, take my word for it. I think if you got to the bottom of it, you'd find our friends, the Russians, there. I want you to work on that, see what you can pick up this week . . .'

'Yes, sir,' Garbrecht said. What a wonderful man Seedorf is, Garbrecht thought. How astute, how correct in his intuition. How worthy of faith. He stood up. 'Is that all, sir?'

'That's all.' Dobelmeir handed him an envelope. 'Here's your money. You'll find two weeks' pay I held back in the beginning are added to this week's money.'

'Thank you very much, sir,' Garbrecht said.

'Don't thank me,' said the Major. 'You've earned it. See you next week.'

'Next week, sir.' Garbrecht saluted and went out.

There were two M.P.'s standing at the door, in the clear winter sunshine, their equipment glittering, their faces bored. Garbrecht smiled and nodded at them amused now, long in advance, as he thought of himself scornfully carrying the delicate parts of the first bomb past them, right under their noses.

He walked briskly down the street, breathing deeply the invigorating air, patting the small bulge under his coat where the money lay. He could feel the numbness that had held him for so long deserting him, but it was not pain that was taking its place, not pain at all.

Walking Wounded

He wondered what had happened to the curtains. He lay stiffly on the bed, listening, with the old, irritated tightening of the nerves, to the wild and grating hubbub of the Cairo street outside his window, the insane wailing of newsboys, the everlasting iron drip of garry-horses' hooves, the pained yelps of peddlers. The sun, bright and hurtful as hot nickel, cut in through the open windows. On the floor lay the curtains, torn, with bits of cord still running from them to the top of the windows, like a ruptured spider web.

'What happened to the curtains?' he asked. His voice felt dry and sandy in his throat, and the right side of his head began to ache.

Mac was shaving at the washstand. His beard made a crinkly, Spartan sound against the razor. 'Last night,' Mac said, without turning. 'In the excitement.'

'What excitement?'

'You pulled the curtains down.'

'Why?'

Mac shaved quietly and intently around the short, soldierly moustache. 'Don't know,' he said. 'Either you wanted to throw me out, or throw yourself out, or just tear down the curtains.'

'Oh, God!'

Mac scrubbed his face with water. 'Pretty drunk, Peter,' he said.

'What else did I do?'

'Two lieutenants and a major. In the lounge. Ten minutes of insults.'

'A major! Christ!' Peter closed his eyes.

'I think you hit a lieutenant.' Mac's voice was muffled in a towel. 'Anyway, you hit something. Your hand's all cut up.'

Peter opened his eyes and looked at his hand. Across the back of it there was a wide, ugly wound, just beginning to puff up around the edges. As he looked at it, he realised that it was hurting him.

'I poured iodine over it,' Mac said. 'You won't die.'

'Thanks.' Peter let his hand drop, licked his dry lips. 'What did I say to the major?'

' "Base wallah." "Imperial vulture." "Gezira bloodsucker." "Headquarters hangman." '

'That's enough.' The right side of Peter's head hurt very strongly for a moment.

'You were a little unfair,' Mac said calmly. 'He was a nice type. Been in the desert three years. Just come back from Sicily with dysentery. Wounded twice. Been attached to Headquarters four days.'

'Oh, Christ,' Peter said. 'Oh, Christ.'

The room was silent as Mac put on his shirt and combed his hair.

'Get his name?' Peter asked finally.

'Major Robert Lewis. Might be a good idea to say good morning.'

'How about the lieutenants?'

Mac took out his notebook. 'MacIntyre and Clark,' he read. 'They await your pleasure.'

Peter sat up and swung his legs over the side of the bed. The room faded and glittered for a moment, and he had to hold on to the bed when he stood up.

'Some day, soon,' he said, 'I have to stop drinking.'

'A little whisky,' Mac said kindly, 'is good for the soul. Anything I can do for you?'

'No thanks.'

Mac stood at the door.

'Mac . . .'

'Yes, Captain . . . ?' Tiny, astringent, helpful mockery in the title.

'Mac, this is the first time anything like this ever happened to me.'

'I know,' Mac said softly. He went quietly out of the room.

Peter walked slowly over to the wash-basin, looked at himself in the mirror. The familiar long, thin face, the uneven dotted crenelation of his wound across his forehead, the strange dark mark in the eye that had been blind for three weeks, all seeming to tremble slightly now in the bitter sunlight, as it had trembled for two months.

He shaved carefully and went to take a shower. He came back, feeling better, and put on fresh clothes. He switched his tabs with the three pips to his clean shirt, looking absently and

334

automatically to see if there was any lipstick on them. Three and a half years ago, at Arras, there had been lipstick one morning, and he had walked around all day long, ignorant, wondering why smiles hid on sergeants' lips.

Then he went down to apologise to the major.

He sat at his desk, sweating. The heat of Egypt was like the inside of a balloon. The balloon was being constantly filled; the pressure getting greater and greater. Typewriters clicked dryly in the swelling air, and flies, the true owners of Egypt, whirled cleverly and maliciously before his eyes.

Sergeant Brown, his thick glasses clouded with sweat, clumped in and put a stack of papers on his desk, clumped out again. The back of Sergeant Brown's shirt was soaked where he had been pressing against the back of a chair, and sweat ran in trickles down his infantryman legs to the heavy wool socks and gaiters.

Peter stared at the stack of papers. Ruled forms and tiny and intricate notations that had to be gone over slowly, corrected, signed.

Outside, a donkey brayed painfully. It sounded like an immense wooden machine in agony, wood grating against wood, incredibly loud. It made the little, paper-stacked room seem hotter than ever.

Peter re-read the letter he had received that morning from Italy. ' . . . I am taking the liberty of answering your letter to Col. Sands, who was badly wounded last week. I am afraid there is nothing we can do about requesting your being posted to this regiment, as there is no provision in our establishment for medically graded officers.'

The donkey brayed again outside. It sounded like the death of all the animals of Egypt on this hot morning.

Peter stared at the papers on his desk. Three flies danced over them, lighted, swept off. The typewriters rattled flatly in the heat. He took the top paper off the pile, looked at it. The figures leapt and wavered in the heat, and a drop of sweat fell from his forehead and mistily covered a 3, a 7, an 8. His hands glistened in little sick beads, and the paper felt slippery under his fingers. Hobnails sounded on the marble floor in the corridor, ostentatious and over-military among the clerks and filing cabinets. His throat burned dryly with the fifteenth cigarette of the morning.

He stood up jerkily and took his hat and went out. In the

corridor he passed Mrs Burroughs. She was a tall, full-bodied girl who wore flowered prints and always seemed to manage silk stockings. She was going home to England to divorce her husband, who was a lieutenant in India. She was going to marry an American Air Force major who had been switched to London from Cairo. She was very pretty and she had a soft, hesitant voice, and her bosom was always oppressively soft and noticeable under the flowered prints.

She smiled at him, hesitant, polite, gentle. She had two rose-buds clasped in her dark hair. 'Good morning,' she said, stopping, her voice cool, shy, inviting in the drab corridor. She always tried to stop him, talk to him.

'Good morning,' Peter said stiffly. He never could look squarely at her. He looked down. No silk stockings this morning. The pretty legs bare, the skin firm and creamy. He had a sudden, hateful vision of Mrs Burroughs landing in London, running to be crushed in the arms of the American major in the press of Waterloo Station, her eyes bright with tears of love and gratitude, her husband, used and forgotten, in India . . .

'I'm going to Groppi's,' he heard himself say, surprisingly. 'Tea. Would you like to join me?'

'Sorry,' Mrs Burroughs said, her voice sounding genuinely sorry. 'So much work. Some other time. I'd be delighted . . . '

Peter nodded awkwardly, went out. He hated Mrs Burroughs.

The street was full of heat, beggars, dirt, children with fly-eaten eyes, roaring army lorries. He put on his hat, feeling his forehead, wet and warm, rebel under the wool. A drunken New Zealander, at eleven o'clock in the morning, wobbled sorrowfully in the full glare of the sun, hatless, senseless, reft of dignity, 7,000 miles from his green and ordered island.

Groppi's was cooler, dark and shaded. The red-fezzed waiters in the long white *galabiyehs* moved quietly through the pleasant gloom. Two American sergeants with gunners' wings on their shirts solemnly were drinking two ice-cream sodas apiece.

Peter had tea and read the morning paper. The birth-rate had gone up in England, and an American magazine had suggested that Princess Elizabeth marry an American. The *Egyptian Mail* reprinted it with approval in a flood of Anglo-American feeling. After six years, somebody said in Parliament, men in the forces were to be sent home. The Russians were pouring across the Dnieper. Peter always saved the Russian news for last. Every step the Russians took was that much nearer home, nearer the rugged and manly weather of Scotland, near Anne . . .

He tried to think of Anne, what she looked like, what her skin felt like. He looked up at the ceiling and half closed his eyes to shut out the tea and ice-cream shop, to close out Egypt, summer, war, army, distance, absence, close out everything but his wife. But he couldn't remember what she looked like. He remembered the dress she wore when they were married and the inn they'd stayed at after Dunkirk and what they'd played at the concert the last night in London, and he remembered that he loved her. But her face, the sound of her voice . . . lost. She refused to have photographs taken of her. Some whim or female superstition, far away in England . . .

He paid and went out and started back to his office. But when he stood in front of the peeling, ornately balconied, sandbagged building and thought of the small, hot office, the endless papers, the sweat and hobnails, he couldn't go in. He turned and walked slowly down the street. He looked at his watch. Still an hour before the bars opened. He walked on the shady side, erect and soldierly, slowly, like a man with a grave purpose. A horribly dirty woman with a horribly dirty child, as dirty and street-worn as only Egyptians can be, followed him, whining, for half a block. Peter didn't walk any faster, although he felt his nerves jerking at the sound of the woman's voice.

The woman left him finally, and he walked deliberately through the crowded streets, stopping from time to time to peer into shop windows. French perfume, women's dresses, mangoes, books, photographs, his mind recorded heavily. He went into the photographer's and had his picture taken, refusing to smile, looking soberly square into the camera, intimidating the photographer. He would send the picture to Anne. Three years. How long could a woman be expected to remember a man? His face would stare solemnly at her morning, noon, and night, crying, 'Remember me, remember your husband . . .'

Out in the street again he resumed his grave pacing down the shady side of the street. Fifteen minutes more and the bars would open. He grinned crookedly to himself as he thought of his pose before the camera, frozen Scotch passion grimly and puritanically peering across three years and two oceans. Anne would probably giggle at the absurdly stern, accusing face.

'Officer, wanna lady, wanna lady?'

Peter looked down. A tiny, filthy ten-year-old boy, barefooted, in a torn, bag-like single garment, was smiling up at him conspiratorially, pulling at his blouse.

'French lady,' the boy whispered wickedly. 'Fine French lady.'

Peter stared at him disbelievingly, then broke into a roar of laughter. The boy, after a moment of doubt, also laughed.

'No thank you, sir,' Peter said.

The boy shrugged, grinned up at him. 'Officer,' he said, 'cigarette?'

Peter gave him a cigarette and lit it for him, and the boy darted off to try the French lady on a Polish corporal.

The bar had a nice beery smell and was dark and cool and the bartender drew eight glasses at a time, letting the foam settle whitely on the glass rims.

'The two lieutenants,' Peter was saying, 'were a little stuffy, but the major was fine.'

'I knew he would be,' Mac said. 'I talked to him last night.'

'I had breakfast with him' – Peter waved for two more beers – 'and he said he guessed he'd be doing the same thing himself if he had to hang around this town five months.'

Mac comfortably drained his beer.

'The birth-rate in England,' Peter said, 'has gone up. I read it in the *Mail* this morning. There're three million Englishmen out of the country and the birth-rate's rocketing . . . ' He heard his own voice loud and angry and humourless. 'How in the name of God do they dare print things like that?' He saw Mac grinning widely, but he couldn't stop. 'Who're the fathers? Where're the fathers? Bloody damned newspaper!'

'My,' Mac said, 'you have it bad today.'

Suddenly Peter realised that Mac, placid and tolerant, was bearing a great deal of the burden of Peter's nerves.

'Mac,' he said quietly, 'forgive me.'

'Uh?' Mac looked at him surprised.

'Wailing Wall Chrome. Agony, Cairo division.' Peter shook his head in disgust. 'I keep feeding it to you seven days a week.'

'Oh, shut up. I've lived with lots worse.'

'Any time I get on your nerves, sing out, will you?'

'Sure thing. Drink your beer,' Mac was embarrassed.

'I must be going a little crazy.' Peter looked at his hands, which had taken to trembling in the last few months. The cigarette jerked minutely between his fingers, in a spasmodic rhythm. 'This town. When I was with the regiment . . . Oh, hell. . . ' The truth was that out in the desert, under the guns, on a pint of water a day, and the sudden air often dire with Stukas, he had been much happier. There were no women in the desert, no reminders of a civilised and normal life. There was clean, sterile sand, the noise of armour, thousands of grumbling, good-humoured men intimate with an equal death, and above all there was the sense of immense and hardy effect and accomplishment, as first they had held the Afrika Corps and then driven it back. Cairo then had been a beautiful town, two days at a time, a hot bath and unlimited Scotch, and sweet, clean sheets and relief from the guns. But now, under the dry flood of paper, under the stiffness and pettiness of head-quarters politics, under the cheap weight of men who had clung to soft jobs for three years, with the streets full of barelegged girls, with the war on another continent a thousand miles away . . .

Now the regiment, what was left of it, was broken up. Most of them were in graves on the road to Tunis, others were in hospitals, the rest scattered among other units, after the four years that had started in France. Mac, who had been his platoon sergeant at Arras, calmly instructing the untrained men how to load and fire the guns they had never used before, then taking them out into the fresh May fields of France hunting for parachutists. Himself, who had crawled through the Ger-man lines to Dunkirk, who had entered Tripoli the first hour, who had been blown up in the jeep outside Mareth, with his driver dead in the air beside him . . . Now, both of them clerks in small offices, chained to paper and civil servants.

'Six years,' he said, 'some bloody M.P. said we'd be sent home after six years. What do you think a woman thinks when she reads that she'll get her man back in only six years?'

'Always remember,' Mac grinned, 'what Monty said. "The war can't last more than seven years. We'll run out of paper." '

'If only I could get back to England,' Peter said, 'and sleep with my wife for two nights, everything would be all right. Just two nights.'

Mac sighed. He was a quiet, efficient, small, matter-of-fact man, noticeably greying, and sighing was strange and incon-gruous to him. 'Peter,' he said, 'can I talk plainly?'

Peter nodded.

'Peter, you ought to get yourself a girl.'

They sat in silence. Peter played sombrely with his beer. In France, even though he had just been married, he had been the gay young officer. Handsome and debonair, he had played joyfully and thoughtlessly with the pretty ladies of the country towns at which he'd been stationed, and in Paris, when he'd had a month there, a charming, beautifully dressed wife of a French captain stationed in Algiers.

But when he'd got back to England with the grey-faced remnants of his regiment, after the hideous, bloody days of the break-through, and had taken his wife silently into his arms, all frivolity, all smallness and lack of faith had seemed wanton and irreligious in the face of so much ruin, such agony. Leaving England for Africa, he had felt that behind him he had to leave the best part of his life orderly and decent.

'Maybe,' he said to Mac, 'Maybe . . .'

'A man's got to be practical,' Mac said. 'Three years. Oh, my God!'

Peter had to smile at the drastic expression on the practical man's face.

'You'll just explode,' Mac said, 'and blow away.'

Peter laughed loudly, nervously. 'Whisky,' he said, 'provides certain compensations.'

'Whisky,' Mac said grimly, 'will send you home a doddering wreck. You'll do no one any good that way.'

'Maybe. Maybe . . .' Peter shrugged. 'Anyway, I hate these women out here. Having the best time of their lives. Ugly, impossible girls no one would ever look at in peacetime, just because there are a hundred men for every woman . . . Snobbish, over-confident . . . Bitches, all of them. A man has to sacrifice all decent, male pride to chase after one of these . . .' He talked faster and faster, all the bitter observation of the past years flooding to his tongue. 'They demand abasement, homage, the ugliest, horrible and meanest of them. Women,' he said, 'have been among the most horrible of the war's casualties. All humility's gone, all normal value, all friendship. They're man-greedy. They're profiteering on the war, like the worst usurer and manufacturer of machine tools, except that their profits are lieutenants and generals, not cash. After the war,' he said, 'we should have rehabilitation hospitals for women who have been in troop areas, just like the hospitals for maimed men, to teach them how to live normal lives again . . .'

Mac was laughing by now, helplessly, into his beer. 'Enough,'

340

he said. 'Enough, John Knox! All I wanted to say is that I have a date tonight, and my girl has a friend who's just come from Jerusalem, and it might do you a world of good just to have dinner with a woman for once. Do you want to go?'

Peter flushed, looked down at the beer-ringed table. 'I won't even know how to talk to a woman any more.'

'Do you want to go?'

Peter opened his mouth, closed it. 'All right,' he said. 'All right.'

'Jerusalem is nice enough . . . ' It was on the dance floor at the Auberge des Pyramides, under the stars, with the three great tombs standing huge and a rebuke to time in the darkness just outside the lights and the music. Joyce was talking as they went slowly and painfully around the dance floor. 'The city's clean, and the King David's an amusing hotel, but the people're simply dreadful.' She had a brittle, drawling voice, pitched just high enough so that everyone nearby could hear clearly what she was saying. 'There,' she said brightly, as Peter managed a full turn, 'we're doing much better, aren't we?'

'Yes,' Peter said, sweating in the heavy Nile heat, only slightly tempered by night, as he tried to concentrate on the beat of the music. Joyce's voice distracted him and put him off, and somehow she never seemed to stop talking. She worked in the consular service, and by 9.30 Peter had a full store of information on the doings of the Consulate in Jerusalem for the last year and a half, at which time Joyce had come out from England. He had hardly said a word all night, stammering, half finishing sentences, suffering, feeling like the clumsiest farmer. Still, she was pretty, most desirable in a full white evening gown. ('We always dress in Jerusalem') with full, sleek shoulders bare and daring under the gay lights.

'That's King Farouk . . . ' For the first time all evening her voice dropped a bit. 'Isn't it?'

Peter looked. 'Yes,' he said.

'Isn't he attractive? What an original beard!'

Peter looked at King Farouk. 'He looks like a fat, self-satisfied young man,' Peter said, the first full sentence he had got out all evening. 'And I understand he grew the beard because he has a terrible case of acne.'

'Dance around the edge of the dance floor,' Joyce whispered. 'I'd like people to see me.'

Dutifully and heavily, Peter danced around the edge of the

341

floor until the music stopped. He followed Joyce to the table. Joyce smiled vivaciously at seven or eight officers seated at various tables throughout the establishment.

'It's amazing,' she said brightly and loudly, 'how many men I know in Cairo.' They sat down. There was an awful silence while Peter wondered where in the name of God Mac was, and his girl, and Joyce smiled prettily first at one table, then another.

'Are you married?' Peter heard his voice, crooked and rasping asking inexplicably. For the first time that evening Joyce gave him her undivided attention.

'Why,' she said, looking at him queerly and coldly, 'what a strange question!'

'It's just that there's a girl around my office,' Peter said, almost dazedly. 'Married to a lieutenant in India. Marrying an American major in London . . . ' The expression on Joyce's face became more and more strained. 'I don't know what made me think of her,' Peter said lamely.

'No,' Joyce said coldly, 'I'm not married.'

'I am,' Peter said, despairingly.

'Really.' Joyce smiled automatically at a colonel four tables away.

'My wife,' said Peter, not knowing why he was talking, feeling his tongue too loose from the drinking that had been continuous since six that evening, 'my wife is a woman of admirable character, although I can't remember what she looks like. Her name is Anne. She works for the Air Ministry in Manchester. After Dunkirk, I was stationed on the beach at Dover for five months. I used to manage to get away week-ends. We'd just stay in one room and just look at each other. After France . . . I felt as though my wife had healed me of a dreadful disease. She healed me of mud and death and friends dying on all sides. She's most beautiful, but I don't remember what she looks like. She's very calm and simple and her voice is low, although I don't remember that, either. I sent her my photograph today. Six years is too long for a man to expect a woman to remember him. Someone ought to tell Parliament that . . . Don't you think?'

Joyce was staring at him, her mouth frozen to one side. 'Yes,' she said.

'If I could only see her for two nights . . . ' Well, finally, the thought crossed his consciousness, the lady from Jerusalem is listening to me. 'Right before I came out here, I was moved to another beach. It was raining. Autumn and miserable and barbed wire at the high-tide marks and mines all over the beaches. I called her long-distance and she told me she had a week and asked me if she should come down. I told her no. It was so miserable. Cheap little shacks waiting for the Germans in the rain. I knew we were leaving for Africa and I didn't want our last days together to be dreary, in that abominable place. I told her no, but she said, "You wait right there. I'm coming down tonight." ' Suddenly, above the dance music in the Valley of the Nile, Peter remembered what his wife's voice had sounded like, merry and sensual and confidently commanding over the faulty wires on that autumn night on a wet beach on the English Channel. 'She came down and we had the week together, and the rain and the barbed wire made no difference at all. I've never been so gay, and it was early in the war, and we always had a coal fire and hot rum and lovely heavy breakfasts, with the curtains still drawn. And never a tear when she left. And I started for Africa singing in my heart.' He was talking straight ahead to the Pyramids in the ancient desert darkness now, not to the silly, bare-shouldered girl across the table. 'I haven't heard from her in two months. Not a letter in two months.' He shrugged. 'After the war,' he said, 'I'm going to go in for politics. I'm going to stand for Parliament. There must be somebody in Parliament who knows what a war is like, who knows that one war is enough, six years is too much . . .'

'Why, Joyce, how nice!' It was the colonel, standing gallantly at the table. 'Dance?'

Joyce looked doubtfully at Peter. Peter stood up, a little unsteadily. 'Delighted,' he said ambiguously. Without looking at Peter, Joyce went off with the colonel, smiling impartially at dozens of officers in Sam Browne belts as she danced on the edge of the floor.

Peter hazily watched the flashing plump white dress among the brave khaki and brass pips. He passed his hand over his eyes, thinking, as he remembered his outburst, God, I must be going crazy.

He saw a captain step in and dance with Joyce, then an American major. 'The world,' he said softly to himself, 'is full of American majors.' He laughed gently to himself, stood up, walked slowly out of the night club. Outside, with the music thin and distant in his ears, the Pyramids loomed, crumbling in the darkness, in memory of the unremembered dead.

343

He got into a cab and started for Cairo.

When the cab got to Gezira Island, he tapped the driver on the shoulder. 'Sporting Club,' he said.

The old, wheezing taxi laboriously turned. 'I need a drink,' Peter told himself seriously. 'I need a drink very badly.' He thought of old Mac caught there with two girls and the tremendous bill. He felt bad about it, but he'd pay his share, although it would mean considerably less drinking for the rest of the month. But he couldn't stay with that damned girl. The truth was he couldn't stay with any girl. Anne, unphotographed, in Manchester . . . Still, she should write more often than once every two months . . .

The bar at Gezira was still open. There were some South Africans and some American fliers lounging against it. One of the American fliers was singing, in a soft Southern voice, 'Oh, Susannah, don't you cry for me . . .'

'Scotch,' Peter said to the bartender, feeling for the first time that evening a cessation of loneliness, his constant climate.

'Fo' Ah'm gawn' t' Alabama, with mah banjo on meh knee . . .' the American pilot sang sweetly and happily.

'Gin and lime,' said one of the South Africans, a gigantic captain with huge, bare arms, whom the others called Lee. 'Gin and lime all around.' He turned to Peter. 'What're you drinking, Captain?'

'I've ordered, thanks.' Peter smiled at him.

'Man says he's ordered,' the American pilot sang. 'What do you know about that? British captain says he's ordered. Order again and again, oh, Captain, order again . . .'

The bartender put two Scotches in front of Peter, grinning. The huge South African captain poured it all into one glass. They lifted their glasses.

'To South Africa,' one of the Americans said.

They drank.

'To sergeants.' The American who had been singing grinned at a large South African lieutenant with a moustache. The lieutenant looked around him uneasily. 'Quiet, please,' he said. 'I'll be in jail five years.'

'This gentleman looks like a gentleman.' Lee put his arm around the lieutenant with the moustache. 'Doesn't he?'

'Yes,' said Peter.

'Jail,' said the lieutenant with the moustache.

'He's not a gentleman. He is a sergeant. He is my bloody sergeant from my bloody company.'

344

'Ten years,' said the lieutenant with the moustache.

'We're all A.W.O.L., Sergeant Monks, lieutenant for the evening, Lieutenant Fredericks . . . ' He waved to a slightly smaller red-headed South African down the bar. 'And myself. We're farmers. Independent men. When the bloody O.C. said "No leaves," we said farewell. Sixty miles out on the desert for three weeks. Miserable little clerk of an O.C. Sergeant, I said, here's a pip. Take off those bloody stripes. We wish to show you the glories of Shepheard's and Gezira, so that you can come back and dazzle the poor bastards in the other ranks with tales of the high life of Cairo.'

'I've been talking to brigadiers all afternoon and evening,' Monks complained. 'Wearing on the nerves.'

'If the O.C. shows up, it's all taped,' Lee said. 'I grab Monks by one arm, Freddy grabs him by the other. "We've just arrested the bugger, sir," we say. "Impersonating an officer." '

'Ten years,' Monks said, grinning. 'This round is on me.'

Peter laughed. He lifted his glass. 'To sergeants everywhere.' They all drank.

'On my right,' said Lee, 'is the American Air Force.'

The American Air Force raised its glasses at Peter and the pilot who sang started in on 'Chattanooga Choo-choo.' There were two lieutenants and a twenty-four-year-old major.

'The American Air Force is going home,' said Lee. 'Their tour is over. Home by way of England. The infantry's tour is never over. Oh, the poor, stinking, bloody infantry, their tour is never over . . . '

'Unskilled labour,' one of the pilots said calmly. 'We're delicate and highly sensitive mechanisms. We are war-weary. Our Schneiders are low as an Egyptian whore. We've bombed too many places. We've seen too much flak. We are lopsided from wearing ribbons. We are going home now to instruct the young how to shoot.'

'I am going home to play with my wife,' the twenty-four-year-old major said soberly.

'The infantry is not under the same Awful Strain,' said the pilot who had been singing. 'All they have to do is walk in and be shot. Their nerves are not stretched to the breaking point like ours, Captain,' he said, leaning back and talking to Peter, 'you look a little war-weary yourself.'

'I'm pretty war-weary,' Peter said.

'He looks sensitive,' the major said. 'He looks fine and sensitive enough to be at least a navigator. He looks like Hamlet on a rough night.'

'I was in the ranks,' Peter said.

'It's possible,' said the major, 'to get war-weary in a tank, too, I suppose.'

'It's possible,' Peter said, grinning.

' . . . breakfast in Carolina . . . ' sang the musical pilot.

'When're you leaving for home?' Peter asked.

'Six a.m. tomorrow: 0600 hours, as they say in the Army,' said the major.

'Five or six glorious days in London among our brave English Allies and cousins,' said the other pilot, 'and then the Stork Club, the Harvard-Yale football game, all the blonde, full-bosomed, ribbon-conscious, lascivious American girls . . . '

'London,' said Peter. 'I wish I were going with you.'

'Come along,' said the major expansively. 'We have a nice empty Liberator. Pleased to have you. Closer relations with our British comrades. Merely be at the airport at 0600 hours, as they say in the Army.'

'Did you see,' asked the singing pilot, 'in the *Mail* today? Some idiot wants Princess Elizabeth to marry an American.'

'Excellent idea,' said the major. 'Some upstanding representative citizen of the Republic. Post-war planning on all fronts. My nomination for Prince Escort is Maxie Rosenbloom.'

Everyone considered the suggestion gravely.

'You could do worse,' the pilot said.

'Infusion of sturdy American stock into an ageing dynasty,' the major said. 'The issue would be strongly built, with good left hands . . . '

'Do you mean it?' Peter asked. 'You really could take me?'

'Delighted,' the major said.

The singing pilot started in on 'All Alone', and everyone but Peter joined in. Peter stared unseeingly at the glasses and bottles behind the bar. In three days he could be home. Three days and he could walk into Anne's room, quietly, unannounced, smiling a little tremulously as she looked up unsuspectingly. Maybe it was possible. He had had no leave since he'd come to Africa, except for two weeks' convalescence. He could go immediately to Colonel Foster's apartment, explain to him. Colonel Foster liked him, was very sympathetic. If he gave him a written order, releasing him from duty for twenty-one days, he, Peter, would undertake to get transportation back. Somehow, somehow . . . He would take all the responsibility himself. He was sure that Colonel Foster, who was a good soul, would do it.

Peter stood up straight. He spoke to the American major. 'Perhaps I'll see you at six o'clock.'

'Fine,' the major said heartily. 'It's going to be a great trip. We're loaded with Scotch.' He waved as Peter turned and left the bar.

'All alone, by the telephone . . . ' the wailing, mocking voices quavered in the night. Peter got into a taxicab and gave Colonel Foster's address.

He felt he was trembling. He closed his eyes and leaned back. It was all absolutely possible. England was only three days away. Two weeks there and the desert and the guns and the dying and ruled paper and heat and loneliness and insane expanding tension would disappear. He could face the rest of the war calmly, knowing that he would not explode, would not lose his reason. It was possible. Men were going home to their wives. That American major. All so cheerful and matter-of-fact about it. England in three days, after the three years . . . Colonel Foster would most certainly say yes. Peter was sure of it as the taxi drove up to the dark building where Colonel Foster lived. Peter paid the driver and looked up. The colonel's window was alight, the only one in the entire building. Peter felt his breath coming fast. It was a symbol, an omen. The man was awake. His friend, who could give him England tonight with five strokes of a pen, by luck was wakeful in the quiet night, when all the rest of the city slept around him. It would be irregular, and Colonel Foster would be running some risk, but he had rank enough and was independent enough to take the chance . . .

Peter rang the night-bell to the side of the locked doors of the apartment building. Far in the depths of the sleeping stone and brick, a forlorn and distant bell sang weirdly.

As he waited for the hall-boy to open the doors, Peter hastily rehearsed his story. No leave in three years. The tension getting worse and worse. Medically graded, no chance of getting to an active unit. Regiment disbanded. Work deteriorating. Given to sudden fits of temper and what could only be described as melancholia, although a doctor wouldn't believe it until it was too late. He knew the British Army couldn't provide transportation, but here were these Americans with an empty Liberator. He'd get back somehow.

As he went over it, in the darkness, with the far-away bell

347

sounding as though it were ringing at the bottom of a troubled sea, Peter was sure the logic was irrefutable; Foster couldn't refuse.

When the hall-boy finally opened the door, Peter sprang past him, raced up the steps, too impatient to take the elevator.

He was panting when he rang Colonel Foster's bell, and the sweat was streaming down the sides of his face. He rang the bell sharply, twice. He heard his breath whistling into his lungs, and he tried to compose himself, so that Colonel Foster would think him absolutely calm, absolutely lucid . . .

The door opened. The figure at the door was silhouetted against the yellowish light behind it.

'Colonel,' Peter said, panting, 'I'm so glad you're up. I must talk to you. I hate to disturb you, but . . . '

'Come in.' The door was opened wider and Peter strode down the hall, into the living-room. He heard the door close and turned around. 'I . . . ' he began. He stopped. The man who was standing there was not Colonel Foster. It was a large, red-faced man, bald, in a tattered red bathrobe. He had a moustache and tired eyes and he was holding a book in his hand. Peter looked at the book. *The Poems of Robert Browning.*

The man stood there, waiting, pulling his bathrobe a little tighter, a curious little smile on his weary face.

'I . . . I saw the light, sir,' Peter said. 'I thought Colonel Foster would be up and I took the liberty of . . . I had some business with . . . '

'Colonel Foster doesn't live here,' the man said. His voice was clipped and military, but tired, ageing. 'He moved out a week ago.'

'Oh,' Peter said. He suddenly stopped sweating. He swallowed, made a conscious effort to speak quietly. 'Do you know where he lives, sir?'

'I'm afraid not. Is there anything I can do, Captain? I'm Colonel Gaines.' He smiled, false teeth above the old robe. 'That's why when you said Colonel, at the door, I . . . '

'No, sir,' Peter said. 'Nothing, sir. I'm dreadfully sorry. This time of night . . . '

'Oh, that's all right.' The man waved a little embarrassedly. 'I never go to sleep. I was reading.'

'Well . . . Thank you, sir. Good night.'

'Uh . . . ' the man looked hesitantly at him, as though he felt that somehow Peter should be helped in some dubious, obscure way. 'Uh – perhaps a drink. I have some whisky I was just going to – for myself.'

'No, thank you, sir,' Peter said. 'I'd better be getting along.'

Clumsily, they went down the passage together to the door. The man opened the door. He stood there, red-faced, huge, British, like a living Colonel Blimp, lonely and tired, with Robert Browning in the foreign night.

'Good night, sir.'

'Good night . . . '

The door closed and Peter walked slowly down the dark stairs.

Peter started towards his hotel, but the thought of the disordered room and Mac lying there, steadily asleep, steadily and slightly snoring in the next bed, was impossible.

He walked slowly past the dark policemen standing quietly with their rifles on the street corners. Down the street garry-lights, small and flickering and lonesome, wandered past, and the sound of the horses' hooves was deliberate and weary.

He came to the English Bridge and stood on the banks of the river, looking at the dark water swirling north towards the Mediterranean. Down the river a felucca, its immense sail spread in a soaring triangle, slowly made its way among the shadows from the trees along the shore. Across the river a minaret, poignant with faith, shone sharp and delicate in the moonlight.

Peter felt spent and drained. A nervous and hysteric pulse pulled at his bad eye and a gigantic sob seemed wedged into his throat.

Overhead, far away, there was the sound of a plane. It came nearer, passed across the stars, died away, going somewhere.

The wedge dislodged and the sob broke out like tears and blood.

Peter closed his eyes, and when he opened them again the wild pulse had stopped, his throat was clear. He stared across the river at the minaret, faithful and lovely in the light of the moon, by the side of the old river.

Tomorrow, he thought, tomorrow there may be a letter from home . . .

The Dry Rock

'We're late,' Helen said, as the cab stopped at a light. 'We're twenty minutes late.' She looked at her husband accusingly. 'All right,' Fitzsimmons said. 'I couldn't help it. The work was on the desk and it had to . . . '

'This is the one dinner party of the year I didn't want to be late for,' Helen said. 'So naturally . . . '

The cab started and was halfway across the street when the Ford sedan roared into it, twisting, with a crashing and scraping of metal, a high mournful scream of brakes, the tinkling of glass. The cab shook a little, then subsided.

The cabby, a little grey man, turned and looked back, worriedly. 'Everybody is all right?' he asked nervously.

'Everybody is fine,' Helen said bitterly, pulling at her cape to get it straight again after the jolting.

'No damage done,' said Fitzsimmons, smiling reassuringly at the cabby, who looked very frightened.

'I am happy to hear that,' the cabby said. He got out of his car and stood looking sadly at the fender, now thoroughly crumpled, and his headlight, now without a lens. The door of the Ford opened and its driver sprang out. He was a large young man with a light grey hat. He glanced hurriedly at the cab.

'Why don't yuh watch where the hell yer goin'?' he asked harshly.

'The light was in my favour,' said the cabby. He was a small man of fifty, in a cap and a ragged coat, and he spoke with a heavy accent. 'It turned green and I started across. I would like your licence, mister.'

'What for?' the man in the grey hat shouted. 'Yer load's all right. Get on yer way. No harm done.' He started back to his car.

The cabby gently put his hand on the young man's arm. 'Excuse me, friend,' he said. 'It is a five-dollar job, at least. I would like to see your licence.'

The young man pulled his arm away, glared at the cabby. 'Aaah,' he said and swung. His fist made a loud, surprising noise against the cabby's nose. The old man sat down slowly on the running board of his cab, holding his head wearily in his hands. The young man in the grey hat stood over him, bent over, fists still clenched. 'Didn't I tell yuh no harm was done?' he shouted. 'Why didn't yuh lissen t' me? I got a good mind to . . .'

'Now, see here,' Fitzsimmons said, opening the rear door and stepping out.

'What d'*you* want?' The young man turned and snarled at Fitzsimmons, his fists held higher. 'Who asked for *you*?'

'I saw the whole thing,' Fitzsimmons began, 'and I don't think you . . .'

'Aaah,' snarled the young man. 'Dry up.'

'Claude,' Helen called. 'Claude, keep out of this.'

'Claude,' the young man repeated balefully. 'Dry up, Claude.'

'Are you all right?' Fitzsimmons asked, bending over the cabby, who still sat reflectively on the running board, his head down, his old and swollen cap hiding his face, blood trickling down his clothes.

'I'm all right,' the cabby said wearily. He stood up, looked wonderingly at the young man. 'Now, my friend, you force me to make trouble. Police!' he called, loudly. '*Police!*'

'Say, lissen,' the man in the grey hat shouted. 'What the hell do yuh need to call the cops for? Hey, cut it out!'

'*Police!*' the old cabby shouted calmly, but with fervour deep in his voice. 'Police!'

'I ought to give it to yuh good.' The young man shook his fist under the cabby's nose. He jumped around nervously. 'This is a small matter,' he shouted, 'nobody needs the cops!'

'Police!' called the cabby.

'Claude,' Helen put her head out the window. 'Let's get out of here and let the two gentlemen settle this any way they please.'

'I apologise!' The young man held the cabby by his lapels with both large hands, shook him, to emphasise his apology. 'Excuse me. I'm sorry. Stop yelling police, for God's sake!'

'I'm going to have you locked up,' the cabby said. He stood there, slowly drying the blood off his shabby coat with his cap. His hair was grey, but long and full, like a musician's. He had a big head for his little shoulders, and a sad, lined little face and he looked older than fifty, to Fitzsimmons, very poor, neg-

351

lected, badly nourished. 'You have committed a crime,' the cabby said, 'and there is a punishment for it.'

'Will yuh talk to him?' the young man turned savagely to Fitzsimmons. 'Will yuh tell him I'm sorry?'

'It's entirely up to him,' Fitzsimmons said.

'We're a half-hour late,' Helen announced bitterly. 'The perfect dinner guests.'

'It is not enough to be sorry,' said the cab-driver. '*Police* . . .'

'Say, listen, Bud,' the young man said, his voice quick and confidential, 'what's yer name?'

'Leopold Tarloff,' the cabby said. 'I have been driving a cab on the streets of New York for twenty years, and everybody thinks just because you're a cab-driver they can do whatever they want to you.'

'Lissen, Leopold,' the young man pushed his light grey hat far back on his head. 'Let's be sensible. I hit yer cab. All right. I hit you. All right.'

'What's all right about it?' Tarloff asked.

'What I mean is, I admit it, I confess I did it, that's what I mean. All right.' The young man grabbed Tarloff's short ragged arms as he spoke, intensely. 'Why the fuss? It happens every day. Police are unnecessary. I'll tell yuh what I'll do with yuh, Leopold. Five dollars, yuh say, for the fender. All right. And for the bloody nose, another pound. What do yuh say? Everybody is satisfied. Yuh've made yerself a fiver on the transaction; these good people go to their party without no more delay.'

Tarloff shook his arms free from the huge hands of the man in the grey hat. He put his head back and ran his fingers through his thick hair and spoke coldly. 'I don't want to hear another word. I have never been so insulted in my whole life.'

The young man stepped back, his arms wide, palms up wonderingly. 'I insult him!' He turned to Fitzsimmons. 'Did you hear me insult this party?' he asked.

'Claude!' Helen called. 'Are we going to sit here all night?'

'A man steps up and hits me in the nose,' Tarloff said. 'He thinks he makes everything all right with five dollars. He is mistaken. Not with five hundred dollars.'

'How much d'yuh think a clap in the puss is worth?' the young man growled. 'Who d'yuh think y'are – Joe Louis?'

'Not ten thousand dollars,' Tarloff said, on the surface calm, but quivering underneath. 'Not for twenty thousand dollars. My dignity.'

'His dignity!' the young man whispered. 'For Christ's sake!'

352

'What do you want to do?' Fitzsimmons asked, conscious of Helen glooming in the rear seat of the cab.

'I would like to take him to the station house and make a complaint,' Tarloff said. 'You would have to come with me, if you'd be so kind. What is your opinion on the matter?'

'Will yuh tell him the cops are not a necessity!' the young man said hoarsely. 'Will yuh tell the bastidd?'

'Claude!' called Helen.

'It's up to you,' Fitzsimmons said, looking with what he hoped was an impartial, judicious expression at Tarloff, hoping he wouldn't have to waste any more time. 'You do what you think you ought to do.'

Tarloff smiled, showing three yellow teeth in the front of his small and childlike mouth, curved and red and surprising in the lined and weatherbeaten old hackie's face. 'Thank you very much,' he said. 'I am glad to see you agree with me.'

Fitzsimmons sighed.

'Yer drivin' me crazy!' the young man shouted at Tarloff. 'Yer makin' life impossible!'

'To you,' Tarloff said with dignity, 'I talk from now on only in a court of law. That's my last word.'

The young man stood there, breathing heavily, his fists clenching and unclenching, his pale grey hat shining in the light of a street lamp. A policeman turned the corner, walking in a leisurely and abstracted manner, his eyes on the legs of a girl across the street.

Fitzsimmons went over to him. 'Officer,' he said, 'there's a little job for you over here.' The policeman regretfully took his eyes off the girl's legs and sighed and walked slowly over to where the two cars were still nestling against each other.

'What are yuh?' the young man was asking Tarloff, when Fitzsimmons came up with the policeman. 'Yuh don't act like an American citizen. What are yuh?'

'I'm a Russian,' Tarloff said. 'But I'm in the country twenty-five years now, I know what the rights of an individual are.'

'Yeah,' said the young man hopelessly. 'Yeah . . . '

The Fitzsimmonses drove silently to the police station in the cab, with Tarloff driving slowly and carefully, though with hands that shook on the wheel. The policeman drove with the young man in the young man's Ford. Fitzsimmons saw the Ford stop at a cigar store and the young man jump out and go into the store, into a telephone booth.

'For three months,' Helen said, as they drove, 'I've been trying to get Adele Lowrie to invite us to dinner. Now we've
finally managed it. Perhaps we ought to call her and invite the
whole party down to night court.'

'It isn't night court,' Fitzsimmons said patiently. 'It's a police
station. And I think you might take it a little better. After all,
the poor old man has no one to speak up for him.'

'Leopold Tarloff,' Helen said. 'It sounds impossible. Leopold
Tarloff. Leopold Tarloff.'

They sat in silence until Tarloff stopped the cab in front of
the police station and opened the door for them. The Ford with
the policeman and the young man drove up right behind them
and they all went in together.

There were some people up in front of the desk lieutenant, a
dejected-looking man with long moustaches and a loud, blonde
woman who kept saying that the man had threatened her with
a baseball bat three times that evening. Two Negroes with
bloody bandages around their heads were waiting, too.

'It will take some time,' said the policeman. 'There are two
cases ahead of you. My name is Kraus.'

'Oh my,' said Helen.

'You'd better call Adele,' Fitzsimmons said. 'Tell her not to
hold dinner for us.'

Helen held her hand out gloomily for nickels.

'I'm sorry,' Tarloff said anxiously, 'to interrupt your plans
for the evening.'

'Perfectly all right,' Fitzsimmons said, trying to screen his
wife's face from Tarloff by bending over to search for the
nickels in his pocket.

Helen went off, disdainfully holding her long formal skirt up
with her hand, as she walked down the spit- and butt-marked
corridor of the police station towards a pay telephone. Fitzsimmons reflectively watched her elegant back retreat down the
hallway.

'I am tired,' Tarloff said. 'I think I will have to sit down, if
you will excuse me.' He sat on the floor, looking up with a frail,
apologetic smile on his red face worn by wind and rain and
traffic policemen. Fitzsimmons suddenly felt like crying, watching the old man sitting there among the spit- and cigarette-
butts, on the floor against the wall, with his cap off and his
great bush of musician's hair giving the lie to the tired,
weathered face below it.

Four men threw open the outside doors and walked into the

police station with certainty and authority. They all wore the same light-grey hats with the huge flat brims. The young man who had hit Tarloff greeted them guardedly. 'I'm glad you're here, Pidgear,' he said to the man who, by some subtle mixture of stance and clothing, of lift of eyebrow and droop of mouth, announced himself as leader.

They talked swiftly and quietly in a corner.

'A Russian!' Pidgear's voice rang out angrily. 'There are 10,000 cab-drivers in the metropolitan area, you have to pick a Russian to punch in the nose!'

'I'm excitable!' the young man yelled. 'Can I help it if I'm excitable? My father was the same way; it's a family characteristic.'

'Go tell that to the Russian,' Pidgear said. He went over to one of the three men who had come in with him, a large man who needed a shave and whose collar was open at the throat, as though no collar could be bought large enough to go all the way around that neck. The large man nodded, went over to Tarloff, still sitting patiently against the wall.

'You speak Russian?' the man with the open collar said to Tarloff.

'Yes, sir,' Tarloff said.

The large man sat down slowly beside him, gripped Tarloff's knee confidentially in his tremendous hairy hands, spoke excitedly, winningly, in Russian.

Pidgear and the young man who had hit Tarloff came over to Fitzsimmons, leaving the other two men in the grey hats, small, dark men with shining eyes, who just stood at the door and looked hotly on.

'My name is Pidgear,' the man said to Fitzsimmons, who by now was impressed with the beautiful efficiency of the system that had been put into motion by the young driver of the Ford – an obviously legal mind like Pidgear, a man who spoke Russian, and two intense men with grey hats standing on call just to see justice done, and all collected in the space of fifteen minutes. 'Alton Pidgear,' the man said, smiling professionally at Fitzsimmons. 'I represent Mr Rusk.'

'Yeah,' said the young man.

'My name is Fitzsimmons.'

'Frankly, Mr Fitzsimmons,' Pidgear said, 'I would like to see you get Mr Tarloff to call this whole thing off. It's an embarrassing affair for all concerned; nobody stands to gain anything by pressing it.'

Helen came back and Fitzsimmons saw by the expression on her face that she wasn't happy. 'They're at the soup by now,' she said loudly to Fitzsimmons. 'Adele said for us to take all the time we want, they're getting along fine.'

'Mr Rusk is willing to make a handsome offer,' Pidgear said. 'Five dollars for the car, five dollars for the nose . . . '

'Go out to dinner with your husband,' Helen muttered, 'and you wind up in a telephone booth in a police station. "Excuse me for being late, darling, but I'm calling from the 8th Precinct, this is our night for street-fighting." '

'Sssh, Helen please,' Fitzsimmons said. He hadn't eaten since nine that morning and his stomach was growling with hunger.

'It was all a mistake,' Pidgear said smoothly. 'A natural mistake. Why should the man be stubborn? He is being reimbursed for everything, isn't he? I wish you would talk to him, Mr Fitzsimmons; we don't want to keep you from your social engagements. Undoubtedly,' Pidgear said, eyeing their evening clothes respectfully, 'you and the madam were going to an important dinner party. It would be too bad to spoil an important dinner party for a little thing like this. Why, this whole affair is niggling,' he said, waving his hand in front of Fitzsimmons's face. 'Absolutely niggling.'

Fitzsimmons looked over to where Tarloff and the other Russian were sitting on the floor. From Tarloff's face and gestures, even though he was talking in deepest Russian, Fitzsimmons could tell Tarloff was still as firm as ever. Fitzsimmons looked closely at Rusk, who was standing looking at Tarloff through narrow, baleful eyes.

'Why're you so anxious?' Fitzsimmons asked.

Rusk's eyes clouded over and his throat throbbed against his collar with rage. 'I don't want to appear in court!' he yelled. 'I don't want the whole goddamn business to start all over again, investigation, lawyers, fingerprints . . . '

Pidgear punched him savagely in the ribs, his fist going a short distance, but with great violence.

'Why don't you buy time on the National Broadcasting System?' Pidgear asked. 'Make an address, coast to coast!'

Rusk glared murderously for a moment at Pidgear, then leaned over towards Fitzsimmons, pointing a large blunt finger at him. 'Do I have to put my finger in your mouth?' he whispered hoarsely.

'What does he mean by that?' Helen asked loudly. 'Put his

finger in your mouth? Why should he put his finger in your mouth?'

Rusk looked at her with complete hatred, turned, too full for words, and stalked away, with Pidgear after him. The two little men in the grey hats watched the room without moving.

'Claude?' Helen began.

'Obviously,' Fitzsimmons said, his voice low, 'Mr Rusk isn't anxious for anyone to look at his fingerprints. He's happier this way.'

'You picked a fine night!' Helen shook her head sadly. 'Why can't we just pick up and get out of here?'

Rusk, with Pidgear at his side, strode back. He stopped in front of the Fitzsimmonses. 'I'm a family man,' he said, trying to sound like one. 'I ask yuh as a favour. Talk to the Russian.'

'I had to go to Bergdorf Goodman,' Helen said, too deep in her own troubles to bother with Rusk, 'to get a gown to spend the evening in a police station. "Mrs Claude Fitzsimmons was lovely last night in blue velvet and silver fox at Officer Kraus's reception at the 8th Precinct. Other guests were the well-known Leopold Tarloff, and the Messrs Pidgear and Rusk, in grey hats. Other guests included the Russian Ambassador and two leading Italian artillerymen, also in grey hats." '

Pidgear laughed politely. 'Your wife is a very witty woman,' he said.

'Yes,' said Fitzsimmons, wondering why he'd married her.

'Will yuh for Christ's sake *ask*?' Rusk demanded. 'Can it hurt yuh?'

'We're willing to do our part,' Pidgear said. 'We even brought down a Russian to talk to him and clear up any little points in his own language. No effort is too great.'

Fitzsimmons's stomach growled loudly. 'Haven't eaten all day,' he said, embarrassed.

'That's what happens,' Pidgear said. 'Naturally.'

'Yeah,' said Rusk.

'Perhaps I should go out and get you a malted milk,' Helen suggested coldly.

Fitzsimmons went over to where Tarloff was sitting with the other Russian. The others followed him.

'Are you sure, Mr Tarloff,' Fitzsimmons said, 'that you still want to prosecute?'

'Yes,' Tarloff said promptly.

'Ten dollars,' Rusk said. 'I offer yuh ten dollars. Can a man do more?'

'Money is not the object.' With his cap, Tarloff patted his nose, which was still bleeding slowly and had swelled enormously, making Tarloff look lopsided and monstrous.

'What's the object?' Rusk asked.

'The object, Mr Rusk, is principle.'

'You talk to him,' Rusk said to Fitzsimmons.

'All right,' Officer Kraus said; 'you can go up there now.'

They all filed in front of the lieutenant sitting high at his desk.

Tarloff told his story, the accident, the wanton punch in the nose.

'It's true,' Pidgear said, 'that there was an accident, that there was a slight scuffle after by mistake. But the man isn't hurt. A little swelling in the region of the nose. No more.' He pointed dramatically to Tarloff.

'Physically,' Tarloff said, clutching his cap, talking with difficulty because his nose was clogged, 'physically that's true. I am not badly hurt. But in a mental sense . . . ' He shrugged. 'I have suffered an injury.'

Mr Rusk is offering the amount of ten dollars,' Pidgear said. 'Also, he apologises; he's sorry.'

The lieutenant looked wearily down at Rusk. 'Are you sorry?' he asked.

'I'm sorry,' said Rusk, raising his right hand. 'On the Bible, I swear I'm sorry.'

'Mr Tarloff,' the lieutenant said, 'if you wish to press charges, there are certain steps you will have to take. A deposition will have to be taken. Have you got witnesses?'

'Here, Tarloff said with a shy smile at the Fitzsimmonses.

'They will have to be present,' the lieutenant said sleepily.

'Oh, God,' Helen said.

'A warrant will have to be sworn out, there must be a hearing, at which the witnesses must also be present . . . '

'Oh, God,' Helen said.

'Then the trial,' said the lieutenant.

'Oh, God!' Helen said loudly.

'The question is, Mr Tarloff,' said the lieutenant, yawning, 'are you willing to go through all that trouble?'

'The fact is,' Tarloff said unhappily, 'he hit me in the head without provocation. He is guilty of a crime on my person. He insulted me. He did me an injustice. The law exists for such things. One individual is not to be hit by another individual in the streets of the city without legal punishment.' Tarloff was using his hands to try to get everyone, the Fitzsimmonses, the lieutenant, Pidgear, to understand. 'There is a principle. The dignity of the human body. Justice. For a bad act a man suffers. It's an important thing . . .'

'I'm excitable,' Rusk shouted. 'If yuh want, yuh can hit me in the head.'

'That is not the idea,' Tarloff said.

'The man is sorry,' the lieutenant said. wiping his eyes; 'he is offering you the sum of ten dollars; it will be a long, hard job to bring this man to trial; it will cost a lot of the taxpayers' money; you are bothering these good people here who have other things to do. What is the sense in it, Mr Tarloff?'

Tarloff scraped his feet slowly on the dirty floor, looked sadly, hopefully, at Fitzsimmons. Fitzsimmons looked at his wife, who was glaring at Tarloff, tapping her foot sharply again and again. Fitzsimmons looked back at Tarloff, standing there, before the high desk, small, in his ragged coat and wild grey hair, his little worn face twisted and grotesque with the swollen nose, his eyes lost and appealing. Fitzsimmons shrugged sadly. Tarloff drooped inside his old coat, shook his head wearily, shrugged, deserted once and for all before the lieutenant's desk, on the dry rock of principle.

'O.K.,' he said.

'Here,' Rusk brought the ten-dollar bill out with magical speed.

Tarloff pushed it away. 'Get out of here,' he said without looking up.

No one talked all the way to Adele Lowrie's house. Tarloff opened the door and sat, looking straight ahead, while they got out. Helen went to the door of the house and rang. Silently, Fitzsimmons offered Tarloff the fare. Tarloff shook his head. 'You have been very good,' he said. 'Forget it.'

Fitzsimmons put the money away slowly.

'Claude!' Helen called. 'The door's open.'

Fitzsimmons hated his wife, suddenly, without turning to look at her. He put out his hand and Tarloff shook it wearily.

'I'm awfully sorry,' Fitzsimmons said. 'I wish I . . .'

Tarloff shrugged. 'That's all right,' he said. 'I understand.' His face, in the shabby light of the cab, worn and old and battered by the streets of the city, was a deep well of sorrow. 'There is no time. Principle.' He laughed, shrugged. 'Today there is no time for anything.'

He shifted gears and the taxi moved slowly off, it's motor grinding noisily.

'Claude!' Helen called.

'Oh, shut up!' Fitzsimmons said as he turned and walked into Adele Lowrie's house.

Faith at Sea

Lieutenant Peter Gifford Lawrence stood on the fore-deck of the S.S. *Rascoe*, holding on lightly to the canvas sheathed three-inch gun as the bow dipped and trembled in the harsh chop of the North Atlantic. Twelve men of the gun crew stood at ease before him, shifting easily with the soaring lift and fall of the S.S. *Rascoe* as she chewed busily into the slate waves that had been hacking at her for six days, getting stronger and stronger as the 6,000-ton tramp steamer ploughed at nine knots towards England.

'The duties of the gun captain,' Constantini was chanting, like a child in school. 'A, on manning gun, reports through sightsetter to group control officer when gun is ready. B, operates plug as necessary. C, calls "Ready", to pointer when breech is closed . . . '

Lawrence only half listened as Constantini's voice droned on, in the regular Thursday afternoon gunnery class that Lawrence conducted to keep the Navy gun crew alert and interested on the long, monotonous trips. He looked at the twelve men outlined in mufflers and coats, against the low-hanging cold sun. These, plus the four men on duty now at the rear gun, had been given him by the Navy to guard the grey and shabby and valuable life of the S.S. *Rascoe*, and as always, when he saw them assembled he felt a mixture of amusement and pity how old he was.

He was only thirty-five, but except for Farrell, the Chief Petty Officer, who was older than he, and Benson, the gunner's mate, who was twenty-five, all the men were twenty-one or under, their faces bronzed and unlined and boyish, always solemn and youthfully important when they were assembled like this for any official function, and especially solemn today because they had lost the convoy the night before in a storm and were now plodding over the grey wastes towards port, vulnerable and alone.

'He is responsible for the conduct, efficiency and spirit of the crew,' Constantini was saying, 'and must be made to realise that he is the representative of his battery officer.'

'Very good,' Lawrence said. 'Harris.'

'Yes, sir,' Harris stood stiffly at attention.

'The duties of the sight-setter.'

'To set the sights,' Harris rattled off glibly, 'and to transmit all communications between gun and group control officer.'

Lawrence looked up over Harris's head to the bridge. Captain Linsey, his head patchy and crooked in the wind, was peering angrily down at what he called the Navy kindergarten.

'To call "Set",' Harris was saying, 'to pointer when sights have been set . . .'

Suddenly Harris stopped. Lawrence turned from looking at Linsey on the bridge. The man next to Harris, William Doneger, was on his knees by Harris's side, gripping Harris's arm with a tortured, clutching hand. Harris stood there stupidly, frightened, looking blankly at the sweating tense face.

'Doneger . . .' Lawrence started towards him. Doneger let loose his grip and dropped, bent over and rocking, to the deck.

Constantini sank swiftly to his knees and took Doneger's head in his hands, tenderly.

'What is it?' Lawrence kneeled beside the two of them, with the other men crowded silent and helpless around them.

Doneger looked up at him wildly, the sweat breaking from his forehead, even in this bitter winter evening.

He's been sick all day, sir,' Constantini said, his hands almost unconsciously going slowly and soothingly over his friend's forehead. 'Terrible belly-ache, sir.'

Lawrence looked down at the suffering boy. His lips were bleeding from biting them and his face had grown terribly, greenly pale, morbid and alarming in the cold Atlantic dusk. His legs pulled spasmodically and unreasonably as he lay on the wet deck.

'Let's get him below,' Lawrence said. 'To my quarters.' There was no doctor on board and Lawrence's quarters had the medical chest and served as a clinic for the Navy men.

Constantini got Doneger under the armpits and one of the other men got him around the knees and they started down with him. Constantini was a broad, powerful boy and held his friend firmly and lightly and manoeuvred him delicately up the steps, his face tense and wary as he attempted to beat the cruel roll of the ship which at any moment threatened to smash the sick boy against a bulkhead.

Lawrence looked out across the ocean for a last survey. The water hissed by the S.S. *Rascoe* and the grey waves piled endlessly and monotonously on top of each other and the clouds came down, and that was all. He swallowed a little drily, thinking of Doneger lying racked and contorted in his room, then braced his shoulders consciously and walked slowly towards his quarters.

When he opened the door, Doneger was lying on the extra berth and Constantini was whispering to him a steady, soft stream of comforting words. Constantini had a deep, melodious voice, like a singer, and it sounded like a lullaby as he whispered to his friend.

'Nothing at all, William, nothing at all.' He was the only one on the ship who called Doneger 'William'. All the other men called him Bill and Billy, but Constantini gave him his full and proper name, like a doting mother, at all times. 'Something you ate. I've had belly-aches in my time . . . ' Constantini was seventeen years old. 'I thought I was going to split down the middle and two hours later I'd be out eating two plates of spaghetti and a quart of dago red . . . '

When he saw Lawrence come into the room, he stopped his whispering and stood up at attention, trying to make his face impassive and military. But he had a child's face with deep soft-brown Italian eyes, with heavy, curled black eyelashes, and a full, almost girlish mouth, and the military mask at the moment was not deceptive.

Lawrence looked down at the suffering boy. Doneger looked up at him wanly. 'Sorry, sir,' he whispered.

'Ssssh,' Lawrence said.

'He's been puking, sir,' Constantini said. 'All day, sir . . . '

Lawrence sighed and sat down on the berth next to Doneger. That's what it's going to turn out to be, he thought, as he put his hand on the boy's side. The worst possible thing . . .

The right side was swollen and tight and Doneger jumped even with the slightest pressure.

'He has a very sensitive belly, sir,' Constantini was speaking quickly and anxiously, as though somehow his words and explanations could make the disease less. 'I took him to my cousin's wedding and he got drunk faster than anyone else, even faster than the sixteen-year-old girls .. . We had a stew yesterday that was a little greasy, and maybe . . . '

'He has appendicitis, Salvatore,' Lawrence said slowly.

Constantini looked at his friend's face in silence. Doneger closed his eyes. Lying down here, in the warm stateroom, on a dry bed, he seemed more comfortable, better able to meet the pain.

'Everything will be all right, William,' Constantini murmured to Doneger. 'The lieutenant has already diagnosed the disease.'

The door opened and Captain Linsey came in. He stood above Doneger, staring down at him, without a word, his mouth curled, as always when he had anything to do with the Navy men on board his ship, into a sour and ancient snarl.

'Sick,' Linsey said. 'This son-of-a-bitch is very sick.'

'Yes,' Lawrence said. Captain Linsey would make amusing conversation after the war at dinner parties in Boston. Crusty old merchant seadog. Ignored the Navy. Ignored the war, even in the middle of a pack of submarines.

'This son-of-a-bitch'll die.' Captain Linsey leaned over and peered harshly into the pale, suffering face.

Very amusing after the war at dinner parties, Lawrence thought. Right now I'd like to kill him.

'We'll take care of him,' Lawrence said.

Suddenly Captain Linsey poked Doneger in the side with a huge, wrinkled finger. Doneger cried and jumped. 'Sorry, Sonny,' Captain Linsey said. He turned to Lawrence, 'Ready to bust. Boy out with me on the way to Wilhelmshaven in 1931 died in three days. Same thing.'

Out of the corner of his eye, Lawrence saw Constantini look quickly down at Doneger, then look up and take a long, deep breath.

'Please,' Lawrence said. 'I'll come up to the bridge later and you can tell me whatever you . . . '

'This son-of-a-bitch needs an operation.'

'There's no doctor on board.'

Captain Linsey sucked at the wet ends of his moustache, looked with crazy slyness at Lawrence. 'We won't make port for seven days. At least. He ain't going to last no week.'

I'd like to kill him, Lawrence thought, looking up at Captain Linsey's old, harsh seaman's face. I'd like to kill him, but he's right, he's right.

'I thought we could freeze it,' Lawrence said. 'After all, we have ice. Maybe it'll subside . . . '

'Too late.' Captain Linsey wagged his head finally. 'Surgery. Surgery or nothing.'

'There's no surgeons here,' Lawrence said loudly. 'If you insist on arguing, let's get out of this room.'

'You ever see an operation?' Captain Linsey asked.

'Yes.' Lawrence's brother-in-law was a fashionable surgeon and over a period of ten years Lawrence had seen seven or eight operations. 'That isn't the same thing.'

'There was a Dutchman we took to Capetown in 1927,' Captain Linsey said. 'A doctor. Studied in America. He left a book on board. All kinds of operations. Every once in a while I read in it. Very interesting reading. I bet it's got appendicitis in it.'

That's ridiculous,' Lawrence stood up and went over to the door. 'Thank you for your interest, Captain . . . '

Captain Linsey touched Doneger's head. 'Fever. I bet it's over 104. An operation really isn't so much. A little common sense and a little nerve. What the hell, what has this boy got to lose?' He leaned close to Doneger and spoke with surprising softness. 'Sonny, you got any objections to being operated on?'

Doneger stared at Constantini. Constantini turned away, giving no answer one way or another with his eyes.

'I have no objections,' Doneger said faintly.

Captain Linsey strode briskly towards the door. 'I'll send the book down,' he said cheerfully. 'We'll save the son-of-a-bitch yet.' He clapped Lawrence on the back. 'I'd do it myself only I'm old and jumpy and I've drunk too much whisky in my day. I'll be on the bridge. I'll keep this tub as steady as possible.'

He went out quickly.

Lawrence closed his eyes so that he wouldn't have to look at Doneger or Crowley or Constantini, all standing stiffly watching him.

A moment later a seaman came in with a worn and broken-backed book. He put it on the table and went out. Crowley and Doneger and Constantini and Lawrence all looked at the fat, dog-eared book, lying on the table. Lawrence stood up and went over and opened to the index. Under A Pg. 941 – Appendectomy.

The first time he read through it, the words were a weird and incomprehensible blur. He looked up once or twice only to see the staring, serious eyes of the three other men scanning his face, as though they somehow could tell from that distance whether or not the words he was reading were of any value to him.

Lawrence took off his coat and started slowly to read it from the beginning, once more.

Before operating, try to locate the situation of the appendix. The incision should be over the seat of the disease. In the rare left-sided cases and in the median cases, the incision is median . . .

The words began to group themselves in his mind into English sentences, capable of being understood by a man who could read and write.

In an acute case in a man I separate the muscular fibres Battle's incision at the outer edge of the rectus muscle is preferred by many surgeons . . .

In a biology course in college he had dissected the earthworm, the frog, the white rat – but all dead, beyond the reach of pain, unmoved by clumsiness or error.

If there be infection, surround the region involved with packs of plain gauze, each strip being two and a half inches wide, fifteen inches long, and four layers in thickness. Pass a ligature through the meso appendix as shown in Fig. 691, A, tie the ligature and . . .

Fig. 691, A, was very simple and if flesh and muscle and organ were anything like the diagram, it was conceivable that a deft, though unpracticed man might be able to manage . . .

'William,' Lawrence said. 'Are you sure?'

Doneger sighed. 'I'm sure.'

'Crowley,' Lawrence said. 'Go to the galley and get a pot of boiling water.'

'Yes, sir,' Crowley said, and went out softly, already making a hospital out of the room.

Lawrence went back to the close print of the book. He read and re-read, studied the diagrams until he felt he could draw them with his eyes closed.

He stood up and unlocked the medical chest. He threw open the doors and stared at the rows of bottles, the serried bandages, the fateful gleaming instruments. Behind him he heard the soft child's voice of Constantini, rough with the accent of the streets of New York, soft with compassion and fear.

'It ain't hardly nothing, William. A cousin of mine had this and he was operated on and three days later he slept with the nurse.' Constantini had a cousin for all eventualities of discussion, naval and civilian. 'Everybody ought to have his appendix out. They don't do you no good. None at all. If I had the time I'd have 'em out myself . . . '

Lawrence stared at the bottles, the bandages, the steel instruments. He made his eyes go slowly and calmly from one thing to another in the chest, taking a deliberate inventory. The thing is, he thought, not to hurry. After all, men have done more difficult things than this. The instruments are there, the one can of ether, the bandage, the scalpel, the needles, the catgut, the clamps, the sponges, the alcohol, sulfanilamide. And the Navy had given him a course in First Aid. How to stop bleeding. How to avoid gangrene. How to set a broken leg.

'You hardly feel it,' Constantini was saying in his deep melodious boy's voice. 'You take a little nap. You wake up. Appendix absent. You feel a little stiff for a day or two, you get a good rest, the other guys stand your watches, you read the magazines and drink hot soup. You get to England, you get three weeks' sick leave, you'll have the time of your life. The English girls're crazy about American sailors. I got a cousin in the merchant marine and he says that an American in London is like a king, far as the girls're concerned. They can't do enough for them . . . '

Why, Lawrence thought with a remote and bitter detachment, did this have to happen the first time we lost a convoy? In a convoy the boy could be transferred to one of the cruisers accompanying them and there a first-rate naval surgeon in a shining, brilliantly equipped operating-room would do the job as a matter of simple routine in ten minutes.

Crowley came in with the pot of hot water and Lawrence put the scalpel, the needles and the clamps into it.

'Anything I can do,' Constantini said, as Lawrence watched the steel gleaming dully as it sank among the bubbles of the boiling water, 'Anything at all.'

Lawrence nodded. 'There'll be plenty for you to do. Clear that table and get a sheet out of the locker and spread it over it.' Constantini listened eagerly and nodded. 'Wash your hands first.'

While Crowley and Constantini scrubbed their hands and the strong smell of the soap pricked his nostrils, Lawrence re-read, slowly, the entire description of the operation.

Even after he had finished and after the gentle watery sound of scrubbing behind him had long ceased, he sat with his head in his hands, staring at the page before him.

He stood up. Well, that was that . . .

He turned briskly and without words he and Constantini and Crowley lifted Doneger on to the white-covered table. He washed and scrubbed his hands with alcohol. Gently, he shaved the slight, downy fuzz from the boy's belly. Then he washed it with alcohol.

Crowley behaved wonderfully. He was a little, impassive Irishman to whom all things seemed to come as a matter of course, promotion, overwork, murders, drownings, wars. Lawrence was glad it was Crowley who had silently volunteered for this job.

Constantini, too, handled Doneger with soft hands, lifting him gently and securely, making no unnecessary move. Together they bound Doneger to the table with linen bandage, so that the roll of the ship would not throw him off the table.

Lawrence noticed that the ship had swung around and was heading directly into the wind and was much steadier now. He would remember to thank Captain Linsey later.

He took the ether cone and stood at Doneger's shoulder. Doneger and Constantini and seven or eight of the other boys had had their heads shaven when they were last in the States. They had done it as a kind of joke, after Lawrence had complained at inspection that they were letting their hair grow too long. All seven of them had marched solemnly back on to the S.S. *Rascoe* from their shore leave and had with one gesture swept their hats off their heads as they reported in. Lawrence had stared at the seven shining pates, scarred with the incredibly numerous battles of childhood, and had lowered his eyes to keep from laughing and had said, 'Very good.'

They had saluted and swept out and he had heard them roaring with laughter on the deck . . .

Doneger's head, now with a slight baby fuzz standing up all over it, lay flatly, in the shadows, on the table in the small cabin as the old plates on the S.S. *Rascoe* creaked and wailed under the attack of the sea . . .

'All right, William,' Lawrence said softly. 'Are you ready now?'

'I'm ready, sir.' Doneger spoke in a whisper and smiled up at him.

Lawrence put the cone gently over the boy's face and said 'Breathe deeply.' He poured the ether in and the smell, sweet and deadly, leaked into the cabin, making it strange and deathly suddenly. 'Count,' Lawrence said. 'Keep counting.'

'One, two, three,' Doneger said clearly. 'Four, five, six, seven, eight . . . ' The young voice began to blur and thicken. 'Nine, ten, eleven, twelve, thir – thir . . . ' The voice mumbled heavily and wearily through the cone. The long chubby body on the table relaxed for the first time and Crowley gently straightened the legs out. The voice died away completely and the noise of the creaking plates of the old ship was the only sound to be heard.

Lawrence lifted the ether cone. Doneger's face was calm and showed no trace of pain. He gave the cone to Constantini. 'If I tell you to,' he said, 'put this over his face. In case he moves . . . '

'Yes, sir,' Constantini said, and moved quickly to Doneger's head.

Lawrence went to the pot of boiling water, and with a forceps took out the instruments he had put in there to sterilise. Crowley had arranged a clean towel on the bunk and Lawrence put the instruments there in a neat and shining row, remembering how dentists who had filled his teeth had done the same thing.

He picked up the scalpel and arranged the lamp so that its full glare fell on the bare stomach of the sleeping boy.

The skin was very pink, and there was a firm, small layer of fat under it. Doneger was very young and his belly still had a round little baby-swell. He was breathing softly and the muscles trembled rhythmically and gently in the harsh light of the single lamp.

How smooth, how subtle, how complex, Lawrence thought, how close to death. How vulnerable to knife and powder. How irrevocably naked to damage. He closed his eyes for a moment, unable to look any more at the smooth, childish skin. With his eyes closed and the moaning and creaking of the tumbling ship in his ears, it all seemed dreamlike and impossible. He, Peter Gifford Lawrence, gently reared, nursed and fed and tended all his years by mother and aunt and teacher and doctor, every boyhood scratch mercurochromed and overbandaged, soft-blanketed sleeper in neat, well-ventilated rooms, student at Harvard, where he had taken notes on Plato and Geoffrey Chaucer, on the architecture of the Renaissance and the metrics of John Milton, Peter Gifford Lawrence, gentlemen, formal guest at pleasant dinners, polite talker to old ladies at Lenox garden parties, dealer in books and fine prints, now standing scalpel in hand in the cramped, peeling First Officer's quarters of the wheezing freighter groaning and heaving in a

Middle Atlantic gale, with four miles of black sea water and countless drowned sailors under the keel, the prey of deadly vessels that struck unseen and mortal in the turn of a man's head . . .

Battle's incision at the outer edge of the rectus muscle is preferred by many surgeons . . . After opening the peritoneum examine very gently to detect the situation of the . . . This divides the mucous membrane, submucous tissue and muscular coat . . .

He opened his eyes and looked up. Constantini was staring at him. In the soft, girlish eyes, beside the worry for his friend's agony, there was deep trust, deep confidence that this kindly efficient, understanding, courageous man, this officer who had been designated by great authority to guide his war-time fate, would, this time and all times, do well what had to be done. There was no doubt in the soft, steady eyes of Salvatore Constantini.

Lawrence bent his head and firmly made the necessary incision . . .

When the operation was over and Doneger had been gently lifted into the extra bunk and Constantini had silently taken the watch at his side, Lawrence opened the door and stepped out on to the deck. The black wind flung bitter spray into his face and he had to half-shut his eyes against it. But he stood there holding on to the rail, peering sightlessly into the roaring darkness, hardly thinking, hardly feeling, rolling crazily and aimlessly with the roll of the ship.

He stood there drunkenly for a long time, then suddenly turned and went into his room. Doneger was lying there, steady and still, the ether still in control. Constantini sat quietly at his side, never taking his eyes off the pale, exhausted face.

Lawrence lay down in all his clothes and slept immediately.

When he awoke, he opened his eyes slowly and came up deeply from the well of sleep, as though he had slept for weeks on end. Slowly he became aware of Constantini sitting across the room from him; still looking steadfastly at Doneger, as though he hadn't moved all night.

Lawrence opened his eyes wide.

'Good morning, Lieutenant.' Constantini smiled shyly at him. His eyes were sunken and he rubbed them like a sleepy infant.

'Morning, Salvatore.' Lawrence sat up suddenly and looked at Doneger, remembering in a rush that across from him lay a man whom he had operated upon the night before. Doneger was awake, and drowsily smiled, his face creased by a kind of remote pain.

'Hello, Lieutenant,' Doneger whispered.

Lawrence jumped out of his bunk. 'How are you?'

'Fine,' Doneger whispered. 'First class. Thanks.'

Lawrence peered at him closely. There were wrinkles of pain in the boy's smooth face, but there was a little colour in the cheeks and something in the eyes that seemed to announce that death had once and for all passed by.

Lawrence looked at Constantini. 'You get any sleep last night?'

'Not much, sir. I'm pleased to watch William.'

'Get below and get some sleep. Someone else'll watch William.'

'Yes, sir.' Constantini looked shyly at him and then turned to Doneger. 'My God,' he whispered as Lawrence poured some water to wash, 'will you have a picnic with those English girls . . .'

And he touched his friend's forehead lightly and chuckled as he went out and deep, deep, from the depths of his eighteen years and recovery from death, Doneger chuckled softly in return.

Later in the day, Lawrence started forward towards the bow gun, where the men were assembled for the interrupted examination in gunnery. The sun was shining and the ocean was a sharp, wintry blue, with the white-caps in the distance looking like the bobbing sails of a regatta with a million entries. He had left Doneger smiling and sipping tea and the bright wind felt festive and alive against his freshly shaven face. He saw the cluster of blue uniforms and the ruddy faces of the gun crew around the gun and heard Constantini's voice, melodious and terribly earnest, chanting in final review before his arrival. Lawrence smiled to himself and was proud of the Navy and the red-faced, earnest boys, and the gun and the S.S. *Rascoe* and himself, abroad, dependable and unafraid, on the wide ocean.

' 'Tention!' Benson called as he approached, and the boys stiffened rigidly, their faces stern and set, their hands tight at their sides. Lawrence looked sternly at them, carrying out his share of the military drama.

He looked at them and felt once more with the old amusement and pity how old he was at the age of thirty-five, confronted by and responsible for these large, determined, valuable, fearless children.

'At ease,' he said.

The tight little knot relaxed and the men shuffled about, making themselves comfortable. They kept their eyes on Lawrence, seriously. Constantini's lips mumbled inaudibly as he ran over the list of questions he might be asked to answer.

'We'll go right into it,' Lawrence said. 'Harris . . .' he started with the boy nearest him. 'What're the duties of the first loader?'

'To receive the shell from the second loader,' Harris said. 'And to load the gun.'

'Levine.' Lawrence spoke to the next man. 'Duties of the second loader?'

'To pass shells to the first loader,' Levine said carefully. 'To arrange shells on deck in rear of gun in probable arc of train.'

'Constantini . . .' Lawrence went down the line. He saw Constantini's face tense almost painfully with anticipation. 'What are the duties of the third loader?'

Constantini's lips started to move. Then he licked them uneasily. He took in a deep breath, looked suddenly, blankly and despairingly at Lawrence. Lawrence glanced at him and saw that all knowledge had fled from his head, like an actor on opening night, with four weeks of rehearsals behind him, who is stricken dumb by the overpowering desire to do well.

A deep red flush surged up over Constantini's collar and stained his cheeks, his ears. He licked his lips in misery, looked straight ahead, hopelessly . . .

Lawrence looked away, called the next man, Moran, went on with the questioning.

Moran answered the question briskly.

One by one, Lawrence went down the line of men. Each man snapped out his answer, their voices ringing clear and triumphant in the bright wind. Once more it was Constantini's turn.

Lawrence looked surreptitiously at him. He went next in line and he was standing as stiff as though all the admirals of all the fleets of the world were passing him in review. His jaws were clenched and the muscles stood out in them like rope. His eyes stared ahead of him like a man watching the execution of his father, wild, hopeless, full of guilt.

Lawrence knew in his heart that no matter what question he put to Constantini, no answer would come from that mourning brain, no word pass those locked, despairing lips. For a moment Lawrence thought of passing him up and going on to the next man. But then, to the shame of Constantini's ignorance and defection would be added the ignominy of official pity.

'Constantini,' Lawrence said as crisply as he could, hoping to shock him out of his trancelike trauma. He carefully sought out the simplest, most transparent, easily answered question in the whole book. 'Constantini,' he said, slowly and clearly and loudly, 'what is the purpose of shrapnel?'

Constantini did not move. The tongue froze between the lips, the eyes stared without hope across the Atlantic Ocean, while no answer came to show this good man, this Boston Lieutenant who had done a brave and noble thing to save his friend's life that he, Salvatore Constantini, loved and admired him and would be grateful to him for the rest of his life. The blush settled like a permanent blight on his cheeks, but no answer came from the rockbound brain. The deep, ordinary thanks that a man could give by the crisp performance of his duty could not be given. William lived and Salvatore failed the man who had saved him.

Suddenly the tears started from his eyes and rolled down his rigid cheeks.

Lawrence looked at the weeping boy, staring blindly out to sea, among the men who kindly stared out to sea with him. Lawrence saw the bitter tears and almost put out his hand to comfort the boy, but held back just in time, since comfort now, before his ten friends, would be agony later.

Lawrence glanced once more at him and tried to call the next man's name and ask him the purpose of shrapnel, but the name stuck in his throat and he turned his back on the men and wept and felt the tears cold on his cheeks without surprise.

When he finally saw her, he nearly failed to recognise her. He walked behind her for a half block, vaguely noticing that the woman in front of him had long legs and was wearing a loose, college-girl polo coat and a plain brown felt hat.

Suddenly something about the way she walked made him remember – the almost affected rigidity of her back and straightness of throat and head, with all the movement of walking, flowing up to the hips and stopping there, like Negro women in the South and Mexican and Spanish women carrying baskets on their heads. For a moment, silently, he watched her walk down Twelfth Street, on the sunny side of the street, in front of the little tired gardens behind which lay the quiet, pleasantly run-down old houses. Then he walked up to her and touched her arm.

'Low heels,' he said. 'I never thought I'd live to see the day.'

She looked around in surprise, then smiled widely, took his arm. 'Hello, Paul,' she said. 'I've gone in for health.'

'Whenever I think of you,' he said, 'I think of the highest heels in New York City.'

'The old days,' Harriet said. They walked slowly down the sunny street, arm in arm, towards Sixth Avenue. 'I was a frivolous creature.'

'You still walk the same way. As though you ought to have a basket of laundry on your head.'

'I practised walking like that for six months. You'd be surprised how much attention I get walking into a room that way.'

'I wouldn't be surprised,' Paul said, looking at her. She had black hair and pale, clear skin and a long, full body, and her eyes were deep grey and always brilliant, even after she'd been drinking for three days in a row.

Harriet closed her coat quickly and walked a little faster. 'I'm going to Wanamaker's,' she said. 'There're a couple of things I have to buy. Where are you going?'

'Wanamaker's,' Paul said. 'I've been dying to go to Wanamaker's for three years.'

They walked slowly, in silence. Harriet's arm in his.

'Casual,' Paul said. 'I bet to the naked eye we look casual as hell. How do you feel?'

Harriet took her arm away. 'Casual.'

'O.K. Then that's how I feel, too.' Paul whistled coldly to himself. He stopped and looked critically at her and she stopped, too, and turned towards him, a slight puzzled smile on her face. 'What makes you dress that way?' he asked. 'You look like Monday morning in Northampton.'

'I just threw on whatever was nearest,' Harriet said. 'I'm just going to be out about an hour.'

'You used to look like a nice big box of candy in your clothes.' Paul took her arm again and they started off. 'Viennese bonbons. Every indentation carefully exploited in silk and satin. Even if you were just going down to the corner for a pint of gin, you'd look like something that ought to be eaten for dessert. This is no improvement.'

'A girl has different periods in clothes. Like Picasso,' Harriet said. 'And if I'd known I was going to meet you, I'd've dressed differently.'

Paul patted her arm. 'That's better.'

Paul eyed her obliquely as they walked: the familiar, long face, the well-known wide mouth with always a little too much lipstick on it, the little teeth that made her face, when she smiled, look suddenly like a little girl's in Sunday school.

'You're getting skinny, Paul,' Harriet said.

Paul nodded. 'I'm as lean as a herring. I've been leading a fevered and ascetic life. What sort of life have you been leading?'

'I got married.' Harriet paused a moment. 'Did you hear I got married?'

'I heard,' Paul said. 'The last time we crossed Sixth Avenue together the L was still up. I feel a nostalgic twinge for the Sixth Avenue L.' They hurried as the light changed. 'On the night of January ninth, 1940,' Paul said, holding her elbow, 'you were not home.'

'Possible,' Harriet said. 'I'm a big girl now; I go out at night.'

'I happened to pass your house, and I noticed that the light wasn't on.' They turned down towards Ninth Street. 'I remembered how hot you kept that apartment – like the dahlia greenhouse in the Botanical Gardens.'

'I have thin blood,' Harriet said gravely. 'Long years of inbreeding in Massachusetts.

'The nicest thing about you,' Paul said, 'was you never went to sleep.'

'Every lady to her own virtue,' Harriet said. 'Some women're beautiful, some're smart – me, I never went to sleep. The secret of my great popularity . . .'

Paul grinned. 'Shut up.'

Harriet smiled back at him and they chuckled together. 'You know what I mean,' he said. 'Any time I called you up, two, three in the morning, you'd come right over, lively and bright-eyed, all the rouge and mascara in the right places . . .'

'In my youth,' said Harriet, 'I had great powers of resistance.'

'In the morning we'd eat breakfast to Beethoven. The Masterwork Hour. W.N.Y.C. Beethoven, by special permission of His Honour, the Mayor, from nine to ten.' Paul closed his eyes for a moment. 'The Little Flower, Mayor for Lovers.'

Paul opened his eyes and looked at the half-strange, half-familiar woman walking lightly at his side. He remembered lying close to her, dreamily watching the few lights of the towers of the night-time city, framed by the big window of his bedroom against the black sky, and one night when she moved sleepily against him and rubbed the back of his neck where the hair was sticking up in sharp little bristles because he had had his hair cut that afternoon. Harriet had rubbed them the wrong way, smiling, dreamily, without opening her eyes. 'What a delicious thing a man is . . . ' she'd murmured. And she'd sighed, then chuckled a little and fallen asleep, her hand still on the shaven back of his neck.

Paul smiled, remembering.

'You still laughing at my clothes?' Harriet asked.

'I remembered something I heard some place . . . ' Paul said. ' "What a delicious thing a man is . . . " '

Harriet looked at him coldly. 'Who said that?'

Paul squinted suspiciously at her. 'Oswald Spengler.'

Uhuh,' Harriet said soberly. 'It's a famous quotation.'

'It's a well-turned phrase,' said Paul.

'That's what I think, too,' Harriet nodded agreeably and walked a little faster.

They passed the little run-down bar where they'd sat afternoons all winter drinking martinis and talking and talking, and laughing so loud the people at the other tables would turn and smile. Paul waited for Harriet to say something about the bar, but she didn't even seem to notice it. 'There's Eddie's Bar,' Paul said.

'Uhuh.' Harriet nodded briskly.

'He's going to start making his martinis with sherry when all the French vermouth runs out,' Paul said.

'It sounds horrible.' Harriet made a face.

'Is that all you have to say?' Paul said loudly, remembering all the times he'd looked in to see if she was there.

'What do you want me to say?' Harriet looked honestly puzzled, but Paul had never known when she was lying to him or telling the truth, anyway, and he hadn't improved in the two years, he discovered.

'I don't want you to say anything. I'll take you in and buy you a drink.'

'No, thanks. I've really got to get to Wanamaker's and back home in a hurry. Give me a rain-check.'

'Yeah,' Paul said sourly.

They turned up Ninth Street towards Fifth Avenue.

'I knew I'd meet you some place, finally,' Paul said. 'I was curious to see what would happen.'

Harriet didn't say anything. She was looking absently at the buildings across the street.

'Don't you ever talk any more?' Paul asked.

'What *did* happen?'

'Every once in a while,' he started, 'I meet some girl I used to know . . .'

'I bet the country's full of them,' Harriet said.

'The country's full of everybody's ex-girls.'

Harriet nodded. 'I never thought of it that way, but you're right.'

'Most of the time I think, isn't she a nice, decent person? Isn't it wonderful I'm no longer attached to her? The first girl I ever had,' Paul said, 'is a policewoman now. She subdued a gangster single-handed in Coney Island last summer. Her mother won't let her go out of the house in her uniform. She's ashamed for the neighbours.'

'Naturally,' Harriet said.

'Another girl I used to know changed her name and dances in the Russian Ballet. I went to see her dance the other night. She has legs like a Fordham tackle. I used to think she was beautiful. I used to think you were beautiful, too.'

'We were a handsome couple,' Harriet said. 'Except you always needed a shave. That electric razor . . . '

'I've given it up.'

They were passing his old house now and he looked at the doorway and remembered all the times he and Harriet had gone in and come out, the rainy days and the early snowy mornings with the milkman's horse silent on the white street behind them. They stopped and looked at the old red house with the shabby shutters and the window on the fourth floor they had both looked out of time and time again to see what the weather was and Paul remembered the first time, on a winter's night, when he and Harriet had gone through that door together.

'I was so damn polite,' Paul said softly.

Harriet smiled, knowing what he was talking about. 'You kept dropping the key and saying, "Lord, Lord," under your breath while you were looking for it.'

'I was nervous. I wanted to make sure you knew exactly how matters stood – no illusions. Good friends, everybody understanding everybody else, another girl coming in from Detroit in six weeks, no claims on me, no claims on you . . . ' Paul looked at the window on the fourth floor and smiled. 'What a fool!'

'It's a nice, quiet street,' Harriet said, looking up at the window on the fourth floor, too. She shook her head, took Paul's arm again. 'I've got to get to Wanamaker's.'

They started off.

'What're you buying at Wanamaker's?' Paul asked.

Harriet hesitated for a moment. 'Nothing much. I'm looking at some baby clothes. I'm going to have a baby.' They crowded over to one side to let a little woman with four dachshunds pass them in a busy tangle. 'Isn't it funny – me with a baby?' Harriet smiled. 'I lie around all day and try to imagine what it's going to be like. In between, I sleep and drink beer to nourish us. I've never had such a good time in all my life.'

'Well,' said Paul, 'at least it'll keep your husband out of the Army.'

'Maybe. He's a raging patriot.'

'Good. When he's at Fort Dix I'll meet you in Washington Square Park when you take the baby out for an airing in its perambulator. I'll put on a policeman's uniform to make it proper. I'm not such a raging patriot.'

'They'll get you, anyway, won't they?'

378

'Sure. I'll send you my picture in a lieutenant's suit. From Bulgaria. I have a premonition I'm going to be called on to defend a strategic point in Bulgaria.'

'How do you feel about it?' For the first time Harriet looked squarely and searchingly at him.

Paul shrugged. 'It's going to happen. It's all damned silly, but it isn't as silly now at it was ten years ago.'

Suddenly Harriet laughed.

'What's so funny?' Paul demanded.

'My asking you how you felt about something. I never used to have a chance . . . You'd let me know how you felt about everything. Roosevelt, James Joyce, Jesus Christ, Gypsy Rose Lee, Matisse, Yogi, liquor, sex, architecture . . .'

'I was full of opinions in those days.' Paul smiled a little regretfully. 'Lust and conversation. The firm foundations of civilised relations between the sexes.'

He turned and looked back at the window on the fourth floor. 'That was a nice apartment,' he said softly. 'Lust and conversation . . .'

'Come on, Paul,' Harriet said. 'Wanamaker's isn't going to stay open all night.'

Paul turned up his collar because the wind was getting stronger as they neared Fifth Avenue. 'You were the only girl I ever knew I could sleep in the same bed with.'

'That's a hell of a thing to say to a girl.' Harriet laughed. 'Is that your notion of a compliment?'

Paul shrugged. 'It's an irrelevant fact. Or a relevant fact. Is it polite to talk to a married lady in this way?'

'No.'

Paul walked along with her. 'What do you think of when you look at me?' he asked.

'Nothing much,' Harriet said carefully.

'What're you lying about?'

'Nothing much,' Harriet said flatly.

'Don't you even think, "What in the name of God did I ever see in him?" '

'No.' Harriet put her hands deep in her pockets and walked quickly along the railings.

'Should I tell you what I think of when I look at you?'

'No.'

'I've been looking for you for two years,' Paul said.

'My name's been in the telephone book.' Harriet hurried even more, wrapping her coat tightly around her.

379

'I didn't realise I was looking for you until I saw you.'

'Please, Paul . . . '

'I would walk along the street and I'd pass a bar we'd been in together and I'd go in and sit there, even though I didn't want a drink, not knowing why I was sitting there. Now I know. I was waiting for you to come in. I didn't pass your house by accident.'

'Look, Paul,' Harriet pleaded. 'It was a long time ago and it was fine and it ended . . . '

'I was wrong,' Paul said. 'Do you like hearing that? I was wrong. You know, I never did get married, after all.'

'I know,' Harriet said. 'Please shut up.'

'I walk along Fifth Avenue and every time I pass St Patrick's I half look up to see if you're passing, because I met you that day right after you'd had a tooth pulled, and it was cold; you were walking along with the tears streaming from your eyes and your eyes red and that was the only time I ever met you by accident any place . . . '

Harriet smiled. 'That certainly sounds like a beautiful memory.'

'Two years . . . ' Paul said. 'I've gone out with a lot of girls in the last two years.' He shrugged. 'They've bored me and I've bored them. I keep looking at every woman who passes to see if it's you. All the girls I go out with bawl the hell out of me for it. I've been walking around, following girls with dark hair to see if it'll turn out to be you, and girls with a fur jacket like that old one you had and girls that walk in that silly, beautiful way you walk . . . I've been searching the streets of the city for you for two years and this is the first time I've admitted it even to myself. That little Spanish joint we went the first time. Every time I pass it I remember everything – how many drinks we had and what the band played and what we said and the fat Cuban who kept winking at you from the bar and the very delicate way we landed up in my apartment . . . '

They were both walking swiftly now, Harriet holding her hands stiffly down at her sides.

'There is a particular wonderful way you are, joined together . . . '

'Paul, stop it.' Harriet's voice was flat but loud.

'Two years. In two years the edge should be dulled off things like that. Instead . . . ' How can you make a mistake as big as that? Paul thought, how can you deliberately be as wrong as that? And no remedy. So long as you live, no remedy.

He looked harshly at Harriet. Her face was set, as though she weren't listening to him and only intent on getting across the street as quickly as possible. 'How about you?' he asked. 'Don't you remember . . .'

'I don't remember anything,' she said. And then, suddenly, the tears sprang up in her eyes and streamed down the tight, distorted cheeks. 'I don't remember a goddamn thing!' she wept. 'I'm not going to Wanamaker's. I'm going home! Goodbye!' She ran over to a cab that was parked at the corner and opened the door and sprang in. The cab spurted past Paul and he had a glimpse of Harriet sitting stiffly upright, the tears bitter and unheeded in her eyes.

He watched the cab go down Fifth Avenue until it turned. Then he turned the other way and started walking, thinking: I must move away from this neighbourhood. I've lived here long enough.

Night in Algiers

It was late at night in Algiers and in the Army newspaper office the clatter of typewriters had long since died down. Most of the men had gone to sleep upstairs and the halls were empty. The wisecracks and decisions and sudden laughter were over for the day, and in another building the presses were comfortably turning out the next day's paper.

On the walls, the pictures of all the pretty girls with big bosoms looked a little weary in the dim light. Down on the street outside the Red Cross building, late-travelling soldiers whistled for hitches in the dark and a soldier who had had some wine was singing the 'Marseillaise' in English, the brave words and the brave tune floating up a little uncertainly through the darkness until a truck stopped and picked the singer up. In the office the radio was on and Tchaikovsky's piano concerto was coming in, moody and sorrowful, from London.

An assistant editor with sergeant's stripes on his sleeves came in and sat down wearily in front of the radio. He stared at it, remembering many things that had nothing to do with his job, remembering home and what his college campus looked like in June and how it had felt to sail out of New York harbour in the rain.

Have some wine,' said the reporter who was sitting there listening to the music. The reporter had no stripes on his sleeves at all. The assistant editor took the wine and forgot to drink, just sitting there holding the bottle.

'There's a bar in New York,' the assistant editor said. 'Ralph's. On Forty-fifth Street. Ugly little joint. I like to drink there. Ever been there?'

'Uhuh,' the reporter said.

'Scotch whisky,' the assistant editor said. 'Cold beer.'

The concerto ended in wild, mournful thunder and a polite English voice said it had been Toscanini conducting and Horowitz at the piano, the names sounding strange on the night-time African coast. The polite voice said good night and the reporter got Berlin. There were waltzes on from Berlin, very prettily played, lilting through the small, paper-littered room. A polite German voice described the waltzes and once more the violins and trumpets swept out of the radio.

'The Germans,' the assistant editor said. 'They should be deprived of music for fifty years. Should be part of the peace treaty.'

A rewrite man, a corporal, on his way up to bed, stuck his head in. 'Anybody want a gum-drop?' He brought out the box. 'Just got my rations today.'

The assistant editor and the reporter reached out. They chewed consideringly on the gum-drops, listening to the waltz.

'Nice music,' the rewrite man said.

'Fifty years,' said the assistant editor.

The rewrite man yawned and stretched. 'Going to bed,' he said, and started out. 'Maybe when I wake up tomorrow the war'll be over. Good-night.' He went out and the assistant editor washed down the rationed gum-drop with a little wine.

'Did you ever eat a gum-drop in civilian life?' he asked.

'No,' said the reporter.

'Neither did I.' He rolled the wine around reflectively in the bottle. 'God, it's dull around here. I wish I could have gone to Italy.' The radio turned to Hungarian dances and the assistant editor stared gloomily at it. He drank a little wine. 'That's the trouble, though. Now that the invasion has come at last, other guys are covering it. Other guys'll write great stories. I'll be sitting here on my can in Africa. The editor. The assistant editor . . . When I got out of college I wrote better than I do now. Eight years ago.' He rubbed his bald spot thoughtfully. 'Somehow I got to be an editor. Eight years.' He finished the wine. 'Maybe I should've got married.'

'Probably wouldn't make any difference,' said the reporter, who was married.

'Probably not. The assistant editor shrugged. 'There was a girl back in college in my sophomore year. She was a year older than me. You had to date her up in October for the spring prom. There was a fellow with a car who used to drive her to breakfast, lunch and dinner and send her flowers every day, but she used to take walks with me and lunch sometimes. She did the most marvellous thing that anyone ever did for me. I was a kid then and maybe it oughtn't to seem like so much to me now, but it still does. She broke a date with this other guy and went to the spring prom with me, I gave her orchids and we went to a couple of speakeasies and it was the best night I ever had in my whole life.' He sat back, remembering the orchids and the speakeasies. 'I introduced her to a friend of mine that summer. He had a lot of dough and called her long-distance three times a week and six months later they got married. You can't blame a girl. Want to see her picture?'

'Yes,' the reporter said.

The assistant editor took out the picture, yellowed and ravelled at the edges. It was of a pretty, graceful girl, in a white dress, sitting erect, a hint of strength in her face, mixed with ancient coquetry. 'I don't know why I keep it,' the assistant editor said, looking at the picture. 'Maybe for luck.' He put it back carefully into his wallet. He leaned back and his thick glasses and square, angular, plain, decent face shone in the dim light, clearly and painfully the face of a man who all his life might expect to find his best friends taking his girl.

'There was another girl. A Danish girl,' the assistant editor went on. 'I met her at a party in the Village. She'd come down from Boston with a friend, to be an actress. She worked at the Filmarte as an usher. I must have seen the last part of *Grand Illusion* twelve times.'

He smiled.

'I'd go around for the last reel or two of the pictures,' he said, 'and take her out to Sunnyside. She lived there with her friend. She liked me, but she wouldn't have anything much to do with me, even though I used to sleep out on the living-room couch five times a week. We had a fight and she decided she didn't want to be an actress and she went home to Boston. I guess I would've married her then if I hadn't fought with her so much.' He took off his glasses and stared wearily at them. 'About six months later she came down to New York on a visit and it was different. She moved right in and we had a wonderful time. We'd go out on week-ends in the country. Just drive around in the summertime and stop in for drinks here and there and go swimming and laugh. She met me in Provincetown and we stayed with a Danish family. There was a great party. Provincetown, on Cape Cod. I don't think I've ever had a better time and I keep remembering it . . . Maybe I should've married her. I don't know.'

The assistant editor leaned over and put the bottle down. On the street below, three Frenchman passed, singing loudly.

'I'm thirty years old and I write worse than I ever did. I

384

don't know what I'll do after the war. Once, when I was in the Engineers, I sent her a letter. She was married, she wrote me, and she was having a kid on May seventeenth. She was going to call it David, after her husband's uncle, she said. She asked me to pray for it. I haven't written back. Well, what's the difference?' He put his glasses on again. 'The Filmarte Theatre.' He laughed and stood up. 'I wish I had two hack writers I could throw stories to and know they'd come out right,' he said. 'I wouldn't get so tired. Well, it's pretty late. Got to go to bed. Tomorrow's another war.'

The radio was sending out American jazz now, the deep familiar horns of America pounding like all the music in all the dance halls and all the night clubs and at the spring proms any American ever went to, any girl in a white dress ever danced at.

The assistant editor listened, his eyes blinking behind the thick lenses of his glasses. When it was over, he got up and walked into his own room slowly, his shirt dumpy and wrinkled, to take one last look at his desk and made sure everything was all right before going to bed.

Preach on the Dusty Roads

Nelson Weaver sat at his desk and wrote, 'Labour . . . Bridge-port plant . . . $1,435,639.77.' Then he put his sharply pointed hard pencil down among the nine other sharply pointed hard pencils arrayed in severe line on the right side of the shining desk, below the silver-framed photograph of his dead wife.

He looked at the leather clock on the back edge of his desk: 10.35. Robert wouldn't be along for ten minutes yet.

Nelson Weaver picked up his pencil and looked at the long sheets of paper, closely covered with typewritten figures, to his right. 'Depreciation . . . $3,100,456.25,' he wrote.

The tax sheets for Marshall and Co., Valves and Turbines, were nearly done. He had sat at this desk for thirty-five days, working slowly and carefully, from time to time deliberately putting down a number on the page, like Cézanne with his six strokes a day on a water-colour, until the huge elaborate structure of Marshall and Co.'s finances, which reached from bank to bank and country to country, from Wilmington, Delaware, where it was incorporated, to Chungking, China, where it sold electrical equipment to Chiang Kai-shek; until all this sprawling, complex history of money paid and money gained and credit offered and rejected and profit and loss, palpable and impalpable, was laid bare and comprehensible on five short pages of his clean accountant's figures.

Nelson looked at the leather clock: 10.40. The train was leaving at 11.15. Robert had better hurry.

Nelson looked at the $3,100,456.25 he had written. For the thousandth time he admired the delicate, tilted, book-keeper's 2 he had early in his career learned to make. Somehow that 2 was to him a badge of his profession, a sign of his talents, an advertisement of the difficult rare world of figures in which he moved skilfully and at ease, turning sweat and clamour, heat and smoke, bonanza and disaster, into clear, rigid, immutable tables.

10.43. Where was Robert? Nelson got up and went to the window and looked out. He looked down the steel and granite fifty stories to the street. He laughed a little to himself when he realised he was trying to pick his son out of the hurry and confusion of Forty-ninth Street, five hundred feet below.

He went back to his desk and sat down and picked up the sheet of paper on which he had been working. Tax sheets represented a formal and intricate game in which the players solemnly and conventionally juggled abstractions, like Spinoza proving God, to bring about very real tangible results, like the great man who, in 1932, proved that J.P. Morgan had no taxable income. Once, in 1936, Nelson, in a rare burst of capriciousness, had made up two tax sheets. One, that Marshall and Co. had actually submitted to the Government. And the other, with a change here and there to conform more to the actual realities of iron and sweat rather than the formal accountant's symbolism of numbers and deductible percentages. There had been a difference of $700,962.12. Nelson had carried the second sheet around with him for his private amusement for a week and then burned it, wisely.

This year, with the blossoming expansion of Marshall and Co. for war orders and the jump in the surplus profits tax, the difference between the real and the formal would be immense — over a million dollars, Nelson figured Marshall and Co. paid him $40,000 a year. He was quite a bargain, he told himself grimly.

10.47. No Robert yet. Nelson put down the paper because the figures were beginning to jump before his eyes. More and more frequently he found that happening to him. Well, along with the waistline that grew an inch a year and the tendency to wake at five in the morning and his lack of shock at overhearing people calling him a middle-aged gentleman, that had to be expected of a man who had led a quiet, rather unhealthy life at a desk and was now over fifty . . .

The door opened and Robert came in in his new lieutenant's uniform, with the rawhide suitcase Nelson had given him in his hand.

'On our way, Pop,' Robert said. 'The U.S. Army is waiting on tiptoe.'

They smiled at each other and Nelson took his beautiful grey Homburg out of the closet and put it carefully on before the mirror.

'I was afraid you wouldn't make it,' he said, delicately fingering the brim of the hat.

Robert was over at the window, staring out at New York, shining all around in the early summer sun, with the Hudson a flat blue highway against the cliffs of New Jersey and the buildings piled against each other like stiff confectionery in the light morning air. 'Lord, Lord . . . ' Robert murmured. 'What a place to work! You ought to be sitting here writing the Ninth Symphony, Pop.'

Nelson smiled at him and took his arm. 'I'm not writing the Ninth Symphony.' He would have liked to carry Robert's bag for him to the elevator and even made a move for it, but Robert detected it and switched the bag without a word to the other hand.

There was a pretty, dark-haired woman in a fine, severe black dress that looked on her as black dresses are supposed to look on smart women who work in fashionable businesses, and rarely do. She had her hair swept up for the summer morning and she looked pert and sharp and pretty and grown-up all at once, and she looked coolly and approvingly, Nelson noticed, at his tall son, standing beside him, very slender and straight and self-consciously handsome in his new dark-green lieutenant's blouse with the proud gold bar shining on each shoulder.

Robert smiled a little to himself, conscious of the cool, approving stare, helplessly and a little ashamedly pleased with himself for provoking it.

'Sometimes,' he said as he and Nelson got out of the elevator and walked towards Fifth Avenue, with the woman lost behind them, 'sometimes, Pop, they ought to be allowed to arrest a man for the thoughts that pass through his head.'

They grinned at each other and Robert took a deep full breath, looking around him, the smile still on his lips, before he got into the taxicab and said, 'Grand Central, please.'

They sat quietly as the cab dodged through the streets. Nelson looked steadfastly at the shining rawhide bag. You saw bags like that, he thought, on Friday afternoons in the summertime, on station platforms where people in summer clothes gaily waited for trains going to New England, to the Adirondacks, to Cape Cod . . . Somehow, he felt, to make the picture complete, there should be a tennis racket lying beside it, in its bright rubber case, and a girl's voice, light and excited, dominating the scene, saying swiftly, laughing, 'Olive oil and

388

vinegar in equal parts and a few drops of glycerin and just smear yourself, darling, every hour. There was this lifeguard at Hobe Sound and he was out in the sun twelve hours a day and that was all he used and he was as brown as the outside of an old piece of roast beef . . .'

But instead it was Robert's voice saying, 'Five medium tanks . . .'

'What was that?' Nelson looked at his son apologetically. 'I'm sorry I didn't quite . . .'

'When I get back,' Robert said, 'I'm put in command of five medium tanks. Twelve tons apiece, with a crew of four men. They represent an investment of about three hundred thousand bucks. And I've got to tell them, start, stop, go here, go there, kindly demolish that hot dog stand to the left, would you be so good as to put six shells into that corset and lingerie shop five blocks down the street.' He grinned widely. 'Me. I never even ran a set of electric trains before in my life. The faith that the U.S. Government has in me! I'm going to develop a beautiful case of stage fright when the time comes for me to look those five medium tanks in the eye.'

'You'll do all right,' Nelson said soberly.

Robert stared at him seriously for a moment, the smile gone. 'I suppose so,' he said.

The cab wheeled into Grand Central and they got out.

'We have fifteen minutes,' Robert said, looking up at the clock. 'How about one quick one, to oil the wheels?'

'Is anyone else seeing you off?' Nelson asked as they walked through the dim, shuffling, echoing vault, towards the bar of the Commodore Hotel. 'No girls?'

'Nope,' said Robert, smiling. 'Can't start that. If you invite one you've got to invite them all. It'd look like a reunion of Vassar graduates, classes of '38 to '41, inclusive.' He laughed aloud. 'I wouldn't like to make such a showy exit.'

Nelson smiled at the joke, but was aware that the joke covered the fact that Robert had saved his final private good-bye before he went to war with his father. He wished there was some way to tell Robert he understood and was grateful, but whatever words he could think of would be clumsy and tragic, so he said nothing. They went into the Commodore and stood at the long bar, quiet now and cool and dim in the eleven o'clock pause before the day's drinking began.

'Two martinis,' Robert said to the bartender.

'I haven't had a drink in the morning,' Nelson said, 'since Arthur Parker's wedding. 1936.'

'What the hell,' Robert said. 'There's a war on.'

There was the pleasant sound of the ice clinking in the mixer and the faint, strange smell of the gin rising in the empty bar and the pungent, tiny smell of the lemon peel that the bartender twisted delicately over the full cold glasses.

They lifted their drinks and Nelson looked past his son's lean, well-loved head, capped and young and martial, with the gold and leather of the United States Army shining on it. Nelson looked along the bar into the dim recesses of the low-ceilinged, long room, as neat and orderly and expectant with its empty and regular tables and chairs as only a bar or restaurant prepared for the day's eating and drinking can be. How many farewells had been said in this room, this drinking place next to the trains that spread out across the whole huge continent. How many final goodbyes. How many last kisses between husband and wife. How many gulped and tasteless drinks, how much shock of alcohol to take the first terrible edge off the pain of loss and distance. How many farewelling ghosts sat at those regular tables, their endless irrevocable goodbyes echoing among the frivolous glasses. How full the company of grieving leave-takers, each of them tasting death in this snatched last moment over whisky, before the train rolled out . . .

Nelson looked squarely, steadily at his one child's military head. He raised his glass a little higher, touching his son's glass. 'To a quick end of the business,' he said.

They drank. The drink tasted powerful and rich and burning and immediately effective against his morning palate. Robert drank with zest, tasting the full savour of the drink happily, rolling it over his tongue. 'You'd be surprised,' he said, 'how hard it is to get a good martini in the Tank Corps.'

Nelson watched him drink and remembered a day in the country, three years ago when Robert was twenty. It was summertime and they were both on vacation and had a house in Vermont and Robert had been out swimming all afternoon and had come in, wet-haired, tan, barefoot, wrapped in a huge white bathrobe, with a faded blue towel swung around his shoulders, summertime printed on his freckled nose and the tan backs of his lake-washed hands . . . He had swung through the screen door, singing loudly, 'Stormy weather, since my gal and I ain't together . . . ' He had padded along barefoot, leaving high-arched stains of lake-water on the grass rugs directly to the kitchen. When Nelson had gone into the kitchen, he saw Robert sitting at the porcelain table, still humming 'Stormy Weather', with an open bottle of cold beer in one hand, the moisture condensing coolly on the glass, and in the other hand a huge, ludicrous sandwich he had made for himself with two great jagged slices of rye bread and a quarter pound of Swiss cheese and two mountainous slices of cold baked ham and a tremendous cold beefsteak tomato cut in three fat, meaty slices. Robert was sitting there, tilted back in the flimsy kitchen chair, the late afternoon sun shining obliquely on him through the high old-fashioned window, slowly dripping lake-water, the giant of a sandwich and the bottle of beer happily in his hands, his mouth full of cheese and tomato and ham and bread and cold beer, the song somehow working out of his throat in a bumbling joyous monotone. He waved the sandwich airily at Nelson when Nelson appeared at the door.

'Starving,' he mumbled. 'Swam four miles. Got to keep my energy up.'

'You've got to eat dinner in an hour,' Nelson said.

Robert grinned through the food. 'I'll eat dinner. Let nobody worry.' And he took another fabulous bite from the monstrous sandwich.

Nelson watched him eat, smiling a little to himself.

'Want me to make you a sandwich?' Robert asked.

'No, thanks.'

'Great maker of sandwiches . . .'

Nelson shook his head, smiling. 'I'll wait for dinner.' He watched his son eat. The full white teeth shining in the sun-burned face, biting strongly and evenly into the food, the lean muscles of the strong throat, rising out of the white bathrobe, moving calmly as he tilted the bottle back and gulped the beer . . .

'When I was your age, Nelson said, 'I ate just like that . . .'

And suddenly Robert had looked at him very soberly as though seeing his father twenty years old – and loving him – and seeing the long years that came after with pride and pity . . .

'Well . . .' Robert ate the olive at the bottom of his glass and put the glass down with a little flat tinkle that ran lightly through the quiet bar. 'Well, the train's waiting . . .'

Nelson looked around and shook his head and the Vermont

kitchen and the sunburned boy and the bottle of beer beaded with icebox cold all disappeared. He finished his drink and paid, and together he and Robert hurried across the station to the gate where Robert's train was waiting. There was an air of bustle and impatience about the gate, and a soldier and his mother and two female relatives were weeping together in a sodden mass, and somehow he and Robert shook hands and there was a last wave and no words because they each knew that any word through the tortured throat would bring with it sobs – and Robert went down the long incline to the dark station below. His rawhide bag gleamed among the descending passengers and he was gone . . .

Nelson turned and walked slowly towards the street. As he walked he thought of the capped head and the rawhide bag going down the long incline to the waiting train, to the medium tanks, to the waiting guns, the waiting agony, going lightly and zealously and unquestioningly off to war. He remembered, although a little mistily, with the martini and the shuffling steps on the marble floor, and the weeping at the gates of the soldier's women, all serving to blur and confuse and make remote, he remembered watching Robert playing tennis last summer. Robert played very smoothly and well, lanky and easy over the court, like those tall kids in California who play 365 days a year in a kind of lazy, expert boredom. Robert had a habit of talking jovially and half-irritably to himself when he missed a shot, looking up to heaven and muttering under his breath, 'Weaver! *Weaver!* Why don't you just give up? Why don't you just go home?' He had seen his father looking down at him, smiling, and knew that his father understood the mumbled tirade he was delivering to himself. He had grinned and waved his racket and slammed the next three services so hard no returns were possible . . .

Nelson walked up Madison Avenue towards the office of Marshall and Co. towards the formal and intricate sheets of figures waiting on his desk, towards the neat, professional, book-keeper's 2 he was proud of . . .

As he walked he wondered where his son would be sent to meet the enemy. Africa? Australia? India? England? Russia? Desert, plain, mountain, jungle, seacoast – and a twenty-three-year-old boy, ex-swimmer, ex-tennis-player, ex-eater of great sandwiches and drinker of cold beer, ex-lover of his father, hungry and full of jokes and ready for any climate, while his father full of his slack fifty years, walked daily to his office . . .

392

Nelson walked along Madison Avenue before the windows of the fine shops. Two women passed him and a high woman's voice said, 'Taffeta. Baby-blue taffeta, shirred, with the back bare down to the hips. It has a startling effect.'

It never occurred to me it could happen, Nelson thought, walking slowly and blindly away from the station where his son had set off to battle. There was one war and that was all. It's my fault. I had a son, but I didn't take my responsibility seriously enough. I worked and I dressed him and fed him and sent him to a good college and bought him books and gave him money to take out girls and took him with me on vacations to Vermont, but I didn't take my responsibility seriously enough. I worked, and it wasn't easy, and I was poor for a long time and only the poor know how hard it is to stop being poor. I worked, but for the wrong things I've added millions of rows of figures, detailed the manoeuvrings of many corporations, year by year, and sometimes it was eighteen hours a day and no time for meals . . . Nonsense! I'm guilty. I should've been out stopping this . . . I am nearly the same age as Hitler. He could do something to kill my son. I should've been doing something to save him. I'm guilty. I should be ashamed to stand in the same room with my son in his lieutenant's green blouse. Money . . . I thought about the grocer, the insurance man, the electric light company . . . Nonsense, nonsense . . . I've wasted my life. I'm an old man and alone and my son has gone to war and all I did was pay rent and taxes. I was playing with toys. I was smoking opium. Me and millions like me. The war was being fought for twenty years and I didn't know it. I waited for my son to grow up and fight it for me. I should've been out screaming on street corners, I should've grabbed people by their lapels in trains, in libraries and restaurants and yelled at them. 'Love, understand, put down your guns, forget your profit, remember God . . . ' I should have walked on foot through Germany and France and England and America. I should've preached on the dusty roads and used a rifle when necessary. I stayed in the one city and paid the grocer. Versailles, Manchuria, Ethiopia, Warsaw, Madrid – battlefields, battlefields – and I thought there was one war and it was over.

He stopped and looked up. He was sweating now and the salt was in his eyes and he had to rub them to see that he was standing in front of the great monument of a building, serene and immutable, in which, in war and peace, Marshall and Co.

conducted its business. His charts and figures were waiting for him, all the clever, legal, evasive, money-saving numbers that a global dealer in valves and turbines could assemble in this bloody and profitable year to turn over in its solemn annual report to the government of the republic. Depreciation . . . $3,100,456.25.

He looked up at the soaring, shining building sharp against the soft summer sky.

He stood there, before the graven entrance, and people jostled him and came and went, but he didn't go in.

The Green Nude

As a young man, Sergei Baranov, although he preferred painting large still lifes of red apples, green pears and very orange oranges, joined the Red Army and did a mild amount of damage in several engagements against the Whites around Kiev. He was a sturdy, good-humoured, dreamy youth who did not like to refuse anyone anything, and since all his friends were joining the Revolution he went along and served faithfully and cheerfully, eating the soldier's black bread, sleeping on the soldier's straw, pulling the trigger of his ancient rifle when the people around him ordered him to do so, advancing bravely when everyone else was advancing and running in fear of his life when that seemed like the necessary thing to do. When the Revolution was over, he retired from the military, equipped with a modest decoration for an action at which he was not present, and took up quarters in Moscow and began once more to paint red apples, green pears, and very orange oranges. All his friends were enthusiastically convinced that the Revolution was an excellent thing, and Sergei, never one to strike out on his own, amiably and decorously concurred. The truth was that he was only really interested in his highly coloured fruits and vegetables and when, in his studio or in the café which he frequented, discussions would start about Lenin and Trotsky or the new economic programme, he would laugh his hearty and agreeable laugh and say, bashfully, 'Eh, who knows? It is for the philosophers.' Besides, being a decorated hero of the Revolution and an artist to boot, he was treated well, and was assigned an excellent studio with a skylight and permitted heavy labourer's rations. His paintings too, were warmly approved by everyone, since he had the trick of making all his garden products seem marvellously edible. They sold without delay and his work was seen in the homes and offices of many quite-important officials of the new régime, warm and appetising globs of colour on the otherwise bleak and functional walls.

When, in 1923, he met and conquered an ample and beautiful young lady from Soviet Armenia, his painting took a new turn. He began to paint nudes. Since his technique remained the same, despite the change in subject matter, his success increased in leaps and bounds. As edible as ever, his paintings now combined the most satisfactory features of the orchard and the harem, and examples of his work, rosy, healthy, and very round, were much sought after by even more important officials of the régime.

He undoubtedly would have continued thus to this day, happily producing a succession of canvases of hearty, lightly clad, appetising girls, alternating with piled heaps of oversized purple grapes and bananas, going from success to success, honour to honour, if he had not met, at a literary party, the woman who was finally to become his wife.

Anna Kronsky was one of those sharp-featured and over-poweringly energetic women that the liberation of women from the nursery and kitchen has turned loose on the male world. Angular, voracious, and clever, with a tongue like an iron clapper in a new bell, racked by indigestion and a deep contempt for the male sex, she was the sort of woman who in this country would run a department store or report wars for the Luce publications. As one of her friends said of her, in attempting to put his finger on the exact difference between Anna and her more gentle contemporaries, 'Anna does not make up her face when she goes out in the morning – she hones it.'

In Moscow, at the time Sergei met her, she had gravitated inexorably into the education system. With twenty-three day nurseries for the children of working parents under her supervision, and a staff of over five hundred cowed men and women, she had already made her mark on the new population of the growing state. The children under her care were known as the cleanest and most precocious in the Soviet Union, and it was not until 1938 that a routine survey of neurotic diseases disclosed the fact that the graduates of Anna Kronsky's immaculate crèches led all the other population groups of the nation by three to one in absolute nervous breakdowns.

In a necessarily incomplete study, prepared by a thoughtful Artillery Colonel during a slow month on the Southern front in 1944, the estimate was made that the ministrations of Anna Kronsky to the rising generation had cost the Red Army more

396

manpower than a full armoured brigade of the Nazi 9th Army. However, the study was accepted with a grain of salt by the Colonel's superiors, since his O.G.P.U. dossier revealed that he had been the lover of Miss Kronsky between the dates of August 3rd and August 7th, 1922, and had sent into head-quarters a fervent request for transfer to Archangel on August 8th of the same year.

It was this lady, who, flanked by a heroic poet and an ageing test-pilot, set her eyes on the sturdy Baranov as he came through the door, and, in one moment of iron speculation, made the decision that was to transform the painter's life. Her carborundum eyes glittering, she crossed the room, introduced herself to her prey, ignored the beautiful girl from Soviet Armenia who had come with Baranov, and started the neces-sary process which resulted three months later in marriage. Just what it was that made Baranov so immediately attractive to her, none of her friends could decide. Perhaps she saw, in the painter's simple docility and good-humoured health, evi-dence of a fine digestion and an uncomplicated nervous system, excellent attributes for the husband of a busy lady executive who came home each night jangled and worried with the day's thousand cares. Whatever the reasons, Anna left no escape possible for Sergei. He had a tearful scene with his beloved Soviet Armenian, painted one last, pink, fruity nude, and helped carry the poor girl's meagre belongings to the new room Anna had managed to find for her in a slum section three-quarters of an hour away from the centre of the town. Then Anna moved in, bringing with her a new bedspread, three packing cases of pamphlets and reports, and a large goose-neck lamp.

The marriage seemed from the beginning to be a thoroughly happy one, and there was only one noticeable change in Bara-nov, outside of a subtle but growing tendency towards silence in company. He no longer painted nudes. Not one painting, not one sketch, not even a wash from the waist up, of the ripe, unclad female form, came from his studio. Confined once more entirely to the vegetable world, he seemed to have mastered a new understanding of the problems of the apple, the orange and the pear. As edible as ever, a new dust seemed to be powdered over his work, a haunting and melancholy fragrance, as though the fruit he chose to paint came now from autumnal boughs, the last sweet bounty of the closing year, the final, nostalgic yield of trees and vines through whose dying leaves and frozen branches the cruel winds of winter were already moaning.

This new development in Baranov's work was greeted with respectful praise by critics and public alike and examples of the new phase were hung in many museums and public places. Success did not change him, however. More silent than ever, he painted steadily, experimenting with beets and pumpkins in ever darker reds and yellows, going everywhere with his sallow and brilliant wife, listening with model attention night after night as she monopolised conversations in literary, artistic, political, educational, and industrial circles. Once, it is true, at the request of his wife, he went to one of her nurseries and started a painting of a group of children he saw there. He painted for about an hour, then put his brush down, tore the canvas in half and had it burned in the stove, and went into the men's room, where he was reported sobbing uncontrollably. This story was not believed by anyone, as it was retailed by a young teacher who had crossed swords with Anna Kronsky and who was removed later at her instigation as unreliable. Whatever the truth of the matter was, Baranov returned to his studio and went back to his beets and pumpkins.

It was about this time that he took to painting at night, using the goose-neck lamp that Anna had brought with her as part of her dowry. They had their own apartment by now, as a result of their double importance, more than a mile away from the studio, and the sturdy though now slightly bent figure of the painter, trudging through the snow late at night was a common sight on the almost deserted streets between his home and his studio. He became very secretive, locking his door at all times, and when friends asked him about his current work, he would merely smile vaguely and politely and change the subject. Anna, of course, never asked him about his work, as she was a very busy woman, and it was not until the opening of his one-man show, an affair attended by many of the intellectual élite of the Government and the arts, that she saw for the first time the painting that had engaged her husband for the past many months.

It was a nude. But it was no nude that Baranov had painted before, There was no touch of pink anywhere on the enormous and frightening canvas. The prevailing colour was green, that green that lurks in the sky before cyclones and hurricanes, sallow, lurid, oppressive to the eye. The figure itself, of a slack-breasted and lank-haired woman with a wrinkled abdomen and stringy but somehow violent loins, was also done in mottled green, and the staring and demonic eyes under the dry brow were another shade of the dominant hue. The mouth, the most fearful feature of the work, was done in dead black and somehow gave the startling impression of howling speech, as though the painter had caught his model in full flood of maniac oratory. The mouth seemed to fill the canvas, indeed the entire room, with a tumbling, morbid, glittering torrent of horrid rhetoric, and it was to be noticed that the viewers attempted, uneasily, to avoid, as much as possible, looking at that particular section of the work. The background, so different for Baranov's usual arrangement of carefully painted, richly figured materials, was spume and wreckage, jagged stony ruins of temples and tenements against a green and charcoal sky. The only recognisable link with Baranov's past work was a cherry tree in the right foreground. But the tree was stunted and uprooted; a green fungus ate at the branches; a thick and snakelike vine wound murderously around the suffering trunk, and minutely painted green worms munched among the unripe fruit. The entire effect was of madness, genius, energy, disaster, sorrow and despair.

When Anna Kronsky Baranov entered the room, people were standing in muted groups, staring with horrid fascination at the new painting. 'Great,' she heard Suvarnin, the critic for *The Sickle,* mutter. And, 'Incredible,' whispered Levinoff, the painter, as she passed him.

Baranov himself was standing in a corner, shyly and excitedly accepting the awed congratulations of friends. Anna stared incredulously at the painting, then again at her husband, who, with his rosy complexion and pleasantly smiling obedient face, looked not one whit different from the man she had known all these years. She started to go over to congratulate him, although the painting seemed very unlifelike to her, but she was intercepted by two men who ran a tractor factory in Rostov, and she became so interested in lecturing to them about tractor manufacture that she forgot to mention anything about the painting to Baranov until much later in the evening.

From time to time, various of the guests stole sidelong and speculative glances at Anna, especially when she happened to be standing in front of her husband's masterpiece. Although Anna was conscious of their regard and also conscious of something vaguely disturbing in their eyes, she dismissed the feeling, since she was well-used by now to glances of varying intensity from her subordinates in the halls and offices of the nurseries under her command. The real reason for the hurried, measuring appraisals of the people in the gallery she never discovered and no one in the Soviet Union had the courage to apprise her of it. The wild and nightmare face that toppled the terrible body of the green nude bore a family resemblance to Anna Kronsky that no amount of stylisation on the part of the artist could erase. Sisters, twin souls, the painted and the living woman existed in a hideous relationship that escaped the notice of none. The only other person in Moscow who did not know that the artist had painted his wife's portrait was the man who went home obediently each night with her. Ignorant and happy in his new glory, Sergei Baranov took his wife to the ballet that night to celebrate and later ordered three bottles of champagne at a café, most of which was drunk by the two tractor men from Rostov.

The week following the opening of the show marked the high-point of Sergei Baranov's early life. Fêted, pointed out wherever he went, especially when accompanied by his wife, saluted in the Press, urged to create murals to cover acres of walls, he swam in a bright stream of praise. The critic Suvarnin, who had barely acknowledged his greeting before this, even deigned to come to Baranov's studio to interview him, and, breaking all precedent, appeared sober.

'Tell me,' said Suvarnin, squinting at Baranov through his pale, cold eyes, those eyes which had riddled holes in so many canvases before this, 'tell me how a man who has only painted fruit before this comes to do such a painting.'

'Well,' said Baranov, who had recaptured some of his early loquacity and expansiveness in the past week, 'well, it happened something like this. As you know, if you have seen any of my painting recently, my work has become more and more melancholy.'

Suvarnin nodded thoughtfully, agreeing.

'The palette became more and more subdued. Brown, dark brown, entered increasingly into the canvases. The fruit . . . well, the truth is, the fruit began to be withered, frostbitten, sad. I would come here to my studio and I would sit down and cry. For an hour. Two hours at a time. All by myself. I began to dream every night. Dreams of death, dreams of trains going out of stations, dreams of boats leaving me on the dock, in the rain, dreams of being buried alive and being sniffed at by dark brown foxes and other small animals . . . ' Baranov spoke with lively animation, as a perfectly healthy man might describe symptoms of a dreadful disease which he has suffered and proudly conquered. 'The worst dream, and one that I had over and over again, was that I was in a small room and it was crowded with women, only women. All the women could talk, but I couldn't. I tried. I moved my lips. My tongue quivered between my teeth. The conversation around me filled the air deafeningly like locomotive whistles and French horns. And I could not make a sound. You have no idea how terrible this simple thing can be. It was like being committed each night to a new kind of awful prison. I began to fear going to bed. I would come and stare at the blank canvas on my easel, at the arrangement of potatoes and eggplants on which I intended to work, and I could not move my fingers to the brushes. An artist, as you know, must create out of his emotions. How could I transfer how I felt into the image of an eggplant, into potatoes? I felt I was lost. I felt I would never be able to paint again. I contemplated suicide.'

Suvarnin nodded. He even thought of making notes, something he hadn't done for twenty years, since he was of the firm opinion that accuracy in reporting was the foe of creative criticism. He put his hand into his pocket for a pencil, but discovered he had neglected to bring one along with him. He took his hand out of his pocket and gave up the thought of taking notes.

'Suicide,' Baranov repeated, flushed with joy at having the redoubtable Suvarnin pay such close attention to his confession. 'I moaned. I shrieked.' Baranov knew that he had done no such thing, and had, in fact, merely gloomed silently in front of the easel, but he felt that these active expressions of passion would sit well with the critic, as indeed they did. 'I cried out. I despaired.' Suvarnin moved restively, glancing instinctively at the vodka bottle on the table, and licking the corner of his mouth, and Baranov hurried on, feeling anxiously that he had perhaps gone a little far with his synonyms. 'I slashed out blindly at the canvas. I did not guide my hand. I did not search for colours. I did not look at the potatoes or the eggplant. My terrors painted through me. I was the instrument of my dreams. I hardly looked to see what I was doing. I painted all night long, one night after another. I did not know what I was doing . . .' By now Baranov had forgotten that he was trying to make an impression. By now he was letting the simple truth pour out. 'All I knew was, that as the painting grew, a great weight was being lifted from me. My subconscious was being delivered from its prison. When I slept, I no longer dreamed of being struck dumb or being nosed by dark brown foxes. Now my dreams were of vine-yards in the springtime and large-breasted young women I wished to approach on the streets. Finally, when I was finished, and I sat back and looked at the green nude and the ruins, I was as surprised by what I had done as if I had come into my studio and found that another man, a complete stranger, had used my easel while I was away on holiday. And I was grateful to him, whoever he was. And I was grateful to the green lady on the canvas. Between them,' Baranov said simply, 'they delivered me from Hell.'

Suvarnin stood up and silently shook the painter's hand. 'Out of anguish,' he said finally, 'comes the great art. Out of the depth of despair only can we reach to the skies. Look at Dostoyevsky.'

Baranov nodded, although a little uneasily, as he had tried to read *The Brothers Karamazov* three times and had never got past page 165. But Suvarnin did not press the point. 'Read my article on Saturday,' he said modestly. 'I think you will be pleased.'

'Thank you,' Baranov said humbly, resolving to call Anna immediately Suvarnin left to impart to her the heady news. 'I am in your debt.'

'Nonsense,' said Suvarnin, with the concision and gift for a phrase that had made his reputation secure in a dozen cities. 'Art is in your debt. And now,' he asked, 'what is the next painting going to be?'

Baranov smiled happily. 'Cherries,' he said. 'Six kilos of red cherries in a wicker basket. They are being delivered here at two o'clock from the market.'

'Good,' said Suvarnin. They shook hands once more and the critic departed, with only one tentative glance at the vodka bottle.

Baranov sat down, waiting dreamily for the arrival of the cherries, thinking, as he sat there. Perhaps it is time that I started a scrapbook, for my reviews.

On Saturday, Baranov opened the magazine with trembling fingers. There, on the page with Suvarnin's photograph, was a streaming black title, 'FILTH IN THE GALLERIES.' Baranov blinked. Then he began to read, 'Last week,' Suvarnin had written, 'the Counter-Revolution struck one of its most audacious blows at Russian Art. From the bestial brushes of one, Sergei Baranov, who has until now concealed his heretical infamies under bushels of rotten fruit, and who now feels that he can come out boldly and shamelessly in his true colours, we have received a nauseating sample of decadent, bourgeois "art".'

Baranov sat down, trying to get air into his aching lungs. Then he forced himself to read on. 'In this gangrenous excrescence,' Suvarnin continued, using what Baronov, even in his extremity, recognised as a pet phrase, 'the dying world of Capitalism, allied with the Trotskyst bandits, has served notice on the Soviet Union that its minions and agents have wormed their way into the heart of the fatherland's cultural life. By what treachery and corruption the notorious Baranov managed to get his monstrosity hung on a gallery wall, we shall leave to the public prosecutor to discover. But while waiting for the reports on the investigation that will surely take place, we of the art world must join ranks to defend ourselves. We must not permit the insidious Baranov and others of his ilk, slavishly devoted to the fads and aberrations of their plutocratic masters, to desecrate our walls with these samples of dadaistic despair, reactionary cubism, retrogressive abstractionism, surrealistic archaism, aristocratic individualism, religiostic mysticism, materialistic Fordism.'

Baranov put the magazine down carefully. He did not have to read further. He had read it often enough before so that he could have recited the rest of the piece without glancing once more at the page. He sat on his stool, his world in ruins, staring unhappily at the six kilos of bright red cherries, arranged prettily in their wicker basket.

There was a knock on the door. Before he could say, 'Come in,' the door opened and Suvarnin came in. The critic went directly to the table and poured himself five fingers of vodka and drained it. Then he turned to Baranov. 'I see,' he said, gesturing towards the still-open magazine, 'that you've read the piece.'

'Yes,' said Baranov hoarsely.

'Here,' said Suvarnin, taking some manuscript pages out of his pocket. 'You might be interested in reading what I wrote originally.'

Baranov numbly took the sheets and stared at them. Suvarnin poured himself another drink while Baranov read through swimming eyes, ' . . . a great new unfolding of talent . . . a courageous grappling with the problems of doubt and dis-

403

illusionment which are the beginning of understanding . . . a blazing display of technical ability . . . a pioneering plunge into the depths of the modern psyche in paint . . . '

Baranov pushed the pages aside. 'What . . . what happened?' he asked dimly.

'The Committee,' Suvarnin said. 'They saw your painting. Then they saw my review. They asked me to make certain changes,' he said delicately. 'That Klopoyev, the President of the Committee, the one who has made eighty-four portrait heads of Stalin, he was especially anxious.'

'What's going to happen to me now?'

Suvarnin shrugged. 'Nothing good,' he said. 'As a friend, I advise you . . . leave the country.' He went over and picked up the manuscript sheets of his first review. He tore them into small pieces, made a little pile of them on the floor and put a match to them. He watched until the flame had burnt itself out, then carefully scattered the ashes with his foot. He finished the vodka, drinking this time directly from the bottle, and went out.

Baranov did not dream that night. He was up all night listening to his wife.

She spoke vigorously from eight in the evening until eight the next morning, a full-length address in which every relevant topic was stated and developed with a balance and fullness which Edmund Burke, in another country and a more leisurely century, would have wholeheartedly admired. She had been notified that afternoon that their apartment was being taken over by a 'cellist with a cousin on the Central Committee and she had been removed from her position as head of the nursery system at 5 p.m. and relegated to the post of assistant dietician at a ward for backward and criminally inclined children in a penal camp some thirty kilometres outside Moscow. With these facts as a springboard and with her audience of one wanly rooted against the bedpillows, she ran through her eloquent twelve hours of recrimination without noticeably pausing for breath and without repeating herself.

'Ruined,' she said clearly, with no sign of hoarseness, as the eight o'clock factory whistles sounded outside, 'we are completely ruined. And for what? For an idiotic, senseless daub that no one can make head or tail of! A man wants to be a painter. All right! It is childish – but all right, I do not complain. A man wants to paint apples. Silly? All right. But apples can be understood. Apples do not have political implications.

Apples do not turn into bombshells. But this . . . this naked witch . . . Why? Why have you done this to me? Why?'

Dumbly, Baranov leaned against the pillows, staring at his wife.

'Come,' Anna called. 'Come, you must have something to say. You can't sit without speaking forever. Say something. Say one word.'

'Anna,' Baranov said brokenly, 'Anna . . . please . . . ' He hesitated. He wanted to say, 'Anna, I love you,' but he thought better of it.

'Well,' Anna demanded. 'Well?'

'Anna,' Baranov said, 'let us have hope. Maybe it will all blow over.'

Anna glared at him coldly. 'Nothing,' she said, 'nothing blows over in Moscow.'

Then she got dressed and went out to the penal camp to report to her new job in the kitchen there.

Anna's prediction proved only too well founded. Attacks which made Suvarnin's article seem like an unrestrained paean of praise by comparison, were loosed on him in newspapers and magazines all over the Soviet Union. *The New Masses,* in New York City, which had never before mentioned his name, printed, opposite a full page pen-and-ink drawing of Stalin by Klopoyev, a heated diatribe which called him, among other things, a 'traitor to the working class of the world, a lecher after Western fleshpots, a Park Avenue sensationalist, a man who would be at home drawing cartoons for *The New Yorker*'. In a follow-up article, a writer who later joined the Catholic Church and went to work for Metro-Goldwyn-Mayer preparing scenarios for a dog star, used the Baranov case to point out that Michelangelo had been the first proponent of Socialist-realism. In Moscow, a painter's congress, led by the fiery Klopoyev, dropped Baranov from the Painters' Union by the customary vote of 578 to nothing. On one morning, between the hours of ten and twelve, every painting of Baranov's disappeared from every wall in Russia on which they had been hanging. Baranov's studio, which he had held for ten years, was taken from him and given to a man who drew signs for the Moscow subway. Two large plain-clothes men appeared and followed Baranov day and night for three months. His mail was always late and always opened. Anna Kronsky discovered a dictaphone under the sink in the kitchen in which she now worked. Old friends crossed over to the other side of the street when they spotted Baranov in the distance and he no longer found it possible to get tickets for the ballet or the theatre. A woman he had never seen before claimed that he was the father of her illegitimate child and when the case came to trial he lost and was ordered to pay 90 rubles a week for her support and only barely avoided being sent to a work-camp.

Sensing which way the wind was blowing, Baranov put an old camel's brush and the goose-neck lamp into a bag, and, haggard and thin, with Anna at his side, fled the country.

Six months later, in the summer of 1929, Baranov and Anna were established in Berlin. The climate of the German capital at that time was most propitious for artists, and Baranov, who had set to work industriously painting oranges, lemons and apples, in his early edible style, enjoyed an immediate success. 'We will be very happy here,' Anna prophesied, correctly. 'You will paint only fruits and vegetables. You will use dark colours very sparingly. You will avoid nudes and political implications. You will keep your mouth shut and permit me to do all the talking.'

Baranov was only too happy to obey these simple and salutary injunctions. Aside from a certain vagueness of outline, a kind of subtle mist, which seemed to arise from the artist's subconscious hesitancy to come out too definitely on any subject, even the exact location of a lemon on a tablecloth, his work compared very favourably with the first canvases he had done when he returned from the Revolution. He prospered. His cheeks filled out and grew rosy again and he developed a little paunch. He took a small chalet for a summer in Bavaria and rented a superb studio near the Tiergarten. He learned to sit in *rathskellers* and drink Munich beer and say, with a hearty laugh, when politics were discussed, as it often was in those days, 'Eh, who knows? That is for the philosophers.'

When Suvarnin, who had slid from official suspicion to official ostracism in Moscow, as a result of his first, unpublished tribute to Baranov, appeared in Berlin, looking somewhat the worse for wear, Baranov generously took him in and let the critic live in the spare room under the studio, even managing a warm, reminiscent chuckle when Suvarnin told him that the green nude had the most conspicuous place in a new museum for decadent art in Leningrad.

Anna found herself a position as a physical-training instructress in one of the new organisations for young women that were springing up at the time and soon became noted for the vigour of her programme. She turned out battalions of iron-thewed females with enormous hips who could march eighteen hours a day through ploughed country and who could, bare-handed, disarm strong men equipped with rifles and bayonets. When Hitler came to power, she was called into the Government and given command of the entire women's training programme for Prussia and Saxony. Much later, the Bureau of Statistics for the Women's Motherhood-and-National-Honour-Front put out a report disclosing that the graduates of Anna's classes led all other Germans in incidence of miscarriage and death in childbirth seven to one, but by that time, of course, the Baranovs had left the country.

Between 1933 and 1937, the life the Baranovs led was very much as it had been in the good days in Moscow. Baranov painted steadily, and his ripe fruit was hung on many famous walls, including, it was said, the Fuehrer's private gas-proof bomb shelter under the Chancellery, where it considerably brightened the otherwise rather austere atmosphere. Much in demand socially because of Anna's prominence and Baranov's good humour, the couple attended a constant round of parties, at which Anna, as usual, monopolised the conversation, holding forth at great length and with her famous clarity and sharpness on such matters as military tactics, steel production, diplomacy and the upbringing of children.

It was during this period, friends later recalled, that Baranov seemed to grow more and more silent. At parties, he would stand near Anna, listening attentively, munching on grapes and almonds, answering questions with absent-minded mono-syllables. He began to fall off in weight, too, and his eyes had the look about them of a man who slept poorly and had bad dreams. He began to paint at night, locking his door, pulling down the blinds, his studio lit by the functional glare of the goose-neck lamp.

It came as a complete surprise, both to Anna and the Bara-novs's friends when the green nude was discovered. Suvarnin, who had seen both the original and the Berlin canvas, has said that, if possible, the second was even better than the first, although the main figure was, in conception at least, almost identical in the two paintings. 'The anguish,' said Suvarnin, who at that time was employed by the Government as a roving critic of official architecture, a post, he sensibly figured, in which errors of judgement could not be as spectacular and dangerous as those that might be made in the field of easel painting, 'the anguish by now in the painting seemed intolerable. It was heroic, gigantic, god-size. Baranov had plunged to the sub-cellars of despair. [Perhaps it was because I knew of Baranov's nightmares, particularly the one in which he could not say a word in a roomful of conversing women, that I got so strong an impression that this was all humanity, locked in dumbness, protesting, wordlessly and hopelessly, against the tragic predicament of life.] I liked especially the nice new touch of the dwarf hermaphrodite nude, done in pink, being nosed in the left foreground by a brace of small dark brown animals.'

It is doubtful that Baranov was rash enough to contemplate showing the painting publicly. [Whatever necessity drove him to re-creating his masterpiece was adequately served by its completion and his memories of the damage he had suffered in Moscow must have been too fresh to allow him to court disaster in Berlin by unveiling his work.] But the matter was taken out of his hands by the Gestapo, who, in their routine weekly search of the homes and offices of all people who read foreign newspapers (a habit to which Baranov was foolishly addicted) came upon the green nude on the very day Baranov had finished it. The two detectives were simple fellows, but they were well-enough imbued with National Socialist culture to sense defection and heresy here. Arranging for reinforcements and throwing a cordon around the building, they called the chief of the bureau which dealt in these matters. One hour later, Baranov was under arrest and Anna had been removed from her post and sent to work as an assistant dietician in a home for unwed mothers near the Polish border. As was the case in Moscow, no one, not even a fire-eating Colonel in an S.S. Armoured division with whom Anna had quite an intimate relationship, ever dared point out to Anna that her husband had not gone out of his home for his model.

Baranov was questioned by the Gestapo for one month. The questioning, more or less routine, during the course of which Baranov lost three teeth and was twice condemned to death, was aimed largely at getting Baranov to deliver over his lists of accomplices and fellow-conspirators and to confess to certain acts of sabotage in nearby aeroplane factories which had been committed in the past several months. While he was in the hands of the Gestapo, Baranov's painting was put on public view in a large exhibition arranged by the Propaganda Ministry to acquaint the population with the newest trends in decadent and un-German art. The exhibition was enormously successful and was attended by a hundred thousand more people than had ever witnessed a showing of paintings in Berlin until that time.

On the day that Baranov was released from jail, considerably stooped and doomed to eat soft foods for some months to come, the leading critic of the Berlin *Tageblatt* came out with the official judgement of the painting. Baranov bought a paper and read: 'This is Judeo-Anarchism at its most insolent peak. Egged on by Rome (there was a new addition in the background of the ruins of a village church), with the connivance of Wall Street and Hollywood, under orders from Moscow, this barbaric worm of a Baranov, *né* Goldfarb, has insinuated himself into the heartland of German culture in an attempt to bring discredit on our German health and our German institutions of justice. It is a pacifistic attack on our Army, Navy and Air Force, a vile Oriental slander of our glorious German women, a celebration of the lecherous so-called psychology of the Viennese Ghetto, a noxious fume from the Paris sewers of the French degenerates, a sly argument from the British Foreign Office for their bloodthirsty Imperialism. With our usual reticent dignity, we Germans of the German art world, we monitors of the proud and holy German soul, must band together and demand, in respectful, firm, reserved tones, that this gangrenous excrescence on our national life be expunged. Heil Hitler!'

That night, in bed with Anna, who had luckily managed to get a three-day leave to welcome her husband home, listening to what was now a standard twelve-hour lecture on his wife's part, Baranov looked back with something like fondness on the comparatively delicate phrasing of the *Tageblatt* critic.

The next morning he saw Suvarnin. Suvarnin noted that despite the physical ravages of the past month, his friend seemed to have regained some secure inner peace, some great lessening of the weight of an impalpable but soul-destroying burden. Also, despite the night of oratory he had just passed through and the thirty days of police handling, he seemed rested, as if he had been sleeping well recently.

'You shouldn't have done it,' Suvarnin said with mild reproach.

'I know,' said Baranov. 'But I couldn't help it. It just came out.'

'Do you want some advice?'

'Yes.'

'Leave the country,' Suvarnin said. 'Fast.'

But Anna, who liked Germany and was convinced that she could win her way up the ladder once more, refused. And it was inconceivable to Baranov that he go without her. But in the next three months, he was twice beaten up severely on the street by S.A. gangs, and a man who lived three blocks away who resembled him slightly was kicked to death by five young men by mistake; all his paintings were collected and officially burned; he was accused by his janitor of homosexuality and was given a suspended sentence after a trial of four days; he was arrested and questioned for twenty-four hours when he was caught carrying a camera past the Chancellery on the way to a pawnshop and the camera was confiscated. All this would not have shaken Anna in her determination to remain in Germany, but when proceedings were put under way to have Baranov sterilised as a threat to the German bloodstream, she crossed the border with him into Switzerland in the middle of a snowstorm.

It took the Baranovs more than a year to get to America, but as Sergei walked down 57th Street in New York City, staring at the windows of the art galleries, in which the most extreme styles of painting, from lurid Surrealism to sugary Naturalism, were peacefully on display, he felt that all his trials and troubles had been worth while because they had eventually brought him to this harbour. Gratefully and emotionally he made application within the first week for citizenship for Anna and himself. As further demonstrations of his new-born allegiance, he even took to watching the Giants play at the Polo Grounds, although it never became quite clear to him what, exactly, the players were doing around second base, and he patriotically developed a taste for Manhattan cocktails, which he rightly assumed to be the native drink.

The next few years were the happiest of the Baranovs' lives. Critics and patrons alike found that the soft-voiced Russian brought a mysterious European flavour, melancholy and classic, to homely American tomatoes and cucumbers, and his shows almost invariably sold out at good prices. A large wine company used Baranov grapes on all their labels and advertising and a large Baranov still life of a basket of oranges was bought by a California packing company and blown up into twenty-four sheets and plastered on billboards from one end of the country to the other. Baranov bought a small house in Jersey, not far from New York, and when Suvarnin turned up, having

410

left Germany with a price on his head because he had been overheard, in his cups, saying that the German Army could not reach Moscow in three weeks, Baranov gladly invited the critic to live with them.

Heady with his new sense of freedom, Baranov even went so far as to paint a nude, very pink and firm-fleshed, from memory. But Anna, who by this time was attached to a nationally circulated news magazine as an authority on Communism and Fascism, was very firm in her handling of the situation. She ripped the painting to shreds with a breadknife and dismissed the robust, apple-cheeked Czech girl who did their cooking, although the girl went to the rather extreme length of having a reputable physician testify to her virginity in an attempt to retain her position.

Anna's success in America, where men have long been conditioned to listen to women, and where her particular brand of crisp, loquacious efficiency was regarded with stunned fascination by her male colleagues, was even more dazzling than any she had enjoyed in Europe. By the end of the war the magazine for which she worked had put her in charge of the departments of Political Interpretation, Medicine for Women, Fashion, Books, and, of course, Child Care. She even got a job for Suvarnin on the magazine, reviewing motion pictures, a job he held until the autumn of '47, when he lost his eyesight.

Anna became a well-known figure in Washington, testifying at great length as a friendly witness before several important committees, discoursing on such varied subjects as the sending of subversive literature through the mails and the effect of sex education in the public school systems of several Northern states. She even had the exhilarating experience of having her girdle pinched in an elevator by a senior Senator from the West. As was inevitable, she was invited to countless dinners, receptions, congresses, and parties, and to all of them Baranov faithfully escorted her. In the beginning, living in the free atmosphere of literary and artistic America, Baranov had seemed to shed the taciturnity that had set in during the last part of his years in Moscow. He laughed frequently, he sang old Red Army songs without much urging, he insisted on mixing Manhattans at the homes of his friends, he spoke up on all subjects with disarming and agreeable gusto. But after a while he began to sink back into his old silences. Munching peanuts, occasionally muttering a monosyllable, he would stand by Anna's side at parties, watching her closely, listening with strange concentration as she spoke out, clearly and fully, on the destiny of the Republican Party, trends in the theatre, and the intricacies of the American Constitution. It was at this time, too, that Baranov began to have trouble sleeping. His weight fell off and he began to work at night.

Half-blind as he was, Suvarnin saw what was happening. Excitedly, he waited for the great day. In advance, he composed once more the stirring tribute to his friend's genius that he had first written so long ago in Moscow. Suvarnin was one of those writers who hates to see any word of his go unpublished, and the fact that nearly twenty years had passed since he had been forced to jettison his appreciation only made him more eager to get it finally into print. Also, it was a great relief to write about painting again, after the long months of Betty Grable and Van Johnson.

On the morning that, Anna being in the city and the house quiet, Baranov came to him and said, 'I would like you to come into my studio,' Suvarnin found himself trembling. Stumbling a little, he hurried out of the house and followed Baranov across the driveway to the barn which had been converted into a studio. He peered through his darkening eyes for a long time at the enormous canvas. 'This,' he said humbly, 'this is the great one. Here,' he took out some manuscript papers from his pocket, 'here, read what I have to say about it.'

When he had finished reading his friend's eulogy, Baranov wiped a tear from his eye. Then he went over to Suvarnin and kissed him. There was no question this time about hiding the masterpiece. Baranov rolled it up carefully, put it in a case, and with Suvarnin at his side, drove in with it to his dealer. However, by silent agreement, he and Suvarnin tactfully refrained from telling Anna anything about the matter.

Two months later Sergei Baranov was the new hero of the world of art. His dealer had to put up velvet ropes to contain the crowds who came to see the green nude. Suvarnin's tribute now seemed pale and insubstantial in the torrent of adjectives poured out by the other critics. Picasso was mentioned in the same sentence as Baranov countless times and several writers brought up the name of El Greco. Bonwit Teller had six green nudes in their windows, wearing lizard shoes and draped with mink. A Baranov Grapes and Local Cheese, which the painter had sold in 1940 for 200 dollars brought 5,600 dollars at an auction. The Museum of Modern Art sent a man around to arrange about a retrospective show. The World Good Will

Association, whose letterhead boasted the names of many dozen legislators and leaders of industry, requested it as the leading item in a show of American art which they proposed to send, at Government expense, to fourteen European countries. Even Anna, to whom, as usual, no one dared mention the interesting resemblance of painter's wife and painter's model, seemed pleased, and for a whole evening allowed Baranov to speak without interrupting once.

At the opening of the show of American art, which was being revealed in New York preliminary to its trip overseas, Baranov was the centre of attention. Photographers took his picture in all poses, toying with a Manhattan, munching on a smoked salmon canapé, talking to the wife of an Ambassador, looking up gravely at his masterpiece, surrounded by admirers. It was the crowning moment of his life and if he had been struck dead that midnight he would have expired happily. In fact, later on, looking back at that evening, from the vantage-point of the events that followed, Baranov often bitterly wished that he *had* died that night.

For, one week later, on the floor of Congress, an economy-minded representative, enraged at what he called the irresponsible money-squandering proclivities of the Administration, which had put up good American dollars to send this sinister travesty of America to our late allies, demanded a thorough investigation of the entire enterprise. The lawmaker went on to describe the main exhibit, a green nude by a Russian foreigner, as sickening twaddle, Communist-inspired, an insult to American womanhood, a blow to White Supremacy, atheistic, psychological, un-American, subversive, Red-Fascistic, not the sort of thing he would like his fourteen-year-old daughter to see either alone or accompanied by her mother, decadent, likely to inspire scorn for the Republic of the United States in foreign breasts, calculated aid to Stalin in the cold war between American and the Soviet Union, a slap in the face to the heroes of the Berlin air-lift, injurious to trade, an offence to our neighbours to the South, artistic gangsterism, a natural result of our letting down our immigration barriers, proof of the necessity of Federal censorship of the Press, the radio, and the movies, and a calamitous consequence of the Wagner Labour Relations Act.

Other developments followed quickly. A conservative, mellow-voiced radio commentator, broadcasting from Washington, announced that he had warned the country over and over

413

again that new deal paternalism would finally spawn just such monstrosities and hinted darkly that the man responsible for the painting had entered the United States illegally, being put ashore from a submarine by night with a woman he alleged to be his wife.

Several newspaper chains took up the matter in both their editorial and news columns, sending their least civil employees down to the Baranov farm to question the culprit and reporting that a samovar stood in a place of honour in the Baranov living-room and that the outside of the studio was painted red. One editor demanded to know why no cover from the *Saturday Evening Post* was included in the collection of paintings. Leaders of the American Legion filed a formal protest against sending the paintings in question over to the lands where our boys had fought so bravely so shortly before, and pointing out that Baranov was not a veteran.

The House Committee on un-American Activities served a subpoena on both Baranovs and put a tap on their telephone wires, hiring a man who knew Russian to monitor it. At the hearing, it was brought out that Baranov in 1917, 1918 and 1919 had served in the Red Army, and the Bureau of Immigration was publicly denounced for allowing such doubtful human material into the country. Ministers of all three religions circulated a petition calling upon the Government to halt the shipment of the paintings to Europe, a place which all knew was badly shaken in the department of religious faith as it was. A well-known jurist was quoted as saying he was tired of modern art experts and that he could paint a better picture than the green nude with a bucket of barn paint and a paperhanger's brush. A psychiatrist, quoted in a national magazine, said that the painting in question had obviously been done by a man who felt rejected by his mother and who had unstable and violent tendencies which were bound to grow worse with the years. The F.B.I. threw in a squad of investigators who conducted interviews with seventy-five friends of the Baranovs and discovered that the couple had subscriptions to the Book-of-the-Month Club, *House and Garden,* and the *Daily News,* and that they often spoke Russian in front of their servants.

A cross was burned on the Baranov lawn on a rainy evening, but even so, wind-blown sparks ignited a privy on a neighbour's property and reduced it to the ground. Irate, the neighbour fired a shotgun at the Baranovs' Siamese cat, nicking it twice in the rear.

The local Chamber of Commerce petitioned the Baranovs to move away, as they were giving the town a bad name, just at a time when they were trying to attract a plumbing factory to set up business there.

A Communist civil liberties group held a mass meeting to raise funds for Baranov, who denounced them. They, in turn, denounced the Baranovs and demanded that they be deported to Russia.

The Treasury Department, attracted by the commotion, went over Baranov's last five income-tax returns and disallowed several items and sent in a bill for an additional eight hundred and twenty dollars. The Baranovs' citizenship papers were carefully scanned and it was revealed that Mrs Baranov had lied about her age.

At a radio forum on the subject, 'What Should We Do with the Green Nude' Baranov's name was hissed by the audience every time it was mentioned, and the next day the postmaster in a small Massachusetts town announced that a mural of cranberry-pickers and fishermen that Baranov had painted for the post-office in the days of the W.P.A. would be torn down.

Anna Baranov, due to the unwelcome publicity given her, was deprived by her editor first of the Department of Political Interpretation, then of Medicine for Women, then of Books and Fashion, and finally, of Child Care, after which she was allowed to resign.

Baranov moved through all this in a dull haze, dreading more than anything else the long hours of mounting rhetoric which were loosed on him by his wife between midnight and eight each morning. Occasionally, huddled for disguise into the turned-up collar of his overcoat, he would go to the gallery where the disputed painting still hung, and would stare mournfully and puzzledly at it. When, one day, the Director of the gallery took him aside, and told him, not unkindly, that in response to certain pressures, the authorities had decided to disband the show and not send it to Europe after all, he wept.

That night, he was sitting alone, slumped in a wooden chair in the middle of his cold studio. The blinds were drawn because of the habit the small boys of the neighbourhood had developed of hurling rocks through the windows at any moving shadows they saw within. In Baranov's hand he held a small world atlas, opened to a map of the Caribbean and Central America, but he did not look at it.

The door opened and Suvarnin came in. He sat down without a word.

Finally, Baranov spoke without looking at his friend. 'I was at the gallery today,' he said, his voice low and troubled. 'I looked at the painting for a long time. Maybe it's my imagination,' he said, 'but I thought I noticed something.'

'Yes?'

'Suddenly,' Baranov said, 'the painting reminded me of someone. I thought and thought who it could be. Just now I remembered. Suvarnin' – he twisted anxiously in his chair to face the critic – 'Suvarnin, have you ever noticed that there was any resemblance there to my wife, Anna?'

Suvarnin said nothing for a while. He closed his movie-destroyed eyes thoughtfully and rubbed his nose. 'No,' he said, finally. 'Not the slightest.'

Baranov smiled wanly. 'Oh, what a relief,' he said. 'It would be a terrible shock to her.' He spread the book on his knees and stared down at the small red and blue countries of the warm middle Atlantic. 'Suvarnin,' he said, 'have you ever been to the Caribbean?'

'No,' said Suvarnin.

'What sort of fruit,' Baranov asked, pering at the map, 'do you think a man could find to paint in Costa Rica?'

Suvarnin sighed and stood up. 'I will go pack my things,' he said heavily, and went out, leaving Baranov alone in the cold studio, staring at his brightly coloured, repetitious map.

THE END